S0-BRF-761

3 3029 04123 8296

COLONIAL HEIGHTS LIBRARY
4799 STOCKTON BOULEVARD
SACRAMENTO, CA 95820 1/00

WITHDRAWN FROM COLLECTION
OF SACRAMENTO PUBLIC LIBRARY

The
Annunciate

Also by
Severna Park

Speaking Dreams
Hand of Prophecy

The ANNUNCIATE

SEVERNA PARK

AVON · EOS

This is a work of fiction. Names, characters, places and incidents either are the product of the author's imagination or are used fictitiously. Any resemblance to actual events, locales, organizations, or persons, living or dead, is entirely coincidental and beyond the intent of either the author or the publisher.

AVON BOOKS, INC.
1350 Avenue of the Americas
New York, New York 10019

Copyright © 1999 by Severna Park
Interior design by Kellan Peck
ISBN: 0-380-97737-0

All rights reserved, which includes the right to reproduce this book or portions thereof in any form whatsoever except as provided by the U.S. Copyright Law.
For information address Avon Books, Inc.

Library of Congress Cataloging in Publication Data:
Park, Severna, 1958–
The annunciate / Severna Park.—1st ed.
        p.   cm.
        I. Title.
PS3566.A6747A56   1999   99-31434
813'.54—dc21   CIP

First Avon Eos Printing: November 1999

AVON EOS TRADEMARK REG. U.S. PAT. OFF. AND IN OTHER COUNTRIES, MARCA REGISTRADA,
HECHO EN U.S.A.

Printed in the U.S.A.

FIRST EDITION

QPM   10 9 8 7 6 5 4 3 2 1

www.avonbooks.com/eos

For Vicki

My Space Babe

ACKNOWLEDGMENTS

This book is lovingly dedicated to
William Burroughs
for the Algebra of Need.

For years of inspiration, thanks to: Barbara Ehrenreich, Louise Erdrich, Peter Garrett, Michael Ondaatje, Barbara Walker, and Elizabeth Hand in particular, for the first line of *Winterlong*.

Thank you so much for your unflagging support when the going got tough: Anne and Katherine, Bob August, Elizabeth Barrette, Marjorie Fergusson, Keith Ferrell (who said the right thing at precisely the right time), Lois Gresh, Laura Johnson, Tom Myer and everyone at *sfsite.com*, Jim Reichert, Mark Siegel, Steve and Jan Stirling, Ron Toth, Eric Van Jateman, and Andrew Burt, whose tireless dedication to the Critters online writing group (*www.critters.org/critters*) is a wonder to behold.

And many, many thanks to Jennifer Brehl and Richard Curtis, for more than I can say.

THE LANDING SONG

❦

Tether now the outflung star,
O' Mother, none
else would plant a garden there.

Sow thy seeds in barren ground,
O' Father, done
are thy tasks beyond the gates.

Harvest now thy fruitful womb,
O' Daughter, one
night reveals all future days.

Raise up thine Unknown Child for
all and shout,
Hail!
Here is the new world.

ONE

She was in me, tongue and fingers, her voice whispering my name, *Eve*, in the dark like she meant it. But the next morning when she left, I knew she was thinking about other places, other things. Certainly other women.

Naverdi.

I stood outside, hugging myself against the cold as her shuttle vanished into the rust-colored dawn. Here on the mountain, between the cathedral's twisted gates and blackened facade, I could see to the horizon where Kigal's sun welled up, raw as a wound. In the anonymous valley below, seared dirt and scattered bricks showed where villages had been burned and built, and burned again.

Naverdi.

Annmarie and Corey paid her for supplies and information about the fighting on this planet and elsewhere in the Three Systems. What she left with me was free but insubstantial. Her blunt aroma on my skin and the hollow feeling under my heart when I wondered what I was to her—a lover, a trophy, or just a warm companion for the night.

The wind bit around my neck and I huddled in my coat. I could close my eyes and know exactly where she was. The microscopic, self-replicating biobots we'd released yesterday—propagats—had woven themselves into the local landscape. They'd infested every creature and plant, every device, covering this part of the planet with an inescapable Mesh of information that only Annmarie, Corey, and I could manipulate.

I could close my eyes and see everything: tomorrow's weather, yesterday's news. If I concentrated on the dull morning sky, the Mesh would mark the trail of Naverdi's shuttle and pinpoint her location. A hundred thousand propagats would let me peer through the hull to find her tantalizing body, or go deeper to catch a glimpse of her inner wiring. The delicate chrome plug between the tendons under her wrist—her Jack—was part of a less expensive technology, not as powerful or invasive as my Mesh. It was the difference between us, and she shouldn't have been able to hide anything from me. But a hundred thousand propagats still couldn't show me if she'd been sorry to leave this morning, or if she was telling the truth when she said she'd wait for me, over the next set of hills in the city of Tula.

"Eve?"

A rush of freezing wind drove up the side of the mountain, shoving upward to where cast-iron saints lurked in eaves. I turned to see Annmarie, hunched against the weather. Behind her, our ship, the Medusa, was a brassy smudge inside the cathedral's scorched ruins, a big austere ship, dwarfed under the torn-open vault of the ceiling.

She came over to me, her black cloak flapping, her skin dark as tarnish and puckered with the cold. "What're you doing out here?"

"Naverdi just left."

Annmarie squinted at the empty sky, shut her eyes briefly to reference in Mesh. I could feel her do it. A steel taste under my tongue.

She opened her eyes. "I suppose you were with her all night."

I nodded.

She put her arm around my shoulders, motherly, like she'd been for the last seven years, since I was fourteen, and squeezed hard. "I'd never tell you how to run your life, honey, but you can do a lot better than that one."

The day when I would abandon her was too close and still too far away. I gave her a smile that didn't mean anything.

"Go inside," she said. "Corey's waiting for you."

"We're making Staze?" I said. "You've already contacted the locals?"

Annmarie nodded, not so much in agreement but at something below. One man in heavy clothes labored toward us up a trail of loose stones, too far away to make out in any detail.

I closed my eyes and studied him. The Mesh showed him in my head in vivid, anatomic schema. He was in his late forties and his heart was racing from the climb but his adrenaline levels were up as well. He was afraid of us. I opened my eyes and watched him.

He was Jackless, without even a plug, like Nav's, in his arm. In the old economic strata of ThreeSys, he would have been a peasant, but since the start of the Uprising, thirteen years of war had ground most of the survivors—Meshed, Jacked, and Jackless alike—down to the same miserable level.

Except for Annmarie, Corey, and me.

Because we made Staze.

Annmarie touched the middle of her chest where the medal of the Annunciate hung from its chain under her clothes and pulled up the hood of her cloak. "Go inside, Eve."

"I don't want to leave you out here by yourself."

"I'll be fine," she said. "Go inside. Corey's waiting for you."

Usually I did what I was told. Not this morning. I went back into the church, out of sight, and crouched in the shadows where the air smelled of wet soot.

The Jackless man stumbled into view, framed in the splintered remains of the doorway against the steadily lightening sky. He stopped, touched the edge of his fur hat, hesitated, then took the hat off. "Lady," I heard him say, "show me your arm."

Annmarie pushed the sleeve away from her left wrist where there was no plug between delicate tendons.

The man studied it carefully. "You're Meshed?" he said. "You don't look no different from us."

I held my breath in the cold shadows. If it had been me out there, I would have lied and said, All the Meshed have been exterminated. Look! I'm as Jackless as you are. But Annmarie's approach to reality was different than mine.

She pointed into the ruined valley. "Watch," she said. The man turned to look, then clutched his fur hat in both fists as she closed her eyes and showed him our greatest strength.

Below, the crumble of burnt buildings had turned into a dense, green forest. Maybe she'd thrown in a river, or a lake. I could close my eyes for a better look, but we'd done this so many times, I didn't need to. Nothing had changed in the valley of course, but in Mesh, Annmarie could make the propagats in the man's body supply him with the view she wanted him to see, even the scent of flowers.

These old tricks had ruined us. The rest of Meshed history—abusive power and plain thievery throughout the Three Systems—had inspired the Jacked like Naverdi to develop nanovirals to exterminate all the 'gats they could find. There were armies of Jackless peasants devoted to hunting us. After centuries of casting our shadows broad and wide under the three isolated suns, Eostre, Jaganmata and Mara, all we had left were illusions. Except for Annmarie.

She opened her eyes and the vision disappeared. The Jackless man turned the hat around in his hands. "I thought we'd killed you all in the Uprising."

"Not quite," she said.

"There's a high price on you. Enough to win a war. I won't say we haven't been offered money by some who're looking."

Hunters. I felt the back of my neck prickle and wondered how long ago they'd been here.

Annmarie shrugged. To her, the Uprising and hunters in general were only temporary successes for the less-than-Meshed.

"You're the ones selling Staze," he said.

"That's right," said Annmarie.

He squinted at the burned valley. "I've heard it's victory. It's peace."

Of course it was no such thing. Staze was a lure, a lever. It was a kind of insurance. We never touched the stuff.

He pointed across the valley. "See what those Jacked sonsabitches from Tula have done to us?" He nodded at the wrecked village. "They started it ninety-seven years ago. Said we breached their borders, but it was them that breached ours. Matter of fact, my granddad told me that in the beginning—"

Annmarie stopped him. "I don't care who started it. I don't care what it's about. I don't even care who's winning. I'm here to stop it."

He scowled and sucked air through his teeth, trying to see his war from her point of view. He was Jackless, and there were plenty of Jackless just like him. He didn't understand the kind of resolve that grew out of genocide, so to him we were peacemakers without a clear motive, but the only hope for any of the Meshed was Annmarie's laboratory concoction.

"Staze," he said, as if verifying what he'd heard from an unreliable source. "The drug. It goes in their water."

"Or their food," said Annmarie. "Anything they can put in their mouths. The addiction is instant."

"What does it do?"

She nodded down the cliff to the illusion, now gone. "It gives them a beautiful place for half the day. The other half, they'll be making sure they can get their next dose. They won't fight you anymore."

"As long as we keep supplying them."

She nodded, brisk, because this was strictly business.

"Will they die if we don't give it to them?"

"No," she said. "They'll be miserable and one day they might be miserable enough to fight. It's easier to give them what they want. Cheaper, too. They'll be happy. You'll live the rest of your lives in peace." She made a wide gesture, falsely generous. "I guarantee it."

He eyed the burned valley, turning the hat around and around. "We've heard you come back later and addict the winners."

Annmarie flicked her fingers in the cold air, knowing as well as I did that hunters left that rumor, along with the promise of cash. "Whatever you were offered for us doesn't compare to the luxury of being able to live without war."

He pushed the hat onto his head, pulling the fur close over his ears. "I'll come again in the afternoon." He laid his fingers over the inside of his Jackless wrist. "I have to talk with my own people. You understand?"

"If you have hunters looking for us, do yourself a favor. Tell them we're not what you thought we were. Tell them all the Meshed are dead."

"No hunters, Lady." He made a stiff turn as though he didn't want to expose his back and started down the mountain. In a moment, he was out of sight.

Annmarie let out her breath. Wind blew away the shreds and she came into the church, where I was crouched in the dark. "Eve, honey," she said, because she'd known I'd been there all along. "I thought I told you to go inside."

I stood up. "We shouldn't stay. He's already made up his mind."

Annmarie shrugged. "We have this situation every time we contact new buyers. They always threaten us. We always have to be careful. Why're you so worried?"

"I don't know," I said. "It just feels . . . different."

"Did you see something in that man that I missed?"

"No, but—"

"Or is your girlfriend waiting for you?" She narrowed her eyes at me. "Where did you say she was going?"

"I don't know."

She studied my face, not sure if I was lying. For better or worse, the data partitions in Mesh gave us enough privacy to hide the truth from each other. "We'll stay until he shows up with his friends," she said. "Corey'll keep an eye out, like he always does. If we can sell a little Staze, fine. If not, we'll go see their enemies in Tula."

She left me in the engine bay where Corey was setting up to make Staze. He didn't see me at first, blindered in goggles, enveloped in his dusty orange coverall, leveling heaps of white monazite sand in the cramped space between the boxy black Isolator units and the base of the Medusa's drive.

I took my own coverall down from its hook by the airlock, shoved in one leg, then the other. The drive was a monumental gray egg, immobile and immense in its corner, surrounded by Isolators like supplicants. Its narrow top brushed the bay's high ceiling and it towered in an echoing space over Corey as he patted down the sand.

Three years ago, Annmarie'd plucked him out of his limping ship and killed the hunters who were tracking him. He was Meshed, of course. Annmarie wouldn't have bothered to save anyone who wasn't. He was shorter than me by a head, older by a decade. His sand-colored hair was thinning on top, leaving a freckled bald spot. I'd tried to like him. I'd tried hard, but from the moment he'd come onboard, he'd struck me as a body with too much energy, always in fidgety, nail-biting motion, with too many unspoken ideas.

I pulled on the stiff gloves and went to get the second ingredient—Nav's cargo, paid for with a kilo of Staze—the Kevake.

Four crates sat in a row by the wall, each tall enough to reach my waist, open to show hundreds of liter containers of viscous red fluid. Out in the desert wastelands of Jaganmata-Devi, faith healers drained the sap out of a common cactus, boiled it down and mixed it with a dozen other alchemical ingredients. Petals of flowers, tears of virgins, blood of the new-born, and so on. They sold the concoction as a cure for uncontrollable angers, but Kevake's uses as a folk remedy didn't interest Annmarie. Years ago, when she was writing academic papers on psychobiology, back when running for our lives wasn't such a preoccupation, she'd shared in the discovery of Staze. A mix of Kevake and rare earths like monazite, time and temperature. A formula for victory, peace, and control.

For her, Staze was the solution to all our problems. To Corey, the drug was half safety net, half cash flow. And until last night, Staze had formed a precise framework for my future.

'Eve, come with me.'

Naverdi. The invitation was like an opening into a strange, two-dimensional garden where there was no Mesh, no Staze.

No Annmarie or Corey.

'Eve, I want you.'

I gathered up the plastic bottles of Kevake, stuffing them under my arms, holding them against my chest where they felt warm. The cloying smell of cactus sap filled my nose. Naverdi. The flavor of Staze, sweet as licorice on her tongue. No matter how many hours since her dose had worn off, the taste of her addiction had been distinct.

I glanced across the bay at Corey again. If the Jackless man on the mountain decided to buy Staze from us, there would be no reason to go to their enemies in Tula, where Nav was supposed to be waiting. We wouldn't need more Kevake for months, and Nav wasn't our only supplier. Depending on the depth of Annmarie's disapproval, I might never see Naverdi again.

'Eve, you're beautiful.'

Corey patted the last of the sand into place and stood up,

wiping his gloves over his chest. "You're here." He frowned. "Are you all right? You look awfully tired."

"I'm fine."

He studied me and then his mouth spread into a syrupy smile. "You were with that smuggler woman all night long. What's her name again?"

He knew her name. Inside the stiff coverall, I could feel my body bristle. Corey tried his best to know everything about me. At first we'd both pretended it was for the sake of harmony aboard a small ship. As I got older, I understood him more and liked him less.

"Isn't she the smuggler we met on Mara-Macha a month ago?"

She was. Nav with her hair in velvet twists, waiting for us in the crowded sprawl of the black market. She'd been sitting in a blue plastic chair with her fists between her knees, her face dark and focused. To look at her made my mouth go dry.

Annmarie liked her too, mostly because her blue plastic chair was in front of enough Kevake to cure the uncontrollable angers of thousands.

Nav's brown eyes had pinned me, found out everything about me without the benefit of a Mesh. She rubbed the chrome Jack socket under her wrist and reached out to shake my hand. Long fingers. Cool palms.

"Hi," she'd said.

"Nice to meet you," I'd mumbled.

She'd winked at me, then turned to Annmarie to ask for more money than the Kevake could ever have been worth. I didn't remember if they argued or haggled. I couldn't remember anything from that afternoon, except for the way the warm breeze made her shirt ripple around her waist and how her smile made deep, pleasant creases in the corners of her mouth.

Corey leaned on one of the squat black Isolators. "Better watch yourself, young lady. You can't just hop into bed with strangers. Not safe. *Not* safe." He gave a prim little snort. "Didn't Annmarie teach you better than that?"

I set the bottles down. From the beginning, he'd flirted so transparently, *so* outrageously with Annmarie. Before Nav, I'd never thought about him and Annmarie in bed together, but I did now, and their sex was hard for me to picture. Annmarie's dark, sinuous body tangled in with his sweaty, balding intensity. He seemed to me so utterly wrong for her, and it irritated me that she couldn't see this for herself. Whatever they were to each other from day to day—friends, lovers, or partners of convenience—she hadn't chosen him. Just settled.

"She's cute," said Corey. "A bit on the worldly side, though, don't you think? I mean, who knows what she sells besides Kevake." He smirked at me.

I opened one of the bottles and poured the contents onto the sand. Red liquid pooled, glutinous and thick in evenly spaced hollows, like blood on a piece of white paper.

"You know what she's really after," said Corey. "Right? Of course you know."

Staze he meant, and the secrets of Staze-making. I shrugged. "We didn't talk about that."

He laughed like I'd told a dirty joke, but when I looked at him, the expression on his face was like hunger. I moved away, pouring out another bottle, not sure what to think.

He padded after me, rustling in the coverall. He took a couple of breaths and finally almost blurted. "Don't tell me that was your first time."

I didn't say anything. So far I'd only resented him. I'd never been scared of him. I tried to decide if he was scaring me now.

"You have to be *very* careful, Evie," he said, too loud, like he could change the tone of the things he'd already said with enough volume. "She only wants one thing from you. No matter what she says, you can't let yourself get attached to her."

When I was younger, more raw from my own experiences, it was easier for me to believe the things he said about the Jacked and Jackless. His prejudices were anchored in such underhanded passion, it was hard not to agree.

I poured, waiting for him to attack her integrity, her personality, her worthiness, all based on the plug in her wrist.

Instead, he changed the subject. "Do you remember Sofi Zie?"

Another one of our Kevake suppliers. Sofi Zie had been an older man living on a small ship with his daughter and her four children. Like Nav, they were Jacked and essentially gypsies. Traveling in ThreeSys was always risky—crossing disputed areas, or getting in the middle of a long-fought war. We'd lost a number of Kevake suppliers, so when Sofi and his family disappeared two or three years ago, no one was too surprised.

"I picked up a transmission between a couple of smugglers before we landed yesterday," said Corey. "One was Sofi's grandson, I think. They had wind of us somehow. Or at least, there was a rumor we were in the area."

Hunters, I thought, and felt my heart speed up. "Did you tell Annmarie?"

"Naturally. But they weren't interested in us. They were comparing recipes for Staze."

That wasn't anything new. With the right ingredients and enough heat, anyone could make Staze, as long as they knew the proportions.

"Were they right?" I asked.

He chuckled. "Almost. That's how I knew who they were. Did you know Annmarie gave Sofi the exact formula for Staze?"

I hadn't known. Annmarie treated Sofi Zie like he didn't have a brain in his head. "Why would she do that?"

"She found out he was trying to make the stuff himself. She told me he was pretty close—too close. So she gave him the recipe, except for one thing."

"What?" I asked, suspicious. Stories from Corey invariably had a moral for me, or served as cases in point.

"She told him the transition from Kevake to Staze could only happen if he added four kilos of argenta."

"What's argenta?"

"It's a kind of rare gem. At the time, the closest source was Eostre-Epona."

On Epona, the fighting moved from one hemisphere to another, army to army, clan to clan. There were wars everywhere in ThreeSys, but most had occasional lulls. On Epona, the fighting never seemed to stop.

"She sent him there?" I said.

Corey nodded, grinning.

"He was killed?"

Corey raised a meaningful eyebrow. "Sofi was an addict. He would have done anything to have his own supply."

What he was really talking about, of course, was Naverdi. "That was how you knew it was his grandson? They were talking about argenta?"

"It was a good lie," said Corey. "It just goes to show, you can't let your customers get too close."

Good lies or bad ones, what the story 'went to show' was that we probably had competitors. In my own opinion, it didn't matter how many addicts we could claim as our own, only that they were addicted, happy, and incapable of hunting us.

He took another step toward me. "Annmarie and I just want you to be careful. The only reason the three of us are still alive is because we keep to ourselves. Do you know anything about this girl?"

I could have made up some story about how Naverdi's family had fallen from the social graces of Mesh, how she'd been Jacked against her will as a child and condemned to live a life that should have been beneath her. The fact was, I'd already snooped out all the official information I could get. She'd been born in a refugee camp on Jaganmata-Uma, where her cousins had raised her, well enough, I supposed, for a group with such lengthy criminal records. Her own was no match for theirs—yet. She was only nineteen.

"She'll be back," he said, "but don't get the wrong idea about that girl. Your family was killed because they trusted those Jacked bastards. They'd kill us all off, given half a chance.

Even if she tells you she loves you, you have to remember that it's just a plain lie."

No, I thought. You're the liar. And even if what he said was true, what difference did it make? She told me the things I needed to hear.

'Eve, you're beautiful. Eve, I want you. Eve, come with me.'

I poured out the rest of the Kevake into the sand, focused on not saying another word to him. We didn't need to talk. Annmarie had taught him everything about making Staze, the same way she'd taught me. I'd been making two batches of Staze per month since I was fourteen. Twenty-four times seven years. One hundred and sixty-eight batches of Staze. Ton upon metric ton of Staze. It seemed like a lot when the addicts needed so little. Fifty kilos could sustain five thousand for a year.

I emptied the last bottle and sat behind the Isolator control panel in the old armless swivel. Corey finished sweeping up stray grit with a dustpan and turned to me with his eyes shut.

I heard his voice inside my head.

Eve?

I took a breath, picturing a life without him, and closed my eyes.

In Mesh, the bay was no different. Still the bay, with a ceiling as high as a cathedral and Corey standing to one side. We could present as anything we wanted, but in this common vision, our avatars looked the same as we did in the real world.

Around the drive, however, everything was different.

The Isolators showed as a circular stone wall, a metaphor for their protective field. A tall clear cylinder, like a standard graduated lab flask, rose up from the wall with temperature increments marked for every five hundred degrees Fahrenheit. Behind the curve of virtual glass, sand and Kevake were revealed in their separate natures; a narrow strip of beach around a pool of ruddy water. In the middle of the pool, the imposing gray egg of the Medusa's drive revealed itself in schema, its latent physical forces flickering under the water, coded in the ardent, shifting colors of fire.

Under the pool's surface, the warm colors intensified as the drive heated everything inside the virtual glass graduate. Fire, water, and earth. Annmarie's alchemical camouflage. If any of what we were doing was visible to prying eyes, it was as obscured as her forested version of the scorched-over valley outside.

In the real world, the heaps of monazite grit around the drive would be too hot to touch. Condensation from evaporating Kevake would be gathering inside the Isolators' invisible cylinder, fogging just under the high ceiling.

My job was to watch the Isolators and vent the bay as the gases rose upward, separating into purer and purer substances. The core temperature of the drive, which would get up to three thousand degrees, was enough to burn through the hull if something went wrong. Corey was supposed to monitor the drive as it heated, and normally we were a coordinated team.

This time he'd started without me. I leaned forward in the armless swivel. The temperature inside the ersatz graduate was already at three hundred degrees and rising fast. Six hundred. Nine hundred. Usually making Staze was like waiting for water to boil. Now alchemical metaphors showed the puddle bubbling away to bare ground inside the confines of the wall.

Why're you rushing? I said.

No answer.

I glanced across the bay, where his avatar stood alert . . . and unresponsive.

Corey?

He didn't answer.

I slid out of the chair and went over to his image. It stared past me, solidly intent but vacant. The only thing there was a smell.

Blunt. Dull and musky.

Sweat and body heat—and sex.

Corey?

Where *was* he? I made the scent visible and it appeared in the air as a trail of wispy smoke, leading out of the bay.

I checked the boiling metaphors around the drive. Another minute and the vents in the bulkheads could fuse. I made myself weightless and shot after the scent.

The trail curled down the hall, right up to the door of his quarters, a metaphor for the data partitions between us. I banged hard. *Corey!*

No answer. I banged harder. *What're you doing? You can't just leave in the middle of making Staze!*

I checked the heat and the Isolators. Fourteen hundred degrees. I leaned on the door and reached deep into the Medusa's network of propagats.

An emergency, I whispered to them. *Let me through.*

The door swung open. I stepped into his dark room. The smell was even stronger.

There was a rustle at my feet. I looked down. He was there, naked, longer in his arms and legs than he should have been, sprawled on his belly in a warm sticky layer of—something. I took an appalled step backward, half in, half out the door. Was *this* his Mesh environment? Hot and stinking of long sessions of self-indulgence?

Corey?

He turned his head in a blind reptilian motion, his mouth wet and partly open. *What're you doing here?* His voice was muffled, as though he was holding something under his tongue.

Me? What're you *doing? We're in the middle of making Staze!*

He raised himself up on long forearms. *Get out of here.*

We're at fifteen hundred degrees! I shouted.

He let his jaws fall open—a slow, languorous motion—and I saw a stopwatch underneath his tongue. *I'm timing,* he said. *Stop worrying.*

I snapped my eyes open, back in the real world, back in the bay, where boiling fog churned around the Medusa's drive.

Corey's body stood right where he'd left it, calm and relaxed. He could have been at a stopping place in a sleepwalk.

I wiped my palms on the front of my coverall, sweating under the goggles. Had Annmarie ever seen *that*? Was *that* what she liked about him? And how much of *that* had to do with me—and Nav?

I focused on the steam, the temperatures, gripped the solid edge of the swivel chair and shut my eyes.

Inside the glass wall, the sand had turned to slag, heaving up in molten bursts. At the edge of my vision, a warning message flashed about an impending crisis in the hull's structure. At the top of the graduate, too much pressure made the bulkheads creak.

Why aren't you venting? demanded Corey. Nothing in his voice gave any hint of where his mind was, or what he was doing.

I am *venting.* I shrugged in Mesh and the outer mechanism released. Arcane vapors were sucked out by the exit of gas less pure. The warning in the corner of my eye went away.

Inside the Isolator field, the roiling liquid glass had vaporized into a viscous cloud. The temperature rose past twenty-seven hundred. I watched the pressure carefully, ready to vent the last of the contaminants, which would only reduce the paradisical effects of Staze on those caught up in its pleasures.

Ten seconds, said Corey, soft, like he was counting money.

There was a pause. I tried not to think about what he was doing.

Three. Two. One.

I felt him cut the temperature.

I opened my eyes.

Around the drive malevolent red fog boiled against the ceiling. The cooling Kevake, purified of its ritual elements, or perhaps enhanced by the tears of virgins, made a glittering dissipation and turned to scarlet crystals. They hung in the trembling air, light as snow, confined by the Isolators, and drifted down until they formed an even pillow around the base of the drive. The final product. A potent, purified concentrate of the drug, stabilized over a fine grit of silica.

Fifty kilos of Staze—what the addicts called Red.

Annmarie's version of victory and peace, and control.

Corey's body swayed a bit. His eyes snapped open and he turned to me. "Why did you follow me in?"

"What was I supposed to do? You disappeared!"

"We've done this dozens of times, Eve. You take care of the Isolators, I take care of the drive." He made a sharp motion at the venting mechanisms in the ceiling. "You could have breached the hull, Eve. If we'd been in orbit, you might have killed us."

"*You* were the one running the temperature up! Why the hell didn't you answer me?"

He shook his head, a stiff, angry spasm. "Stay out of my places, Eve, unless you want me in yours."

I left him to wade in Staze, bagging it for the sake of self-preservation. His room was on the way to mine, and I made myself *not* look at his door. Inside, everything he owned was in precise order. Sheets folded on the bed, pillows plumped. His shoes were arranged by color, with their toes against the back of the closet. Nothing sticky or smelling of sex. Annmarie's room was next to his. Mine was across from hers. I went in and sat on the end of my bed and thought about which of my things I would take with me when Naverdi took me away.

I didn't have much that mattered.

A necklace. Two fish.

When I was a child, my father was in the diplomacy business, which now I thought the Jacked and Jackless might have called extortion. We had been rich because of it, Meshed and elite, on the high end of the equation where money equals the most powerful technology.

My Mesh came in a needle when I was twelve, an injection of type-1 propagats which took up residence in my nerve cells. A parallel network in my brain, adaptive, interactive, connected to a vast network of information we had no business knowing, all conveyed by the swarm of self-replicating type-2's which, in those days, infested everything and everyone not Meshed. I remember the first time I closed my eyes and found the broad path which put me *there,* where maids and doormen were laid out however I cared to view them—as wiring diagrams of their Jacked interfaces, genetic histories, anatomic studies—or as the seething collections of germs that my mother always insisted they were. I thought they were prettier with scales and so I made them like the pair of fish I had gotten for my birthday, the beautiful exotic ones called *pisca pugnate,* so violent, they had to be kept in separate bowls.

In Mesh, I could see everything about the house staff, except how they hated us.

And then one day the backwash of bad deeds came over us and the servants were gone.

What did they leave behind? In Mesh, only technical information about blood loss and stolen jewelry. In reality, my mother's throat was cut in a scarlet crescent, her ruby earrings torn out. Blood on the carpet. Blood on the new sofa. A puddle of red in my mother's shoe. They took her ruby necklace, but they left the religious medal she always wore, like Annmarie.

I remember my father kneeling in front of me, fastening the cold chain around my neck. He closed my fingers over the flat metal pendant engraved with the Annunciate, the woman standing at the gates of Paradise.

" *'Hail,' "* he'd said, the way they said it in church. " *'Here is the new world.' "*

It was the only time I saw him cry. He sent me to the Sanctuary, a traditional religious boarding school for Meshed children, on Mara's fifth planet, Isla. The Sanctuary had been a Meshed haven for almost three thousand years, tracing its origins to the time when the Generation Ship entered ThreeSys and our Meshed ancestors set foot on the first world, Paradise. Paradise hadn't survived its brush with human habitation and had been blasted from orbit over two millennia ago, deemed a navigational hazard, and assaulted with explosives until its gravitational attachment to ThreeSys was broken. By the time I arrived at the Sanctuary, Paradise was only an old nursery rhyme and the Sanctuary was anything but a refuge. I was surrounded with children and adults all running from disasters like mine, and it wasn't safe.

I sat on my bed, listening to the soft sound of water circulating in the two fish tanks, and ran my fingers over my mother's medallion. It would be easy to carry this bit of stamped metal and all its bad memories away from the Medusa. Taking the fish would be harder.

They circled in their small bowls. *Pisca pugnate.* Not really water creatures, they needed to come to the surface to breathe. Not really land animals, they needed immersion to stay alive. Ignorant of everything, they still wanted to kill each other. One was red with a veil of black fins, the other was black with scarlet. They had everything, like I did. Food and light and water. Being carried away from home in plastic boxes in my hot thirteen-year-old hands hadn't seemed to affect them. So when the Sanctuary was destroyed barely a year after I'd arrived, I knew they could survive it again.

And again, whenever I left the Medusa.

Naverdi.

I wondered if she liked fish.

I rolled over on my stomach, closed my eyes, and dropped into my own place in the Mesh.

Mine was deserted.

Dry. Flat.

Hot, with a few leafless trees. My version of the air was so clear, I could see the pebbles on my horizon, riveting down the bowl of the sky, tight against the ground. In the center of my desert was a shallow pool of water, blue as steel, surrounded by fist-sized river stones.

A private place and a workstation. Here on Kigal, the net of dry branches over my head stood in for the jagged roof of the cathedral. The stones around the pool were metaphors for the Medusa's antigravs. The pool was the window into the rest of ThreeSys, wherever type-2 propagats survived.

I knelt in the damp sand by the water. If Corey came in here, I would have to change everything, or find a way to purify it. Naverdi would be welcome, but her Jack wouldn't support the interface the Mesh required. She could leave a message, even something as complex as a scent, but she would never be able to walk in as an avatar, the way Meshed people could. I'd been in her Jacked environment, though—easy to insinuate myself through the propagats in her ship. Her communications interface was an overly-tactile Jacked construct, like a temple, I thought, thick with velvet and brocade, soft in a fleshy way but without Corey's lascivious stink.

Naverdi.

If she hadn't been addicted to Staze, I wouldn't have known what she saw in me. I peered at my reflection in the polished steel water. Dark eyes. Wide nose. Tender, childish mouth. I'd made this place when I was thirteen, thrown away my clothes and rolled myself in unreal dust until I turned from ebony to ash white. I never let the real years show. Always thirteen, naked, dirt between my toes, warmth soaking into my palms, thighs, the naked skin of my butt. No self-inflicted stress wounds, zits and pimples and pocks.

If I leaned forward far enough, I could see the reflection of the silver pendant Naverdi had made me find last night, a thumbnail-sized gift hanging between my little girl nipples, round and hard as a seed in fruit.

A symbol of knowledge, according to the Mesh.

Last night. Kneeling together in her narrow bed, her hair soft as wool over the brushed-iron color of her skin.

She opened the top of my shirt and I clutched her shoulders, expecting her hands, her mouth, but instead she fished out my mother's medal of the Annunciate and unfastened the chain.

I sat there, hot and cold and hot again. She didn't know I never took it off.

Nav held the medal up to the small light beside the bed. "All you Meshies have this thing."

"It's nothing," I said, breathless.

"The Annunciate." She traced the engraving with her finger. "Have you ever really looked at this?"

I was trembling, close enough to smell her hair. "Looked at it?"

She pointed. "Here's the walled garden—Paradise, right? Nice round circle. Here's the Annunciate in the garden. See how she's at the gates, facing out?"

The frizz of her hair tickled my cheek. "So?"

"So, if she's the first person to step off the Generation Ship onto Paradise, why isn't she outside the garden, trying to get in? I always thought the Ship must've been a nicer place to live. The planet was just a rock, you know."

My heart had stopped pounding with anticipation. Instead, there was a dull pain in my chest. Old memories. "It's just a symbol."

"But didn't you study it?"

I shrugged. "When I was thirteen, I was in a church play about the Landing. I was a flower in the garden and we had to learn The Landing Song. All I remember is being jealous of the girl who got to be the Annunciate. She got the big line."

" 'Hail,' " said Nav. " '*Here is the new world.*' " She smiled. "I always wondered if she wasn't saying, '*Hell! I liked the old world better!*' " She turned the medal over in her fingers. Curious, I decided. At the very worst, uneducated. The last thought came out in Annmarie's voice—not through the Mesh, but from inside myself.

"How do you know The Landing Song?" I said.

"Everybody knows it. It's just that no one remembers what it's really about. It's just a nursery rhyme now." She grinned. "A pointless fable from the old oppressors."

I felt the heat rising behind my cheeks but she laughed and

leaned forward to fasten the medal around my neck. She took my hand and made me trace the metal bud inside her wrist; her Jack, surrounded by smooth scar tissue from the implant surgery.

"Aren't you afraid of us?" I whispered.

"How can I be afraid of you?" she said. "Eve, you're beautiful." She touched her lips to mine. "Eve, come with me."

I would have done anything for her. I bent closer to her mouth and felt her whisper against my lips.

"You're a virgin," she said.

I froze, suddenly terrified it would make a difference. "Yes."

She pressed my fingers between her breasts. "I have something special for you," she said, "if you can find it."

Her shirt fell away from her shoulders and the silent note of released clothing made my body light with heat. She pulled my shirt over my head without ceremony, twisted out of her pants and I writhed out of mine. She pushed me onto my side and caught my hand again, guiding it to the roughness of her crotch, her sticky thighs. Her cold fingers slid into me and curled into a savory grip I could feel all the way up to a place under my teeth.

"Do *that* to me," she whispered, and I did, but more slowly, trailing through slick pathways, searching out strategic hollows. Her arms tightened across my back. Her breath rushed out against my ear, and then I was in *her,* where my fingertips found something hard.

It was a plastic canister, hidden in her vagina, no longer than my thumb, just a bit wider. It had a loop on it, like a handle. "Pull it—" she said, so I did, in what I hoped was an excruciating seduction. The canister slid out and I got a breath of her inner heat. For a second, she smelled of licorice. Then of Staze. That was when I knew she was addicted.

She rolled against me, warm and damp. "Hold out your hand." She snapped off the top of the canister and dumped the contents—a soft rush of metal inside plastic—into my palm.

It was a delicate chain, warm from her body, attached to a heavier silver shape which rolled out last.

I peered at the silver pendant, throat tight with the scent of candy and helpless understanding of why she had any interest in me at all. "It's beautiful," I said. "What is it?"

She laughed. "Eve," she said, "can't you see? It's an apple."

In my desert, I put my knuckles against my teeth, tasting sand and licorice and ash.

Eve?

It was Annmarie. *Yes?*

How much Staze did you and Corey make?

About fifty kilos, like you wanted.

Good. Now change your clothes and come outside.

I stood behind Annmarie on the steps of the burned cathedral. She, tea-colored dark, me, even blacker, both of us wrapped in red coats. The locals, bundled from head to foot in patched-over clothing, huddled on the broken stone stairway below. Every last one of them was Jackless, not even blessed with a metal plug in the wrist. Compared to them, Naverdi was wealthy beyond belief. If you listened to Corey long enough, we were as good as gods.

Wind and stinging grit cut across the stony ridge. I squinted into the distance, trying to sense the presence of hunters with my own gut feelings. If they were here, they would have used nanovirals to destroy our propagats, leaving blind spots in the Mesh. Those could only be detected with enough time. We didn't have that.

The man who'd climbed the mountain this morning stood in front of the rest, holding our sealed bag of red crystals. His companions shuffled on the stairs, wrapped against the weather. The rest of the Staze was still on the ship with Corey, who was ready at the Medusa's controls for a fast exit.

Annmarie stepped forward, her hair twisting in the wind like snakes. "You understand why we're here?"

"Peace!" shouted a man in the small crowd. His face was dirty, his beard was tangled, and he looked hungry. "But we don't *want* peace!"

The man who'd spoken with Annmarie this morning gave us a nervous glance. "I told them," he said. "Buying Staze from you means we win. It's victory. The peace is incidental."

A woman in the back jabbed a finger at the far hills, at Tula. "We don't want your kind of victory. We want justice."

"You mean revenge," said Annmarie coolly, and I could feel her gather herself for the speech she gave to doubters. She had three speeches, which she practiced every few days, either with me or with a mirror. One was for the distrustful. One was for those who had seen what Staze could do, and one was for the devout addicts who believed in Staze as deeply as any religion.

The woman shoved her way forward. "Why not revenge?" Her voice was high and tight. "They've been killing us for generations. My children. My brothers. My *father*."

"Staze is the end of conflict," said Annmarie. "You can call it peace, or victory, or you can call it revenge, but I guarantee, it's easier than fighting. Addict your enemies and they'll come crawling to you for their next dose. Make them placid and you can rebuild."

"I don't *want* them placid," shouted the woman. "I want them *dead*."

Annmarie shrugged. "Then kill them. Addicts can't fight. Staze is *Stasis* and it makes them immobile—mentally and physically. But addiction is a weapon, and you're obviously imaginative people." She raised an eyebrow, doubtful and at the same time encouraging.

There was a short silence.

"If they were addicted, we could enslave them," said one man.

"We could addict their children," said another. "We could hold their parents hostage to their next dose."

"We wouldn't have to stop at the Jacked in Tula," said someone else. "If we had enough, we could use it on those rich bloodsuckers in Giranoi. We could take everything they own."

"True," said Annmarie. She pointed lazily to the bag. "But first you have to pay."

Another long silence. Too long.

I squinted at the overcast morning, mouth dry. No one here had Annmarie's asking price. They'd been sent to stall us, to set us up for an attack we wouldn't see until it was too late. It had happened before.

Annmarie started to turn away. I did, too. A wild gust cut through my thin cloak and clothes. For a moment, I was as cold as if I was standing naked on the stone stairs.

"Wait," said the first man.

Annmarie half-turned. "Yes?"

The man licked his chapped lips. His eyes darted to the bag of Staze, up to the sky, then back to Annmarie. "You'll be over the mountain in Tula by afternoon," he said hoarsely, as though the words took all his courage. "You'll make those Jacked sons of bitches the same offer and I bet you tell them we bought a ton of your poison. If you want us dead, you should stay and do the job yourselves."

Annmarie frowned, but not at him, and blinked. There was a metallic taste under my tongue as she referenced in Mesh.

I see airborne Shrikes, she said. *They're at eighty klicks and closing.*

I made the dull sky give way to information overlays and saw single-pilot attack ships on the horizon. Their targeting hardware showed bright green, their charging weapons as flecks of scarlet. A dozen Shrikes, now at sixty klicks. Hunters.

On the cathedral steps, the Jackless locals elbowed each other, nodding and showing their teeth. They'd been expecting this.

Animals, I thought.

Annmarie grabbed my arm.

We have a thirty-second launch window, Corey's voice muttered inside my head. *Thirty-five and we're in their range.*

I hurried after Annmarie into the shadows of the cathedral. The bag of Staze hit my leg and I turned in time to see the Jackless disappearing down the windblown slope.

Annmarie hauled me through the airlock door and punched in the closure sequence. "Get us up in the air," she panted. "I'll take care of the engines."

I slid to my knees and shut my eyes. Felt sand under my palms and looked up.

Unfamiliar shapes in my familiar blue sky. Here the Shrikes read as birds on my horizon, close enough to make out the patterns in their feathers.

I crouched over the steel-colored pool, focused on the stones, the sky, and the branches in between. The stones rose into the air balanced on nothing but my will. In real time, the floor lurched as the antigravs engaged.

Navigation is set. Corey's voice sounded thick and distracted. *Give me altitude, Eve.*

In reality, the net of branches over my head stood for the jagged hole in the roof of the cathedral. We'd settled through it easily enough when we'd first arrived, but we hadn't been rushing. In Mesh, the stones drifted up, in between branches, barely disturbing dry leaves as birds plunged toward me.

There was a ripple in my air and Corey's image materialized on my hot patch of sand. I stared, open-mouthed at his amazing arrogance, but I should have expected it.

He took in the pool, the birds, the rising stones. *You call this efficient? What're you going to do, fight them off with sticks?* He made a motion with his hands and I felt the Medusa's weapons systems envelop me in a sheath of cold air. Abruptly my desert disappeared and Corey and I were outside the cathedral, high in the gritty clouds. Below us, Shrikes descended on the mountaintop, closing in on the Medusa's bronze-colored bulk as it lumbered upward.

Corey fell away, a vague blur shearing downward. I followed, not a naked thirteen-year-old covered with dust, but an avatar of the Medusa's defenses.

I opened my mouth to the rush of frigid air, eyes tearing in virtual cold as propagats laid out the Shrikes below me in schema. I could see the people inside, their ages and battle scars. The strengths and weaknesses of their little ships. A bad relay in the fuel system. Faulty wiring in the cockpit. The pilot's vital signs—was she any older than I was? I looked closer. The Shrike's original, Jacked technology had been ripped out and replaced with an old-style computer interface.

Too primitive and poor for hunters.

Corey, I shouted in Mesh. *They're not hunters. They're Jackless.* Probably the surviving sons and daughters of the filthy, hungry people on the mountain.

His acknowledgment was a change in pressure. *They get money if they kill us,* he said. *I'll bet they get new ships, new guns. New everything.*

His presence sharpened and the Shrike he'd targeted burst into flames. Below me, the girl's vital signs spiked with fear. She changed her navigation and shot toward the Medusa. I saw her weapons lock.

Do something, Eve. Not a demand. An expectation.

I pushed the Medusa's cold envelope outward. In the Shrike, navigation scrambled. Guidance failed. The girl switched frantically to manual controls, aiming unsteadily for a place to set down on the mountainside. Enough, I thought, for her to live and us to get away.

I felt Corey's ozone presence slide past me.

His heat made a spark in a disintegrating relay between fuel pods. Her terror was something I could almost taste and then the ship caught fire. It veered and smoked and fell, tearing itself to pieces, tumbling across the mountainside, past the ruins of the church.

If you're not going to fight, at least make sure the ship stays on course, snapped Corey.

"You don't have to murder them," I said, and opened my eyes.

I was still crouched in the airlock. Annmarie was bending over me.

"We're out of range," she said.

I wiped my face. "Corey's killing them."

"I know," she said. "I know."

"What you need is a more adult scenario," Corey said to me in the small crew room when we were in orbit. He leaned forward on the compact sofa. "What's that desert all about? Why are you a little girl in it? It's fine to have a fantasy world and all that, but when we're working, you should be somewhere useful."

Pervert, I thought, but not so anyone else could hear.

He turned to Annmarie, who was sitting next to him on the sofa, still wrapped in her red coat. "I'll say this again. You should rethink how you approach the locals. In the old days, when the Mesh was in one piece, we could have set things up for ourselves in a place like this. We wouldn't need Staze. But these people aren't going to cooperate of their own free will. You should sift a little Red into their wells, pay a local supplier to keep up the dosage, and we'll just move on. This wheeling and dealing of yours doesn't work often enough."

Annmarie got up and smoothed her clothes. She didn't say anything to him, just started for the door. I did, too, not wanting to be trapped alone with Corey while he was in the mood to preach to me about my many flaws, real and virtual.

When we were alone in the corridor, Annmarie took my arm. "Eve," she said, "get me all the information you can find on the Jacked in Tula. We'll go and see them next."

TWO

In my room, I prepared my lies.

Nav had given me a map last night—a piece of folded paper with a drawing of the decimated city, Tula. She'd pointed to the northern edge, where a curved line indicated a river.

"When you Mesh to see this part of the town," she'd said, "you'll find barriers—aegistics are what you people call them. Be sure you show them to Annmarie."

I'd looked at her in surprise. We used aegistics to hide the Medusa from the lesser technologies, making the ship appear as something harmless—a Jackless freighter, for example. They were an old but sophisticated masking technique, always a sign of Meshed survivors. I'd studied the northern edge of the map as Naverdi sketched in the rest of the town.

"Who's down there?" I'd asked, but she wouldn't say. Which made me nervous, and made all of Corey's prejudiced exaggerations seem true.

Would Naverdi lead us to hunters hiding in the ruins of Tula? I sat on the edge of my bed, folding and unfolding the map, thinking about the sex and the promises. If I told Annmarie how I'd arranged this rendezvous with Nav last night and that I planned to leave, Annmarie would turn the ship away from Kigal and never go back. Not necessarily because it wasn't safe, but because I was in her vision of her future, forever.

Annmarie's voice came into my head. *Are you ready, Eve?*

In their tanks, my fish broke the surface for one considered mouthful, then another.

I took a breath of the warm algae-smelling air in my room. *Yes.*

I felt her Mesh overlap mine, like a dim room turning light. Instead of algae and water, her place smelled of damp leaves and dirt. She widened her aspect and I found myself sitting across from her in a small clearing. She sat in a carved wooden chair, trimming flowers. Violets and lilies and scarlet amaranth clustered behind her. Red and white roses wound up a trellis in a wash of sunlight. The clearing ended where daylight vanished between the trunks of huge old trees. Last time I'd been here, a month or two ago, this had been nothing more than a kitchen, her metaphorical space for lab work.

You have a forest, I said in surprise.

She smoothed the cut blossoms with her fingertips. *And you still have a desert.*

But where's your workspace?

She pointed over my shoulder, through the tended under-brush where I could just see the edge of a wooden building.

You put in a house?

More of a cottage. I started to expand the kitchen and ended up . . . She made a vague gesture at the dark woods all around us. *Sometimes I wish I never had to leave.*

A breeze rustled in the branches. Tranquil, I thought. As peaceful and serene as I imagined a vision in Staze might be.

Annmarie nodded at Naverdi's folded map. *What did you find for me?*

I let the paper fall open between us on the litter of fallen petals. It spread itself flat, clarified, and became a window in the floor of the forest, peering down from our low orbit, focused on the Jacked city of Tula.

What was left of Tula was a sooty streak between a river delta and a line of hills. The city was a good hundred kilometers from the Jackless cathedral, but it was obvious that the Jackless forces had been pounding it for years. Tula's narrow streets had been reduced to shadows between shadow buildings. Divided avenues were now only wider ruts in the spray of ash and rubble. The Mesh showed the remaining Jacked information networks as red filaments across burned ground, linking troops with defensive perimeters and pockets of survivors. A red diamond in the middle of the ruined city was the local militia headquarters. Names and ranks, the chain of command, security protocols all spun themselves out in the shade of Annmarie's woods, secured against Jackless spies, but wide open for us.

Very thorough. She smiled. *Good practice, too. You'll be doing all of this on your own eventually.*

Every once in a while, she'd bring this up. My own ship, my own life, and a route for distributing Staze. As the Mesh became more and more sparse, that became less likely. I wasn't sure when I'd given up on her dreams for me and come up with my own.

I watched her scan the city until she reached the river and the northern edge where Nav had told me about the aegistics.

She frowned. *Did you see this?*

Maybe I wouldn't have to say anything. If there was a trap, I wouldn't be the one to spring it. *See what?*

Aegistics. She leaned closer to run her fingers over the image. *You can feel them.* She took my hand and made me touch the place where there was a change in the smooth texture of the illusion. Aegistics. They felt like blisters in plastic, too dense to see through.

Her fingers flew over the rest of the map. She was looking right at me, but her eyes were blank and her face a little more slack than I liked to see. *Survivors,* she whispered. *Meshed survivors. They're the only ones who'd have aegistics.*

How can that be? I said, trying not to sound nervous. *Tula's crawling with Jacked soldiers. How could they still be alive?*

I don't know.

Could it be hunters? I whispered.

She shook her head. *They haven't mastered our technology— yet. All they've been able to do is destroy it and we all know how that looks.*

I did know. Big gaps in the Mesh. Things missing from the virtual places where you were certain you had left them.

Her face became more focused. *Get the ship ready. We're taking her down.*

I gave her an amazed look. *Don't you want to contact the Jacked contingent first?*

No. She got to her feet. *We're not going down there to sell Staze. This is the same as when we found Corey. This is for us.*

But they've got bigger guns than the Jackless on the mountain, Annmarie. Maybe we should check things out first . . .

She made an impatient gesture at the window in her forest floor. *I'll fix their targeting systems. You just take care of descent.*

But they'll see us, I said. *There's nowhere to hide.*

Eve, she said tightly. *I want them to know who we are.*

The lieutenant in charge of the Jacked militia in Tula was barely more than a teenager. His left arm hung in a sling and his dirty uniform hung on him. Harsh blue-white lights in the scorched cellar showed lurid burns over the left half of his face.

We sat on the only chairs while the rest of his command staff stood behind him by the door. These boys were far younger than their Jackless counterparts, but just as filthy and frightened. In Mesh, their physical signs rippled through the cold cellar. Heart-pounding fear and new sweat. The smell of them thickened in real time, in the real air, wet and wintry and dank.

Outside the bright rectangle of the broken doorway, the Medusa hunkered in the ruins. The Mesh made the ship invisible to Jack-enabled weapons, but it was frustratingly obvious to the naked eye. Anyone with enough nerve could have tossed a grenade or fired a few shots, maybe damaged the ship enough to keep us here. But then they would have had to face us, and we could fill their heads with enough illusions to make them run through the ashy streets, killing friends, neighbors, and comrades until everyone in Tula was dead.

"We've heard of you," said the lieutenant.

"Have you?" murmured Annmarie. The blue-white lights made her into an iron-colored creature. "From whom?"

"Smugglers," said the lieutenant, and I felt my stomach tighten, certain he meant Naverdi. I'd tried to feel her presence in the ruins, but the blur of the nearby aegistics made it impossible.

"We get a lot of arms traffic through here. We hear all sorts of things." He shifted from one foot to the other, his right hand close to his body, covering his wrist wire. His data-scape was strapped against his hip, hidden under his clothes. We'd inserted diverters in their communications pathways to prevent anything but line-of-sight transmissions. Opinions and suspicions flickered between him and his companions, silent in Jack, perfectly audible in Mesh.

They were trying to decide if we could hear them.

Will they kill us? wondered the lieutenant.

Not unless you tell them the truth, replied one of the soldiers.

"The truth?" said Annmarie.

The lieutenant stiffened. Behind him, heart rates pitched even higher. "What do you want from us?"

If she'd said, *Your souls,* these boys might have found a way to tear them out and hand them over. "Tell me what happened to our people," she said.

Here it comes, I thought. The same old stories. Propagats everywhere. No way to hide anything. Would they tell us the sad histories of their families, I wondered, and the details of their rightful grudges? My father's generation and the generations before him had become rich by stealing and conniving and eventually leaving nothing but a few arbitrary borders for lesser beings to fight over. Seven years and tons of Staze hadn't changed a thing.

The lieutenant's eyes flickered to Corey and rested briefly, despairing, on me.

"We didn't have anything to do with the addiction," he whispered.

My stomach, already a knot, went even tighter.

"Addiction?" said Annmarie, her voice like a knife. "To what?"

Breathless silence.

"Staze," said the boy. Annmarie's expression narrowed and he went on. "I don't know the details," he said and I could hear how his tongue stuck to the roof of his mouth. "All I know is that it was done so they didn't have to be killed."

Corey leaned forward. "So who didn't have to be killed? The Meshed?" The lieutenant nodded nervously. Corey's face creased in the harsh shadows. "The Meshed in this city are still alive?"

"Yes," said the boy. "Yes."

Annmarie stood up. "Take us to them."

If the fighting ever stopped, in another ninety-seven years the ruins of Tula might be lost under grass and flowers. The only remains of the war would be uneven ground, odd boulders, maybe the hint of a wall where two stones still balanced on top of each other. I trailed after Corey and Annmarie as they followed the Jacked soldiers through the remains of the city. In Mesh, the destruction of this part of town had been perfectly clear, but the smell of wet smoke, rot, and the muffled wails of hidden children hadn't been part of the picture. We passed a heap of clothes—a shirt and two unmatched shoes crushed into the mud. For some reason it made me think of my mother's corpse lying spread-eagled on the white carpet.

Blood loss and stolen jewelry. A lack of life signs. The bacterial progress of decay.

I walked faster, away from the shoes and the shirt, resisting the urge to shut out the real Tula for a cleaner, more straight-forward version. In Mesh, things could be simple. Right or wrong. Dead or alive. Jacked or Jackless.

The northern edge of the city was just high enough to have a shallow view of the river. Wrecked foundations of houses showed underneath hummocks of dead grass. Down by the riverbank, I could make out the blackened shapes of an arm-chair and a rolled-up carpet, the remains of someone else's life. Waist-high piles of discolored stone surrounded us. I shut my eyes briefly and almost lost my balance. The aegistic blur made the Mesh useless here. It was like looking through the watery distortions in a fish bowl.

Corey frowned at the piles of stones. "What're those?"

"They live down there," said the lieutenant.

Annmarie opened her eyes and steadied herself. "They're entrances?"

"They're graves," said Corey.

"No," said the lieutenant and pointed down the hill.

Behind us, two people made their way up the windy slope. One was a very old lady supported by a young woman with dark hair, dark skin. Naverdi. I felt myself smile, bigger than I could press down for the sake of grim decorum. All the tension in my stomach evaporated. She squinted at us and waved at me with her free arm. It was all I could do to keep from bolting down the hill, grabbing her and running back to her shuttle, away from here.

"It's the smuggler woman," I heard Corey mutter to Annmarie.

"I can see *that*," said Annmarie.

I made myself hold still, arms crossed tight over my chest as the two of them labored toward us. Every time the wind gusted, Nav would tighten her grip on the old woman, whose wispy white hair lashed around her ears. She seemed weight-lessly sparse and as they got closer, I could see shiny patches of scarring over her face and thin neck. Her breathing had a hot, wounded sound. She clutched Nav's arm, gasping, and I thought she'd been burned, inside and out.

Something about her was familiar and I decided uneasily that it was her condition. She was an addict. She'd been in some terrible accident, turned to Staze for comfort, and gone too long without a dose. We'd seen hundreds of beggars like her, standing in line, Jacked and Jackless, desperate for a favor.

She and Naverdi stopped. The old woman's gaze slid over Corey, hesitated on Annmarie, but I was the one she stared at.

"Little Eve," she whispered. "You know me."

My stomach rolled up like the blackened carpet down the hill. I didn't have to examine the old woman's plugless wrist, or wait for the taste of metal under my tongue. Not just an addict. She was Meshed. I opened my mouth, but Annmarie answered for me.

"How *could* she know you?"

The old woman turned painfully to Annmarie, still clutching Naverdi's arm.

"Rose," said Annmarie.

Then I knew her, under the scars and wrinkles. She'd been my teacher at the Sanctuary before the place was burned to the ground. She'd been Annmarie's friend. Rose Carpho, who we thought had died in the fire. "Doctor Rose," I blurted and put my cold hands over my hot cheeks, afraid I would start to cry.

"How many survived?" said Annmarie. "Are you the only one?"

"I'm the only one from the Sanctuary," said Rose. She made a weak gesture at the piles of stones. "We're thirteen altogether. Not counting the children."

"Why not count the children?" said Annmarie.

"Where are they?" I asked.

Naverdi cleared her throat. "They're below. They were nervous about meeting you."

Corey frowned. "Why?"

"Because they don't fall into any of your categories," said Nav. "The children aren't Meshed."

Annmarie turned to Rose, still not understanding. "You *Jacked* your own children?"

Doctor Rose's knees gave way and she sank to the ground. "No, no," she said. "It wasn't allowed. Part of our punishment. No Mesh, no Jack. They have nothing."

"Jackless," said Corey. *"Jackless?"*

"And you're all addicts?" demanded Annmarie. "Where did you get the Staze?"

Rose glanced at the Jacked lieutenant, whose eyes widened and rolled in Naverdi's direction.

Corey stabbed a finger at Nav. *"You* did this. Why did you do this?"

"Supply," she said. "Demand."

"Idiot girl," said Annmarie. "You don't sell Staze to the *Meshed.*"

"I didn't." Nav pointed to the soldiers. "I sold it to them."

Rose looked up. "You can't leave, Annmarie. Now that you've found us, you have to help."

"Help you do what?" said Annmarie, her voice low with disgust. "Make more Staze? Hell, Rose. You're the one who came up with the whole idea."

Rose shook her head miserably and lowered her voice. "Help us get away."

Underground, the stone warrens were thick with body smells and a cloying licorice sweetness. The lights strung along the ceiling were the same blue-white as in the basement headquarters of the Jacked soldiers, and the bright areas were so blinding that the afterimages made crawling imaginary things in the equally black shadows.

Ahead, Annmarie and Corey followed Doctor Rose, muttering to each other. Annmarie outraged at a Meshed existence

no better than the Jackless, Corey disgusted that an entire enclave of Meshed had let themselves be buried by inferior beings.
Rose, who could no doubt hear every word, said nothing.

I followed Naverdi, wondering what else she hadn't told
me.

We stepped into a block of dense shadow and I caught her
elbow. She stopped and turned. Light from the next room
sliced the oily dark, catching the side of her face.

"How long have you been . . ." Selling Staze to poor Rose,
I thought, but I couldn't make myself ask. "How long have
you been coming here?"

"A couple of years." She smoothed hair away from my
forehead. So casual. So intimate. So easy for her, I almost forgot I wanted to accuse her. "These aren't my customers, Eve.
They're my friends."

I wasn't sure I believed that. Meshed, dependent on Staze.
The wrongness of it made my chest hurt. "Why didn't you tell
me Doctor Rose was here?"

"Annmarie would've found out." She let her hands drop
to her sides. "Rose could hardly wait to see you. When I told
her you were alive, you should've seen her face."

Which made me indescribably happy for a second and then
so sad I had to bite my lips to keep from bursting into tears.

"She said you were like her own daughter," said Nav. "I
know she was Annmarie's friend."

"She used to sing to us," I blurted. "In the orphans' dorm
at the Sanctuary. Doctor Rose and Annmarie . . . they invented
Staze . . ." I stopped myself.

"I know," said Nav. "She told me that, too." She glanced
down the hall after Annmarie. "She's sick, Eve. She can't stay
in this hole much longer."

"We could take her with us on the Medusa. If I went with
you, she could have my room."

I felt the air cool between us, abrupt and physical.

"I know what I said, before." Her voice was too soft, too

apologetic. "There's more you need to know before you decide that's what you really want to do."

My breath hung in the air as steam. I couldn't say anything. In Mesh, she could have seen my heart beating fists against the inside of my chest, but of course, everything I felt was invisible to her.

"Eve?" shouted Annmarie, far ahead, out of sight. "Eve! Where are you?"

"Here," I said and pushed past Nav, down the damp tunnel and into the light of the next room.

It was much brighter. There was furniture—two battered sofas and a big dirty mattress on the floor. I squinted in the glare. Maybe a dozen blank-eyed old people and a handful of raggedy children were sitting or lying down, their bodies slack in the blue-white light. The close air stank of sweat and old food. The survivors of Tula's Meshed population stared past us into empty space, every last one of them addicted to what Annmarie had intended for her enemies.

Doctor Rose hunched in the next doorway, waiting for us.

Annmarie passed her fingers under her nose and made her way across the dirty floor. Corey followed, neck stiff, mouth tight.

Nav took my arm. "Come on."

The next room was a dining area with too many mismatched chairs around a small table. Someone had set out a few teacups and saucers, but there was no tea. In the middle of the table, a stick of incense had been lit to freshen the air. The scent was like charred wood.

Maybe it was the smoke. All I could think of was how fast Annmarie and I had run, seven years ago, through the Sanctuary's gardens, my poor *piscae* sloshing in their water boxes while the fires behind us roared.

Rose sat at the head of the table, an empty teacup in front of her. Annmarie and Corey settled themselves at the other end, as far as they could get from the room full of Stazed Meshed.

I sat next to Rose, feeling how thin she was and how

burned. Nav was still standing in the doorway. Her face didn't tell me anything.

Doctor Rose's rheumy eyes came over to me. "Little Eve. Did you know you're the only child from the Sanctuary who survived?"

"She knows," said Annmarie. "How did you get away, Rose? The whole place was on fire. There were soldiers . . ." She stopped herself. "We thought you'd died."

"Ashes. Ashes. I crawled out of the ashes." Doctor Rose rubbed her forehead. "What about you?"

"I started the fire," said Annmarie.

Just before my fourteenth birthday, the Sanctuary was attacked by the same Jacked mercenaries who'd been paid to protect the place. One afternoon they released viral decoys into the local population of propagats, disabling a huge portion of the Sanctuary's Mesh. When the soldiers entered the campus, the malfunctions made them invisible to all but the unaugmented eye.

I was sitting by the window in Annmarie's lab when a dozen mercenary shuttles landed on the grassy quad. On the walkway below my window, between spreading trees and tended flowerbeds, privileged children stopped and stared when they should have been fleeing for their lives.

Annmarie was on the other side of the room, running psychobiologic simulations in Mesh, eyes shut, her back ramrod straight.

I remember I said, "Look! What's happening?"

I felt her jolt into real time.

I remember she said, "Get your coat."

We ran into the Jacked soldiers halfway down the stairs. In Mesh, we could jam their weapons, but there was nothing we could do to stop them from breaking Annmarie's jaw, her fingers. They would have broken her skull and worse if Annmarie hadn't started the fire in her own lab. Flames billowed into the stairwell and drove the soldiers away and I dragged Annmarie out, through the smoke and scattered corpses. When she could get up, we left the Sanctuary, running.

"Annmarie," said Rose. "Do you remember what Staze was when we first thought of it?"

"The end of violence." Annmarie gave a resentful shrug.

" 'The dream in Red is the dream of peace.' " Doctor Rose peered at the ceiling, the bedrock of the devastated city above. "Isn't that what you used to say?"

"I was wrong," said Annmarie. "Addiction is a weapon. It doesn't have anything to do with peace."

"You're still wrong," said Rose softly. "Staze gives me a beautiful place. Sometimes I never want to leave."

"You *let* them give it to you," said Corey.

Rose shook her head. "The Staze was in the water, or in the food. I don't remember how it happened, but it was a mercy, Annmarie." She stared at her teacup. "Do you know why we've managed to survive here?"

Annmarie didn't say anything, but I knew what she was thinking. This wasn't survival. This was barely an existence.

Rose touched the tip of her tongue with her finger, anticipating her next dab of Red. "We're alive because we're addicted. No one comes hunting for us. We're not a threat anymore. We can live in peace."

"You're alive because you're hiding in a *hole*," said Annmarie. "Staze wasn't supposed to be for *us*."

Rose sighed.

Naverdi came over to stand behind Rose, like an advocate. "We have a business deal for you," she said.

Annmarie snorted. "You want more Staze."

"No," said Rose. "We're self-sufficient. We can make all the Staze we need."

"Then what exactly do you want?" said Corey.

"We have a minimal production," said Rose, "but in a few months, we could be making ten times as much as you can on your ship. In a year, we could be making a thousand times as much."

Annmarie eyed Nav and her face darkened. "*You* want my business. *You* think you can control my markets."

"You don't control your markets," said Nav. "You dodge border disputes and war zones and hunters wherever you go. You're lucky if you can resupply your customers."

Rose leaned over thin burned arms. "You could make Staze for a century and none of us would be any safer than we are right now. What're you going to do in five or six years when there aren't even enough 'gats to give you a navigational bearing? The Mesh is falling apart and one of these days, you're going to get caught. I've made calculations about how much Staze you could have made since the Sanctuary burned down. Even if you had a dozen ships, you still wouldn't have a hundred percent addiction by the time the Mesh is gone. You've given up on the end of violence, because you know you can't do it without help."

Annmarie's bland composure hardened. "Have you spent the last seven years in this pit, second-guessing me?" She pointed her thumb at the middle of her own chest. "*I've* got a ship, Rose. *I* put the theory into mass production. *I've* been the one out there, risking my neck, while *you* gave up right after you crawled out of the damn ashes." She jabbed a finger at Rose. "*You* haven't got the right to question *me*."

Rose went paler, more strained. "Something's changed, Annmarie. We're leaving this planet. The Jacked in Tula don't care what happens to us. They're losing their war. Even if nothing else was different, we have to leave."

"And you were planning on packing yourselves onto my ship?"

"We still have our old transport from the Sanctuary," said Rose. "It's not in the best condition, but it'll do."

Annmarie glanced around the room, through the door at the addicts, and back to Rose. "So what's really changed is that you've got to abandon this hole, and you think you can move in on what I've made for myself. Sorry, Rose." She beckoned sharply to me. "Let's go."

Rose's watery eyes found me, fixed on me like a drowning person. I didn't move.

"Get *up*," Annmarie said to me.

"What's changed, Doctor Rose?" I said.

"We've found a safe place." She sounded almost too exhausted to speak. "A defensible point of production. It could change everything."

"Where?" I said. "What is it? An asteroid? A moon?"

"Let me show you." Rose closed her eyes.

I tasted copper in my mouth and glanced at Annmarie, who fixed Naverdi with a particularly poisonous glare and shut her eyes. Corey did, too. I looked up at Nav, who gave me a noncommittal shrug. I followed them in.

With the aegistics lifted for the moment, the room wasn't much different in Mesh. Only Naverdi was missing. The biggest difference was in the teacups on the table, which had turned to smoldering balls on a pitch-black background—a simulation of the three suns of ThreeSys: Eostre, Jaganmata, and Mara.

I moved closer, wondering what new thing we were supposed to see. There was nothing more familiar than this particular scene, which could have been pulled from a virtual textbook. There might even have been a caption. *'Three suns close enough for commerce, far enough apart to keep from creating an uninhabitable well of heat and gravity. Three thousand years ago, when the Generation Ship settled into orbit around the first planet, Paradise, the trio of suns and their accompanying eleven-each planets were welcome islands in an endless sea.'*

Even on a tabletop, it was clear how isolated we were. The next nearest system was well out of sight—another millennium of travel in any direction.

What are we doing, Rose? said Annmarie.

In Mesh, Rose showed herself the way I remembered her at the Sanctuary when she sang old songs for the orphans, late into the night. A slender woman with gentle blue eyes and an expressive mouth. When she sang, I remembered her forming the words carefully with her lips, opening them wide over straight white teeth. Even if I didn't always understand the lyrics, which were sometimes in different, ancient languages, I could remember how she made the words. Music came into my mind, either from Rose's tenuous connection with me in the Mesh, or from my own memory. The Landing Song sounded in the quiet room.

> *Tether now the outflung star,*
> *O' Mother, none*
> *else would plant a garden there . . .*

Annmarie frowned as though there were other, far more important things for me to be thinking about at the moment, but the younger Rose looked at me with obvious relief.

It's good that you remember. She turned back to the flaring teacups and laid in the borders—red lines over blue, over green over white—a tangle of alliances and disputes involving every planet, moon, and asteroid; wars as old as the human occupation of ThreeSys. *The only secure place would be one where there's never been anything but a Meshed population. We need an uncorrupted race of propagats to stay in control.*

Rose, said Annmarie. *There hasn't been a pure race of 'gats since they blew Paradise out of ThreeSys.*

Rose pointed into the space between Mara's sixth and seventh planets. *Look.*

There's nothing there, said Annmarie.

Watch, said Rose.

The three teacup suns darkened to embers and slowly went out. The surface of the table thickened, no longer a simulation of vacuum but a surface. The thickening turned to a rigid, uneven gray and I realized we were looking at a landscape. The unevenness was a strew of snow-covered boulders and the remains of stone buildings. Fog drifted in clots along the shadowy outlines of grand avenues. For a moment, the scene reminded me of the decimated city above us—broken streets and gutted houses—but this was far older. Even the way the vision felt in the Mesh was different. Not a metal taste, but a dryness, like ashes.

What's this? I whispered.

Little Eve, said Rose. *This is what's left of Paradise.*

That's impossible, said Annmarie flatly. *Half the planet was destroyed when they broke its orbit. Even if part of it survived, it'd be unstable. And even if we decided it was safe to land there, we'd be a target. It's the first place hunters would go to find us.*

If they could see it, I thought. *Why was it invisible before, in the bigger view?*

Because it's infested with propagats, said Rose. *Not modern ones. They're the old breeds. They survived. They multiplied. They've defaulted into hiding the entire planet.*

Then how can we see it? said Annmarie.

Because, said Rose, *I've found out a few things about the old technologies.*

So you're saying it's invisible to everyone except us? said Corey. *What about the Jacked? What about the Jackless? Anyone with a telescope should be able to find it. Interplanetary traffic's bound to notice it. And what about gravitational effects on the planets it passes?*

The room blurred, and in a moment, Naverdi was in with us, standing stiff as a mannequin.

What do you see when you look at the new world, Naverdi? asked Rose.

Only Nav's mouth moved. Not because the Mesh couldn't make her image more realistic, but because it was unseemly to give her the attributes of a higher social station.

In Jack, it shows up as a comet, she said. *There're already warnings out about its trajectory and gravitational effects. No one's saying anything about Paradise.*

Now her stake in this was clear to me. Annmarie, Corey, and I were supposed to help Rose put together a Staze factory on Paradise. Nav would take care of the distribution. Was there a percentage for her in helping me leave Annmarie and the Medusa? I doubted it. We would be safe. Nav would be rich. Once in a while she might invite me to her bed and I would fall on her out of starvation. I felt sick to my stomach. And stupid.

Rose let the vision on the table change to the textbook view again. Between the sixth and seventh orbits, the navigational illusion showed a comet falling slowly toward Mara, like some old harbinger of terrible news.

You've had too much Red, old woman, Annmarie said to Rose. *You think we can secure the whole planet, set up a Staze factory, and get a hook on all thirty-three planets before some petty little general comes and bombs us flat?*

No one's asking you to participate, said Rose. *What we need are . . . assurances.*

And now I understood the rest. Rose would have moved her tiny operation out to the wandering planet in an eyeblink, except for Annmarie. Nav must have told her about Sofi Zie and the others who had disappeared while trying to siphon off Annmarie's business. We were here so Rose could ask our permission to save her own life.

I wrapped my fingers together under the table and opened my eyes. Naverdi sat down next to me.

"We need to talk," she said in a low voice.

"Sure," I said, trying not to sound as though it mattered to me, one way or the other.

I felt Annmarie drop out of the Mesh, then Corey. Across from me, Doctor Rose opened her eyes, reached into her jacket with trembling fingers, and took out a tiny opaque plastic box. I knew exactly what was in it and glanced at the lolling addicts in the next room. I couldn't imagine them doing much more than licking up every grain of Staze they might make.

"Annmarie," said Rose. "At least try to understand our situation."

Annmarie looked away, arms crossed over her chest.

Rose opened the box. Red powder covered the bottom, not thickly. She licked the tip of her finger and dabbed a little

Staze on it. She put her finger in her mouth and her exhaustion disappeared. All the sad lines in her face went soft. Her eyes closed and her body slumped. She looked like she was sleeping.

Annmarie's expression was almost as blank as Rose's, but her mouth was tight around the corners, rigid down to the tendons in her neck. Beside her, Corey tapped his fingers, appropriately horrified and disappointed.

Nav followed us out of the catacombs, wordless. I scrambled up the ladder, emerging from the dank underground into the cold of late afternoon. Far ahead, at the bottom of the hill, the Medusa rested in the debris like a sloping temple of hammered bronze.

Nav came up next to me and caught my arm. "We have to talk."

Annmarie and Corey were already halfway down the hill, well out of earshot. I shrugged. Nav's hand slid away.

"You think I'm only interested in you because of the Staze," she said.

I turned so we were facing each other. Smoke from slow burning fires drifted in the gray air behind her. Artillery rumbled in the mountains. "Aren't you?"

"Listen," she said, "I'm an addict. I do everything—*every-thing*—because of Staze. It's not about you, it's just the way I live. I'm not dangerous, I'm not stupid, and I do like you, Eve. Not just because you can supply me." She tugged my sleeve, apologetic. "If it was just about supply, I'd be sleeping with Corey."

I felt myself twitch. "Did you?"

"Fuck, no." She hesitated. "Have you?"

"No!"

She came a little closer. "Can you at least listen?"

'Eve, come with me.' I wondered if she would say it again and found myself doubting it. Down the hill, Annmarie had stopped and was shading her eyes in our direction.

I touched the silver apple where it hung underneath my

shirt. A symbol of knowledge. A gust of wind blew grit across my face and I wiped my eyes, feeling as though I knew far too much. "Annmarie won't go to Paradise," I said.

"Just because Rose is addicted?" said Nav. "Doesn't that strike you as short-sighted?"

"It's only a matter of time until someone else figures out it's not really a comet."

"If Annmarie was there, she'd make the place impregnable."

It was probably true. I hadn't thought Nav knew Annmarie so well. "Did Rose say that?"

She nodded. "Rose knows she can't do it herself. She isn't very well these days."

"Rose wouldn't dare do it herself," I said bluntly. "She's afraid of Annmarie."

Nav raised her eyebrows, as if this was an obvious point. "Isn't everyone? Aren't you?"

I thought of Annmarie's face as she watched Rose dose herself. "Did Rose ask you to go with them to Paradise?"

She nodded. "I have to keep them supplied with Kevake." She reached inside her brown coat and gave me a folded piece of paper. I opened it and saw her familiar scribble over a low-resolution holo. Another map. Not of Tula this time. It was Paradise.

The planet itself was a grim gray blot. There was a high mass of rock, a rill, which wound around the planet's equator, uninterrupted, like a snake with its tail in its mouth. Nav had gridded the visible surface with pearl-colored lines and made a tiny circle in the middle of one equatorial quadrant.

I pointed to it. "What's this?

"What Rose showed you down below. That's where the biggest city was. There're still buildings. Some machinery, too."

"Machinery?"

"Terraforming machinery. The 'gats must be running it. You saw the fog and the snow. They've started an atmosphere."

I ran my thumbs along the crumpled edges. "You want me to show this to Annmarie. You want me to talk her into helping Rose."

"You talked her into coming here."

Of course I'd done no such thing. We'd come to Tula because Annmarie had caught the scent of old revenges.

"You'll do it?" said Nav.

I folded the map and pushed it into my pocket. "Last night you asked me to come with you."

She blinked. For that half second, I thought I could see everything I needed to know. How close she was to her next dose of Staze and how much she needed it—how much she needed me—and how little of that would ever be love.

She angled her head at Annmarie, who was standing with her fists on her hips by the Medusa's main airlock. "Go to Paradise," she said. "I'll meet you there."

"When?" I said, too sharp to my own ears, too demanding.

"In a month," she said. "I'll be there. We'll get things set up and then we can do whatever you want."

She made it sound so easy. And suggestive. The folded map in my pocket poked me, a joking nudge.

I touched the silver apple where it pressed against my heart. "Goodbye," I said.

She blew me a kiss and walked away.

Annmarie and I drifted in the virtual blackness of the Medusa's navigation, in orbit safely above the fray on Kigal, but not all that removed.

There it is. Annmarie pointed to a nondescript white dot. It wasn't the real image of Paradise. All we could actually see between the sixth and seventh orbits of Mara was a gravitational wobble. Even the illusory comet was missing through the holes in the Mesh.

Hail, I thought. Here is the new world.

Annmarie pondered the prick of light. *Imagine being the first to see it, way back when the Generation Ship arrived. After a thousand years of ship-bound travel, it must have been like water in the desert to them.* She came closer and took my hand. *That was the outflung star, you know.*

I know.

I suppose we taught you all that at the Sanctuary.

Rose, always the historian, had taught us. Old songs in the orphans' dorm about how a lifeless planet, years away from its perigee with the three nearest suns, could have been considered a Paradise. Only desperate people would have landed there. The place was no more true to its name than the Sanctuary. I peered around until I found Isla, Mara's fifth planet, making its wide swing toward Paradise's inward path. The Sanctuary at least had the trappings of safety. I'd fallen asleep to the sound of surf there and played under beautiful old trees.

None else would plant a garden there. . . . Annmarie traced the darkness with one finger, leaving a red trail behind as she moved from Mara-Kigal's cloudy gibbous to the distant fleck where Paradise was supposed to be. The trail thinned to a line, adjusted itself into an arc, and circled the white dot of the returning planet. A plot of a trajectory and orbit for the Medusa.

We're going?

Annmarie nodded. *We need an uncorrupted race of propagats to keep the Mesh in one piece. If Rose is right about the old 'gats, we might be able to put together a new breed. Something immune to the viruses the hunters are using.*

But you said you wouldn't go!

I said I wouldn't go with Rose. She raised an eyebrow. *That old woman's lost her mind, Eve. She's not the same as she was. If she really does manage to get herself and her—her friends to Paradise, you can bet some hunter'll find the place in a matter of months. Every addict in ThreeSys'll know where their motherlode is. Especially with that smuggler woman running supplies in and out. It won't take long.* She gave me a long, hard look. *Naverdi told you about Rose before we went to Tula.*

She didn't. I didn't have any idea what was going on down there.

Annmarie snorted. *You can't let yourself be used. Naverdi's an addict. I can tell you right now, she only wants one thing. I don't want you to see her again.*

I stared at her.

Did you hear me?

I nodded.

She was silent for a while, weighing, I thought, how much of my own will I might have developed over the last seven years without her noticing. *I don't want you off the ship until we get to Paradise.*

She waited for me to say something. When I didn't, she faded, slowly, breaking her connection with the Mesh.

I looked around in the dark, at the three isolated suns, feeling like it was the first time I'd ever really noticed where I was.

Back in my room, I shut my eyes, bare-assed in sand. Outside the dome of my sky, Nav's ship manifested as a thumbnail gleam in hot azure and I peered hard at the glint. She was there. Her ship was crawling with 'gats and I could feel her, but her presence had the tang of Staze. If I wanted, I could see how much she'd taken in the last half hour.

Naverdi had promised to be in Tula, and she was. She would meet me on Paradise in a month . . . she said.

I could find out for sure.

I could slide into her com-interface, her licorice-scented temple, and poke through the brocade until I found her Jacked metaphors for navigation and see where she planned to be in the meantime. Her ship's systems would give me facts, not sultry suggestions. Nav was Stazed. She'd never know I'd been there. She had lied to me—or left out essential truths, any-way—about Tula. I had the right to find my own answers.

I rolled over on my belly. Hot sandy grit against my thighs, azure warmth over the small of my back. A clean, sensual feeling.

She would be lying in her chair, sprawled across crimped velvet, senseless inside the walls of her static garden. Perfectly still.

I would go in, and I would come out.

I moved forward on my elbows until I could see my reflection in my steely pool. My desert quivered in its own heat, then dissolved into nothing as I slid through the watery surface of my interface, transferring my presence from my place to hers.

Naverdi's temple was warm, and dense with perfume. I made my way past gold-framed mirrors, candelabras, and trailing tapestries. The room was exotic and alluring at first glance, but the deeper the intermix between my Mesh and her Jack, the more fake I knew it would feel.

Nav was curled up on a velour divan, the Jackwire trailing from her wrist, across the floor, disappearing under patterned carpets. It struck me as odd that she would dose herself while plugged in, but maybe it heightened the sensation. I would have to ask about that, but not anytime soon. I crouched down beside her. Instead of the usual tumble of dreads, her virtual self had a coif of braids and beads, feathers and shells. Tiny emeralds glittered along the satin edges of her ears. If I touched her hair, for all the decorative doodads, it would be cottony and vague. Her skin would taste like dust. I knew all this and I put my fingers against her cheek anyway. Surprisingly smooth.

I touched her dress, an exaggerated costume made of spangled brocade. It had slipped off her shoulder, leaving a shadowy path across the bare brown skin of her throat and lower, between her breasts. She was as solid, as warm as anything in Mesh. I leaned closer and my body welled up with heat as my palm came against the softness of her breast. I wanted to know if she could feel me, wherever she was, and found myself forgetting why I'd come here in the first place. Was she at the edge of a lake? In a field of licorice-smelling flowers? The urge to get closer, deeper, crowded inside me.

I moved one hand to where the spangled dress split over her thigh and pushed my fingers under stiff fabric. The lining was silk. Hot and inviting. I leaned over her still body, my belly brushing over sequins, my silver apple on its thin chain catching on ruffles. I shifted and the necklace caught on some fabric frill. I stopped and looked up to see my face in one of the gold-framed mirrors.

At first I thought it was Corey.

Ashy and sexless, scrawny and lewd. Crouched over Nav like a scavenger.

I jerked my hands away, shoved them under my arms and backed off, unable to look away from what Nav saw in me. I was gargoylish in the mirror, slack-jawed and depraved, radiating dishonesty, opportunism under the thin layer of dust. I heard myself yell and opened my eyes.

"Eve?" Corey's voice outside in the corridor. "Is everything all right?"

I took a gulp of air. Licorice and perfume flattened into the Medusa's recycled atmosphere. I was in my cabin, in my bed, open-eyed in real time. My hands were still shoved under my armpits, and I clenched them around myself.

"Eve?" I heard him try the lock on the door.

"I'm fine," I shouted, too loud and pitched too high.

"Come up to the control room," he said. "We're breaking orbit."

I nodded, which was pointless since he couldn't see it, and made myself get off the bed. My knees were still trembling from the hot interruption that would not have been sex. I was afraid to blink. Inside my eyelids would be that image of myself, slick with attitude and self-indulgence.

Far below, Kigal's surface was chalky gray with its own cold weather. I hugged my knees in the seat by the control room's starboard window, not sure why Corey had made me come up. He could run the drive without help. Navigation was already set. Annmarie had sequestered herself in her room. I had nothing to do but sit where Corey could keep an eye on me.

Naverdi's shuttle and Rose's ship were in orbit as well. Both were in visual range, in a slightly lower orbit. Rose's ship was closest, between us and Kigal's cloud cover, its battered hull lit harshly from one side. Nav's shuttle was just a trailing glint.

I leaned my cheek against the cool surface of the window and wondered unhappily which of us was worse. Nav, for luring me with the promise of sex and love when all she wanted were the secrets of Staze-making. Or me. Because in the end, with enough 'gats and enough Staze, I could make her into anything I wanted. At least Corey and Annmarie had an equal field of play.

But then again, maybe Nav and I had a better balance of power. Naverdi didn't owe me anything. Corey owed Annmarie his life.

Across the control room, Corey was watching one of the three monitors lined up on the control panel between us. His face was tense and focused, and I peered over to see what was so absorbing.

One monitor showed orbital traffic; a dozen or so blips over a graphic display of the planet. The second showed whatever was in visual range, in this case a zoomed-in view of what I could see out the window, and the third, the one Corey was so fixated on, showed a distorted schematic of Rose's ship.

Which was odd. I got out of my chair and stood behind him. Presumably, Rose would use the same aegistics in transit as she had with her underground enclave, but something was wrong. More than half the ship was visible, as though Rose didn't have quite enough 'gats to make the whole thing disappear.

Corey smiled up at me. A tight smile.

"Where're her aegistics?" I tapped the screen. "We shouldn't be able to see her. Something's wrong."

"No doubt," said Corey mildly. "That ship's probably been

gathering dust for years. They should have kept it on a proper maintenance schedule."

"Anyone can tell that's a Meshed ship trying to make itself disappear. What if there're hunters . . . ?"

Corey's eyes flickered over to the first screen, where the rest of the ships in orbit showed as different-colored blips. Three floated along in a loose formation, each a particular shade of red.

Shrikes.

Bigger ones, with better weapons than the Jackless guerrillas had on the mountainside. I touched the screen, unable to believe that I would see this before the Medusa's systems warned us. The alarms should have been blaring, but there was no sound.

"You saw them?" I whispered. "You knew they were here?"

Corey nodded. "I've been watching them for the last half hour. They haven't seen us. I keep checking."

"But what about Rose?" I said. "She can't run her 'gats like that. She's a target."

"Oh, Evie," he said. "I'm sure she's seen the Shrikes by now."

"She hasn't . . ." I knew *that* and so did he. Rose was still deep in Staze and so were her nodding underground partners. "Call Rose! You can't just sit here and watch it happen!"

He gave me a cool, appraising look, as though I was hysterical and out of control. "All right." He leaned over the control panel and slapped a switch.

There was an empty, rasping noise across the open channel before a sleepy male voice responded.

"Yes?"

"Listen," said Corey, "are you monitoring orbital traffic?"

"Well," said the voice. *"Sure."*

I leaned over the panel. "Three Shrikes are coming right at you," I said. "You understand? They're hunters. They can see you."

"I can't see anything." Silence on the other end, and then an exasperated sigh. *"We're having a couple of system problems. But anyway, we're invisible."*

The Shrikes were close enough to show up on the visual monitor, leaving trails in the clouds over Kigal as they prepared to rush up from underneath.

"You're *not* invisible," I said. "Stand down your 'gats. Everyone can tell what you are."

"I can't," said the voice. *"I'm not Mesh . . . well, wait. I'll see if I can get the Doctor."* The channel hissed and went dead.

I stabbed the internal com button. "Annmarie?"

No answer.

"Annmarie!"

"I think she's got the com turned off in her room," said Corey. "She told me she didn't want to be disturbed."

"But they'll be *killed.*"

Corey just spread his hands.

I ran out of the control room, down the hall to Annmarie's door and banged on it.

"Annmarie!"

No answer, but I could feel her inside. Her resentments and revenges, her razor-edged conceptions of right and wrong. I slid to the floor and closed my eyes.

Intact, the Mesh would have shown Kigal in a spectacular wash of radiating auras—gravity, atmosphere, and magnetic fields. Instead, the planet was a patchy collection of colors over a dull depression in the vacuous dark. Compared to what I could see of Kigal, Nav's shuttle was a blaze of data—size, class, and trajectory. Above her, Rose's ship was easy to spot—an undulating blob of information, partly Meshed, partly not.

The Shrikes, which should have been directly below, were nowhere in sight but I wasn't surprised. Hunters would strip their crafts of propagats with nanovirals, rendering them invisible in Mesh, but I could still track them with the Medusa's Jackless sensors. I would save Rose the same way we'd rescued

Corey. I widened my own aspect to activate the Medusa's defense systems.

And found them already in motion.

It was Annmarie, I thought. She would be an essence outside, arrayed in a net of the ship's defenses. Instead of relief, I was suddenly very afraid for Rose.

I launched my avatar self away from the Medusa and spread my perceptions across the emptiness. The Shrikes were still invisible, not quite close enough to be a danger. Would they attack Naverdi's shuttle? I cast around for her, knowing exactly where she should have been, but the orbiting blaze of data had vanished.

There was no sense in calling out. She wouldn't answer. Her ship was running on autosystems and Nav was as deep in her dose as Rose. I pressed outward, tasting the void for her, directing a pack of 'gats here, a pack there until I found a scatter of ionized particles not far from Rose's ship, more or less the same size as Nav's shuttle. The shape vanished as I tried to focus on it, disappearing from the Mesh like a hole filling with sand. In a moment, it was gone. The effect was familiar. Nanovirals, I thought and spiraled away. If hunters were tracking Rose already, it would make sense for Naverdi to strip her shuttle of complicit 'gats.

I felt a motion between myself and the planet and turned, expecting the 'gats to have pinpointed the Shrikes.

Instead, I saw Annmarie.

She was just where the Shrikes should have been. Her avatar essence fell toward Rose's ship from the same coordinates the Medusa's screens had shown as an enemy.

I checked again. No sign of Shrikes.

Annmarie?

I could feel every bristle of her irritation and surprise. Irritated that Corey hadn't been able to keep me out of her hair, surprised that I had found her so quickly. She angled toward Rose's ship, fast as an angry thought.

On Rose's ship, the shifting blur of information became a

little clearer. Someone was adjusting the Isolators around their drive, a green tint under spotty aegistics. As I got closer, I could see the green field flicker and I realized what Annmarie was doing. Rose's Isolators weren't stable. If they lost power, there was more than enough heat in the drive to breach the hull and burn the ship to a cinder. It would take seconds for Annmarie to skew the unsteady field and from the Medusa's control room, it might very well look like a Shrike attack.

Ashes, ashes.

I was supposed to be watching this disaster in open-mouthed horror while Corey, calmly complicit, made sympathetic noises and Annmarie murdered her old friend.

And Nav. Where the hell was the shuttle?

I dove at Rose's ship. *Stop!* I shouted, at Annmarie, or Rose, or whoever could hear me. I made a wild grab into the darkness, trying to make contact with whoever was running the Isolators, and felt Annmarie's presence slide past me.

Rose's Isolators turned from green to scarlet. The ship quivered, flashed, and balled outward in a silent gritty sphere. I turned out of instinct to shield my face and saw the Medusa hanging well out of range behind me. Raw white light raked across the bronze hull. Annmarie's vindication was a taste under my tongue, bitter and sour and stale.

Naverdi!

If she had been in range, there would be nothing left of her. I turned to the planet, flat and dull as a piece of gray paper. Where Rose's ship had been, there was only a glittering field of data concerning former mass and former occupants.

Naverdi.

I opened my eyes, still crouched in the Medusa's corridor, and found Corey standing over me. He reached down to help me up, but I knocked his hands away.

"You did this," I hissed. "Why did you do this?"

He looked at me, eyes flat and reptilian, and didn't say a word.

THREE

Dinner that night was shredded vegetables and a little meat over rice. The three of us sat too close together around the tiny table in the crew room. Corey poured cold tea into wide ceramic cups, putting one at his own place, one in front of Annmarie, and the third firmly beside my plate.

"Terrible," he said to Annmarie. "Terrible to lose one of our own."

She sipped and nodded, lips pressed together. Her eyes came over to me, but she didn't say anything. I was supposed to agree, or stay quiet. I stared at my plate, sick to my stomach.

> *Tether now the outflung star,*
> *O' Mother, none*
> *else would plant a garden there.*

The song that had started in my head this afternoon had caught.

*O' Daughter, one
night reveals all future days.*

I took a breath over the hot food and knew I would choke
on anything I put in my mouth—or whatever came bursting
out. What could Annmarie possibly do to me, I wondered, if I
had the audacity to challenge her? Leave me on some backwater
world at the mercy of the Jackless? Abandon me on Paradise?
Ignore me? Was I afraid of her, like Naverdi said? I looked across
the table to find her watching me, her food untouched. In that
moment, she reminded me most of the cast-iron saints under the
eaves of the Jackless cathedral on Kigal. Correct and immobile.

"You shouldn't have killed her," I blurted and then wondered who she thought I meant.

Her expression didn't change. I could feel my face getting hot.

"Rose was dead when we found her," said Annmarie.
"She'd been dead for years."

"Eve, honey," said Corey. "We know you're upset about
this. Maybe you'll understand as you get older."

"She understands now," said Annmarie. "She's upset because the smuggler was killed in the explosion."

There was a quick pain in my stomach, sharp enough to
make my vision blur. I couldn't say, You don't *know* that, because she would nod her head with an eyebrow raised and
assure me that she had seen Naverdi's shuttle blown to pieces.
I couldn't tell her that Nav *was* alive, because I didn't know,
and she would sense that. If I said another word about Nav or
Rose, she would wring out my tiny futile hopes until I was as
sure of Nav's death as she wanted me to be.

For a while, there was no sound but forks tapping on the
plates. Then Annmarie cleared her throat.

"The Rose you remember was a different woman," she
said, as though she did have a regret or two. "Rose was never
a strong person, but back in the Sanctuary she could hide the

weakest parts of herself in a crowd." She eyed me. "Even you knew she was weak."

"She wasn't weak," I whispered. "She cared."

"You came to me instead of her," said Annmarie. "You were terrified of the older children in the orphans' dorm. Who did you go to when you wanted to get out?"

"You," I said, "but . . ."

"But?"

But at the Sanctuary, Annmarie had an apartment with an extra room. Rose, her husband, and teenage son lived together in even less space. If Rose hadn't had a child of her own . . .

"You would watch me through the doorway while Rose taught you the old songs," said Annmarie. "I remember how scared you were. I could see it in your face."

I looked down, blinking away tears for Rose, Nav, even the witless addicts.

"You and I," said Annmarie, "are still alive for one reason. We stayed together. Isn't that right?"

I nodded.

She took a sip of tea. "Rose abandoned us the first time she took Staze."

"It wasn't her fault," I said. "The Jacked in Tula put it in the water, or in the food."

"And they were supplied," said Corey, "by Naverdi."

I bit my lower lip, hard.

"You knew Naverdi was going to be in Tula," said Annmarie.

I didn't say anything. Now the circle of accusations was complete. Rose. Nav. Me.

Corey put his fork down. "You should have told us about Rose. Did you think we wouldn't go to Tula if you'd told us?"

"I didn't *know*."

"You lied to me," said Annmarie.

"And you're making it worse for yourself," said Corey.

My stomach wound a notch tighter. I pushed away from the table and started for the door.

Annmarie folded her napkin. "Eve?"

I stopped, knowing it was a mistake, that the correct thing to do was to cover my ears and scream and run until I was behind my own locked door.

"We love you, Eve," she said. Beside her, Corey was nodding.

She held me with her eyes until I realized there was no choice.

"I love you, too," I said.

She nodded her permission and I pushed out of the crew room.

Hours later, her voice came into my head.

Are you sleeping?

I was lying in bed, watching the fish circle in their tanks, coming to the surface for air once in a while. Watching them made me calmer and more desperate by turns. On the one hand, they were trapped by their circumstances. On the other, where else would a pair of exotic fish survive?

I'm not asleep, I said.

There was a long silence.

I'm sorry if I seemed angry at dinner. This has been an upsetting time.

The sensation her voice carried was a delicate sadness. I rolled over. I'd never heard her apologize for anything. Ever. I could have said I was sorry for confronting her, but I wasn't.

Would you come in and see me, Eve? We need to talk.

I nodded, wondering if I should feel vindicated or more suspicious. *All right,* I said, and her lightness came over me.

This time I found myself inside the cottage, sitting at her kitchen table.

Annmarie knelt across the room on a braided hearth rug, arranging kindling in the stone-arched fireplace. Where I had a pool in my desert, she used flame for scrying the Mesh. The first time she'd showed me, I'd thought it was a ponderous way to interface until I decided the building of the fire was ritual, not a necessity. She could bring up flame with a gesture, or she could spend half an hour arranging the elements. Anything I could see in my pool, she could find in the flames, although sometimes I thought she could see considerably more.

I rubbed at the fine dust of flour on the table until the dark wood showed. The kitchen hadn't changed since the last time I'd been invited. Close and warm, the air smelled faintly of yeast. Unbaked loaves of bread, Annmarie's favorite metaphor for bio-simulations, lay on paddles, ready for the oven. Everything here had a formal simplicity, like a laboratory. Green glass jars for metaphorical spices and herbs lined the shelves in alphabetical order. Only her bread oven and the fireplace showed signs of use, and the use seemed painted on.

Annmarie pulled out a long match and struck it on stone until it flared. She held it under the kindling, letting the fire play over the match well after the tiny twigs had caught, then tossed the match in.

Fire engulfed the wood with a gnawing sound. It occurred to me that it looked nothing like the inferno at the Sanctuary. Instead of ravening, this was dangerously considered. If fire was a metaphor for Annmarie's furies, it was under such control that she could aim it, flawlessly directional, sharp and true.

She patted the braided rug beside her and I came over and sat. The fire rippled with a comforting heat, warming my face. I could feel Annmarie gathering herself, and the urge to put my head in her lap was overwhelming. A function of the warmth or her will, I lay down with my head on her knee and she stroked my hair.

Eve, she said, *do you understand that no matter how I try to protect you, there are certain things that I may not be able to control?* Her hand came to rest on my shoulder. Her palm felt hot. *Are you listening?*

Yes.

I've always told myself that because the Sanctuary turned out to be vulnerable, we had to keep moving, and as long as we could use the Mesh, we'd be safe enough. But the fact is, we could be better off in a single location. In a way, Rose was right. In a way, she was wrong.

What do you mean?

It would be easy to make Paradise a central point of production for Staze. The propagats are already terraforming the surface. By the time we get there, the atmosphere might be viable. But that's too limited a vision.

I didn't say anything. The fire crackled, hypnotizing and false.

We can do it again, she whispered. *Plant the garden. Sow the seeds.*

We?

All the Meshed, she whispered. *All the ones who're still alive. We can make the new world over.*

I sat up. *That's crazy. Hunters'll find it—you said that yourself. We'll be killed.*

She shook her head. *Not this time. Paradise is far more defensible than I thought. We can land and we can rebuild. This time we won't be stuck in a fairy tale. We'll be realistic. We'll survive.*

I was afraid to ask how she'd come to these conclusions in such a short time. Rose might have spent years opening communications with the old breeds of propagats. For all I knew, once the aegistics on Rose's ship were gone, Annmarie had simply pried the knowledge out of Rose's mind in the seconds before the poor old woman had died.

Now watch, said Annmarie.

In the hearth, the flames seemed to flatten, a prelude to interface. In my own environment, the pool's mirror surface would have turned transparent. Here, the back wall of the fireplace opened like a door. The fire thinned to a waver of heat and gave way to the same sooty landscape we had seen on Rose's table.

Except this time we were in it, standing side by side at the end of a wide avenue in a faint wash of unreal light. The light had nothing to do with Mara, too far away to be more than a bright speck behind snow-laden clouds. It was supplied by the local population of 'gats. If I closed my eyes, metaphorically in Mesh, the scenery would be the same. What the 'gats gave us wasn't sight. It was a map of their locations, conveyed as a visual impression of where things were, their dimensions and volume.

That was familiar, but there was far more information than I was used to. For one thing, I knew precisely where I was. We were standing on the rill, the planet's physical equator, and I remembered Naverdi's pearl-colored marks on the holo of Paradise. This was the edge of the city where she'd told me she would be in a month. I thought of Tula, just as blackened and torn down, and wondered if she would always arrange to meet me in some decimated location.

What do you see? said Annmarie.

To my right, the crumbled ruins of a building rose from an iced-over landscape to its first set of windows. To the left, foundations no higher than my knees divided up the other side of the road. Behind us, the road sank into the glassy pit of a half-filled crater, not from a meteor but from the attack that had destroyed the city.

I shivered. Annmarie seemed to feel it.

You're cold? she said.

As avatars on Paradise or anywhere else, temperatures shouldn't affect us. I was chilled, but it wasn't the snow, or the ice on the black stone. It was the place. *It feels different.*

Does it? Her voice had a knowing smile in it. *Tell me.*

I wasn't sure there were words. Paradise was on me like a second skin, in me like a breath. I could have told her about the composition of the stone under my feet or given her the median temperature of the entire planet. I could have told her where the human remains on the planet were, crushed to powder by two thousand years of ice. I knew how deep the next snow would be, how fast it would melt into the planet's frozen aquifer, and how high the water would rise as Paradise closed in on Mara.

I looked up at the dull sky, but nothing could hide behind the inconvenience of clouds. Propagats were everywhere: healthy, dedicated 'gats, ready to swarm the tiniest bit of falling debris or the stealthiest Shrike. Nothing could happen on this world without our knowledge. Nothing could survive here without our inclination.

I know everything, I whispered.

Welcome to the Mesh, she said. *The old one. The real one.*

I sat cross-legged in the sand by my virtual desert pool, an imaginary piece of paper in front of me with a list of names written in red ink.

Three hundred names for the new world. The people Ann-marie considered worthy. Meshed in hiding, Meshed in prison. Meshed supposedly dead and buried in undocumented graves. Meshed biologists and doctors, specialists in Mesh propagation. Engineers and architects. Artists. Writers. I recognized two of the names from the Sanctuary. Lila Sphear and Otto Rondelle, both physicists.

There was a common directory I could access in Mesh, no different from what the Jacked or Jackless could find with their equipment, but neither Sphear nor Rondelle would be in it. To trace them, I would have to start with the Sanctuary records on Isla, Mara's fifth planet, where I had been sent for safety as a child.

I leaned over my pool and put my fingers in the water. Ripples widened into a window opening onto the same schematic of ThreeSys as the one on Rose's tabletop diorama. A textbook view of the three suns: Eostre, Jaganmata, and Mara. I trailed my fingers under the surface, focusing on Mara's eleven planets. The first seven, including Kigal, were terraformed. The other four, on the edge of the system, were cold and hostile, and the people there lived in domes, massacring each other for air. Even on Isla there was fighting, but I could ignore it from my viewpoint in the desert.

When I was close enough, I slid into my pond. Face and shoulders. Arms and legs. Wet, but not the same as diving into water. A transition. A leaving of dry land.

I sank toward Isla, immersed in liquid metaphors until I reached the virtual surface.

In Mesh, the Sanctuary presented itself the way I remembered the campus. I drifted over green lawns and flowerbeds, walkways of crushed red gravel and the beautiful trees whose branches had been trained into permanently graceful gestures. I passed the building where Annmarie'd had her lab, and the window I'd been looking out of when the Sanctuary was attacked.

In some places, the visual surface of the Sanctuary seemed tattered—a flowerbed disturbed. Bricks out of place. Raw code showed like footprints in deep mud, where hunters had torn through the formatting to find the digital trails of survivors. I drifted over the torn grass, past broken windows, and then I smelled the flowers.

Their scent enveloped me. White roses on a tree that never bloomed. Blossoms carved into the stone lintel of a doorway. Information stung behind my eyes, and I understood the message. Rose Carpho had been here, and she had left a trail for anyone who knew how to look.

I followed the vague outlines of flowers in the red gravel path until I was at the building that had housed the central offices. Inside, I found myself staring at a row of Sanctuary icons, all sealed with a single red petal. Personnel files. Probably databases that could track individuals by their Mesh accesses. Everything I needed to trace the Sanctuary faculty and student body was here, and it was all locked up tight.

I could rip away the formatting, study the codes underneath and find a way to slip in, but so could any assassin. The security staff would have left booby traps, deadfalls, and a shouting crowd of countermeasures. Rose had put her seals here to protect herself, but would she cut off friends and allies from the same information? Whatever security she had added to the school's, it had already recognized me by showing the hidden flowers.

I hovered in front of the icons and thought about Doctor Rose. Her watery eyes and burned arms.

Maybe all I had to do was say something. I cleared my throat and started to sing. The sound of my voice, even in Mesh, was thin and unsure.

> *Tether now the outflung star,*
> *O' Mother, none*
> *else would plant a garden there.*

Petals drifted away from the security seals. I sang a little louder.

> *Sow thy seeds in barren ground,*
> *O' Father, done*
> *are thy tasks beyond the gates.*

The seals vanished along with the dark antechamber.

> *Harvest now thy fruitful womb,*
> *O' Daughter, one*
> *night reveals all future days.*

The faculty database brightened: warm, welcoming, and too blurry to make out. I kept singing.

> *Raise up thine Unknown Child for*
> *all and shout, Hail!*
> *Here is the new world.*

The virtual space focused and I found myself standing in the middle of an ornate picture gallery.

Portraits hung everywhere, big and small, in clumps and

alone. Here was everyone who had ever been in this enclave: students, staff, and faculty. Gold frames gleamed against flocked wallpaper. There were red velvet couches arranged here and there, and I eyed those uneasily. Red was probably an indication of security measures—maybe even traps for the unwary hunter. What virtual viewer would get tired and need to sit?

Eve?

I jerked around and saw Doctor Rose, elaborately framed.

Is it little Eve? she said, barely moving her lips.

I had no idea what to say to her. It seemed wrong to demand answers about the living from a woman so recently dead. Finally I said, *Do you know where you are right now?*

She nodded, ever so slightly. *I died near the planet Kigal in the Mara System.* She gave yesterday's date.

She said it so matter-of-factly, I was afraid I might start to cry. *I'm sorry,* I said. *I tried to warn you.* The image of Rose gave me a sad look. *Do you know where I am?* I said.

Little Eve, you're with Annmarie Stijl near the planet Kigal in the Mara System.

Do you know where Lila Sphear is, Doctor Rose?

Sphear has been dead for three years. She was in a detention camp, you know.

Where? I said.

On Jaganmata-Durga. Camp 3409 near the city of Hadesta. What did she die of?

Internal hemorrhaging, said Doctor Rose. *She was beaten to death. Tortured, no doubt.*

I had heard about these kinds of detention camps, but I had never seen one. To see one—really see one—was to know that your days were numbered. *What about Otto Rondelle?*

Professor Otto Rondelle has been dead for six years.

Was he killed in a camp, like Sphear?

Professor Rondelle died at the intersection of Dray and Grada avenues in the city of Josta on Eostre-Eire. He died of a skull fracture. Do you need to know the precise time of his death? The hospital recorded it.

Attacked in the street, like a criminal. I pointed to the list. *Can you tell me if any of these people are still alive?*

She studied it. *They're all dead, little Eve.*

So much for Annmarie's vision of the new world. *All of them?* I said, *Are you sure?*

Quite sure.

You can't tell me anything else?

I want to tell you more, little Eve, but I can't. It's a security precaution. But I can tell you this.

What?

Rose's eyes moved to the left, indicating the next set of rooms. *The landscapes in the gallery are lovely. Artful paintings. Some by important masters.*

Landscapes?

Her image gave me a stiff, encouraging nod. *Go on,* she said.

I made my way past the next set of portraits and turned a corner into the next gallery. It was a long, narrow room, almost a corridor, lined with landscapes. Most were bucolic views of rivers and forests, but one showed a version of the Annunciate I'd never seen before. Instead of standing wistfully at the gates, this woman squatted in the middle of an overgrown garden, biting hungrily into an apple. She was pale and naked and pregnant, and behind her, the gates of Paradise were wide open. When I looked more closely, I could see a naked man stepping through the gates, either to confront the swarm of mythical monsters that flew toward the garden or to welcome them in.

Was this what Rose thought I should see? It seemed like a parody of my mother's medal, a little too heretical to be in a place like this. Technically, it wasn't a landscape anyway. I turned away from the painting, confused, and then, on the opposite wall at the far end of the narrow gallery, I saw what Rose wanted me to find.

The landscape was tall as I was, wider than I could spread

my arms. It was set into a heavy frame of gilt roses with a gate across the surface of the painting. Not a real gate, but a flimsy thing made of twisted gold wire.

I went over and stopped in front of it. The gate was fastened to the frame with hinges and had a loop for a handle where its two halves met in the middle of the picture. Of course, the painting was Paradise. Not the bombed-over planet, but the garden from the old stories. A stream rushed down the side of a hill, complete with its own babbling sound. Birds flitted through sparkling air. A deer bounded past. The scene reminded me of a majority of my homework when I'd studied here. Assigned reading usually meant Meshing into the narrative as a character and now I peered through the wires for a glimpse of the Annunciate, because surely it would be Rose. In a minute or two, she would step forward dressed as the woman in the garden and explain that Paradise had returned. The scene would change to show exactly where the planet was and any accumulated messages would play themselves back.

I waited. The stream continued to rush down the hill. The birds flew in and out of sight. The deer grazed in a field of flowers, exited, and bounded in again as the image looped. There was no sign of human beings, real or mythical.

Obviously I was missing something. I tucked my little finger into the golden loop holding the gate shut and eased it open.

The pastoral surface of the painting sheared away in strips. I pulled the gate wider and the birds wilted away. The stream solidified and flattened. The deer and the meadow became mounds of rubble. Trees changed to ruined buildings. I recognized a few of them. It was the same city Annmarie and I had walked through this morning.

I put my palm against the painting's surface and wasn't surprised to find that there was no surface. It was a propagat interface, like my pool, or Annmarie's fire. Rose's link to Paradise. All I had to do was enter the image and I would be elsewhere.

I took a step, found my foot on jagged stone, and wondered briefly if I should run and get Annmarie. I put the thought aside. If Rose had left a message for the surviving Meshed in general, or me in particular, I wanted to see it first. I took another step and turned to make sure I knew where the exit was. Behind me, the gates hung open, framing a view of the Sanctuary's gallery.

I turned toward the city and let my perceptions widen.

Something felt different. The lightless visibility was the same, but the sensation of being swaddled in information was distinctly missing and I wondered if something had gone wrong in the few hours since my visit here with Annmarie.

What I needed was an answer to an easy question.

What's the period of rotation? I cast the query into the cold and felt the answer.

One hundred and four standard hours.

That seemed right, although there was no way to check. I stood in the eerie undark for a moment, deciding that the local 'gats had initialized their relationship with me and were now at my disposal. I could access them when I wanted to without having to worry about being tracked, or giving myself away to people who wanted to sift my brain for its grown-in technology. A strange sort of freedom in such a desolate place. In a month, I might be standing on this very spot, finding ways to fit into Annmarie's vision.

Or finding ways to escape.

I tried not to think about Nav. Tried not to remember how her hair smelled, or the way her body felt. It was easier to imagine her alive than otherwise and I stood in the blank landscape not thinking about what I would say if I ever saw her again.

No matter what I'd seen in the murderous space between the Medusa and Doctor Rose's ship, I *would* see her again. I touched the silver apple where it hung against my chest. It was as solid in Mesh as it was in reality. I would see her again, and I could feel the truth of that.

I started walking toward the city and let my feet come off the ground. The broken ground shrank beneath me and in a minute I was skimming over the broken stone, arms outflung over the ruins of my own history.

At the edge of the city, I landed on the crumbled pavement of the wide avenue where Annmarie and I had gone walking earlier. All the intersections we'd passed were blocked with piles of rubble, as though survivors of the final attack had been able to plow the destruction to one side of the street before the planet, forced from its orbit, became too frozen to support them. I'd been under the impression we'd crossed the city from one end to the other, but now I stopped at a corner where an unfamiliar alley wandered off between crumbling walls. There was something lying in the middle of the broken pavement. Something small and vaguely ruddy in the low light. Probably a marker from Rose. I started toward the shape, expecting a flower.

Instead, I found an apple.

A surreally perfect piece of fruit.

Its scent drifted in the unreal air, crisp and convincing, but I wasn't about to touch it. I crouched about an arm's length away, fingertips pressed to the pavement, ready to spring into the overcast sky and dive for the open gate if I saw anything move. I could just open my eyes if I *had* to get out, but that might compromise the Sanctuary's security. If I left the gates open, I could only imagine what might come crawling into the gallery.

Down the alley I could see a change in the lighting, or more accurately, a lighter change in the dark. I let myself rise into the air, and without touching the apple, drifted toward what looked like the glow of streetlights.

The alley made a couple of sharp turns before I could see where the light was coming from. I could have risen up above the buildings, which seemed taller and more intact, but I didn't want to go any higher for fear of being seen. Querying the local 'gats felt like a fundamental error.

Ahead, the blackened leftovers of the old war were disappearing. Warm-colored stucco walls showed under layers of ash. I could even see a few intact roofs. There was one complete house, then a cluster of them. The alley widened into a proper street and the propagat-light became even brighter. I could see flower gardens and trees. The road rose along the planet's central rill and wound *up* between white walls draped with red blossoms. Their scent was endlessly pure, the smell of unheard-of happiness. Streetlights cast a sleepy, peaceful glow on everything. Soon, I thought, I would find something. A warning, an offering. Or bait.

At the top, what I found was a blue plastic chair in the middle of a deserted plaza. It was exactly the same as Nav's chair on Macha, the first time I'd laid eyes on her.

Naverdi? I whispered and turned to see her, solidly real—not in her physical body but in her temple persona, with the braids and beads and heavy dress of spangled brocade.

She reached over to take my hand. Her palm was dry and warm, her fingers cool.

My heart speeded up. How could she possibly be here—unless Rose had found a way to let her in? *Are you alive?* I whispered.

She smiled.

Annmarie killed Rose, I said and found myself lightheaded with relief. *I tried to tell you what was going on. I thought you were dead. How did you get here?*

Rose opened the gate for me. She smiled again.

Smiling back made the muscles in my face hurt. *Where are you now?*

She made a vague gesture at the sky, as though she didn't quite understand what I was asking. *I'm hungry,* she said.

What?

Hungry. She pulled on my sleeve. *Come on.*

We walked through the deserted plaza until the pavement turned to a cobble of flat stones. The buildings around the plaza vanished behind high walls, draped with more vines and red flowers.

I don't understand what's happening, I said. *How can you interface with a Meshed construct?*

This is a Meshed construct?

That stopped me. Wasn't it? Or could a healthy population of propagats support a virtual environment accessible to both Jacked and Meshed? And if that was the case, did it mean that any Jacked hunter who figured out how to break Rose's petal-seals could also open those gilt-wire gates?

How many times have you been here? I asked.

Twice, she said. *The other time was with Rose.*

Just the two of you?

Of course.

She brought you through the Sanctuary gallery?

Gallery? she said. *Oh, yes. The rooms with all the stories. Now look.* She waved at the road ahead of us, where the walls opened onto another small plaza. This one had a fountain, tables and chairs, and strings of lights across the open spaces between the low buildings. The smell of fried meat drifted in the air, there was music, and the place was packed with people.

Nav hooked her arm in mine and guided me under the lights through a crowd of drunken dancers. Children ran in circles, trailing colored streamers. At one table, four men shared a pitcher of frothing brown beer. Nearby, a man and a woman danced to a song with words I could almost understand. The man sang along, waving his arms while his partner swayed on nail-thin heels, laughing drunk, elegantly thin.

Who're all these people? I asked.

I don't know, she said. *I didn't put them here.*

We passed a cooking cart where two old women chopped vegetables with blinding speed while a third wrapped them briskly in dough and tossed them in hot grease.

Naverdi eyed the frying rolls, but she didn't stop until we came to a narrow passage between two buildings. I followed her up a flight of winding stairs to the second floor, where a landing opened into a small room. Inside, there was a bed, a small round table, and a window tall enough to stand in. Nav pushed the window open and sat on the edge of the mattress.

The scent of flowers drifted in, sweet and dense as perfume, but there was another smell. Fruity and familiar. I sat gingerly on the mattress and saw another apple on the small table. This one was cut into pieces and arranged on a silver plate. My heart started to beat a little faster. This wasn't Rose's vision. It was mine, playing out courtesy of an extinct breed of propagats designed to please every whim. This was a fantasy, like Corey's private worlds. The apple in the road hadn't been a threat, or bait. It was an invitation to do what the local 'gats had decided I was inclined to do.

Naverdi moved closer and kissed me, soft, on the cheek. The scent of Staze was missing from this version of herself. Instead, she smelled of fruit. Her mouth touched my ear, down my neck. I wanted to push her away, but couldn't make myself do it, even though I knew how this would end. The Mesh would entertain me until I seemed satisfied and then everything would vanish. I would find myself lying alone under the black sky, or on the carpet of the Sanctuary's gallery. No Naverdi. No Rose. No answers. *I thought you were hungry,* I whispered.

She kissed me again. *I am.* Her fingers opened the fastenings on my shirt and pulled it down to uncover my breasts. I put my hands on hers and held them still.

Nav gave me an innocently questioning look. The expression seemed wrong for her. *What does the apple mean?* she said.

The question surprised me. *It's a sign of knowledge. Isn't it?*

She shifted closer and touched my mother's medal. *Who is this?*

She's the Annunciate. The woman at the gates of the Paradise.

I know a story about a woman in Paradise, said the creature that looked so much like Nav. *Would you like to hear it?*

Sure, I said. *All right.*

She touched the silver pendant. *Once there was nothing,*

except the first woman and her garden. One day an apple fell from the sky. She picked it up and took a bite and knew all the secrets of the world.

Why would the Mesh volunteer this sort of information if this was just a sexual fantasy? *Then what?*

When she got lonely, she decided to re-pro-duce, so she swallowed the seeds of the apple.

Strange data, I thought, or bad glitches. Obviously something had gone wrong in two and a half millennia of freezing. I wondered if our diagnostics would work on Paradise. *How could she reproduce with apple seeds?*

It was a my-ster-y. The first man wanted to know how she did it, so he took a bite of the apple as well.

Wait a minute, I said. *Where did the first man come from?*

From the sky. Just like the apple.

I looked at her brown hand still pressed against my chest and knew this creature had nothing to do with Nav. There was nothing familiar about her. Not the story. Not her face. Not even her smell.

What happened to the first man after he ate the apple? I said.

He knew everything. And one day, when the first woman wasn't watching, he opened the gates of Paradise and let in all the awful things he knew were outside. She touched my mother's medal with her fingertips; the Annunciate, manless, and I thought of the peculiar, distorted painting back in the gallery. She—it—had seen it, obviously, and made up this arcane story to go with the image.

What happened then?

She shrugged. *Everything in the garden was changed.*

I waited for something more conclusive. *Is that the end?*

Almost. She smiled at me. She caught my hands in both of hers and brushed my fingers against her lips.

I tried to pull away.

I need you to stay, she said. *I need to know everything about you.* She touched my palm with the warm tip of her tongue.

I can't.

She pressed closer, her knees on either side of mine, clasping my hands under her chin.

A panicky rush made sweat start under my arms. *Let go!* I yanked, but her grip was unyielding.

She lowered her face as if to kiss me, then her chin dropped behind our tangle of fingers. I felt teeth sink into my left thumb.

I yelled. I yelled and jerked away and flung myself out of the bed. She let go at the last second before I would have pulled her onto the floor. I ran to the bedroom doorway and stood there, holding my bleeding hand.

What the hell did you do that for? I shouted.

The sound echoed, as though the small room had turned into an enormous empty space. Nav—or whatever she was—sat cross-legged on the bed, licking at the red smears at the corners of her mouth.

I know everything, she said.

She started to climb out of the bed and I jerked around for the stairs. As I turned, the white stucco faded to air. The stairs became a jumble of stones. I was already in motion, my legs running before I could direct them, and I fell hard on my knees into a heap of black rubble. I rolled, ready to kick her away, but everything was gone—the room, the bed, the plaza. Naverdi.

I stood unsteadily and kept turning until I knew where I was. Naturally I was back at the fork in the road which shouldn't have been there. The apple, which should have been lying in the scatter of rubble, was gone.

My hand hurt and I was shivering. I turned in a full circle one more time. The gutted buildings, the heaps of plowed destruction, and the overcast sky were all the same. And the supposedly faithful 'gats?

What's the period of rotation? I asked, half afraid of the answer.

One hundred and four standard hours.

I kicked myself upward, heading for the gilt-wire gate,

thinking that if a figment of the Mesh could bite, it might just as easily lock me in before I could escape. I wondered if it was best to exit slowly, to appear unafraid. But I was afraid. I could feel my heart banging up high in my throat where my body lay in my safe little bed on the Medusa, and I wondered if my hand was bleeding outside the Mesh. I made my angle sharper and went as fast as I could. In a moment, I saw the break of light in the thick dark and I knew the gate was open. I shot toward it, weightless with fright, expecting it to swing shut just before I got there, but it didn't.

I fell onto the carpeted floor of the Sanctuary gallery and scrambled up to twist the gold wires shut. As soon as the gate was latched, the deer, the birds, and the stream reappeared, peaceful and serene.

I stood for a while, catching my breath, and then made my way out, past the paintings and portraits until I found Rose.

Doctor Rose, I said. *It's me again.*

She seemed surprised. *Is it little Eve?*

It was the same response as when I'd first walked in and I felt my stomach sink. Annmarie had killed her too soon. There were things we needed to know and now we would end up guessing. *Doctor Rose.* I pointed in the direction of the other world. *The gates into Paradise—that's your link. You put it there for any surviving Meshed to find, right?*

She gave me a slow, sober nod.

Do you know what's in there, Doctor Rose?

Another nod.

I waited in front of her sad-eyed portrait. *Can't you tell me?*

Little Eve, she said, *I could have when I was alive.*

I looked down at my hand. The bite mark was a neat crescent just under the joint of my thumb. Unreal blood ran down in thin trails to my wrist. *Doctor Rose,* I said, *will your seals be restored when I leave?*

Yes, little Eve.

Goodbye, I whispered.

Goodbye.

*   *   *

I sat up in bed, made the lights go on, and examined every centimeter of my thumb.

There was no sign of a wound.

The cut had been in the Mesh.

By the next morning, I had decided what I could safely tell Annmarie. None of it included Nav.

We sat together in her garden, just outside the cottage. She'd made it rain recently and the roses, heavy with water, lay on the ground, petals spread wide, bruised to the stems by the force of the weather. I glanced down at my wounded thumb again. In Mesh, unlike reality, the mark was still there, appearing to heal over. I'd watched it in fascination while I'd waited for my invitation into the forest. I'd never been hurt in Mesh before.

You got into the Sanctuary records without any problem? asked Annmarie.

I nodded, thinking that Rose must have expected us to go there. She had given me a mental prompt the minute we'd dropped into Mesh together on Kigal. She'd expected something to go wrong. *'Tether now the outflung star . . .'* The song had stayed in my head well after she'd died.

The records are set up like an art gallery with paintings, I said. *I found Rose's picture and she told me I should look around.*

What else did she say?

She knew she was dead, I said. *I asked her about Rondelle and Sphear and she knew about them, too.*

Annmarie ran her fingers over the chair's wooden arm, stained with water. *Then what?*

She has a link to Paradise in there. It's set up like another painting, but it has a gate across it. I could tell by the tight way she held herself that as soon as we were finished talking, she would go inside, start a fire, and study it until she found her way into the Sanctuary gallery. She would open the gates and then what? I had found what was foremost in my mind—

Nav. But I couldn't imagine what would be waiting for *her*. I touched the cut on my thumb, carefully keeping it out of sight.

Well? she said impatiently and I blinked, having missed the question. She raised her eyebrows. *What was in the painting?*

Deer, I said. *And birds and a stream. I kept waiting for the Annunciate, but she wasn't there.*

You opened the gates?

I nodded. *As soon as I did, the scene changed to the way the planet really looks.*

Except?

Except there was a hungry succubus lurking inside the stucco walls of a town which no longer existed. *It felt different,* I said. *The data from the 'gats felt completely different. There was a road we didn't see. Off the main avenue.*

You followed it?

I shook my head. *It felt—I don't know. Spooky, I guess.*

She didn't say anything for a while. *Have you noticed anything different in your desert?*

I thought about that. *No.*

I want you to go there. She stood up. *I'm going to access the Sanctuary site. Stay in your place until I call you. I want you to tell me if anything changes.*

Changes? I said in surprise.

She pointed at the fallen roses. *I had a storm a couple of hours ago.*

And?

She smoothed her hair. *I didn't plan it. It just came.*

I stared at the flowers and then at her. *How can that be?*

It can't be, she said.

In my room, in the stony silence of the Medusa, I ran my fingers over the engraved design of the Annunciate. The flat metal was worn thin, giving it almost a knife edge. In the wavering light from the fish tanks, the woman was faceless with age, her intentions polished to an ambiguous gesture. Against my chest, Naverdi's apple was a smooth, substantial shape.

Whatever had bitten me in the Mesh—tasted me like food—wasn't Nav. It had been a distorted image of her, reflected by aging propagats which still had the wherewithal to sense what I wanted. Except for the bite, I would have called the whole episode a malfunction.

'*I know everything.*'

I wondered again what Annmarie would find behind the gates and closed my eyes.

It was colder in my desert than it should have been.

I huddled by the pool, squinting at my own reflection. Something was wrong with the range of tones. The white dust over my dark skin was gray, and in the pool at least, the sky was overcast. When I checked my arms and the blueness overhead, everything seemed fine, but the reflective aspect of the water was definitely off. And when I put my fingers in, I found icy slush where there should have been nothing but uninterrupted access.

The rest of my tiny environment hadn't changed, at least not on the surface. Sand to the horizon, no twig disturbed on my dead trees. The blue sky was riveted to the ground by stones the size of my fist, all still right where they were supposed to be. I should have insisted on going with Annmarie to the Sanctuary site. What if the Naverdi-succubus met her at the gates, or lured her to the bedroom, or just plain pounced on her? What was I supposed to say when Annmarie came back and demanded, *Did you know she was there? Look what she did to my hand!*

I shifted to sit cross-legged and happened to glance down at the water. Instead of the reflective steel color, something red rippled under the surface. I leaned closer and saw red sofas and paintings in gilt frames.

A view from the ceiling of the Sanctuary gallery. Something in my mind was replaying through the Medusa's 'gats, I thought, but that wasn't right. The ripples went away and I saw Annmarie and Corey.

Whose idea was it to drop the data partitions? I wondered. A ringside seat for me, courtesy of Annmarie? Or Corey? Even less likely. If I was supposed to monitor their progress, maybe warn them if something dangerous showed up, why hadn't either of them bothered to tell me? Typical, I thought. But it wasn't typical.

I crouched in the cold sand, watching as they made their way through the gallery, peering at one portrait, then another, glancing over their shoulders as though they could feel eyes from somewhere. I looked, too, from my higher viewpoint, but the gallery was deserted. When they found Rose's portrait, the two of them stopped.

Rose, said Annmarie, *do you know me?*

The painting didn't answer.

Where's your link with Paradise, Rose? asked Corey.

No answer.

Annmarie kicked at the carpet a couple of times and I wondered if the defaults Rose had left included appropriate responses to a full confession from her former colleague. It didn't look like I would ever know. Corey followed Annmarie out of the gallery and past the red sofas, where landscapes replaced portraits.

The gateway to Paradise was impossible to miss. Annmarie ran her fingers lightly across the gilt wires, as if checking for an electric charge. From my ceiling-high vantage point, I could see the deer and birds and even hear the burbling water. There was something different in the landscape, though. Corey saw it almost immediately and pointed through the wires at a tiny figure in the distance, slowly making its way toward the gates.

The skin between my shoulder blades prickled.

Naverdi? Or Rose?

Corey fingered the latch, and I almost yelled, but he didn't try to open the gate or reach through the painting's false surface. The figure came closer, more distinctly female, her long white dress fluttering in a light breeze. Closer, I could see that

it was Doctor Rose. She leaned against the gate. Her thin
burned hands clutched the wires.

There is a new opportunity for our survival, panted Rose.
*I've found a secure place with an undisturbed population of pro-
pagats.* She pointed up where the gate's gold wires were now
curved into a line illustration of ThreeSys. The vacant space
where Paradise was, was circled in bright red. *The old world has
returned,* whispered Rose in her burnt voice. *Hail. Here is the
new world.*

Annmarie peered into the illusion of Paradise. *I'll be
damned if that's how it looks,* she said. *Let me in, Rose. I still
have questions.*

Rose didn't answer, just walked away, turning now and
then to beckon. The deer and the birds straggled along behind
her, and after a few minutes, they all disappeared into the trees.

This must be the link, said Corey. *There's no recognition fac-
tored in. She'll say the same thing to anybody as long as they're
Meshed.*

She didn't say anything to Eve, said Annmarie. *Eve said there
was nothing here but birds.* She motioned at the bright air. *And
bees. That sort of thing.* She tugged at the flimsy twist of wire
which held the gate shut.

You're going in? said Corey.

Are you kidding?

She pulled and the gate eased open, but the flowers, the
trees, the stream, and the sky remained intact. The vision was
far more intense this time, even as removed as I was. The waft
of warm spring air was so welcoming, I found myself wanting
to dive into my own cold water, to rush through the Sanctuary's security seals and the gallery, just to be able to roll in the
grass. It felt so close and real, I had the impression I could
reach through this imaginary window and give Annmarie the
push she needed to step over the boundary. Someone would
have had to push her. She showed no sign of moving forward
on her own.

This feels wrong, said Corey.

Does it? she said, but she sounded like she agreed. *How does it feel wrong to you?*

I don't know . . . He reached tentatively into the fragrant air. *If we go in, we might not be able to find the way back . . . unless we had bread crumbs, or a long rope. It's not what Eve said it was.*

Not anymore.

Do you think she was telling the truth?

Annmarie nodded and closed the gates, careful to secure them. *I don't think she'd lie to me about this.*

She lied to you about the smuggler.

That was different.

Was it?

I realized I was holding my breath. They didn't know I was watching. The data partitions, which should have kept me from eavesdropping, were gone.

Which shocked me. I'd had to bang on Corey's door and declare an emergency to get into his private spaces. I always had to wait for permission to come into Annmarie's woods. But this was worse than a simple malfunction in protocols, like Annmarie's storm and the ice on the surface of my pond. The data partitions between the Medusa and the Sanctuary—the gates separating the Sanctuary and Paradise—were just illusions.

Annmarie made a dismissive motion and the gallery faded. It should have been the end of my eavesdropping, but it wasn't. In another moment, I had a perfect view of her and Corey sitting by the fire in her cottage.

It's still here, said Corey. *Can you feel it?*

He was talking about *me*. It was *my* eyes they'd felt in the gallery. Annmarie frowned at the windows, then the ceiling, seeing nothing. She got up slowly and made her way through the kitchen, where virtual loaves of raw dough lay in stasis, waiting to rise.

Finally she went back to the fireplace and squatted in front of the embers, palms down on the brick hearth. The fire leapt up again and I knew the next thing she would check on was me.

I leaned away from the pool, innocent in my empty space. The water opaqued to steel. It would take a moment for her to connect with me here. The bite on my thumb throbbed once, and I felt a chill between my shoulders. I squinted at my sky. Just as blue as ever, but now it felt too thick, too easy to hide behind.

Annmarie? I whispered, but I already knew it wasn't her.

Corey was waiting for us in the control room, a shade paler than normal, fingers laced into knuckle-white fists between his knees.

"We have a problem," he said. "An hour ago, our onboard aegistics were fine. Now we've got two huge holes in our shielding."

Annmarie sat down in front of one of the monitors and began paging through the displays designed for a Jackless crew. She stopped at one. Then another. Her mouth tightened into a bloodless line. "We might as well put up a sign. Anyone out there's going to be able to spot us."

Just like Rose, I thought. "Can't we fix it?" I said.

"I've tried." Corey's knuckles got even whiter. "There's a problem with the onboard 'gats. About ten percent in each of the specialty units aren't responding. They've been corrupted." He glanced sideways at Annmarie, sweat showing under his lower lip. "I told you we shouldn't have landed on Kigal. We've got a virus."

"We don't," said Annmarie. "A virus would've knocked out all our 'gats at once. Not ten percent here and ten percent there."

"What else could it be?" demanded Corey. "Someone must've hacked our system—there must've been hunters—"

"If it was hunters, we'd be drifting." She moved to one side so we could see the display on the screen. It showed navigational options for plotting trajectory and destination. Instead of prompts and blanks, the screen was filled with zeros.

Corey craned forward. "What's *that?*"

"It *was* our navigation," said Annmarie. "Now it's a default. We're heading for Paradise, and there's no way to change that. Any virus capable of *that* would've loaded us into someone's cargo bay by now." She came over to sit in the chair across from me. "Did you notice anything different in your desert?"

"I could see you," I blurted. "When you went to the Sanctuary site. I didn't have to code myself in. I was just there."

"Watching from the ceiling?"

I nodded.

"What else could you see?"

"I could see into your cottage."

"Anything else?"

"No."

She turned to Corey. "Have you been in your places lately?"

He shook his head, a nervous jerk.

"Our data partitions are falling apart," she said. "The way the 'gats are behaving, in a few days, there won't be any separation between private environments. In a week or two, we'll probably be able to walk through each other's landscapes."

"That can't happen," said Corey.

"It can," said Annmarie, "and it's because of Rose."

"Rose?" I said, but I shouldn't have been surprised. Annmarie could match Rose's painted avatar, blame for blame.

Annmarie nodded. "You remember the aegistics over her enclave on Kigal? The first time I saw them, I thought they were augmented." She angled a thumb at the useless navigation screen. "I think Rose had access to the Paradise 'gats for years. She must have lost her data partitions, too, but she obviously figured out how to solve that problem and her defenses were stronger for it." She nodded darkly at the view out the window. "Before we get to Paradise, we need to unify our systems with the old technology. If we can do that, we'll be able to hide the ship while we're in transit. And if we need to, we'll be able to fight."

"Or change course," I said.

Corey shook his head. The color had come back into his face. "There's nowhere else for us to go. This is fate, or a stroke of luck. If we pass this up, we'll be wandering for the rest of our lives."

"Like the old explorers," whispered Annmarie, soft and full of feeling. "This is our obligation. Our right." She reached over and took my hand, her nails across my palm. "It's your future, Eve."

FOUR

Annmarie's voice was bodiless and clear in my desert air.

Eve, she said, *can you hear me?*

If I looked into the water, I would have been able to see her peering up through a veil of flame. I ran my fingers through dry sand, adding to aimless patterns by the pond, not answering.

One week closer to Paradise, with three weeks to go. Our data partitions had become as thin as cardboard walls, barely intact enough to hide us from each other. Even though Annmarie had managed to fix most of the aegistical holes around the Medusa, the ship wasn't ours anymore. What Corey called *assimilation* could as easily be a hijacking. We were on our way to Paradise, and the navigation was untouchable.

I touched my thumb where the bite had healed to an itchy, markless place under my skin. We were only passengers now.

Or pilgrims.

Or food.

In some ways, it was a good thing. I was discovering how Annmarie and Corey fought.

I heard the sound of hard shoes on a stone floor as Annmarie crossed her virtual kitchen.

Have you finished cleaning? she said to Corey.

Relax, he said. *I'll get it done. There's no rush.*

Cleaning what? I wondered, but I had a suspicion.

Annmarie let out a frustrated breath. *How can you be so calm?* she demanded. *Everything on this ship's about to fall apart and you just* sit *there.*

I'm calm because things aren't that bad.

Things are *that bad. The last time you made Staze with Eve, she saw one of your nasty little holes. In another week, she'll be able to see them all. I want you to get rid of your interface sites, or change them, or make them wholesome, or something.*

He was quiet for a while. *You want me to make sure she can't tell you've been in there with me.*

Get rid of them, she snapped, *and shut up. I think she can hear us.*

She left. I could tell by the change in air pressure, like a door slamming. I heard Corey sigh and start moving around in a space suddenly closer and wetter than Annmarie's cottage. In a second, the chemical smell of cleansers drifted over my sand, along with the sound of unhurried scrubbing. In another moment, Annmarie's voice came into my head.

Eve? I need to show you something.

I leaned over the water, hoping against any stray glimpse of Corey, scouring away his nasty old subroutines. Instead, the Sanctuary's tended grounds rippled under my surface, green and full of flowers. Annmarie floated over the crushed-gravel path, heading for the gallery. She glanced up at me and beckoned. She'd dragged me to the gallery twice already, supposedly to search for survivors, even though Rose had declared them all dead. It was just busywork to keep me out of her hair and away from Corey while he cleaned up his sordid personal locales. Most of the time, I would end up standing by the gilt-wire gates, where Rose would appear and repeat her short speech, then vanish into the garden. I was too afraid to follow.

I slid through the surface of my pool feet-first, braced against the change in temperature outside our private environ-

ments. Ever since our first brush with Paradise, the greater
Mesh had turned cooler and now it was as brisk as early winter.
In three weeks, no doubt the temperature would drop even
more, until the cold inside our minds matched the cold on the
surface of the planet.

The oaks and elms of the Sanctuary site surrounded me,
full-leafed despite the chill. I drifted over the red gravel paths,
prickled from head to foot with gooseflesh. Autumn, I decided,
had never been written in by the eternal optimists who'd designed this place.

Rose's painted eyes followed me as I scuffed through the
musty rooms. Annmarie was sitting on one of the red sofas
with an ornate table pulled up like a desk. It was covered with
navigational charts.

You're here, she said. *Good. Are you finished?*

Finished canvassing the portraits of the dead, she meant.
My list of questions was short: *Are you alive?* So far, the answer
had been a unanimous *No.* There was no point in rushing that
I could see. A job that should have taken three or four hours
had stretched into days.

I have a few more. I glanced at the portraits which gazed
blankly back. The feeling of unwelcome eyes was stronger some
days, weaker on others. Today the place felt ominously vacant.
Why're you working in here?

It's quiet, said Annmarie.

It makes me nervous, I said.

It makes Corey nervous, too, she said. *He hardly ever comes
in.* She moved over on the sofa and patted the seat. *Sit down.*

I touched the sofa gingerly. *What're you doing?*

She smoothed one of the navigation charts and traced Paradise's trajectory toward Mara with her finger. *I was trying to
decide how much Staze we should make in the next four or five
months. By the time we pass Mara's inner planets, we could be
dumping it into reservoirs.* She grinned. *We could addict almost
a quarter of the population in this system. We might even get to
the point where we could demand protection money. You know*

what I mean? We could say, Pay us not *to dump Red in your
drinking water.*

I smiled, making an effort to look sincere. It surprised me
to hear her talking like this. The point of Staze was to keep
the hateful masses placid. It didn't have anything to do with
cash. I wasn't about to ask where she planned to get the hundreds of liters of Kevake she'd need for that kind of output.

I should get started, I said, but she caught my hand.

I found something you should see, she said. *Come on.*

She led me through a labyrinth of smaller rooms until we
came to the pictures of children from the dorms. Annmarie
turned a corner and stopped.

A portrait of a young girl hung in the center of the near
wall. Her skin was as dark as polished stone. The scarf covering
her hair shaded her eyes, too, erasing any childish innocence
from her expression.

It took me a minute to recognize her.

It's me! I blurted.

The portrait studied me, still wearing the soft brown dress
my father had sent me away from home in. I wondered if
Annmarie wanted me to ask it if I was still alive, but she pointed
at something laying against the dress.

What's that hanging around your neck? she said.

My mother's . . . Medal, I wanted to say, but it wasn't. It
was round, not flat.

Annmarie leaned closer to touch it. The pendant—a cardboard approximation of the silver apple Nav had given me—
moved lightly over the canvas.

The portrait's painted eyes blinked as though she'd been
pinched. My bitten hand began to throb where I'd been bitten
and, abruptly, I recognized the presence behind the eyes.

Different face. Same succubus.

Annmarie picked at the canvas and managed to pull the
false apple away from the surface.

Leave it alone, I said.

What the hell is it?

The painting answered in a soft girlish voice. *An apple.*

Annmarie twitched, but she didn't let go. She peered up at the portrait. *Why are you wearing this? Where did it come from?*

It's a sign of knowledge, said the painting, not taking its eyes off me.

Would it tear itself out of the canvas and fall on us with bared teeth? I tugged at Annmarie's sleeve, wanting to run. *It's a glitch,* I said. A thin spot, or an undetected opening in the Mesh between us and Paradise. *Something's wrong with this part of the gallery.*

Annmarie let the pendant fall back against the canvas. *A sign of knowledge . . . ?*

I know a story about the first woman in Paradise, said the painting. *Her name was Eve, the first to set foot in the garden. Eve, the great mother who knew the secrets of the world.*

I stared at it as it stared at me. If it could get into the gallery with the gates still firmly shut, how long before I saw it eyeing me from under the water in my pool? How long before it reached up with succubus arms to drag me under?

Annmarie . . . I whispered.

Annmarie rubbed her chin. *You're right. It must be a glitch. The system's got you confused with some kind of old myth.* She angled a finger at the painting. *Tell me your name.*

I'm Eve DeJardin, said my portrait.

And where are you now?

The painting hesitated, like it wasn't sure how to answer.

Where are you? said Annmarie.

The brown eyes went opaque. One painted hand came up to caress the apple. *I'm everywhere,* it said. *I know everything.*

Over the next few days, the Sanctuary gallery began to shrink and we stopped going in. From our overhead viewpoints, we watched the rest of the Sanctuary vanish. First the children's wing, then three rooms of landscapes, including the bizarre painting of the Annunciate. One morning, only two weeks away from Paradise, I looked down into my pool to find nothing but Rose's painted avatar, the gilt-wire gates, and one red sofa.

Things weren't any better on the Medusa. My desert, which had *seemed* big enough for the last seven years, had diminished to a sandy spot and a puddle, lost between Annmarie's towering forest on one side, and Corey's world on the other.

Corey's new world. I got up from where I was squatting by the pool and wandered to the edge of the sand. Gauzy shreds of what had been my sky hung between me and a big square of spotless white carpet with a single, cream-colored armchair in the middle. I'd watched him sitting in that chair, staring into space, supposedly interfacing with the greater Mesh, but I couldn't see any sign of a useful metaphor, like a pond or fire. If his new environment had a window in it—and I had my doubts—it was a small one.

Maybe it was time to change my own scrap of space. Make the pond into an ocean. Make a building, like Annmarie's cottage. Something for privacy. I scuffed at the sand. Being naked and childish and covered with white dust was starting to feel embarrassing. Clothes might be a good neutral option.

Through the trees, I heard hinges squeak and Annmarie appeared at the edge of her woods. She eyed me as I stood nude, barefoot, and dusty. She made a halfhearted beckoning motion and I scuffed my way over to her, passing from sand to crisp dry leaves.

Inside the cottage, I slumped in a kitchen chair, half a dozen raw, rising loaves arranged in front of me. These weren't metaphors for bio-simulations, as far as I could tell. She was as nervous as I was, but in Mesh, at least, she had something to keep her busy.

I watched her crack eggs over the side of a wide earthenware bowl and tap in teaspoons of herbs from green-glass jars labeled AYAHUASCA, HEMP, and MUGWORT. She put the jars back in their places, wiped off a long wooden spoon, and stirred at the unmixed dough.

You seem very worried, said Annmarie.

Aren't you? I said.

I was a little concerned about the changes in the gallery, she said, *but now I think the Sanctuary designers may have decided to shut down the site when there were no more survivors.* She broke another egg into the mix. *Rose probably wrote augmentations in to keep her link open to Paradise. Even if everything else disappears, the gates'll still be there.*

But what about us?

She reached for a bowl of flour and sifted it in. *What do you mean?*

We're survivors, I said. *Why would it shut down if it knew we were still alive?*

Obviously, she said, *the site wasn't as intact as it appeared to be. And it wouldn't surprise me if the codes have been sabotaged by hunters. They've probably been digging through the main site for years.*

You don't think the gallery disappearing has anything to do with what's happening to our data partitions?

She picked up a wooden spoon and stirred until the dough began to thicken. *There may be a relationship.*

A relationship? I said. *We're losing systems by the* hour *and we* still *don't know if it's an infestation or an upgrade.*

Obviously the elder 'gats are more aggressive than we expected. They're active enough to force our systems into compatibility and we're bound to have problems while the programs unify.

It's like a virus, I said.

Yes, it is, said Annmarie, *but at least it's our virus. It'll take a few weeks for us to stabilize and that'll be the end of that.*

But what if you're wrong? I said. *What if we still can't navigate when we get to Paradise? What if we can't land? Or what if—*

Eve, said Annmarie sharply, *Rose was an* addict *and she had everything under control. If she could handle this, we can, too.* She dusted her hands with flour and plunged them into the bowl, digging up dough from the bottom. *The only reason we should be worried is if we knew there was some kind of contamina-*

tion piggybacking from Paradise. But our 'gats aren't in any shape to give reliable diagnostics.

She pushed loose strands of hair away from her face. *If the Medusa's been contaminated, it would explain a lot.* Her attention was fully on me, not the bread. *Do you have any thoughts about that, Eve?*

Thoughts? I said uneasily.

Think about how dangerous that might be. What if we thought our systems were assimilating, but in fact they were being destroyed? We might be left with nothing. The only way to cleanse the ship and get control would be to exterminate every propagat on board.

I took a breath. An amazed breath. *With nanovirals? You'd do that? You'd kill off the 'gats and turn the ship around?* It wasn't what she meant, but the vision caught me. *No more Mesh?* I blurted. *No more Paradise? And we wouldn't need to make Staze anymore—we'd be Jackless.*

She ground her hands angrily into the bowl and I knew I'd missed her point.

The doorway darkened and Corey stepped in, soaking wet.

Kill off the 'gats? said Corey. *That's the last thing we'd ever do.* He pulled out a stool, squeezed water out of his lanky hair, and sat.

He'd been in my pool. He smiled at me, water running down his neck. He'd waited for me to walk away with Annmarie and then he'd gone in.

Worse. She'd told him to do it.

You were in my water, I sputtered, meaning both of them.

I was in the gallery, he said. *I was* trying *to find the source of the contamination.*

Contamination?

Annmarie banged the bowl down on the table with such force, the whole room echoed with the sound. I jerked in the chair. Even Corey flinched.

Eve, she snapped. Something *came through with you the first time you went in. You won't tell us about it, so we have to find out what it is for ourselves.* She jabbed a finger at me. *I keep asking you to help, but you won't do it. I don't understand your reasons. You've put the ship in danger, you've put us all in danger. I just cannot understand your reasons.*

I'd never seen her so furious—at me. Part of me was too scared to do anything but blurt out the honest truth, but another part was muttering, *This* was what would have happened if you'd told her Naverdi was waiting in Tula. I glanced at Corey, still dripping, eyeing me with smug, righteous disapproval. Had the succubus bitten him too? I peered at his hands. Bitten nails. That was all.

Eve, said Annmarie. *I'm waiting.*

Corey raised an expectant eyebrow.

I took a shaky breath. She would never turn back, no matter what I told her. We were going to Paradise, whether we wanted to or not. And she *wanted* to. We should have been running for our lives, but she would find a way to rationalize away the truth. And the truth—whatever that really was—would save me from only one thing. I couldn't spend the rest of my life hiding from her in my room. I couldn't.

Okay, I said. *I'll tell you what happened.*

She turned the bowl over and shook it as hard as she could. The dough fell onto the table in a damp, sticky heap.

Well, I said. *When I went through the gates the first time, I was thinking about Naverdi and after I walked a little while, I saw her. In there.*

Corey nodded. *And?*

Well, I thought it was the local 'gats picking up on what I wanted to do. I could feel my face getting hot. *So she took me to a room and I thought. Well. You know.*

Just tell us what happened, said Annmarie.

I traced a circle on the table. *She told me she was hungry. And she bit me. And it scared me. So I left.*

Annmarie pressed the dough into a wad and kneaded it against the table. Tiny air bubbles cracked inside. *Bit you?*

I pointed to the thin, crescent-shaped scar on the ham of my thumb. In real time there had never been a mark. *Here.*

She drew blood?

I nodded.

And then what?

I just ran. The room disappeared and I ran to the gate and shut it.

Corey rubbed his chin. *Did she say anything else?*

She told me a story about the first man and the first woman and how they reproduced with apple seeds.

Apple seeds? said Corey.

Annmarie eyed me. *The portrait of you in the gallery. It was wearing an apple.*

It was a gift, I said lamely. *Naverdi gave it to me.*

Annmarie rolled the dough slowly into three long worms. She didn't say anything for a while. *Corey, if this is true, there's something wrong with the old 'gats. They're corrupted somehow. Maybe this was a mistake. Maybe I was wrong.*

I felt my mouth fall open in amazement, but Corey laughed.

You're not wrong, Annie. She had a little fantasy in there. She's obsessed with that smuggler woman. The elder 'gats picked up on it and played it out for her. She's sexually inexperienced and it felt— What would you say, Evie? More real than the real thing? He showed his teeth. *That's all it was. I was just in there. I went five hundred klicks to each compass point and I didn't see a thing. The terraforming looks fine. Most of the ice is gone, at least in the equatorial areas. By the time we get there, the atmosphere could be breathable.*

Annmarie twisted the worms of dough together, tucked the ends underneath, and wiped her hands. *You didn't see anything?*

Corey shook his head, all smiles. *The best thing we can do is stay calm and organized. In fact, I think we should start planning our own 'Landing.' It doesn't have to be anything fancy. Just a little ceremony to celebrate the beginning of something new.*

Or a repeat of the same old mistakes. I started to object, but Corey was way ahead of me.

I think you'd be a perfect Annunciate, Eve.

I glared at him.

Annmarie nodded at me, half-hopeful, as though this was the one positive thing I could do for her—for us—for all the Meshed, alive or long dead. *Like the Landing play we used to do with the kids in the Sanctuary. Eve, didn't you have the lead the year you were there?*

I was just a flower.

But it's an easy part. Corey slapped his thighs and got up. *We'll help you rehearse.*

Maybe it was the fact that the last time I'd thought about the stupid play was when I'd been in bed with the real Naverdi, savoring a new direction in my life. Maybe it was because the two of them were treating me like someone too young and silly to know what a real danger was. Or maybe it was because it finally occurred to me that if we went to Paradise, the last I would see of Annmarie would be some image in Mesh about blood loss and stolen jewelry.

And that scared me more than anything else. More than wanting Naverdi. More than staying on the Medusa for the rest of my life.

I stood up and banged the table with my fist. *I won't do it,* I yelled.

Annmarie and Corey stared at me.

It's just a play, said Corey.

What's the matter with you? said Annmarie.

We should exterminate our 'gats—all the 'gats onboard, I shouted. *If we weren't Meshed, we could go wherever we wanted. No one would care about us, or bother us, or try to kill us for money.* My tongue was sticking to the roof of my mouth and my heart had contracted into a cold painful knot. I took a breath, afraid the words would fail me. *We can't go!*

Annmarie stood up. If there was a list of things never to say to her, I had just said them all.

Are you finished?

I nodded.

She came around the table and grabbed my arm. I could feel angry heat radiating off her. *Even though hunters have failed to eliminate us, Eve, you* think we should throw away the things *our ancestors fought and died for—not just mine, but yours, Eve. My* mother died of natural causes, in her bed. What about yours?

Corey *tsked* at me. *All we want is a bit of bare rock to call our own.*

But, said Annmarie, *you don't have the nerve for that.*

I wiped away hot tears, wishing I'd said it differently, thinking I should have said, I'm afraid you'll die.

Annmarie snapped her hand away, as though I was dirty. She straightened and turned and stalked out the door. Corey shook his head and followed her.

I laid my head on the table with the rising loaves and sobbed.

After that, Annmarie made a schedule so each of us could have eight private hours in Mesh. I suppose she had things to do to fill up the time, but I didn't, and I knew Corey didn't. Still, it was good to be alone.

I sat cross-legged by my pond, thinking about the things I wasn't supposed to do. I wasn't supposed to go into the gallery anymore. Through the icy surface of the water, I could see Rose's portrait, and beyond her, the golden gates.

The other forbidden thing was to wander outside of my own environment. Annmarie probably had ways of knowing if I disobeyed. I was starting not to care. But I didn't have the nerve to go sneaking through her garden—not yet.

I slid through my water into the velvet chill of the Sanctuary gallery for one last talk with Rose.

No matter what kind of self-perpetuating augmentations she'd written for herself, by the time we made planetfall, I was certain she'd be gone. I dragged the last red sofa over in front of her portrait and sat with my fists between my knees, deciding what it was safe to ask. My deepest fear was that the succubus was hiding inside the painting, ready to answer with Rose's voice and manner. Had Rose been bitten? I wondered. Was it her I'd spoken to when I'd first found my way in, or had the succubus been lurking in here all along?

Rose watched me with her usual melancholy expression. Behind her, a meadow of spring flowers rose into gentle hills. A line of trees was silhouetted against pretty white clouds. I hadn't paid any attention to the background before, but now I thought I recognized the place. It wasn't the Sanctuary campus. Was it somewhere Annmarie had taken me? But that didn't seem likely. What war-torn world had meadows and rolling hills? Which city full of hostile, Mesh-hating Staze addicts had a sky like that?

Rose, I said finally, *what's the place behind you?*

Little Eve, she replied, as though she'd waited a long time to answer, *it's Paradise.*

I pushed myself off the couch, palms suddenly damp. The view behind Rose was the same as the one through the gilt-wire gates.

I went closer and hesitantly touched the surface. The meadow shredded into blackness, giving way to a stony surface stippled with uneven holes, each filled with icy water.

The outline of the ruined city showed in silhouette on the high rill, which meant my point of view was from somewhere on the plain below. I craned up on my tiptoes, holding onto the edges of the painting. Everything was just as stagnant and still as I remembered. Except for a flicker of motion at the edge of the canvas.

I was certain the next thing I would see was the succubus and jumped back, so scared of being grabbed or chewed, I almost opened my eyes right then. The flicker moved again, closer this time and more distinct.

It wasn't Nav, or the succubus.

It was Corey.

He was floating over the barren landscape, arms spread, head turning this way and that, scanning the ground for something. He landed gracefully on the balls of his feet and walked over to one of the water-filled holes, peered in but didn't seem to find what he was looking for. He moved on to another pool.

Rose, I said, *Doctor Rose, what's he trying to find?*

She didn't say anything, but the viewpoint of the painting shifted abruptly. Instead of the city, I was looking down at a dark puddle. Disorienting reflections of clouds scudded across the surface and I tried to pick out what Rose was trying to show me.

All I saw was a ripple in the water. Just a ripple from the wind.

Or from something underneath.

The idea of the succubus breaching upward from the pool made me jerk. I stumbled backward, away from Rose's portrait, groped for the sofa, and touched bare skin instead.

I gasped in a breath of cut fruit, whirled around with a yelp, and saw the succubus on the sofa.

What're you doing here?

It patted the cushions. *Come and sit.*

I backed up against the opposite wall instead. This time it didn't look quite like me, or even quite like Nav, but there was a resemblance to both of us in its face. There was more convincing detail as well. Tendons moved in its neck. Its dreads had a distinct bristle of texture. Its fingers fidgeted with each other, ragged and short in the nails, and I wondered if it'd started chewing them.

Something about that was oddly familiar. Naverdi? I tried to picture her flat, moon-colored nails. Naverdi was too careful to reveal her insecurities in such an obvious way.

Corey bit his nails.

Corey saw you, I said. *Did you bite him, too?*

It smiled. *Why should I? He gave me what I asked for. He was much easier than you.*

What did you want from him? I said, dreading the answer.

Seeds, she said. *Like in the story.*

The bed in the tower. The balcony overlooking the plaza. The scent of flowers and the apple in pieces. He'd been in there with this *thing* and lied to Annmarie. Lied about everything. *What did you do with his seeds?* I said and knew the answer as soon as the question was out of my mouth. *God,* I said, *are you—pregnant?*

The succubus gave me a look I couldn't quite interpret. *I'm learning,* it said carefully, *about being preg-nant.*

Could it be? No, I thought, because whatever lurid, perverse things Corey had been up to in his spare time, it was all virtual. *Propagats*—not sperm. *Information*—not ova. I wondered if the succubus knew the difference.

What about those things in the pools on Paradise? I said. *Did you show him those?*

I showed him those. It touched its hair, patting it into place.

What are they?

They're me, it said. *And one day you. And him. And the other ones.*

It glanced upward. Overhead, the ceiling glimmered like the underside of clear water.

It was my pool.

It knew how to open up my environment and Corey had probably shown it how.

The succubus stood and crouched, ready to jump straight up.

Wait! I said. *Wait!*

It didn't wait. It billowed upward, disappearing through the top of the room with a fluid kick. I shot up after it, broke my own surface, and crawled, soaking, out of the water onto the sand.

The succubus wasn't there, but I could see its prints beside my pool and taste its pectin tang. The footprints led off, arrow-straight, to Annmarie's forest. I scrambled up, following them to where they disappeared in scattered leaves, and hesitated, uninvited, at the edge of the crisp deadfall. The soft rustle of leaves was no different than when Annmarie was here to enable things. I took a step into her world and another, and finally went in without her.

In the garden, the roses were a little bruised, but not crushed the way they had been last week after the unexpected rainstorm. I made myself slow down, peering under flowers for the glint of succubus eyes, breathing deep for its scent. Nothing.

The air was warm and yeasty inside the cottage. Neat rows of stoppered green-glass jars lined the shelves. Loaves of raw dough lay undisturbed on the wooden table. If the succubus had come in, there should have been tracks in the perpetual dusting of white over everything, but there was no sign of that. Still, in a virtual environment where gravity was only an option, a succubus could certainly dispense with leaving a visible trail. I hesitated in the doorway, thinking how much more angry Annmarie would be when she found out I'd been here without her permission. I might as well lift myself into the air and hide my own evidence, but I'd already lost so much of her goodwill. . . .

There were a hundred places to hide in the cottage and I could *feel* the thing somewhere nearby. I made my way across the room to crouch in front of the fireplace. Black marks from ersatz smoke made a velour lining inside the hearth. The faint smell of baked bread drifted out from the enclosed stone oven, but the heap of ash between andirons was untouched. No sign of something crawling in, or out.

Back in the kitchen, I peered anxiously into the corners, but the stuffy feeling of something *else* in the cottage had faded. Gentle light from outside lay over the table and the rising loaves. Annmarie's green-glass herb jars shimmered like the surface of seawater and the coating of flour on the floor turned silver.

Maybe the succubus had slithered away, bored with being chased. I pushed my hands through my hair, determined to at least have a close look at everything so I would know, later, if something had been disturbed or changed.

I went over to the shelves of jars and squinted at the powders and crushed leaves.

ARUM, AYAHUASCA, BELLADONNA . . .
HEMP, HENBANE, HENNA.

Something moved in the gleaming surface of the bottle-green glass and my heart banged inside my ribs. I made myself look closer. A dozen reflections eyed me, but at least they were my own. I moved down the row, mouthing the names on labels.

MUGWORT, MYRTLE, OLEANDER . . .
THORNAPPLE, TOBACCO, WORMWOOD.

Wormwood. The last jar on the shelf. I put my fingers against the cool glass, turning the jar so I could see past the label, and stopped. My reflection was sharp, without any distortion, almost solid enough to have been pressed inside the jar along with the crumble of splinters and powder. A thought stored away—or hidden. I looked closer.

An ineffectual, dirty girl stared back. Not the child sent out in traveling clothes, like the picture in the Sanctuary gallery. Not the self-involved fiend sneering out of the mirror in Naverdi's Jacked temple. This face hadn't changed at all since the Sanctuary fire had smeared it with soot.

Flat behind the eyes. Narrow in the mouth.

Too young to be dependable. Too old to be so needy.

Pressed into a green glass jar where I wouldn't be any trouble.

Her opinion of me, always in plain sight, in a place I would never notice.

I turned away, steadying myself against the edge of the

table, stumbled out into the forest garden, and found Annmarie standing there, fists on her hips.

What the hell's going on, Eve?

That thing *crawled in from the gallery!* I pointed at the cottage. *It was in there!*

She pulled me along until we were standing together in the doorway. My footprints in the flour wandered around the room. Over by the jar full of wormwood and judgments, they became a confused shuffle and then trailed out the door. Of course, there was no sign of the succubus.

But these are your tracks, said Annmarie. *What were you doing in here?*

Looking *for it,* I said, which was the truth at least. *It's here—Corey's seen it, too.*

Where?

Out there— I pointed to my pool. *It said he gave it seeds.*

Her expression made me think of wormwood. *I've been out there, too,* she said. *We've gone out together and we haven't found anything. Do you understand? There's no* thing *out there.* She crossed her arms, as though she was very, very tired of dealing with me.

It's talked to him, I whispered, but the words felt useless. *He gave it* seeds. *Don't you know what that means?*

She let her breath out in an impatient gust and vanished in the gilded air.

I sank into one of the garden chairs. Annmarie's cottage sat in the gloom under the trees, thick with false food and comfort. Around it, the tended shrubs seemed overgrown and dark, her flowers rotten.

Annmarie's disapproval and the damp smell of ruined roses washed over me. I put my fists between my knees and stared at the ground. A few of the blossoms had fallen and lay soiled in the wet earth. One was missing half of its petals.

The bite marks in the blossom were distinct.

FIVE

Annmarie clenched her jaws to keep from shivering in the cold of the control room and pulled a gray blanket over her shoulders. The sallow light from Paradise gave her dark skin a waxy, sickly sheen. She looked older, harder than I'd ever seen her.

Corey leaned over her, breath steaming as they watched the stony rill and blackened craters below. The destruction was easy to see, preserved in the archive of vacuum.

I sat behind them in the chair by the monitors, bundled in layers of heavy clothes and thick socks. Over the last few days, everything from life support to automated food prep had been overwhelmed by the elder 'gats. The temperature inside the ship had fallen until even the food was crusted with ice. As far as we could tell, the ship's internal environment was changing to match what was current on the surface of Paradise. *Why,* was anyone's guess.

Annmarie jabbed at the useless controls again, trying to access the Medusa's Jackless landing protocols and that made me want to scream with frustration. Unless Annmarie was willing to purge the Medusa, turn, and run, she might as well trust the elder 'gats to bring us down without killing us. They'd kept us alive for the last three weeks, after all, even though the temperature was cold enough to give you pneumonia. Personally, I had a lot less confidence in the old propagats, and I had already stowed my *piscae* in the same leak-proof waterboxes I'd used to carry them away from the Sanctuary.

Corey came behind me to check the two functioning monitors. The one for orbital traffic showed nothing but a few far-off blips—ships close enough to come into orbit but which showed no signs of doing so. The other ran straight visuals. He zoomed that one until it showed the surface of Paradise from an altitude of three or four hundred klicks.

Dirty-looking clouds swept past the screen. Water glinted in chasms where eons of ice had scored the surface and in craters left by bombs or meteors. Corey studied the view in silence, chewing at his thumbnail. His reflection bowed in the screen's fisheye reflection like a hunched-over gnome.

"What're you looking for?" I asked, knowing perfectly well what he was looking for.

He blinked. "A place to land."

If he was lucky, the succubus could only show itself in Mesh. If not, we would all see it on the surface, waving its panties at the sky and shrieking his name.

"We're not going to get a choice about where to put down," I said.

He put his hands under his armpits. "*Obviously,* Eve."

I glanced over at Annmarie, still focused on the view out the window, huddled in her gray blanket. Whatever silent agreement she and I'd had for the last three years concerning Corey, now it was broken. I sat up straight and stabbed a finger at a random shadow flitting past on the screen. "What was *that?*"

He tensed. His eyes darted to where I'd pointed, but the shadow had passed out of range. "What was what?"

It felt good to torment him. "I thought I saw . . ." I leaned forward, pretending to search the dirty clouds.

Annmarie eyed me over her shoulder.

"I . . . guess it was . . . nothing," I said with what I hoped was dramatic hesitation.

His face turned hard.

"We're too far away to see anything on the surface," said Annmarie.

"Yes," said Corey tightly. "We are."

For a second, the sound of his voice hung in perfect counterpoint to hers. In the pallid light of Paradise, I looked up and clearly saw the structure of their relationship—a net tightly woven—as vivid as any virtual diagram. Her fundamental beliefs required his lies. His survival balanced on her demands. The cold crept deeper into my chest and I was afraid that if I kept staring, I would see my part of their tangle.

Not an integral strand but a ragged knot to be cut out.

The dull vibration of engines changed as the Medusa angled for descent. Annmarie groped for the safety harness, fastening it over her blanket with an effort. Corey glared at me and sat beside her, strapping himself in.

I belted into my own webbing as the bleak world rolled closer. Hail, I thought unhappily and swallowed against the changing cabin pressure.

The ship swung leeward. The engines changed pitch and the floor shuddered as we dropped. Clouds blew past the windows in shredded rags. Dirty sleet rattled against the hull and I heard Corey make a small comforting noise in his throat. He was gripping Annmarie's hand on the armrest between them and I suddenly wondered if I was wrong about everything, and perhaps the girl in the jar was the truth of myself. Then she pulled her hand away and wrapped it in the blanket. He gave her a questioning look. She kept her eyes on the looming planet.

The clouds broke apart, revealing vast fields of rubble left by heat and cold and old battles. All rock, ebony and gray under a violet twilight, without a trace of green. The basalt rill rushed below like an undulating worm in the frozen lava chop.

Mara's dim light winked up from scattered pools, as flat and smooth as polished hematite. Every once in a while, a segment of decimated road would show itself, leading nowhere in particular, never quite arriving at its point of origin or destination, visible for a moment, then gone.

The drive cut off into ear-ringing silence. My stomach lurched as the antigravs took over and the Medusa gyred for landing, nose upward. The view out the windows swung from broken stone to ragged sky. Above us, Mara was the brightest light, but still too far for comfort.

" *'Tether now the outflung star,'* " whispered Annmarie. " *'O' Mother, none else would plant a garden there.'* " She nudged Corey. "Go on."

" *'Sow thy seeds in barren ground,'* " he intoned obediently, " *'O' Father, done are thy tasks beyond the gates.'* "

" *'Harvest now thy fruitful womb,'* " said Annmarie, " *'O' Daughter,'* " and when she said "daughter," I felt a deep pain in my heart, like she'd somehow reached in and pierced me, just by saying the word. " *'One night reveals all future days. Raise up thine Unknown Child for all and shout . . .'* " She turned in her seat as well as she could, eyes gleaming, but her face said, *Wait . . .*

In front of me, the monitor showed us descending into an uninviting netherworld punctuated with sharp rocks. A hopeless view of a hopeless place whose time was a long way past.

The floor shifted. Paradise became still. We were there. And that was all.

"Hell," I said, forgetting the words and ready to cry. "Oh, hell."

Annmarie and Corey stood, deep in Mesh, between the open doors of the drive bay. We were approximately three klicks from the old city and the charred silhouettes of broken buildings were just visible, flat as cardboard against the violet horizon. Paradise's atmosphere was the equivalent of some extreme mountaintop and far too thin for survival. Corey had reset the Isolators to extend a bubble of breathable air around the ship and added a couple of tall stalky halogen lamps, but our tiny pocket of light and heat was no match for the chill of the old world.

I stood inside, shivering in my heavy clothes, ashamed of myself in spite of everything for Saying It wrong.

Hail! Here is the new world.

Annmarie was ignoring me, eyes shut, framed in the indeterminate dawn, or twilight, beyond the bay. Corey stood motionless beside her, deep in Mesh.

I wandered over to the bay's airlock and stepped down in my thick socks from steel plate to the frigid ground. My shadow spread weakly on the basalt. The first human shadow for twenty-five hundred years in a landscape so empty, so utterly devoid of life, that the words of The Landing Song seemed cynically blunt. *'None else would plant a garden there.'* I made my way across the rubble until I found the shimmer where the Isolator bubble separated me from the rest of the planet. Beyond the shimmer, an uneven plain vanished into its own darkness, rimmed by the bowl of sky. For a moment the familiarity of it was overwhelming. I knew this place. I'd been coming here for years. The sand and the pond made it look different, but what was Paradise except another kind of desert?

I turned to see Annmarie and Corey—silent, lanky shapes in the yellowish light. If things had been as tense on the Generation Ship as they'd been on the Medusa lately, I could understand the dancing, the leaving, the garden and the gates. Naverdi was wrong. The comforts of the old world, the Generation Ship and now the Medusa, had turned rank and poisonous. I rubbed my arms, chilled through the heavy fabric, and turned toward the horizon where the ruins of the city groped at the sky.

Corey's voice broke the silence.

"The surface seems stable. By this time next month, it should be lighter, probably warmer."

Annmarie nodded. "Get the environment suits out." She

shaded her eyes against the halogens. "Eve? Eve, what're you doing out there?"

"Nothing," I said from the cold, stony dark.

"Well, come in. We're going to have a look around."

We could have stayed inside the Medusa, wrapped up in blankets while we flitted across Paradise in Mesh, but there was no sense of discovery in that. Besides, the ship was freezing and no matter how hideous and uncomfortable the environment suits were, they were warm. Despite my gut feeling that the succubus was just outside, waiting hungrily for any tendril of contact, I was exhausted with being cold.

I stuck my feet into the legs of my suit, taking a last breath of clean air before sealing myself into the stink of stale plastics and old sweat. The suits were helmeted coveralls, airtight, with an antigrav coil winding around the neck and knees. Annmarie had found them pawned off somewhere, years ago, and at first glance, they looked anything but flight-worthy. They were greenish-khaki, with a rebreather helmet and a faceplate. They had sewn-in gloves and finned booties which provided the illusion of physical control. For all I knew, the original owners had fallen out of the sky and died in them.

I toed into my booties, pulled up the suit, struggled into the helmet, and turned to the greater challenge of the antigrav unit.

The antigrav came in two separate parts. The first was built into the spine of the suit. The second was housed in an external coil, which was a white plastic hose as thick as my wrist. The coil had to be twisted once in the middle to form a figure eight or an infinity sign and the crossover was supposed to connect at the small of your back. The top part of the external coil went around your neck. The bottom loop went around your knees like a hobble. When the antigrav was activated, all the lines of force had to be within certain parameters for it to work correctly. Flailing or pointing in mid-air could cause a fatal drop, so there were straps to bind your legs together and buckles to hold your arms at your sides. Sensory information and guidance were routed through the Mesh anyway, so it didn't matter that you were bound hand and foot, flying through the air half-blind.

Annmarie and Corey stepped into their white plastic coils and looped the hoses around each other's necks. They watched through scratched faceplates, expressionless while I struggled with mine. The coil was too flexible and writhed with a life of its own when I tried to duck into it.

"Here." Annmarie's voice muffled through the respirator. She caught the coil in both hands. "Stop." She spread it for me to step into. "Put your feet there." I did, cartoonishly clumsy in the short fins. "Turn around." I did, facing the unconcerned bulk of the drive. I felt her tighten the straps around my knees and arms until I couldn't budge. She twisted the hose across my back, pressed the connecting assembly almost hard enough to knock me off balance, and wrapped the rest around my throat.

It was tight. I coughed and felt her checking the buckles and straps. She yanked on something and the pressure on my throat seemed worse.

For a second, I was terrified. How angry was she?

"Annmarie?" I choked.

She adjusted something and the coil loosened. "There you go."

I turned, breathing too hard. Her face showed me nothing, hidden behind scratches and patchy reflections.

Beside her, Corey rose up, feet splayed, angling out the door into the morning or the evening of our first day. "Aren't you coming?"

Annmarie strapped herself together with one smooth motion, raised her feet, and floated after him. "Eve?"

"I am," I said, all my fears muffled in the helmet. "I am."

There was just enough light from Mara to cast shadows. Ours rippled across the landscape, flickering in the small pools.

Heads and long torsos, tapered legs and short fins trailing. The suit was warm inside, and despite the smell and the pressure of the hose at my throat, flying like this made me feel freer, happier than any weightless overlay in Mesh.

In the mental distance, I could hear Corey and Annmarie comparing notes, analyzing the constant flow of data supplied by the elder 'gats. I let myself skim in the wake of it, one eye turned inward, one watching the ground nervously for signs of—whatever—but there was nothing new. The old Mesh supplied us with all the useless details we could possibly want to know: The period of rotation, ancient, volcanic history, the mix of atmospheric gases, and information about the weather. There was nothing suspicious. No succubus.

Most of Paradise was fairly flat, except for the basalt rill and the ever-present signs of bombing. The remains of roads and buildings were intermittent, separated by fields of rubble. Pools of water welled to the surface wherever the ground dipped a little or cracked open, but none were remarkably large and none deeper than a few meters.

"Nothing big enough to fish in," said Corey, his voice blurred in the helmet's speaker, and Annmarie laughed in my ear.

"Say, Eve," said Corey, "when things're a bit warmer, maybe you could breed your fish and let a few of them go."

"They're both males," I said.

"They are?" said Corey. "But you could clone them. It'd be nice to have fish in a place like this. Eventually we'll be planting and building. Why not have a little wildlife?"

"But they'd *all* be males," I said. "When they found each other, they'd fight to the death. After a while, they'd die out."

"Isn't that what's going to happen to the ones you have now?" said Annmarie.

"Well," I said. "Yes. I guess so."

"What's the point of having them?" said Corey. "I mean, if they're just going to die."

"They're pretty," I said, too defensive. "They're mine. I *like* them."

"What're their names?" he said.

I frowned behind my dirty faceplate. "I never named them."

"No kidding?" said Corey. "What's the point of having a pet if you don't name it?" He hesitated. "I know. What about Cain and Abel?"

"Who're they?" I said.

He laughed, not answering.

Annmarie interrupted, in Mesh. *The pools are sinks into an aquifer. Can you see how the whole subsurface is honeycombed?*

I was noticing that, said Corey. *Anywhere you could dig, you'd find water.*

I shut my eyes, tapping into what she saw. Below, the ground laid itself out in schema, the old lava riddled with channels, as porous as a loaf of bread. One drop of water could probably travel the entire substrata, given enough time.

Might be hard to put in foundations, said Annmarie.

Corey laughed. *We don't have to worry about that yet. Let's get comfortable—let's see how much Staze we can make. We should get used to the place. Then we can start building.*

"You're right," she said, and I could hear the smile in her tone, as though she really believed his plans matched hers.

We flew on. An hour. Two hours. The data began to repeat itself and after a while, the conversation stopped.

For a hundred kilometers, there was no change in the landscape. Not to the naked eye, or in Mesh. Just the crystalline structure of basalt, patterns of geologic stress, the night sky, the cold ground. I yawned in the warm helmet. I could sleep, I thought, tethered in Annmarie's wake. The suit would fly on without prompting.

My eyes were almost shut when Corey swerved, swung around, and stopped. His wake in the Mesh went large, and I made the suit slow down until I was hovering next to him.

Annmarie had been farther ahead. Now she twisted in the air, angling toward us. "What's wrong?"

Corey nodded stiffly at the black stone below. "What the hell is *that?*"

My heart jumped. The succubus, I thought, first panicked, then wildly relieved that Annmarie would finally *see* it. I felt Annmarie's attention focus downward and pushed myself into the cool factuality supplied by the elder 'gats.

Below was a tiny, *tiny* anomaly in the vast lava desert.

Whatever it was, the Mesh showed it chemically—organic amines and DNA strands, and a cloud of excreted ammonia.

I heard Annmarie catch her breath. "That's *alive.*"

"Kind of," said Corey.

We angled lower, swooping down to land on a flat of stone. I struggled to pull my arms out of the confining straps as Annmarie excised herself in one enviable, fluid motion. Corey crouched over something, shining a handlight onto icy stone. I hunkered closer, my faceplate fogging from the inside. Through the mist, I could see an area of discoloration on the surface of the rocks—yellowish, with a crusted texture.

Annmarie squatted beside Corey. "Fungus?" she said. "Is it a fungus?"

"Looks like a fungus. Smells like a fungus." Corey laughed at his own joke, since all he could smell inside his helmet was himself.

He gave Annmarie the light, took a sample bag and a sterile-sleeved knife out of his pocket, and picked at the stuff on the rock until he had a yellow flake of it. He dropped that into the bag and held it up for Annmarie to see.

She shone the light over the fleck. "I'll bet it's not native. It probably fell onto the planet while the atmosphere was frozen and now it's trying to make itself at home."

Not the succubus, I decided uneasily, not sure if I was glad or not. "Why didn't we see it before?" I said, but neither of them seemed to be listening.

"It won't last long," said Corey. "Not at this rate of terraforming. Talk about landing in the wrong place at the wrong time." He bent over the fungus and shook an admonishing finger at the remaining smear of yellow. "Doomed is what you are. Doomed."

In my ear, Annmarie let out a cough of a laugh, hesitated, and then giggled like a schoolgirl.

The fact that the fungus had crept up on us—not in a literal sense, but by being beneath the notice of the Mesh—made me more nervous. On the way back to the ship, I tried to scrutinize every bland detail supplied by the elder 'gats. Ambient temperature. Lacy paths of subterranean water. All of it seemed too obvious. No succubus, but its presence was an itch I couldn't quite reach. I wanted something I could point to and say to Annmarie, There! I told you we should never have landed. The more I thought about *that,* the less likely it seemed that I would ever find *anything* awful enough to make Annmarie nod grimly in agreement. *That,* I realized, was the dream. What was real was that we were stuck on Paradise, and on Paradise we would stay.

Hail.

Since I'd ruined the mystical ritual of our arrival, Annmarie had resigned herself to making our Landing into a scientific investigation. We had to do something with the fungus besides let it bloat the specimen bag with ammonia, so Annmarie decided it should be nurtured.

Over the last seven years, she'd collected a certain amount of lab equipment in her quest to make the purest, most addictive version of Staze, and it fell to me and Corey to drag it all out and set up a makeshift biology lab in the drive bay.

I found boxes and boxes of different-sized culture dishes and a spherical quarantine field generator which hissed like a snake when I suspended it over two wide lab tables and turned it on. In one of the Medusa's closets, I found a narrow wheeled cart with drawers full of medieval-looking picks and scissors and needles. There were dissection tools, magnifiers, and hypodermics. The variety of junk far exceeded what I would have attributed to researching Staze. None of it was designed for use in Mesh. Annmarie'd collected it the same way she'd gotten the dubious environment suits—from pawn shops and backstreet markets where people sold precious things from blankets spread out on the ground.

When we'd finished setting up, Annmarie came into the bay, carrying her environment suit limp over one arm and a bowl of something hot, steamingly fragrant, in the other. She draped the suit across a chair, where it lay like the husk of an unforgivably ugly mermaid.

"What's wrong with the suit?" I said and saw what she had in the bowl. My mouth started to water. "Soup?" I said. "How did you get hot soup?"

"The food units are finally working. That's the good news. The suit, on the other hand . . ." She set the bowl down and tapped the helmet. "Something's wrong with the rebreather. It'll fly, but that's about it."

Corey came over and scratched his chin, stubbly where he hadn't shaved. He'd already deposited the fungus into a sterile dish and had been watching it for the last half hour. The fungus, which already seemed bigger, gave the bay a light stink of ammonia despite the quarantine field. "We'll have a viable atmosphere pretty soon. You won't need a rebreather."

"Can't you fix it? I can't be grounded."

He shrugged. "We don't have a lot of specialized supplies, Annie. You just have to be patient."

Annmarie turned to the lab table, where tools and dishes were laid out like a setting for an inedible meal. She sniffed the air.

"It stinks," I said. "The quarantine field's not working."

Annmarie gave me a humorless smile. "A little ammonia won't hurt you, Eve. We'll make a few adjustments. It'll be fine." She picked up the bowl again, warming her hands with it. The food might've been hot, but the bay was still frigid. "We're online in the control room," she said to Corey. "The rest of the systems seem to be coming up, but it's slow." She rubbed her forehead. "If we had to lift off, I don't think we could."

"Stop worrying." Corey gave us both a huge grin. "I can see this place in five or ten years. Trees and flowers everywhere. Animals and birds. Can't you?"

Annmarie smoothed her hair, let out her breath. She turned to the doorway and the black world framed in our own weak light. I watched her try to make her shoulders relax.

Corey turned to me. "Birds and bees," he said. "Can't you just see it?"

"Sure," I said. And Staze. I could see plenty of Staze in his vision. Addicts falling from the sky.

I woke up sweating in my room, my nightshirt soaked through. The air was warmer than it had been in weeks and I kicked the covers off.

Fire. I'd been dreaming about fire.

I lay there, wide-eyed, taking in deep breaths through my nose.

No smoke.

In the corner, the orange glow from the fish tanks rippled against the wall. My *piscae* drifted in what passed for sleep. I sat up, groped for a sweater, and pulled it over my damp night-shirt. There *was* a smell. Coming from the corridor.

I found my pants and socks and went out, shivering in the heat.

The door to the bay was open. Inside, Annmarie sat perched on a stool, arms crossed on her knees, her eyes wandering over the clutter of plates on the table. The bay stank— *stank*—of ammonia.

I stood in the doorway for a minute, thinking of the flames in the stairwell at the Sanctuary. Thinking of Annmarie's face when the soldiers twisted her arm up, out, and snapped it at the elbow. Her eyes had been focused elsewhere, her mind clawing at the mechanics of fire. They'd understood this and knocked her head against the wall to break her concentration, but it was too late. Smoke in the stairwell, filling my nose and mouth and eyes. They'd left her to be burned alive, and me, crouching next to her, fingers wound in the torn cloth of her sleeves.

I thought about Corey trying to hold her hand as the ship descended and tried to imagine myself being bold enough to shriek at her about the succubus and what it was doing to the ship—to us—but she wouldn't believe me unless Corey validated the things I'd said.

And he wouldn't. He had other plans. Maybe she did, too.

As long as I was a sad dysfunctional face in a jar, he was better in Annmarie's mind. More dependable. Smarter.

My throat got hot, tightening with upwelling tears. I'd saved Annmarie's life. That should have sealed our relationship, but in her mind, I owed her for the last seven years. I could almost accept that. If she'd abandoned me after the fire, I would never have survived. I rubbed the tears away. What if it'd been Corey in the blazing stairwell with her? I told myself she would have burned to a cinder. But maybe not. Maybe the things they'd seen in each other the moment he'd come aboard would have been visible in the smoke and flames. I took a shallow breath of the fungal reek. There was no succubus. A little ammonia wouldn't hurt her. There was no way to rescue Annmarie if she wouldn't believe in the danger. On Paradise, redemption was out of my reach.

I coughed. She looked up.

"Isn't the ventilation working?" I said.

She straightened on the stool and rubbed her neck. "Is it that bad?"

"It's awful."

She got up stiffly, went to a panel box in the wall, opened it to touch a switch, and came back to the table. Overhead fans shuddered into motion and I felt a breeze against my cheek.

She leaned against the table. "It's late. You should be in bed."

"It's too hot in my room." I went into the bay and stood opposite her across the table. My body felt transparent, like I was still asleep. "What about you?"

"Oh," she said, "I can't sleep. Not with all this." She settled on the stool, her chin on her fists. "You're not happy to be here."

"No," I said. "I guess I'm not."

"I'm sorry about that. I really am." She sighed. "You're practically an adult. You should be able to do what you want. But it's impossible for you to leave. You understand." She hesitated. "Don't you?"

It was such an unlikely question from her, I was almost positive I was still asleep. My reflection in the green glass came back to me. I wanted to ask her, Have I ever been anything more than an obligation to you? and realized for the first time, I didn't *want* to know what she might say. My illusions and assumptions over the last seven years were far more comforting than her truths.

Her eyes stayed on me, full of the easy answers she wanted to hear. I turned away without saying anything, went to the open airlock, and stood there in the dark. She sighed again, like she hadn't expected anything else. Stupid girl, I thought. To her, I'm just a hopelessly stupid girl. I looked down at the cold stone of Paradise, where freeze marks crisscrossed the surface.

"Where do you think you're going?" she said.

I hadn't known until she'd asked. "Out," I said and stepped down.

Corey'd added a few more lights to the Isolator-enclosed environment, but beyond their halogen glare, the planet only seemed blacker than before, as though the night had thickened in direct correlation to how much light we threw into it. I picked my way to the edge of the Isolator field where Annmarie couldn't see me.

Here I could feel the basalt curve downward, fissured by the stresses of its journeys. I found a crack about as wide as a bucket, full to the brim with icy water, and sat down beside it. I wished hard for the succubus to leap from this puddle, bare its breasts at Annmarie, and scream out the facts about Paradise. Instead, it was utterly quiet.

In the distance, the old city showed stars through empty windows. A meteor arced across the horizon and I looked down at the water, half-expecting the ebony surface to clear to a deeper vision. What I saw was myself.

Not the dust-covered thirteen-year-old, or the sooty parasite in Annmarie's cottage. My real face was haloed in rough hair, half-lit by halogens. I searched the reflection for any sign of a second presence in the eyes, or the angle of the mouth, but all I could see was my own awkward surprise. My expression was so ridiculous, I had to laugh. It was only me. My breath made the surface of the water ripple.

Like the pool behind Rose in her Sanctuary portrait.

I watched my own smile vanish and glanced up at the city.

The mild sky and pretty hills had shredded away to show . . . this? Was *this* the pool Corey'd been hovering over, searching for something the old Mesh refused to show?

I looked at the water again. Anything could be in there. More fungus. The succubus. Things I couldn't imagine.

My skin prickled in the chill, and I shut my eyes. The casual deluge of information, the old Mesh, the elder 'gats, swept over me. The pool turned a dull pewter, silver, then transparent. Under the water, a velvety darkness lined the sides of the hole in the rock. Not fungus. This was bumpy-soft, like one of Nav's fancy brocades. I enlarged the image. The velvet texture turned mossy, looming and motionless in the lack of current. Magnified even more, its frondlets were stunted, blunt and ugly, shedding bits of themselves, too oriented for survival to be bothered with prettiness. Was it a plant? I watched the detritus fall away, drifting downward in an unformed constellation, like petals dropping from a flower.

Rose hadn't been trying to show me vegetation. I looked

deeper into the ash-colored water, magnifying everything hugely.

And then I felt the worm. Felt it before I saw it.

It rose like the basalt spine of the planet, looming under drifting offal, immense and wrinkled in its tiny puddle. It raised itself like one of my *piscae,* without a leap or a jump, just the lazy motion of one world sliding against the wet belly of another. It *inhaled,* and the drift of dead moss rushed into some hidden worm orifice.

The moss quivered in the sudden current.

The worm sank out of sight, a behemoth in its black pool—and was gone.

I opened my eyes and scrambled away on cold stone, bruising my knees. The elder 'gats had reluctantly exposed the fungus for us, but we'd seen no sign of these things at our very *doorstep.* I got to my feet, shivering in the long dawn. Languid ripples crossed each other in the water, glinting in the halogens. Outside the bubble of the Isolators, I could feel the entire planet stirring sluggishly in the distant warmth of Mara.

"Annmarie?" I shrieked in the morning twilight. "Annmarie? *Annmarie!*"

"We'll name them after you," said Corey. "We'll call the moss *Evie foundus.*" He grinned. "And we'll call the grub *Evie screamedus.*"

I hugged myself in the thick blanket. "It isn't f-f-funny."

The things lay submerged in sterile dishes, joining the crop of fungus on the crowded table. As soon as I'd started screaming, Annmarie had come running. Corey'd stumbled out, half-asleep, then bolted back to the Medusa to return encased in his environment suit. He'd plucked a piece of the moss out and stuffed it into a sterile bag. For the worm, he'd plunged his arm into the pool up to his shoulder and found it—plus another five, exactly like it.

He was calling them grubs. As if they might mature into something else.

Annmarie opened a small box of dissection tools and set it beside a plastic tray where one of the grubs was already cut down the middle and pinned open to frame its own innards. It was small. Harmless. About the size of an open hand.

"There's no mention of these things in any of the historical texts," said Annmarie. "If the fungus fell onto the surface over the last two and a half thousand years, I could buy that. But the worm and the mitochondria are water-based. Where did they come from?"

"I think that's obvious," said Corey. "Paradise was never heavily populated. It was such a rock, no one expected to find life here. The grubs and moss were probably in a dormant stage at the time of the Landing, and no one ever noticed them."

"Dormant stage?" I said. "But they're all over the place. How could anyone miss them, dormant or not?"

"If it's cold and dry, I bet they dry up to practically nothing," said Corey, like he had it all figured out. "These kinds of organisms can hibernate for hundreds of years and still be viable, like seeds. A little water, a little heat, some light, and *zap!*" He snapped his fingers and raised an eyebrow at Annmarie, who just looked doubtful.

Corey peered at the mutilated grub in front of her. "Why're you dissecting it? The Mesh should tell you everything."

"It should. Everything on this table is swarming with 'gats. The Mesh *should* have let us know about every single thing on this planet, living or dead. But it didn't." She prodded the grub with the scalpel.

"I don't see any organs," said Corey. "Or muscles. Or even a brain."

"There isn't one, as far as I can tell. It can't think. It can barely move, but it *can* eat." She pulled up a thread of tissue with the tip of the blade. "This seems to be the digestive tract, but it's hard to tell which end is which." She pointed to the top of the carcass. "This is the mouth, I think. Although it could be the anus. And look at this." She poked the thing in the side and liquid oozed into the dish. "When it ingests, I think the nutrients must disperse through its body through osmosis along with the water." She poked again. "It's like a sponge. When it's dry, it's probably no bigger than your thumb."

"How does it reproduce?" said Corey.

"I'd bet it's asexual," said Annmarie.

"Can't you tell?" I said.

"It should be too complex to depend on mitosis," said Annmarie, "but I can't find anything it could use for reproduction."

"What about the moss thing?" I said.

"It's not a moss." She pushed the dead grub aside and took a dish full of brackish fronds out of the quarantine field. She found a steel needle-tool and used it to lift the fronds up so they draped, slimy and translucent, across the edge of the glass dish.

"What a beauty," said Corey.

"It's not a plant," said Annmarie. "The best I can get from the Mesh is that it's an organized collection of single-celled animals."

"Like coral," said Corey.

"Not that complicated." She let the frond drop. "It has more in common with mitochondria. The closest thing I've seen to this would be an archaea."

"I saw the worm eating it," I said.

She glanced up at me. "You saw it take a *bite*?"

"No, I mean the plant—the moss-thing—was shedding and the worm sucked in the waste."

"Obviously they're symbiotic," said Corey. "The moss probably absorbs shit from the grub and the grub feeds on slough from the moss. Very simple. Nice and neat in a place where there isn't any food."

"There has to be more to it." Annmarie studied the moss in front of her. The brackish color was fading to a brittle brown as it dried. "You're talking about biological perpetual motion. That's not possible."

"Maybe the grubs get a snack once in a while." Corey eyed the fungus, which had taken on a fragile frothy texture. "Look how big that's getting," he said. "It's ready to spore."

"What if the spores land in the worms, or the moss?" I said. "Aren't you going to separate those things?"

"Grubs," said Corey. "Not worms. But that's a good question. I wonder what happens when all these organisms run into each other?"

"Why would they?" said Annmarie. "The fungus prefers a dry surface, as far as I can tell, and those other organisms live in the water."

Corey picked up a pair of tweezers and extracted a wide flaking section of fungus. "What do you think would happen if I mixed them up?"

"The fungus would probably drown," said Annmarie. "Don't . . ."

Corey dropped the fungus into a dish with one of the grubs. The crusty yellow flake drooped over the gray worm.

"Damn it," said Annmarie. "I'm doing *research*."

"It's not going to hurt anything." Corey leaned over the table and closed his eyes briefly, taking in the invisible details. "I guess we'll see," he said.

Annmarie scowled at the dissection tray. "What I really want to know is why the Mesh didn't see these things until we practically tripped over them."

"The Mesh isn't working," I said. "That's why."

They both looked at me. Annmarie glanced across the table at the collection of helpless alien lives. "We need to make a bigger survey," she said. "I want to know what else is out there."

We didn't go anywhere, in spite of needing a "bigger survey." Annmarie stayed in the drive bay with the mix of grubs, moss, and fungus. Corey sat cross-legged in the control room, eyes shut, ostensibly monitoring the assimilation of the Medusa. My job was to find the parts to fix Annmarie's suit so we could all go out again—together. I decided to take my time. I fed my fish. Picked up my room. And finally went hunting for spare parts.

There weren't a lot of places to look, as the Medusa only had two main areas for storage. One was a deep closet set into the wall between my room and the drive bay, where we normally stored crates of processed Staze. The next biggest was a narrow space behind a folding door in the crew room. Each of our rooms had a closet as well, but those were the size of lockers and hardly big enough to hold anything except underwear and socks.

I went to the crew room first and pushed the flimsy folding door to one side. Annmarie's lab equipment had taken up most of the space in here for years. Now the only things left were a half dozen waterproof, airtight, high-impact bioboxes for keeping live samples. They were made of dull red plastic, about the size of a small suitcase, and I remembered when Annmarie had bought them, years ago, from an elderly Jackless woman who'd assured us they would make wonderful containers for fruit. I opened them all, in case someone had decided they'd be a good place to keep spare electronics, but there was only the musty smell of live things which had died, crumbled away, and been mostly washed out.

There was nothing else in the closet but a zippered bag of flowered sheets. I crawled out backward and went down the corridor to the closet where we kept the Staze.

From here, I could see into the control room. Corey and Annmarie leaned together in close conversation, their faces nearly touching. Their reflections showed vaguely in the curve of the window, never turning my way, and I wondered what had happened in Annmarie's makeshift lab. Something important enough for her to walk away from it and tell Corey.

Had the succubus finally shown itself?

I went into the bay and stood at one end of the table.

Instead of vague groupings of grubs and moss and fungus, there was a straight row of a dozen sterile dishes. The acrid stink of ammonia was gone and the fungus, which had been doing so well, was relegated to one corner. Instead of sheaves of healthy flakes, it looked distinctly smaller.

There were twelve grubs, one to a dish, each paired with a piece of moss, like a rotting garnish. Each dish had a number taped next to it, 1 through 12, and the first six—as though Annmarie and Corey had reached a compromise—contained a flake of blossoming fungus as well.

Twelve grubs? Of the original six, one was splayed and dead on the dissection tray. Where had the rest come from? Had they reproduced somehow? The succubus's interest in pregnancy came into my mind, sharp, as if the thing was standing somewhere nearby. I took a step and kicked something heavy. One of the red bioboxes, open and half-filled with water. Two more grubs and some of the mossy archaea wallowed at the bottom.

Corey had gone out for more. The planet was infested. Grubs and moss as thick as propagats. The idea made my skin crawl.

I stepped over the biobox and took a closer look at the arrangement on the table.

In dishes 1 and 2 and 3, the fungus reeked of ammonia, soggy but intact, despite keeping company with the grubs and moss. It was a healthy yellow-gray with blisters where it was ready to spore. But in dishes 4, 5, and 6, the fungus seemed to be the loser in the mix. It was smaller, less of a sulfurous yellow, and more the brackish color of the grubs. In 7, 8, and 9, I could hardly see any difference between the fungus and the moss. I sniffed. No ammonia. And in 10, 11, and 12, the fungus was gone. Killed. Eaten, or absorbed somehow. The grubs and moss must have iron constitutions, I thought, to be able to digest something so completely foreign.

I sniffed again over dish number 12. There was a delicate wisp of another scent. Sweetish, but sharp. I breathed in through my mouth and the smell clarified. A distinct pectin tang.

Saliva started under my tongue. My hand stung and I shut my eyes, almost against my will, needing to know if it was *here.*

In Mesh, as if from a huge distance, I saw the succubus kneeling at the edge of my pond. Its presence seemed to fill the space, leaving no room for anything else, real or virtual. I hung somewhere in the air, staring down, disoriented in the place I'd made for myself, feeling my innards throb with fright.

Its hair coiled like a raveling rope of black snakes. It was naked, lustrous as metal, and it opened its fists to show something pulpy, yellow—its virtual version of the fungus. It smeared the pulp against its mouth and neck and shoulders. The yellow faded where it touched the succubus's body, becoming more the shade of its dark-coffee skin. The succubus pressed one hand, still thick with metaphoric fungus, down between its thighs and bent to peer after it, not quite sure what to do next. The shockingly clear smell of apples wafted upward as it explored its own crotch, rocking its hips, slathering itself, face closed with focus—not orgasmic pleasure, but studious, as though there was information it might miss if it didn't concentrate.

Someone touched my shoulder. I gasped and swung around, half-in, half-out of Mesh.

"There you are," said Annmarie. She smiled at me—really smiled.

"What?" I said. "What's wrong?"

"Nothing." She was wearing a white lab smock, happily professorial like she had been back in the Sanctuary. I couldn't remember the last time I'd seen her this way. "I wanted to show you," she said. "We've had a bit of a breakthrough."

She led me to where Corey was standing over the lone dish of fungus.

He grinned at me. "You remember how that stuff was growing in an isolated area?" he said.

I nodded, swallowed the fruity taste in my mouth.

"The only reason it survived was because it was all by itself.

Now look at this." Annmarie pulled me over to dish number 12. "See any fungus?"

I could see a grub and its companion moss: two damp heaps in a clear puddle. "No," I said. "Was there some?"

"Corey put a piece of it into this dish six hours ago," said Annmarie.

I tried to push away the image of the succubus smearing itself with yellow pulp. "What happened to it?"

"The grubs and the moss absorbed the fungus," said Annmarie. She beamed like this was the revelation of the ages.

"Digested," said Corey, and his tone was dismissive. "This is strictly a predator-prey situation. The grubs and moss ate the fungus. No mystery. Case closed."

Annmarie shook her head emphatically. "It isn't digestion," she said. "As far as I can tell, they can't digest the fungus. There's something else going on." She crossed her arms, head cocked to one side, more animated than I'd seen her in a long time. "I started one of these cultures every half hour. The fungus is an aggressive colonizer and the first thing it tries to do is poison everything nearby with ammonia. But when it started to attack the grubs and the moss, they started sending out what the Mesh calls organelles."

"Organelles?" Seven years of making Staze had dulled what I could remember of biology classes at the Sanctuary. "Bacteria—right?"

"More or less," said Corey.

"You might as well call them missionaries," said Annmarie. "They spread into the fungus and mark out the parts of the DNA which control the fungus's ability to produce ammonia."

"They disabled the fungus's defenses," said Corey, as if I couldn't figure this out for myself. "Then they ate it."

"They didn't *eat* it," said Annmarie. "They—they analyzed it. They gathered genetic information. And when they knew enough, they—sort of—converted it."

"Converted it to what?" I said.

"Food," said Corey.

"No," said Annmarie with just a hint of impatience. "They told it to stop trying to adapt—to stop its aggression."

Corey rolled his eyes.

"Once the aggressive tendencies are gone, the missionaries start exchanging chemical information. In a sense, they 'feed' the fungus with their own biological matter until the fungus starts to lose its biological identity. Eventually it resembles the grubs and moss so much"—she pointed to dishes 10, 11, and 12, where there was no sign of fungus—"the threat is gone."

"Or eaten," said Corey.

Annmarie touched the nearest dish with her fingertips. "At first, I thought the grubs and the archaea were two variations on the same life form, but now I think they're completely unrelated. What's happening to the fungus also happened to the moss at some point. The grubs and moss 'de-developed' together until the end result is what we think of as symbiosis. They're co-dependent." She raised an eyebrow at Corey. "We agree on that, right?"

"Right," he said. "They could've come from opposite ends of the universe, for all we know."

Annmarie pointed to the middle dishes where the yellow fungus struggled to hold its own. "Even though it disappears, the fungus isn't dead. It's been simplified. It becomes part of the existing eco-system. And it's quick. The whole process takes less than six hours. In effect, the grubs and moss 'teach' the fungus how to be part of the local ecology."

Corey laughed. "You're making it way too complicated, Annie. I mean, it's an interesting approach to survival, if you're right, but evolution is a simple process. Eat or be eaten. Fight or flee. Survival of the fittest."

"There's nothing complicated about it," said Annmarie. "It's co-dependency instead of competition. And it makes perfect sense in a place with such limited resources. None of these organisms have the energy to waste fighting to the death."

"Can it absorb us?" I said.

"Not unless you go swimming with them for six hours," said Annmarie. "You'd freeze to death first."

I glanced over at the table, the luckless fungus. "Can that ever change back?"

"I don't think so," said Annmarie. "The physical changes seem permanent. The fungus isn't equipped to reach back for its original identity." She drummed her fingers on the table. "It'd be interesting to see how the process works on something more complicated."

I found myself wondering how to kill the grubs—by stepping on them, or throwing them against a wall.

"It's assimilation," I said.

"Yes," said Annmarie. "Exactly."

"Like our propagats being overwhelmed by the ones here on the planet," I said.

She started to nod, then shrugged off the metaphor. "Close enough."

"It's addiction," I said.

They both looked at me.

"What?" said Corey.

"Like Staze."

Corey's face stayed expressionless, but I could see that this idea hadn't occurred to Annmarie. "The grubs make the fungus dependent," I said. "It eliminates their violent natures. Like Staze."

Neither of them said anything.

"There's a parallel anyway." Annmarie ran her fingers through her hair. "Maybe not the best analogy."

Corey smiled. "Maybe not the best."

I finally found the repair kit buried behind the two twenty-five kilo crates of Staze we'd made for the ungrateful mountain guerrillas on Kigal. The crates were too bulky to move out into the corridor, so I dug between musty cardboard boxes and bags of old clothes until I found a bag marked SPARE PARTS. I spent the next two hours in my cabin with Annmarie's suit, too preoccupied with my latest image of the succubus to do much but make the damage worse.

The grubs *were* the succubus. That's what she'd told me in front of Rose's portrait.

They're me, she'd said. *And one day you. And him. And the other ones.*

Assimilation. Addiction.

Fight or flight.

Her face peering up from my pool. Alien things hidden under the surface of half-frozen water. If someone had asked me to explain the connections I could feel in the hollows of my chest, I wouldn't have been able to, but they were there.

All I wanted to do was run.

Which made me think about Naverdi.

After weeks of agonizing over what I might have done to save her, I'd discovered it was most comforting to think of her as an opportunist with schemes so vast, she couldn't afford to die. From her blue chair on Macha, to the addicted Meshed in Tula, to me. Every time I'd seen her, she was thinking ahead. She must've known her life was in danger the minute Annmarie'd connected her to Rose's addiction.

Naverdi *was* alive, I told myself again. She was too clever and too greedy to leave me stranded with Annmarie and Corey on the blasted remains of a mythical planet when I had the means to give her everything she'd ever wanted.

I pushed the wires and shreds of plastic from Annmarie's rebreather onto the floor where her environment suit lay prone, its helmet lolling, half-attached to the neck. I curled up against my pillows to watch my fish circle in their tiny worlds, almost tired enough to sleep. Corey's ridiculous idea of cloning hundreds of males for release came into my mind again. Cloning for extinction was what it boiled down to, but the vivid image of scarlet and sable *piscae* swimming freely in the current of some swift creek held my tired imagination until I closed my eyes and the Mesh flowed around me.

*   *   *

There was no sign of the succubus in the depths of my pond. There was no sign of anyone and that made me feel safer than I should've. I went over to the edge of Corey's sandy carpet, pushed the gauzy sky to one side, and stood barefoot in front of his chair. Maybe his view was strictly directional? I dropped onto the soft cushions and examined the empty air in front of me. Not a damn thing. Even his sky was colorless.

I tugged at the fabric on the chair searching for hidden openings. There were none, but when I pulled at the deep pile rug with my toes, I felt it give. I got down on my hands and knees, grabbing fistfuls of white shag until I found an area looser than the rest. When I looked carefully, I found a square cut into the carpet, like a trapdoor. In Mesh, the join was nearly invisible. I traced the edges with my fingers, found a likely corner, and peeled it up.

Underneath was a dark little hole, and through the hole was Paradise, laid out as a view from orbit. Much more than a blackened husk. The obligatory geology was there, but from Corey's point of view, so were the grubs and the moss.

Here were the scattered pools—all over the planet—pole to pole, each with a minimum of three grubs and three separate clusters of moss, all in different stages of thawing. I was willing to bet he hadn't shown them to Annmarie.

There was more. Between the pools were threads. Not on the surface, but like the aquifer, weaving everywhere under the volcanic stone, crisscrossing the entire planet like a ball of black string. Maybe it was a root system for the moss? A kind of filament link between the grubs? Annmarie's dissection had made those look pretty self-contained. I sat back, thinking of the dark insight I'd had on the way down through the atmosphere—Corey and Annmarie tied together by their own dependencies. I leaned down for a closer look. Put my arm through the opening and slid into Corey's secret world.

In a moment, I was on the virtual surface, the same as my first time.

Paradise, in shades of indigo and violet. A wink of water

here. A crust of ice there. I was standing on a high point where the corner of a building might have been, in the middle of a town or another city. All gone. Stars arched above it all in a great wash, unaffected by the pressing matters of tiny lives, endless wars, and persecutions.

Why here? The unrelenting flow of information told me I was nowhere near the rill, or the old city and its imaginary population. Obviously Corey knew things he wasn't sharing.

I shuffled down the hill, through loose shale and the stipple of ice, trying to imagine Paradise with rivers, trees, and grass. The surface was so desolate, all I could picture was a few scrawny weeds among the boulders.

And then I heard a moan.

Not a painful moan. The other kind.

Corey and the succubus. I was certain of it.

I hunkered down behind a rock, wanting to spy but not wanting to see the details, which I was sure would be disgusting.

Another moan.

I peered over the top of the rock.

Corey was pulling up his trousers in a small clearing in the rubble. The succubus reclined on the ground in front of him, its face a weird, half-familiar mix of my features and Nav's. It was voluptuous, entirely naked, and the insides of its thighs were smeared with sticky, milky wetness. It touched its crotch and put the finger against its tongue.

No, said Corey, *that isn't food.* He leaned forward to touch its privates. *For us, this is a reproductive orifice.*

The succubus eyed him. *I know that. I know everything.*

You don't know how to reproduce, said Corey.

It gave a languid shrug. *Apples. Seeds. It isn't so hard.*

He scratched his bald spot. *Where in the world did you get that idea?*

From the picture of the first woman in the gallery.

I had a sudden vivid image of the succubus standing for hours at the gates of Rose's link, staring down the narrow gallery at the incomprehensible painting of the Annunciate. What bizarre stories had it come up with, guided by the elder 'gats, which tried to inform it with ancient abstract mythologies? A hungry woman in a garden, pregnant and threatened and abandoned. How much of that could it really understand? In terms of apples and seeds, obviously not very much.

Corey sighed and changed the subject. *Can you please explain why you put the fungus into your genital area?*

I wanted to see if it knew how to re-pro-duce, like you do.

But I told you it couldn't, he said. *It would need different organs. Besides, there are lots of ways to exchange genetic matter. For example, when you find something new, you know a way to absorb it.*

Food, it said.

No, he said, *you change it. You found a way to make the fungus part of yourself and it changed. Its color changed.*

I find ways to understand new things, it said, as though he was unforgivably ignorant. *I bite into them, like the first woman, and I know everything about them.*

It meant me.

The succubus spread its legs and examined its wet thighs. *Why re-pro-duce?*

To make sure our species can survive, said Corey. *How does your species guarantee its survival?*

The succubus shrugged.

There's only one of you. Isn't there?

The succubus frowned at its nails.

The grubs and the archaea—the moss. Those things are you—aren't they? They're how you appear in the physical world, right? And all of them are connected, right?

Yes.

Corey pressed on. *What happens when a few of those grubs, or some of the moss dies? How do you get more?*

Dies?

You know, he said. *It no longer functions. We've killed one*

*of the grubs already. Annmarie cut it open after we took it out
of the water. It's not alive anymore. Don't you feel that?*

No, it said.

Do you know what injury is? he asked. *Can you feel pain?*

The succubus scratched its nose, bored, and I squinted at
it in the weird propagat-light. Not bored, I decided. This *thing*,
which was sophisticated enough to manifest in a virtual space
provided by our own elder 'gats, simply didn't have the intelligence or the experience to answer him.

Is Annmarie the other female? asked the succubus.

Yes, said Corey. *Remember, I want you to stay away from
her. It's for your own safety.*

Safety, repeated the succubus.

She's very powerful, said Corey in a tone reserved for children or idiots. *She wouldn't hesitate to kill you.*

Kill?

Like food, said Corey. *She'll kill you. You'll be food to her.*

The succubus studied him. *You mean die?*

That's exactly right.

The succubus nodded. *I understand die.*

You don't, said Corey. *To understand death, you have to
understand reproduction.*

The succubus got to its feet and swung its naked sticky legs
over his lap so it was sitting astride him, its chest pressed against
his. It rubbed its teeth against his bare neck. *Give me more
genetic matter so I can understand you.*

Not right now, he said. *I'm tired. Let me teach you a song,
instead.* He cleared his throat. *Here's how it starts. 'Tether now
the outflung star . . .'*

I opened my eyes, ready to leap out of bed, grab Annmarie,
and show her everything. I swung my legs over the side of the
mattress, stiff in my back. My feet were freezing and my head
felt numb, like I'd been asleep for too long. I checked the
time. Four *hours?* I pushed myself out of bed, scrubbed at my
eyes, and looked around.

Something was missing. A familiar noise. A smell. I turned, half-asleep, almost knowing what was gone.

The fish.

The tanks—everything—gone.

I bolted out of my room and down the hall, thinking with dull half-awake paranoia that Corey had stolen them because I'd taunted him in the control room. But that was wrong.

My fish were on Annmarie's lab table in the drive bay, side by side in matching cylindrical glass containers.

A grub and a portion of the moss floated with each of them.

Their tanks had been dumped out and colored gravel lay in a gritty heap in the bottom of a bucket. I stood by the table, fighting back tears as the fish moved sluggishly past the grubs, under the dank fronds of moss. Their ebony veils were gone. Red scales had faded. My beautiful *piscae* were as gray as wet cardboard.

Annmarie watched me, her face a mask of false sympathies. "You were asleep," she said. "I didn't want to upset you with this." She made a little beckoning gesture. "At least let me show you what's happened."

"They're dead," I said.

She shook her head. "They've lost their violence. They're assimilating."

She led me to the table and made me look at the ruins of my pets. One bobbed to the surface, took a breath and sank again.

"See how close they are." She ran her fingers over the glass where the two cylinders touched. "They should be all puffed up, right? Full display for the other male?"

Their displays were nothing. They were like fish dressed in rags.

Annmarie picked up a pair of blunt-ended tongs. She plucked one unresisting fish out of the water and let him sink into the container with the other male. They drifted together, colorless, nameless.

"Under normal circumstances?" she prompted me.

"They'd kill each other," I said numbly.

"Never again." She bent next to me and I could see our faces distorting on the opposite side of the glass container. Hers was wide and optimistic. Mine was narrow and ashy, as though stained by fire.

SIX

Later, when I thought it was morning, Annmarie came to my room. She sat on the bed beside me.

"I'm sorry about your fish," she said. "I took them out of the tank before they were completely assimilated. You can have them back."

Rag-fish. They could share a bowl. Save space.

"Eve, honey," she said, "if it makes you feel any better, I took genetic samples from both of them. You could clone them, like Corey was saying. You could make a hundred new fish." She touched my hair. "It's not the end of the world, Eve."

"No," I said.

She didn't say anything for a while and then stood up. "I want you to help Corey today. He's collecting specimens from different locations on the surface. I don't like it when he's out there by himself."

"He's not by himself," I said.

If she had any idea what I meant, she didn't show it. "Please, Eve," she said.

After she left, I got up and washed and put on clean clothes. My room seemed utterly empty without the sound of the aerator and the light smell of algae. The absence made me feel like I was a visitor, and that the room I'd lived in for so many years was only a borrowed space from which I was free to leave whenever I liked. Or whenever I felt unwelcome. I thought about Rose's ship bursting into silent flames and Naverdi's shuttle disappearing in its wake. I thought about the fire in the Sanctuary stairwell and the way Annmarie had grunted with such pain as I'd dragged her, choking, down the stairs with all my thirteen-year-old strength. I thought about the fish and wondered why I'd never named them, when that should have been such a natural, loving thing to do.

Had I loved them?

Or was it because I'd saved them, I'd felt obligated to take care of them?

How could you love a fish anyway?

Or a stupid girl?

I brushed my fingers across the place where the fish tanks had been and went out into the corridor, heading for the drive bay.

My *piscae*, such as they were, floated grubless, mossless, just under the surface. They were dying, and I made myself not look. Other things in the bay had changed as well.

Grubs and moss were everywhere, not just in dishes on the lab table but on the floor, too, in buckets and bowls, even water glasses. I took a step and kicked over a coffee cup with a grub in it. The grub slopped onto the floor in a puddle of oily water. It was the same ugly color as decaying fruit. The skin had a texture like wet paper and it oozed like a sponge. It was as big as my fist, but I had the impression that it could fit into almost anything. Just keep pressing until all the liquids were squeezed out and maybe half a dozen grubs could fit into a thimble.

And how would the succubus look then?

Annmarie was watching me from across the room. I stepped over the grub without touching it.

Corey appeared just outside the open airlock, swung two bioboxes up into the bay, and climbed in after them. More grubs. More moss. He looked around at the scatter of various containers and grinned at Annmarie with boyish enthusiasm. "Think we've got enough?"

"Where'd you get these?"

"From the southern half of the third quadrant." He rubbed his gloved hands together and slapped at his shoulders like he was cold. "Something's wrong with my heater. Is there any of that tea left?"

"A little. It should still be hot."

He trotted past me, all smiles, and stopped when he saw the hapless grub lying on the floor. He picked it up with great care and put it into the empty coffee cup. A pointless act of mercy, since the cup had no water in it.

I turned to Annmarie. "I don't want to go with him."

"I don't want him out there by himself. The suits are in bad enough shape. I don't want anyone stranded in the middle of nowhere."

"*We're* stranded in the middle of nowhere."

"You know what I mean," she said sharply. "And we're *not* stranded." She put her palms flat on the table, trying not to yell.

Corey came in with two cups of tea. He set one down for Annmarie and took a gulp from his own. "Ready to go, Evie?"

"Go where?" I said.

"Northern half of the third quad. Everything's pretty much melted up there. You won't have to dig." He mimed using a pick hammer. "When we have samples from all over the planet, we can start checking for differences due to habitat."

"There's nothing different about their habitats," I said. "The whole planet's the same and you know it."

"*Eve,*" said Annmarie, and there was no room for argument

in her tone. I walked over to my suit and began putting it on as slowly as I could.

Chatty as he'd been in the drive bay, Corey didn't have much to say once we were airborne.

Below us, melting ice made a glistening web of pathways between heaps of broken black stone. Watery runnels turned silver across the ebony surface and the effect was briefly magical. I turned my attention to the soles of Corey's flippered feet instead, rehearsing the things I wanted to say to him, all the accusations.

"Why don't you tell Annmarie about that thing in the Mesh?" I said.

"Thing in the Mesh?" His surprise sounded patently artificial, even through my suit's tinny earphones.

"You *know* what I'm talking about. You told it to stay away from her."

He was quiet for a while. "Eve," he said finally. "Annmarie thinks of Paradise the same way she thinks of Staze. For her, it's our only chance of survival. She'll accept that the ship's been completely assimilated by the elder 'gats, but if I showed her everything I've found out about this planet, she still wouldn't believe we might be in danger. It doesn't fit into her plan and she just doesn't want to hear it."

"You don't want her to know what's really going on," I said, "and she won't listen to *me*. You told that *thing* she'd *eat* it if it showed itself."

"She would," he said. "Metaphorically speaking, anyway. It's bigger than she is, and you know Annmarie doesn't like to be challenged."

In the back of my mind, I tried to open a narrow filament between myself and Annmarie—to send a sense of urgency to the Medusa without actually dropping into the Mesh. If I was careful, she could listen in.

"You've lied to her about everything," I said. "Whenever

she thinks she's figured out something about the grubs, you tell her she's wrong and steer her off in some other direction."

"I think that's a little unfair," said Corey. I'd expected him to get angry, maybe even yell, but he only sounded disappointed. "Annmarie's already figured out what the grubs and moss are, in their visible sense. This whole planet's like a beehive, or an anthill. That's the dynamic, anyway. The grubs and moss've probably always had an awareness of each other, but when they started absorbing the elder 'gats, their connections became more complex. They gained a sort of sentience, but not a real intelligence."

"How can you say it doesn't have intelligence?" I said. "It's *learning.*"

"It's hungry," he said. "It doesn't have any other motivation—not even reproduction—it doesn't have the capacity to understand that. It just wants to eat."

"You're teaching it to have sex!" I shouted. "You're showing it how to absorb human beings!"

He laughed. "Don't be ignorant. It can't hurt you unless you go swimming with it and stay in long enough to let it exchange biological material."

"What if it figures out how to crawl out of those puddles?"

"It doesn't have the imagination for that, Eve. It's a simple organism with a tendency to imitate its prey—part of its assimilation behavior, I think—but it doesn't have much mental capacity. Every time I try to explain reproduction, it starts talking about that painting it saw in the Sanctuary gallery and the fairy tale about the apple and the seeds." He laughed again. "I've been trying to make it understand what death is, but I think you'll have to take over for me."

The way he said it made my stomach lurch. I blinked into Mesh, dispensing with desert and pond to make direct contact with Annmarie. No response. I groped in the mental darkness, but it was like a door had slammed shut between me and her.

I opened my eyes. Corey was gone. Not gone, because he couldn't have flown out of sight in just a few seconds. I twisted awkwardly in the confining suit and caught a glimpse of him above me, falling toward me with his arms free of the restraining buckles.

He landed on my back, knees clamped along my sides, fingers digging into my arms. I gave a breathy croak of a scream, pinned into position with him riding me. My suit couldn't hold both of us up and sank toward the rocks below—not fast enough to kill, or even hurt.

"What're you doing!" I shrieked. "What do you think you're *doing*?"

"I know how you feel about this place," he said in my earphones. "I know how you feel about me. I would have liked for things to be different, but . . ."

The pressure over my throat went tight as he grabbed the coil of my antigrav unit. I saw the flash of a sterile-sleeved knife out of the corner of my eye. Blades of sharp lava drifted upward and I ripped my arms out of their straps—ripped the straps right out of the suit's stiff fabric.

Freezing air rushed in around my thighs. I grabbed at my throat for the antigrav unit. The dirty white coil came loose in my hands, sliced in half. We were falling, no more than a meter or two from the ground. Corey pushed himself off me and I landed hard on the rocks, banging my knees and elbows, rolling in sharp gravel, the wind half knocked out of me. By the time I scrambled to my feet, he was already strapping himself into his suit.

"You're not hurt?" he said.

I stumbled toward him in my fins over the broken stones. I was scared witless. My right leg hurt and everything was moving with a nightmare motion.

He stuck his arms into their straps and rose up, out of reach.

"You *killed* Annmarie," I shrieked. "You *bastard*!"

"She's not hurt. She's asleep. I put a little something in her tea. She'll wake up in a few hours."

"Staze!" I choked. "You *Stazed* her!"

"Oh, no," he said. "I'd never do that to her. Or you."

"You can't *leave* her!" I bellowed.

He floated above me, expressionless and bound. "I can't stay. She's too focused on making this place into something it's never going to be. Did you know we can't move the ship or send communications offworld? Everything seems to be working, but the systems won't act. Not in Mesh or with the manual controls."

The inside of my chest went tight with dread certainties— like dying here. "How're *you* going to leave?"

I could hear a faint grin in his voice. "Evie, if *you* ever want to get off this rock, you should be asking, '*Why* can't we move the ship?'"

"Because it's full of contaminated propagats! I keep *telling* you. The succubus—that *thing*—doesn't want us to leave."

"Is that what you're calling it?" He laughed hoarsely. "I think it likes you. That's why it still looks so much like Naverdi."

"You can't get away," I yelled. "No one can land without getting infested with old 'gats."

He rose up higher. "Naverdi has nanovirals."

Naverdi.

She was alive. She was coming to him for Staze.

Not to me.

All my faith in her ability to survive was overwhelmed by what I knew about him.

He would take her ship and leave.

"Is she here?" I whispered.

"Why don't you check?"

Close my eyes, he meant, and he would be gone when I opened them. He was already starting to drift away.

"Wait!" I shouted at him. "*Wait!* You can't just leave me here!"

He hesitated, savoring what he saw or repelled by it, or just wanting to hold the moment in his mind.

"Start walking, Eve," he said in my ear. "It's not that far."

And then he flew away, ignoring every curse, all the threats I shrieked into the revealing night, long after I couldn't see him anymore.

My suit was torn just above the knees where I'd yanked out the restraining straps. Cold air crept up and down my bruised legs as I picked my way between boulders and grub-infested puddles. At ground level, Paradise was immense. I was hours from the ship. As many hours as it would take for Corey to steal Annmarie blind and leave with Naverdi—or with her ship. What could he want from her except convenient transportation?

And sex. The idea made my stomach hurt.

Was she here? I twisted my face up inside the helmet. Wispy clouds drifted between me and the stars. I wondered if I could feel her without the benefit of the Mesh, but that sort of contact would have meant an emotional connection I wasn't sure we'd ever had. I closed my eyes, dispensing with my desert to scan the propagat-image of the planet. Paradise spread itself out in my mind, thick with as much information as it took to make a secret of grubs and moss, and the possibility of approaching ships.

I widened my perception to include the area of a standard orbit, but beyond that, there simply weren't enough propagats—new or old—to tell me anything. I peered around for the succubus. Maybe it was waiting for me to call. For the right favor, it would probably show me everything. I didn't have time to be proud or even wise.

There was a pool practically at my feet with a surface texture like half-congealed oil. I couldn't imagine how anything could live in it. I touched the water with the very tip of my finger. The ripple spread like a signal.

In Mesh, the succubus stood right in front of me, without even a change in the scenery. Its teeth were luminous in the indigo night. Its naked body seemed to flicker, ethereal and vague.

Where's Naverdi? I said. *Where's her ship?*

It pointed to the puddle. The surface glimmered, transparent to some other vision. I crouched down without turning my back, nervous about its metaphors, so obviously borrowed. Corey's sarcasm echoed in my head. *I think it likes you . . .*

Naverdi's shuttle appeared under the surface, parked in a flattened former town. Nav was standing beside it in her own environment suit, newer and far less ratty than ours. Her helmet tilted awkwardly backward as she searched the sky. She went to the other side of the ship and leaned against the battered hull. Probably low on Staze, I thought, and wondered how long she'd been there. Hours, maybe. Even days.

Why can't I see this myself? I said.

Because, said the succubus, *I'm hiding it from you.*

Corey told you to do that?

It nodded. *He said he'd give me more seeds if I did.*

I wondered uneasily how much control this creature had over the elder 'gats. More than Corey would admit to, apparently, or maybe more than he knew about.

How far away is this ship? I said.

The succubus came closer. *Why should I tell you?*

I wasn't sure what might pass for a good reason. *I have to go with her.*

It brushed its fingers along my arm. *Corey said there was only room for me.*

Room for you? I echoed.

He has part of me. He said there was no more room.

You're saying he has some of the grubs and moss with him? Your, um, other manifestations?

It nodded.

Grubs and moss in a biobox. Grubs and moss infested with corrupted elder 'gats, floating in murky water. Grubs going offworld in Naverdi's hold, along with this succubus consciousness. I shuddered with cold and under that, I felt a spark of real fear. Why would Corey do that unless it was worth more than his relationship with Annmarie—more than Staze? I glanced at the image in the pond, expecting Corey to appear any minute. How much time did he need to rob Annmarie of all her Staze, pack it into the shuttle with a couple of bioboxes, and go? We'd spent almost an hour in the air between here and the Medusa, but we hadn't been going very fast. If there was a way to stop him, I had to figure it out pretty damn soon.

Why is he taking you with him? I said.

To re-pro-duce, said the succubus, as if this was the most obvious thing in the world.

Even Corey would think twice before plunging in with the grubs and moss to 'exchange biological information.' More likely he'd mixed sperm in with the grubs the way he'd mixed in the fungus. But what kind of results would he get from that? Just another assimilation—certainly not *'re-pro-duc-tion'*. Maybe it was all just a bad idea at this point—a virtual hypothesis hidden somewhere under that white carpet. Then I had a sudden awful vision of Naverdi, Stazed to the gills and slathered with curious grubs.

Look, I said weakly. *About those seeds. Corey probably hasn't told you everything.*

But I know everything, said the succubus. *The apple. The seeds. He showed me.*

I'm sure he did, I said. *But did he tell you Naverdi was different than us?*

Its face furrowed with concern. *What do you mean?*

If you look, you'll see that she doesn't have the capacity to use propagats. She's like the fungus you found just before you found us. Very simple.

The succubus gave me an eager look. *Simple? Like food?*

I felt my heart speed up and knew one day I would regret every word I was saying. *Sort of like food.*

But he said she was genetically compatible with him. He said the three of us could make her re-pro-duce. That's what he said.

How ridiculous, I said. *Could he make the yellow fungus reproduce with you?*

It shook its head. *It didn't know how.*

Are you sure Naverdi knows how?

It hesitated. *There's a disease on her ship. I don't know everything.*

The nanovirals. No doubt Nav had purged her ship as she landed. Without propagats, Naverdi was a mystery to the succubus—and to Naverdi, the succubus would be no more than ugly biologic samples. *Well,* I said, *before you go with Corey, I think you should be absolutely sure you can trust what he says.* I paused for effect. *I don't.*

Why not?

He left me here. I can't get back to my ship. He did something to—to the other female, and I can't contact her, so I'm trapped in a place where I can't survive for very long. If he did that to me, why wouldn't he do that to you?

Its eyes seemed to cloud. *But he gave me seeds.*

I shrugged. He gives everybody seeds. He's got an endless supply. They don't mean anything to him.

The succubus studied me. *If I took you to the shuttle, would you leave without me?*

If I took you to the shuttle . . . ? *No,* I said flatly, *of course not.* It was too easy to lie to this thing. I wondered how soon it might learn to interpret the physical signs of falsehoods. *Is there a way to . . . uh . . . get me there?*

Its face, so much like Naverdi's and so unlike hers in its meager range of expressions, pushed together in a pout of difficult thought.

Maybe, it said.

At first, I didn't think anything had happened. Then it was darker. And then the dark went hot enough to make me sweat inside the suit. I thought the succubus was the vague phosphorized shape in front of me. I reached out and felt a new viscosity in the air. The night became closer, colder, oppressive, and *scary.* It was hard to breathe and I opened my eyes in a panic, expecting the real surface of the real world.

Not there.

The dark was directionless. I grabbed my knees, falling,

but there wasn't any gravity, only a half-frozen thickening. My stomach clenched. I thought I was going to throw up in the helmet—and then there was light.

It was bright. Bright as normal daylight. I was in Corey's blinding forest of halogens.

I was up to my neck in water. A *pool* of water, full of grubs and moss.

I yelled and hauled myself out as freezing water poured in through the tears in my suit where I'd ripped away the restraining straps. I rolled over the stones, banging my head on the inside of my helmet, slapping at my legs and arms to crush all the awful spongy things I imagined had fastened onto my skin, thinking *this* was my unspoken bargain with the succubus—it wanted *me*, and it didn't care about Corey or his *seeds*. I stripped off the suit, screaming and skinning myself on gravel, twisting naked under the harsh lights until I'd examined every centimeter of gooseflesh. No grubs. I sat, shaking and hugging myself until it occurred to me that there hadn't been a grub in that pool for days. Corey'd relocated them to Annmarie's lab table and dissection trays. The succubus had done me a favor, dropping me into an empty hole.

Two favors.

I wobbled to my feet. The Medusa's bronze-colored bulk loomed under the halogens and I stumbled toward it, feeling as though I should pinch myself awake, but this was no Mesh vision and no dream. I was *here,* fifty klicks from where I'd been seconds ago. There was nothing in human technology which could do *that.*

Simple organism? Like hell.

I climbed into the drive bay, naked, wet hair hanging in my eyes, and saw Annmarie lying on the floor.

The teacup was still on the table. My fish floated belly-up in their tank across the room. Buckets and cups and sterile dishes full of grubs and moss covered the floor. In spite of everything, I knew I would murder Corey if he'd killed her. I crawled over to touch Annmarie's throat and listened to her chest. Her pulse was slow. Her eyes moved in dreams behind her eyelids. She was composed, confident. Still the strong beautiful woman I had fallen in love with as a girl. The woman I had trusted as my foster mother. This was the last time I would be able to see her that way. I got to my feet, half-frozen, grateful and miserable at the same time that there would be no goodbyes between us. Just my disappearance—if I was lucky. If not, we'd be trapped together for the rest of eternity on Paradise, or until we killed each other.

In the storage closet, there was only one crate of Staze, which meant Corey'd already been and gone. I was sure he'd be back for the rest. Whatever he planned to *'re-pro-duce'* with a couple of grubs, some moss, and Naverdi, Staze was a known quantity. If all else failed, Corey would make sure he was rich. Two crates of Staze would guarantee that.

I went into my room, stepping over the headless corpse of Annmarie's environment suit. I pulled on my warmest clothes and dropped into Mesh to see where Corey was.

The succubus was by my pool, looking apologetic in an underpracticed sort of way. *I brought you to the wrong place.*

Which was true, although it hadn't occurred to me. It was supposed to have taken me to Naverdi's shuttle, not the Medusa. *That's okay.* I wanted to ask how the *hell* it'd transported me partway across the planet, but the explanation probably wouldn't be any more detailed than the usual *'I know everything.'* Better to pretend I would ask questions later when we were safely aboard Naverdi's ship.

Where's Corey? I said.

Here. It smoothed the water with its palm. My gesture. I wondered how long it'd been watching me.

The view of Nav's shuttle was from much higher this time. Corey appeared as a bright shape moving from the shuttle toward the Medusa, returning for the second crate. The bright red speck on the ground, well out of walking distance from Nav's shuttle, was the first crate of Staze. He'd left it where she couldn't get at it, staging his delivery.

The distance between the Medusa and Nav's ship was no more than a twenty-minute flight at the most. I didn't have much time.

Have you moved Corey around the planet like you moved me? I said.

No, said the succubus.

Does he know you can do that?

No, said the succubus.

Would you do it if he asked you to?

It gave me a look of unlikely innocence. *I wouldn't. He's been lying to me.*

I nodded. *That's right. You can't believe anything he says. Understand?*

Yes, said the succubus.

Can you take me to Naverdi's ship the same way you brought me here?

It chewed a thumbnail. It was *so* like Corey. *If I do, your physical body will be in with mine.*

Which meant, I assumed, that I really would find myself plastered with grubs when I crawled out of the next murky pool.

I don't want to do that, I said. *I don't want him to see me. He might try to stop us. Can you hide me the way you hid Naverdi's ship?*

Yes. It stood there while I waited for a different sensation, but there was none.

I hesitated. *Am I hidden now?*

It nodded.

I'd find out soon enough if we were *all* lying.

I dragged my useless, soggy environment suit into the drive bay and shook it out. Worse than useless—flightless. There was no antigrav coil. No way to pinion myself with the torn restraints. I wasn't going anywhere.

I stood still, my heart pounding so high in my throat, I thought I would choke. Then I remembered Annmarie's suit.

It was lying in pieces on the floor of my room. Her rebreather was shot, but *mine* worked. All I needed was a few seconds to reconfigure the antigrav settings in Mesh. I grabbed my helmet and dodged through the buckets of grubs, back to my room.

Her suit was bigger than mine. I kicked away the dismembered parts and struggled into it, waltzing idiotically with the uncooperative loop of antigrav cable before I managed to snap it into place. I squeezed my eyes shut to configure the settings.

And found Annmarie waiting for me.

If we'd been in my desert, I would have turned for the pool and thrown myself in, disappearing long enough to change settings and get away. But there was no desert. No cottage, either. There was nothing. The privacy of our spaces in Mesh had changed. Bright hues of blue sky, white shag, and green trees had become a liquid mix of colors, every solid vision draining into a sticky, inescapable murk.

Annmarie stood in the center of it all, black as burnt wood. Hair writhed around her face, twisting with hurtful words, a licking fury beyond betrayal. She was holding the green glass jar and my younger self peered out, eyes dull with fear. She shook the jar as hard as she could.

You make me so angry, she hissed.

She must have been Meshing through Corey's sedative, half-awake. Her perceptions were distorted, and I'd fallen into them—impossible with working data partitions—but of course, those were *long* gone.

She made a motion with her hand. Flames roared up, as though an invisible wall had caught. The heat was intense and real enough to make me sweat. A few wild sparks landed next to me and I stamped them out, not sure how destructive the metaphor might be, but there were hundreds and I couldn't get to them all. The fire lit the vision and behind her, I saw stairs. Familiar blazing stairs from the Sanctuary.

Annmarie stood in the middle of her inferno, legs burning, arms on fire. She held the jar above her head, then smashed it down.

Shards flared up in vivid magnesium greens. My dirty, sooty girl-self stumbled into the circle of flame beside Annmarie like some reluctant spirit.

Help me, Annmarie whispered to the terrified child and reached for her with flaming arms. *Help me.*

My girl-self backed away.

Annmarie fell to her knees, her twisted limbs engulfed. *Help me!*

I took a step toward them both. Annmarie *hadn't* been burning. Injured, yes. Bleeding, breathless with awful pain, but it hadn't been like *this.* My girl-self turned, mouth open in a terrified scream. Fire washed over her and she fled, vanishing with a wail, leaving Annmarie swathed in her own burning dream.

This was how she'd always thought of me. An undependable stupid girl, ready to run at the first sign of danger.

I could have gone to her, shaken her awake, and soothed her, because in reality, she was lying in the drive bay. In reality, I could have stayed with her, knowing that I was the root of her deepest fears. I could have spent the rest of my life finding ways to extinguish seven years of limitless, scorching distrust and stayed on Paradise until the embers of our feelings went cold. I could have let Corey leave with the second crate of Staze. I might have made myself forget about Naverdi, but I doubted it.

I covered my face and focused on the suit's configurations. And when that was done, I opened my eyes, sweating in the coolness of my own room.

Even the air in the Medusa felt different. Charged and static at the same time. I grabbed my helmet and ran clumsily for the drive bay, where Annmarie was awake. I didn't have to see her struggling to sit up to know it.

She watched as I buckled myself into her suit.

"You can't go," she whispered.

My eyes were hot, scratchy. I didn't want her to see me cry. I fumbled with the helmet. "I have to."

"You'll lose everything," she whispered. "Your Mesh. Your freedom. You'll be killed out there, Eve. This is the only place we belong."

I clamped the helmet down over my burning ears and secured it.

She pushed herself up on one elbow. Her voice shook. "I need you, Eve. The outflung star, the garden, the fruitful womb. *All* of that depends on you."

"I don't like it here," I whispered, but I didn't think she could hear me.

Annmarie pointed a long finger at me. "I tried to give you everything. You've never understood what that meant. Never."

I buckled my ankles together and hobbled sideways to the edge of Paradise's revealing night. "Hail," I said, my voice blunted inside the helmet, and kicked myself up into the sky.

From above, the Medusa was a smudge of bronze under white lights. I made the suit go faster. The horizon curved before me and I angled eastward, throat on fire with childish swallowed-back sobbing.

Below, the grim obsidian chop stretched to the skyline and I watched for the dull khaki color of Corey's suit. When I did see him, he was on the ground beside the Staze crate, shining a light over the stones. The crate had tipped, broken open, and spilled its contents. At least one of the styrene bags had torn. Red powder blew with the mild wind into a wide spray across the dark rocks and the pools. Staze. It was everywhere.

Corey made a wide unselfconscious gesture of helpless anger and leaped into the air, heading for the Medusa.

I sank to ground level. I didn't need a light to see the details.

Fine red dust covered everything. Staze floated on the surface of a shallow pool a few meters away. A grub rose to the surface, its papery skin clotted with wet powder.

It all had the look of a horrible ecological disaster, which would probably keep Annmarie occupied for a good long time—if Corey ever told her about it. I ran my fingers over the tight pile of styrene bags, packed with red crystals. For me to leave Paradise without some kind of currency was idiotic. If nothing else, Staze would give me the same leverage with Nav that Corey already had. I grabbed three intact bags out of the crate, stuffed them into the leg pockets of my suit, and glanced at the contaminated pool again.

Grubs. Moss. Succubus.

Staze.

Every grub on the planet was connected through the aquifer and the wiry tendrils I'd seen in Mesh. If one grub was full of Staze, wouldn't they all be affected? *Could* they be affected? If Staze made humans fall into a silent addictive ecstasy for ten or twelve hours . . . what would it do to the succubus?

And what if the succubus wanted more?

I kicked myself upward, and as Corey's accident faded into shadow, I thought I smelled apples in the helmet.

The metallic glint in the distance became a small shuttle. I was breathless with nerves. I hadn't thought of what I'd say to Nav when I saw her, but there was only one thing I wanted to know.

Was it Staze she'd come for? Just Staze?

Stiff, leggy braces stuck out from the shuttle's dented body, angled like the limbs of a wary animal, ready to jump away if anything surprised it. There were two slender towers a few meters away from the ship, which showed the perimeter of an environmental enclosure, like the one Corey'd established outside of the Medusa. A set of metal stairs extended down from the bay, half-lit from the open cargo door.

I dropped to the ground, unstrapped myself, kicked off my fins, and nearly tripped over a stack of bioboxes at the edge of the environmental field. I didn't have to open them to know what was inside. I yanked off my sweaty apple-smelling helmet and ran for the open door.

"Naverdi?" My voice was a burst of steam. "Nav?"

No answer.

I banged up the metal stairs and stood in the hatchway. At first, all I could see were bio boxes. A half dozen or so, one or two propped open. Grubs and moss floated under oily-looking water, feeding off each other.

Then I saw her, sitting against the wall.

Her face was as slack as any other addict's, probably hours past her dose. She saw the styrene bags sticking out of my pockets and tried to get to her feet.

"Uh," she said. "It's you."

I wanted to go over and throw my arms around her, but she would just make a grab for the Staze. She would tear the bags open and stuff red powder into her mouth. I couldn't bring myself to offer her any. It was her strength I wanted, not this weak leeching shadow. "Are you all right?" I whispered. "Did he hurt you?"

She got onto her hands and knees and began to crawl toward me. I took a backward step. She let out an awful little noise.

"Give me some," she whimpered.

"Why's Corey loading grubs on your ship?" I said. "What does he think he can do with them?"

She rolled her eyes. "Grubs?"

Why would Corey tell her anything? I hesitated, then took one of the bags out of my pocket, twisted it open, and dumped a tiny bit of red powder into my hand. Fine red grit in a neat pile. I looked up to see the hunger in her face. It wasn't as if this was her first dose. I did not addict her I told myself, but of course I had, in some way.

"Come here," I said, and she crawled over eagerly, pressed her mouth into my palm, and lapped up every grain with her hot tongue.

For the first time in my life, I wondered if Staze had a taste.

When it was all gone, she sat up suddenly, frowning as though she'd just noticed she wasn't alone. Then she lay down on the floor of the cargo bay and shut her eyes.

It would be twelve hours before I had any answers from her. I stood there, wiping my hand on the suit's stiff fabric, wondering how long before Corey showed up. I could have dropped into Mesh to find out, but the image of Staze coating the black water, the grub sinking under it, was too vivid, and I was *really* afraid of how much more the succubus might know about *everything* now. All I knew for sure was that no grubs or moss would leave Paradise on this shuttle.

I hefted a biobox off the top of the nearest stack. It was heavy, sloshing inside with water. I staggered down the steps with it, lost my footing, and lost my grip. The box slid out of my arms and hit the ground, rolling unevenly across sharp stones.

The lid came off and water gushed out. Wads of moss and a pair of grubs slithered wetly onto the stones and lay there, limp and dying. They reminded me of my *piscae*. I got up to grab them and throw them into the nearest pool and stopped myself. These weren't my fish. If these were the physical manifestation of the succubus, it was stupid to give it *more* awareness that I was about to leave it behind.

I went into the shuttle, grabbed the next box, and kicked it down the stairs. The lid burst open. Grubs, moss, oozing everywhere over the broken lava. I threw another after it and staggered in the doorway, thinking of Annmarie's neat rows of sterile dishes. Grubs, trapped in her vision of investigation and proof. My poor damn fish, trapped in a bowl without any escape. Me, on the Medusa, under the fishbowl sky of my own desert. My face, framed in a jar of green glass and nightmares of fire.

Years of trust.

Eve, she'd said to me. I love you.

She hadn't meant it any more than I had.

I turned, sweating, the suit stuck on like an extra skin, and dragged the last biobox to the hatch. It caught on the lip of the airlock and I heaved it, end over end, down the stairs. Somehow the lid stayed closed. I banged down the stairs and kicked it, heels and toes, until the lid popped and the creatures inside bled out.

I stood panting on the metal stairs, tugging at the suit where it stuck against my chest. At the horizon, the sky had brightened to a profound sapphire, cut off sharply where it met the ragged surface. My last view of Paradise. Halfway down the metal stairs, I leaned over the railing and spat.

From somewhere far away, there was a bellow. An awful angry noise.

I looked around stupidly, half-believing it was the succubus, suddenly audible in the real world.

It was Corey.

He plunged out of the indigo sky, landed hard, and tore off his helmet. "What the *hell* do you think you're doing?"

From halfway down the stairs, I screamed at him. Wordless screams, so loud and raw I thought the sounds had to be coming from someone else. The scream emptied me and faded into cold silence. For a moment, Corey and I stood at equal distances from each other, suspended in genuine surprise.

Then he charged across the broken stones. I turned and ran for the shuttle door, but he was on me, squeezing my waist, throwing me down. My cheek hit the metal stair. He let go and pushed himself up to get ahead of me, into the shuttle and away. I grabbed his legs and rolled. He toppled over the side of the stairway, hands wound into my hair, pulling me along.

We fell into the pile of broken-open bioboxes, grunting like animals. He pulled away to swing his fist, but I grabbed his arm and twisted it so hard he yelped. He was no heavier than I was. He was no taller. These things rushed into my mind as I shoved him backward with all my strength, knowing suddenly and deeply that I was stronger, younger than him, that I could hurt him, and more than anything, I *wanted* to. He lunged up and I shoved him down. The bioboxes bumped into each other underneath us and his mouth made an "O" of pain as the small of his back hit a corner. He tried to grab me, tried to get up. I knocked his hands away, beat his stomach with my fists. His expression changed with each strike, a catalog of surprise. I hit him until he crumpled on the sharp black lava, then I stood over him, gusting steam from my mouth and nose. His fear rose off of him. I could smell it. I could feel it between my teeth like grains of sand and the sensation ground inside my mouth, bitter and salty.

I kicked him between his legs and left him rolling in the gravel with his fists between his thighs.

I ran up the stairs, weightless with victory or fear or disbelief, and punched the closing sequence for the cargo door. The stairs ratcheted up. The pressure door hissed shut, smelling of machine oil. The airlocks clamped shut, leaving me with a smudged circular window to see out of. Corey crawled over to the shuttle and disappeared, too close to see from the window's narrow angle. In a minute, I could feel the door vibrating as he beat on it with his fists.

I wound my fingers around the door's steel frame.

He could get in. It wouldn't even be a challenge.

All he had to do was drop into Mesh and smash through Nav's Jacked interfaces until he found the airlock controls.

I closed my eyes.

On the Medusa, I would have raised the ship with my own icons—stones, water, and sky—but those were Mesh conventions, and it would take time to figure out how to apply them in a Jacked context. Instead, I slid into Nav's temple interface, easy access even for the corrupt old propagats of Paradise.

The brocaded room was familiar, warm, dense with the scent of licorice. I could sense subroutines in the fancy embroidery. Coordinates for her orbiting transport were woven into a tapestry. Launch protocols were part of a glitzy red sheath flung over a divan. It hadn't occurred to me before, but I could picture how Nav would run the shuttle: slipping into the dress and dancing through the room to touch the beautiful things on the wall, but there wasn't time for me to do that.

For the Mesh, Nav's intricate overlays were as easy to brush away as dust on a tabletop. In a second, all the frills and silks and velvet were gone. The room went square and dark. The controls showed as simple icons arranged in rows along one wall, the temple stripped to naked code.

I reached for the icon that would activate the engines. Something touched my shoulder and I turned to see the succubus, nude and smeared with red powder. Its expressions were clumsy and exaggerated, but it knew what I'd done with all those bioboxes. I could see that much.

You lied to me, it said. *Just like he did.*

I'm sorry, I said. *But you can't leave the planet. I'm sorry.*

You can't leave without me. It pulled its lips away from its teeth, eyes bright and predatory. I could almost see what it was, right then. There was nothing simple or unsophisticated about it.

I turned to jab at the engine controls, certain it would jump on my back and sink its teeth into me. Instead, it threw its hands over its head and twirled on red toes. Nanovirals would cut off the succubus's access, but it was too soon to flood the shuttle. Nanovirals would cut me off, too.

The floor trembled as the engines engaged, but the ship didn't move.

The succubus threw its head back and sang. *Tether the outflung star. Nobody else would grow a garden there . . .*

That's not how it goes. I groped at the displays in desperation. Antigravs, of course. Where were they? *If you know everything, you should at least know how the Song goes.*

The succubus laughed. It was an awful sound, like old metal, twisting.

Antigravs. I found the icon, punched it, and the vibration in the floor changed. The ship was rising.

The succubus came over and stood next to me, far too close. I could feel it starting to comprehend. *'Harvest now thy fruitful womb, O' Daughter, one night reveals all future days.'*

That's not how it goes, I whispered, but that was just another lie.

I stabbed at the icon for nanovirals. At first, there was no difference. And then it was darker. The icons vanished. The room vanished. It all went away. The succubus, the worlds of my childhood, my powers and strengths.

I opened my eyes. Outside the hatch window, I could see Corey's face through smudged, cloudy plastic. For a panicked moment, I thought we were still on the ground, but we were rising, and the color of the sky behind him changed as we gained altitude. I thought he would be pleading to get in, but he wasn't. He hung on—no helmet—in the thinning atmosphere, his skin bloodless and pinched with cold.

He cursed, silently, enunciating so I would know which words he was using.

Finally he let go, falling as we ascended.

Away from the outflung star, high above the hateful garden.

SEVEN

Outside the hatch window, the sky turned blacker.

I couldn't see anything.

I was hanging on to the airlock's metal frame but I couldn't feel my fingers anymore.

Behind my eyelids, there was nothing, would never be another thing, just salty tears and stinging eyeballs.

Below, night crept across Paradise as the shuttle passed into the planet's shadow. The new world all but vanished, its place in the heavens marked only by the stars it obscured.

I blundered over to where Nav lay on the floor and sank down beside her, watching her in Staze-sleep with my new blind eyes.

Hail.

We docked with her transport half an hour later. The airlock swung open onto two dim corridors. One went left, marked as a cargo access. The other went right and, I assumed, led to Nav's living quarters. I decided to carry her to bed. But first I had to find her bed.

In contrast to the baroque quality of her Jack environment,

Nav's transport was old, inelegant, and dirty, but it had nearly the same layout as the Medusa. The bridge, the kitchen/crew room and three private cabins were all connected by a short central corridor. The only real difference was that the two rooms which would have been Annmarie's and Corey's were combined into one large space, and that was filled with junk.

Exotic junk. Holos in expensive frames leaned against the walls. There was a sofa upholstered in torn pink velvet and an ornate desk. Strange junk. There was a *boat*, painted blue with a single oar.

I went across the hall and found her bedroom where mine would have been.

Her clothes lay in heaps on the floor. There was nothing on the walls—not a holo or a drawing or a note to remind her of something—just industrial-beige paint. Her unmade bed sat in the dead center of the room, pillows balled up to one side. A datascape lay on the blankets with its Jackwire trailing loose between the sheets.

I went back to the shuttle for Nav, carried her awkwardly to the bed, covered her, and sat on the edge of the mattress.

Was she charming and childlike with one arm flung out and the other across her chest? Did the way her dreads coil over the wadded pillows make her seem innocent, or seasoned? Stazed, her face was tense instead of blissfully relaxed. Her eyes darted under closed lids. Her lips were dry and lined with cracks. A dusting of stray red crystals glittered in the fine hairs above her upper lip. Her dark skin had an ashiness to it from so much time under artificial light.

She looked older than nineteen. From the stresses of her life, or perhaps she'd been ill lately, but most likely the Staze had affected her. Staze wasn't restful for the body. In the half-day between doses, Nav needed to eat, sleep, and make a living. If Staze cut her waking time in half, she would have to live at twice the speed to make up for the hours spent in beautiful imaginary places. Maybe she was closer to forty years old in Staze years. Set in her ways.

'Eve, come with me.'

What would she do when she found out I'd taken her up on an empty offer?

I got off the bed and stepped over the scattered clothes. There were obvious things I could do to stay busy. By the time I ran out of things to clean, maybe she'd be used to me.

The kitchen was a mess, with dirty dishes in piles all over the table. I searched the cold unit for something edible, but all I found was a liter carton of beer, a damp hunk of white cheese wrapped in foil, and a container of gluey noodles. I ate some of the noodles, but I couldn't bring myself to touch anything else, and went down the hall to the room with the boat in it.

I couldn't tell how much time Naverdi spent here: a lot or none at all. Maybe this was storage.

I picked my way through boxes until I was in a clear space between the torn velvet sofa and an antique video set. The set was beautiful, with a polished crystal screen. I ran my hands over the turquoise-colored, molded lacquer housing until it blinked on. Blue light behind the crystal coalesced into two women standing in a sparsely furnished room.

The controls were badly adjusted, making the images flat and willowy thin. I hunched in front of the screen, trying each delicate control for volume. The images brightened, got hazier or sharpened. I found a knob which brought up static noise, but the two women never made a sound, moving their mouths with intent expressions. I tried to guess what they were saying, but gave up after I realized they reminded me of all the endless, wordless disagreements I'd had with Annmarie. I turned the set off and wandered through the rest of the room, searching for anything that might reveal Nav's inner purposes.

Nothing seemed to be in any order, so I pawed through the junk at random until I found a wooden box with two books in it.

I'd never seen real books and these were ancient. I opened the thinnest of the two, carefully, but as I turned the pages, the paper crumbled, brown and fragile. It was a math primer, with chapters and chapters on analogous equations, which I remembered vaguely from my classes at the Sanctuary.

$$\{3 + 3\} - \{3 + 3\} = 0$$
$$\{6 + 6\} - \{6 + 6\} = 0$$
$$\{9 + 9\} - \{9 + 9\} = 0$$

I closed it and put it away. The other book was in better condition. Instead of pages, it had sheets of thin plastic, mirrored on both sides. When I held it up, my reflection stretched into infinity, and I guessed it was supposed to amuse little children, but to me, it seemed more like a faulty tool for divination. Eve past, present, and future, a hundred dark-eyed, pensive faces—never changing. I closed the book and put it away with its crumbling companion. I *had* changed. If someone had told me, even six months ago, that I was destined to knock Corey down and leave Annmarie so I could run away with a woman I'd slept with once, I would have laughed.

In another box, I found toys, dried fruit in colorful boxes, and a real stuffed dog under a stack of men's shirts. The dog was a white terrier with a sharp, nasty expression. It wore a plaid dog-sweater and slouched on a piece of fiberboard with its fangs bared, glass eyes gleaming. I set the dog on the floor while I rummaged through more stuff, but it made me nervous and eventually I put it back, covered again with the bag of shirts.

Had it been Naverdi's dog? The more I thought about it, the more I was sure it wasn't. And as I dug through the clothes and silverware, costume jewelry and expensive vases, I realized that these were things Nav had collected in trade. People had given their life's belongings in exchange for Staze.

Which made her—what?

Generous? A woman of saintly nature, handing out Red by the bag to a thousand poor souls in exchange for whatever they could afford? I went over to the other side of the room and began searching the desk.

Now *here* was something.

In the top drawer was a small box with holos in it. Quick shots of people having a party in someone's backyard. The girl in a green dress with the sheaf of dreads, blurred with her own action—was that Nav? I spread the pictures over the desktop. I didn't see her in any of the others. Maybe she was the one taking the pictures. This tall man with the easy smile, though, would that be her father? And this woman laughing as a toddler wobbled toward her, was that her mother, or maybe an aunt? Here was the house. Two stories high with pink concrete walls. Flowers in tended beds and benches set on grass between brick walkways. I could see through a window in one shot: a child sleeping on a sofa, with a big gray cat sprawled comfortably beside her. I found that if I put seven or eight of the pictures side by side, I had a fully circular panoramic view of the back-yard and a glimpse of the rest of the neighborhood.

Modest houses. More people in the distance. Blue sky with a few white clouds.

I knew Naverdi had grown up in a refugee camp, but it'd never occurred to me that we'd both lost the same things—house and home and family.

I stared at the pictures, as perfect and pure as a storybook illustration.

I wanted *this* more than anything else.

I touched the chains around my neck, ran my fingers along the warm metal until I found the clasp for my mother's medal and unhooked it. I laid it in the center of the circular panorama of the house, its flowers, and safely sleeping children.

The Annunciate exiled to a life behind a pair of golden gates where the simple pleasures of any world were visible, but well out of reach. The Annunciate, locked in a false Paradise, where no one could see the desperation in the polished-away metal of her face and the only escape was to wither into nothingness.

I refastened the chain and tucked the medal inside my shirt. I made the pictures into a stack and put them back in the drawer, out of sight.

"How are you?" I asked hours later.

She sat up, puffy and unfocused. "Eve," she said.

"You were expecting Corey," I said, hoping she would say no.

"No, no," she said. "Don't be silly." She glanced around the room, as if to make sure we were alone. "Is Corey here?"

"No."

"What about Annmarie?"

"No."

She gave me an uneasy look. "Do they know you're gone?"

I wondered if she thought I might have killed them. "They know. They can't come after us. The Medusa won't move."

"Why's that?"

"It's hard to explain," I said. "We found some . . . organisms."

She raised an eyebrow. "Organisms?"

"It wasn't human. They—it—had a presence in Mesh. I think it was a predator. And then Corey was teaching it about reproduction. It wanted us to stay." There was so much more.

"No shit," she said.

"No shit." I tried to smile, but my mouth seemed to twist on its own and I had to bite my lips to keep them still.

"You look awful," she said. "What's the matter with you?"

I took a shaky breath. "I lost my Mesh."

She nodded slowly. "When you launched the shuttle. The nanovirals. You had to. You couldn't have gotten off Paradise any other way."

Amazingly hot tears slid down my cheeks. She put her hand on my shoulder.

"What about the cargo Corey was loading?" she said.

"I threw it out," I whispered.

"It was the organism," she said.

"It was dangerous."

She took her hand away and got out of the bed. "You know how much that was probably worth?" she said and walked out of the room.

I tried to make coffee for her in the hot unit. It turned out thin and she didn't drink it, just let the cup steam on the unwashed table while she wrestled a fork through glutinous noodles. The sweating cheese lay in its foil wrap between us.

"Do you want some beer?" I said, since that was the only other thing in the cold unit.

She shook her head, chewing.

"I couldn't find anything else to eat," I said.

"I'm scheduled to meet a storeship this week." She frowned. "What day is it?"

I told her.

"Tomorrow," she said. "They'll be here when I come off my dose. I have it all planned."

"Oh," I said. Annmarie would never have been caught foodless. To be in need was to be a victim, or a target, or both.

Naverdi pushed the noodles away, sipped at the weak coffee, and leaned back in the chair.

"Are you all right?"

She got up and took the beer out of the cold unit. "I don't usually drink right after I get out of bed," she said, took a sip. "Just need something with bubbles." She drank, closed the carton, and left it on the table. "Better check navigation," she mumbled and left me sitting there.

*   *   *

On the bridge, I found her lolling in the command chair, holding her belly like it hurt. The datascape was in her lap and she was plugged into the ship, eyes closed.

Beside her, a monitor showed the sparse local traffic. Two red blips at the sensors' extreme range of detection were military cruisers. Closer, a squad of long-range Shrikes flanked a couple of transports. There was no storeship in sight. I flipped through the monitor's displays until I found the rearward view. Paradise. Of course, it showed as a comet.

"What're you doing?" Nav snapped the monitor's display back to its original setting. "Don't play with that." She tapped her Jacked wrist. "Everything's connected."

"Sorry."

She fiddled with the plug in her arm and finally pulled it out. "See those patrols?" She pointed to the red blips, the military cruisers. "We need to stay out of their way."

"Where's the storeship?"

"Probably hiding. He's not part of a legal franchise. The cruisers are military cops from Isla, and they'd probably rob him blind."

"What if they see us?"

"They can't. Rose showed me how to integrate the aegistic technology she was using. We should be invisible."

"Oh." I waited to see if she was going to plug in again. Between Staze and her Jack, I could see long, lonely times ahead, but the Jackwire and the datascape stayed in her lap, unconnected, while she studied the manual versions of the controls.

"So," she said, trying to make her voice light, conversational. "You were telling me about these organisms."

I didn't want to. "They were like worms." I said. "They looked like they'd come apart in your hands. Their skin . . ." Like damp curls of peeling paper, or wet rot. I rubbed my knees.

"That's how they looked in Mesh?"

I shook my head. "It looked human in Mesh."

"Really?" She sounded surprised.

"It would say, *I know everything.*"

"It could *talk?*"

"It was learning from us," I said. "Corey was telling it all sorts of things."

"Like what? How to reproduce?"

I stared at her. "Corey told you."

She flushed under dark skin. "You told me that, Eve."

"Corey contacted you from Paradise," I said and wondered *how*. "What did he tell you?"

She made a blameless gesture. "He said he'd found something better than Staze. He didn't give me any details. He said there'd be plenty of money for it. That's all."

"How could you believe that?" I demanded. "He would have told you anything."

"Sure." Sweat gleamed under her lower lip and she wiped it away. "He would have hitched a free ride on my ship. Just like you."

"You came because of the Staze."

She nodded, suddenly tense. "Didn't you bring any?"

"Yes." It was too soon for her next dose.

"Where is it?"

It was still in the shuttle, in the pockets of my environment suit.

"I just want to know where you put it." She pushed herself stiffly out of the chair and started down the corridor. I followed her into the room where I'd found the stuffed dog and the holos of her family. She went through the desk drawers until she found a medical scanner and an envelope. She opened the envelope, took out a blue transdermal patch, lifted her shirt, and pressed the patch just below her navel. She put her legs over the desktop and shut her eyes. In a few minutes, her face relaxed.

"Are you sick?" I said.

She shook her head. "Eve," she said a little thickly, "do

you think we're going to romp along through ThreeSys having romantic adventures and good clean fun?"

"I know how to make Staze," I said. "Isn't that what you want?"

She licked her lips. "Annmarie showed you how? She always struck me as a pretty secretive lady."

"I've been making it for seven years."

"She trusted you?"

I wound my fingers together until the joints hurt. "Yes."

"Did she teach you to bargain?"

"What do you mean?"

"Tell me how to make Staze, Eve. Tell me everything."

I hesitated.

Nav rolled her head sideways to face me. "Now. What do you want from me?"

"I want to stay with you."

"You want sex? Is that going to be enough?"

I couldn't tell if she was teasing me or disgusted by the whole idea. "Yes," I said and knew instantly that I wanted more. I wanted love. Real, honest love, and permanence. I opened my mouth to say it and realized that those were precisely the things that Naverdi would never be able to give me.

The understanding shook me. I looked around for a second chair, but there wasn't one. Nav opened the wrong drawer to put the scanner away and I pointed desperately to the stack of holos lying there.

"Who are those people?"

Nav picked up the pictures and flipped through them. "No idea."

"But they're in your desk."

"It's not my desk."

"Whose is it?"

She dropped the pictures on the floor. "I don't remember their names, Eve. I just take their stuff in trade."

"For Staze?"

"What else?"

"You don't ask for money?"

"Of course I ask for money, but if they don't have it, what am I going to say? Too bad for you, no Red today?" She shrugged. "Nobody wants to do business like that."

I pointed at the stacks of boxes. "What're you going to do with all this junk?"

"I trade most of it for Kevake."

"You do?" I had a sudden startling image of the faith healers on Jaganmata-Devi exchanging liter bottles of warm cactus sap for the stuffed dog in its plaid jacket. "Don't they know what Kevake's worth?"

She shook her head. "I never tell them why I want it. It's an economy of information. I know a little about what Annmarie does. The faith healers on Devi know a little about what I do." She raised an eyebrow at me. "But you know everything."

I picked up the holo of the woman and the toddler, wanting to change the subject. "I thought this was your family."

She let out a sharp laugh. "I never had much of a family. You're the one who lucked out."

"I did?"

"You had stability," said Nav. "Your mother didn't just drop you off somewhere. You decided when to leave home."

My mother, lying on the floor with her throat slit from ear to ear. My father covering my eyes. "I didn't . . ."

She grinned. "You can't tell me Annmarie kicked you off Paradise. That was your choice. She probably begged you to stay."

"Annmarie's not my mother."

Nav gave me a look of unguarded surprise. "She sure acted like your mother, always telling you to do this and do that and keeping you locked up in that ship."

"Well, she *isn't*," I snapped. "My mother's dead."

"Big goddamn deal," said Nav. "So's mine."

There was no sign in her face of grief, or loss . . . or anything. "What happened?"

"She was sick," said Nav. "Sick in the head. At least, that's what my cousins told me. I was just a little kid. I don't remember."

"Not at all?"

She shrugged. "I remember her yelling at me. She would throw things." She cocked her head. "Did you have any brothers or sisters?"

"No."

"I had a little brother," she said. "She killed him just after he was born. I don't remember, but they told me all about it."

I couldn't help staring. "Why did she do that?"

"Because." Nav tapped the side of her head, indicating insanity. "My cousins told me. When I first went to live with them, my one cousin, Treisa—she's the one who raised me—used to always say she could feel herself turning into her mother. I didn't know what she meant and it scared the shit out of me. I was afraid I'd get to a certain age and *bang*, I'd be throwing things and screaming and killing babies." She shifted in the chair, as though she wasn't quite convinced there was no danger of this happening. "I'm glad she died. Otherwise I would have stayed with her. She would have killed me, I think. Or she would have taught me to be crazy. You have to break that cycle. That mother-daughter thing. You know what I mean?"

I didn't say anything.

She touched the patch on her stomach. "Do you remember your mother?"

"Not really."

"Well," said Nav. "You spent so much time with Annmarie, you'll probably turn into her."

I frowned, not sure how to react, but she was smiling. It was a dopey smile, supported by the painkillers.

"Are you feeling better?" I said.

She nodded. "I can't feel a damn thing."

Later she went back to the bridge and plugged herself in, but I thought she was sleeping. I sat beside her for a while, hoping she'd wake up and talk some more. I wondered if I should clean up the mess in her living quarters, but the task was overwhelming and I wasn't sure she'd even notice. So I sat in the low light until my eyes began to close. Which made me think of the desert I would never see again. Which made me so lonely I could have wept for days, but I was too exhausted.

I shut my eyes, expecting sleep.

Instead, I stood barefoot in cool sand, staring at my familiar world—not trampled and shredded like it'd become on the Medusa, but pristine. Here was the still humidity of water and the empty blue sky. This desert wasn't surrounded by Annmarie's forest and Corey's obscuring white carpet. It was my own place.

Not a dream, either.

I hunched down, fingers pressed into damp sand, wondering if this was a terrifying new succubus trick. But the more I thought about it, the more I knew it wasn't. Naverdi's nanovirals killed Type-2 propagats. The Type-1's that had been injected into my body seven years ago were internal servers with different tasks, infesting me alone. They provided a solid enough environment for me inside my own head, but were useless for gathering information, or acting upon the larger world without a corresponding population of Type-2's.

Which meant I was alone in a room without windows or doors. My reflection stared up from the motionless water, naked and dusty. I tried to clear the surface to test the interface with the greater Mesh, but there was nothing.

Nothing greater than me.

I slept on the sofa in the storage room, woke up hungry, went to the kitchen, gave in, and ate the cheese. I found Naverdi in bed, this time with a bag of Staze on the covers beside her. When I went to check the leg pockets of my environment suit, which was still on the floor of her shuttle, all three bags of Staze were gone.

There was no point in looking for them. I knew how to make Staze and that was what she really wanted. I went to the storeroom and watched the silent images on the video set until I went to sleep again.

Hours later, Naverdi wandered in to bang the desk drawers open and shut. I sat up as she stuck two blue painkiller patches onto her belly.

"The storeship's here?" I said.

She shook her head. "They're having trouble with the patrols. I'm rescheduled for tomorrow." She came over and sat heavily on the sofa.

"How're you feeling?"

She touched the patches, her belly. "It hurts. Feels like my period, but it's the wrong time. There's a guy on the storeship who knows about drugs. I'll ask him for something stronger." She put her hands on her knees, fingers taut. "Eve."

"Yes?"

"Did Annmarie do anything different with that last batch of Staze?"

"No," I said. "Why?"

"Something's changed in my Staze place."

"Staze place?"

"You know what I'm talking about." She leaned back on the sofa. "I have a place I go. It's always the same. Except for now." The blue patches were already seeping into her system and her shoulders began to relax. "I have a river in Staze. And when I'm *in*, I'm on a bridge, right over the middle, looking down at the fish. I have beautiful fish. Hundreds. All different colors and sizes. I've met other people with the fish dream. They get all poetic about it, but it's a pretty place. You can't blame them."

"Other people have the same . . . Staze place as you?"

She squinted like I should know this. "Of course. Rose and I had the same place."

"You could *see* each other in Staze?"

"No, we couldn't *see* each other. It isn't like *Mesh*."

"Then . . . how did you know?"

"We talked about Staze," said Nav. "We're addicts. We don't have real lives anymore, so we have to talk about something." She frowned. "It's funny. Now that Rose is dead, I feel like she's on the bridge with me. Like that was the part of her that stayed alive."

"I wish it hadn't happened," I said and realized I was apologizing for Annmarie.

Nav didn't answer, lost in the idea of Rose surviving inside her Staze vision, or just lost in the painkillers.

"So," I said after a while. "Everyone sees the fish and the river and the bridge? How long can you talk about that?"

She blinked. The drugs were making her punchy, but also remarkably candid. "You make it sound ignorant."

"I'm sorry," I said. "Are there a lot of . . . Staze places?"

"At least a dozen." She began counting on her fingers. "There's the forest with the waterfall and birds. The jungle with deer drinking from a waterhole. There's a lake with boats. The meadow with the stream running through it." She hesitated, trying to remember the rest.

"They all have water?" I said.

She nodded. "You know what Rose used to say?"

"What?"

"She said if we could move in our Staze places—and you *do* know we *don't* move, right? We just sit around and smile."

"I know."

"She said if we could follow the river or the pond or whatever to its source, we'd probably find a Red pool of dreams."

"What does that mean?"

Nav spread her hands. "I hardly ever knew what Rose was talking about. She was so obsessed with *community*, though. That's probably what she meant."

Was that what she'd been hoping for in the dark stinking tunnels under Tula? "A community of addicts?"

"What else?" She gave me a lopsided grin. "If you think

Rose was bad, you should see the nutcases who think Staze has a big cosmic meaning."

Annmarie's Staze disciples. "I've met a few."

She laughed. "Did they get down on their knees when they saw Annmarie?"

"Practically," I said. "She had a special sales pitch for them."

Nav giggled. " 'The dream in Red is the way of peace.' "

A direct quote. "How'd you know . . . ?"

"I've heard all sorts of stories about Annmarie," said Nav. " 'Red will make us all as one. Red is eternal life. Red is the end of death.' " She snorted. "What a load of shit."

I wasn't about to defend Annmarie. "They were dependable customers."

"I'll bet," said Nav. "I've heard them preach once or twice. Did you know they quote her, word for word? People call them Staze-Fakers because they pretend they can make the stuff themselves." She held up her thumb and forefinger, with a tiny space between. "They have about this much real Red, just to keep their converts happy. They pretend it's magical. They say each of the Staze dreams are symbolic. The boat in the pond means stability and wealth. The deer at the watering hole means imminent danger."

"What if your life changes?" I said. "Can you change dreams?"

Nav shook her head. "That's the thing. Staze is stasis." She made a self-conscious gesture at the messy room. "Nothing ever changes. I'm stuck, they're stuck." She raised an eyebrow at me. "You're stuck."

"What about your fish dream?" I said. "What's that stand for?"

"They're a sexual image." She grinned, but it vanished almost immediately.

"What's the matter?"

"They've all turned gray."

"What's turned gray?"

She pressed the heels of her hands against her eyes. "My beautiful fish."

I felt my heart lurch. "What? how?"

"I don't know *how*. They just turned gray. I check when they go under the bridge. The trees are still green and the water's still clear and all the stones on the bottom are the same as before, but now the fish are gray."

"Are they dying?" I whispered and she turned to look at me with an expression of dull fright.

She seemed to feel better that afternoon. We sat on her bed with a digital notepad. She keyed it to record and held it in front of me.

"Now," she said. "Tell me how to make Staze."

I hadn't expected her to be so blunt. It occurred to me that this was a secret she planned to sell to her friends on the storeship. Once I told her, she'd get rid of me. I was sure the storeship paid bounties for Mesh.

"I don't want to talk about that," I said.

She touched my thigh. "What do you want to talk about?"

My face got hot. I hadn't expected her to be so blunt about this, either.

She leaned closer, kissing my forehead and eyelids. Her lips were wet, but thin-feeling, like damp paper. They reminded me of the grubs' fragile skins and I pulled away.

"What's wrong?"

"Nothing," I said.

She studied me. "Sex for Staze. Wasn't that the deal?"

Blunt was the way to go, I decided. "I don't want to tell you how to make it."

"You mean you can't. I didn't think Annmarie'd give you all her secrets."

"She did," I said. "I know how."

She looked doubtful. "I get it. You can't make it without your Mesh."

Was that true? For an awful second, I thought she might

be right. But the fact was, Staze was a product of simple chemistry. It was only a question of proportion and heat. Anyone could do it.

"I don't need the Mesh." Saying that made me feel less crippled. I sat up straighter on the bed, wondering how Annmarie would have approached this situation. She was always a step ahead of the game at hand. Sex for Staze. Staze for sex. The equation suddenly struck me as hopelessly unequal. Annmarie would have demanded something far more substantial. I couldn't begin to think of what.

"You don't trust me," Nav said in a soft voice and she put her hot palm on my leg again.

It was the truth. I watched her caress my knee.

"Obviously you'll need Kevake," she said. "Anything else?"

I shrugged.

"You have to tell me that, at least," she said and moved closer. "What else?"

"A metric ton of sand."

"Sand?"

I nodded.

Her fingers moved up my leg. "What else?"

"What kind of drive do you have on your ship?"

"Standard fusion." Like it was a trick question. "Isn't that what you had on the Medusa?"

It was. "I'll need sand and Kevake," I said and took a breath. "And a kilo of argenta."

Her hand stopped moving. "Argenta? The gemstone from Eostre-Epona?"

I nodded.

"You know how hard it is to get that stuff? And how much it costs?"

"Yes."

She turned the notepad off and put it on the bed. I knew she would spy on me every time I produced a batch of Staze. I would end up with a magic show to rival Annmarie's and in the end, the chemical change might not be so impressive as my own transformation. Nav was right. I'd be a mirror image of Annmarie before I knew it.

Nav put both arms around me and maneuvered into my lap with perfunctory skill. Her mouth touched mine and this time I let her kiss me. A first installment. I tried not to think about what else she'd paid for like this. Her tongue slid inside my mouth. She tasted starchy, and deeper, I found a faint licorice sweetness.

She rolled me down on the rumpled covers, pushed a leg between my knees, opened my shirt and her own and moved so our breasts touched.

I gave up weighing the exchange.

She rubbed her teeth over my shoulder and I let her guide my hand under the silky waistband of her pants until my thumb blundered into her slickness. She pressed her face against the pillows, shuddering when I touched something she liked, moaning when she liked it more. I slid a finger inside her, and another. Her body quivered. Her tension, genuine or not, was making me sweat. I pushed deeper.

"Eve," she whispered, like she meant it.

Deeper.

"Eve."

Deeper still. And found something. Plastic-hard.

At first, I was surprised, but then I knew what it was. This was the same plastic smuggling tube she'd made me look for the first time. Another gift? I felt for the loop, found it, and gave it a tug, wondering what else she wanted to hang around my neck, but she jerked away.

"What the hell are you doing?"

"You've got one of those canister things in—in there."

Her eyes went flat with suspicion. Whatever romance had been in the room evaporated.

I waited while she felt inside herself. Her mouth went tight. She pulled the canister out, a sheath of cloudy plastic. She held it by the loop. At the opposite end, the lid hung open.

A scrap of something thin and grayish was caught on the inside. Like skin.

Papery. Fragile.

"Fuck," she said.

My palms began to sweat. "Can I see that?"

She pushed the canister at me. I picked at the grayish scrap, peeling it away from the lid until it lay on my forefinger, from tip to middle joint.

There had been a grub in the canister. Corey had forced it in and fastened the lid, but not very well, and it had gotten out. Sex education for aliens. There was only one place it could have gone.

'Harvest now thy fruitful womb.' The succubus, slathered with Red, singing and dancing in the virtual dark as I'd launched us away from Paradise. *'I know everything.'* In the pit of my stomach, I was starting to believe it.

"Do you know what that is?" said Naverdi, without any emotion at all.

"It's part of a grub."

"You mean the organism."

I nodded.

"You mean the goddamn alien organism you found on that goddamn planet."

I nodded.

"Corey," she whispered. "You son of a bitch." She lurched off the bed, hands over her belly. "Fuck!" she shouted and ran stumbling, half-naked, for the crew room.

I bolted after her and found her pawing through the desk. At first, I thought she was digging for more painkiller patches, but she pulled out the medical scanner instead, turned it on, and pointed it at herself.

She made a fist when I tried to come close enough to see. "Stay away from me! You *knew* what he was doing!"

"I didn't!"

"That's why they let you leave!" She was shouting now and her voice lanced off the close walls and ceiling. "Look what you did!" She hurled the scanner. I barely caught it and crouched against the wall, trying to interpret what was on the screen.

Blues and oranges, purples and yellows. The scanner showed everything about her in a confusing mosaic of color—adrenaline levels, heart rate, breathing, and the underlying scarlet of addiction. I found the wire tapestry of Jack where it wove through an artificial joint in her elbow, healed-over fractures in her ribs. I could see how it tapered to a junction in her spine . . .

And then I saw the grub.

Curled into her uterus, shining like a prize. Clusters of defending white cells had disintegrated into a brackish haze under the onslaught of the grub's missionary organelles. Grubbish filaments crept along Naverdi's fallopian tubes, as clear as the images in Mesh on Paradise. Portions of her gut were already infested. Her spleen and kidneys were stained at the edges. It had even tied itself to the inner embroidery of her Jack.

She would die in six hours, just like the yellow fungus.

But that was wrong.

I tried to keep my sweaty, sex-smelling hands from shaking while I calculated the hours since we'd left the planet. She'd been Stazed for twelve. We'd eaten. I'd slept. She'd dosed herself again. Which meant we were a day and a half—at least—from Paradise. Nav was more complicated than a scrap of yellow fungus or a couple of fish, but my *piscae* lasted only because Annmarie had taken them out of the grubby water. In the long run, it hadn't saved them.

"That *thing* has to come *out*," Nav shouted.

I wondered what she thought I could do, imagining all sorts of bloody solutions.

She heaved herself up from the desk. "You have to *kill* it!"

"How?" I whispered.

"Don't you *know*?" she shrieked. "Why don't you get in there with your Mesh and find *out*?"

The nanovirals made that impossible. She remembered and her mouth made a spasm of panic. She blundered past me, down the corridor to the bridge. I went into the hallway and stood there, afraid to follow. In a minute, I heard her shouting at a tinny voice on a speaker.

"Let me talk to the doctor, you Jackless bastard," she cried. "I know he's there! I don't give a damn about the patrols! I have to talk to the doctor!"

I couldn't hear what they said to her, but in twenty minutes the storeship was visible through the bridge windows. It was a blocky ship with storage units that looked like they'd accreted to the hull instead of being mechanically attached. Eight umbilical docking arms stuck out from the bottom and we rushed toward one of them.

Nav sat in the pilot's chair, biting her nails. I stood in the doorway, my pulse going fast enough to make me light-headed.

"Where are the patrols?" I asked.

"Why?" said Nav. "Afraid you might get caught?"

My heart made a painful slam. "Did you tell them I was here?"

She turned to glare at me. "You're an idiot," she snapped. "Why would I do that?"

Nothing had changed for her, I realized. Her panic had condensed into pragmatism. Getting rid of Corey's experiment was an inconvenient extra step between Nav and her greater plans. Not a nightmare, just a waste of time. For a moment, I could see the future the way she did: riches from Staze and the luxuries Annmarie had dismissed. The vision slid away, replaced by my own gut feeling.

One of the storeship's umbilicals began twisting toward us. There was an echoing *bang* as it clamped to the transport's outer lock.

Nav was already out of her seat. She shoved past me. "Come *on*!"

* * *

The doctor, or whatever he was, was a skinny young man with light skin. The short red-haired woman with him was the storeship's owner. I assumed this, as no one had made any introductions. The four of us stood in a small lobby that opened doorlessly into the cavernous storeship. Glass cases filled with frozen meat and metal shelves stacked with containers of preserved food stretched away in long aisles. I could smell fresh bread as well, which made me think of Annmarie.

The doctor stared at Naverdi's image on his medical scanner with obvious disbelief.

"Jeezus," he said.

"Hurry up," said the woman. "The ship's out in the goddamn open."

The doctor just stared at the readings.

Naverdi crossed her arms over her chest. "Just do whatever it takes to get it *out.*"

He nodded and then shook his head. "I'll do . . . I mean, I don't know."

Naverdi's voice rose and for the first time she sounded scared. "I have all the Staze you could possibly want!"

The doctor and the owner glanced at each other. The woman gave him a sharp nod. "You have fifteen minutes," she said. "Half an hour—max."

The doctor hustled Naverdi out of the lobby, into the store. Before they disappeared between the shelves, Nav pointed at me.

"Supplies!" she yelped and vanished.

The red-haired woman pushed her sleeves up to reveal a silver plug in her wrist. I put my hands in my pockets.

"How did that happen to her?" said the woman.

"I'm not sure," I said, wondering if I seemed innocent or guilty.

She studied me. "I haven't seen you before."

I shook my head. "No," I said. "I mean yes. That's right."

She eyed me with an expression meant for damned fools

and angled her thumb at a row of wheeled baskets by the entrance to the store. "Go ahead," she said to me.

"What?"

She made an exaggerated motion from the baskets to the shelves. "Supplies," she said. "Get whatever you need. But you'd better hurry. The patrols from Isla are all over the place. You wouldn't want to get caught."

"No. I wouldn't." I went over to the wheeled baskets and pulled one out. The woman smiled at me. I started pushing it down an aisle and glanced back. Of course she was gone.

I left the basket and bolted after her, down the narrow umbilical access to Naverdi's transport. She was robbing us. Or was she? Were three bags of Staze equal to a cart of groceries and a dubious medical procedure? How was I supposed to know what arrangements Nav had made with these people? And how was I supposed to know what Staze was worth to them, when Annmarie had always taught me that we could overthrow empires with a few kilos?

I swung around a corner and saw the red-haired woman at the end of the corridor, plugging her Jackwire into the airlock controls. She saw me. The door slid open. She stepped through and snapped the wire loose.

"Wait!" I shouted after her.

She didn't even pause. The lock slid shut behind her with a greasy hiss. I caught a glimpse of her red hair through the window as I pounded uselessly.

I stayed too long, banging on the door and yelling and imagining what Nav would say when she found out all her Staze was gone. The woman showed no sign of returning and finally I fled into the store again. Robbery could turn into an equal exchange if I could grab enough.

I snatched up the first plastic container into the first aisle of shelves—a light blue box with white stripes. The lettering on the box was in a garish pink and for a second, I thought that was why I couldn't read the words. But I couldn't read them. The alphabet was completely foreign to me. On the back of the box, I found a dull holo showing a picture of the contents. Gray slimy things. I screamed and threw the box on the floor. It looked just like one of the grubs from Paradise.

Now the whole storeship felt hugely threatening. I raced down the aisle, finding more labels I couldn't read. One had a picture of thick twisting green threads—maybe a vegetable. I grabbed a dozen of those. Another showed blue crustaceans with tiny orange tentacles. Four of those, hoping it was edible. I found metal boxes with holos of blue-nosed reptiles and cellophane bubbles filled with moldy yellow seeds. There were eyeless embryonic things floating in vinegar solutions and finally I found myself crouching in an intersection of aisleways, half-nauseous, a failure even at shopping.

It was time to find Nav and get *out*. What was that so-called doctor doing, and why was it taking so long? What if he killed her by accident? *Or*, Annmarie's voice added darkly in my imagination, *on purpose*.

I left the basket and hurried past packages of feathers and a stack of dried fish. I found sticks of incense as long as my arm and live rats in a terrarium with awful yellow goiters growing under their eyes. A homemade sign hung under the glass tank, showing a cartoon wolf in a fancy jacket, licking its chops. Finally I found a door.

I knocked, carefully at first, thinking there might be some delicate operation going on, but that seemed so unlikely, I began pounding as hard as I could. No answer. I yanked and the door flew open.

Inside, Naverdi lay stretched out on a table, visibly bloated, naked from the waist down, bloody between her legs. I covered my mouth, trying not to howl out in horror.

The doctor—or whatever he was—stood right beside her with his head thrown back, lips slightly parted, posed like an actor in the finale of a religious play. A double wire snaked out of his own wrist socket. One ran into Nav's Jack, the other led to his datascape. Harsh overhead lights glared on his face, showing tired folds of flesh and the motion of his eyeballs under thin grayish lids.

I stood in the doorway, knuckles in my mouth, abruptly understanding every single thing.

He was seeing into her, where the grub curled up all damp and nascent, knotting itself into her body. But he was also seeing *past* that. At some point in Jack, his perceptions would go beyond the ravenous infestation. He would see the succubus in all its predatory charm, and he would stand there gawking, answering questions until . . . until what?

It wouldn't take long for the succubus to figure out that Jack was just a simpler version of the Mesh. It knew all about filament connections—like wires in a wrist—and it would test this new pathway into a virtual world far wider than the surviving population of propagats. It would be *in* Jack.

It would be *everywhere*.

I yelled. I lunged and grabbed the doctor's Jackwire, yanking it out of his wrist and hers.

The datascape clattered onto the floor. The doctor staggered. His eyes flew open.

"Did you see it?" I was shrill, hysterical. "Did you *see?*"

He moved away from me, wiping his hands on his pants. "That thing in her womb is a parasite." He made a tenuous motion at her bloody thighs. "I tried to get a sample, but it's rooted into her."

"But didn't it talk to you?"

"Talk to me?" He shook his head but it was more like a shudder. "Get her to a hospital. In the meantime, give her Staze."

Like poison to the dying. "Staze!"

"Staze'll slow it down. Otherwise, she'll be dead in a week. Even with the Staze, she won't last more than ten or twelve days."

I squeezed past him to grab Naverdi's wrist. She had a pulse. She was breathing, but she wasn't conscious. The doctor pulled a dermal patch off her belly. Naverdi twitched and let out a groan.

There was a rush of footsteps between the aisles outside the small room and the red-haired woman ran in, eyes wide. She took the doctor by his sleeve and pulled him out the door and out of sight. Their quick patter of shoes was smothered by a heavier sound. I went to the doorway to see what was happening and saw the patrol soldiers swarming between aisles of groceries, red and blue uniforms and weapons, and the glint of chrome metal in the skin of their wrists.

EIGHT

Nav lay half-naked on the table with her eyes rolled up in her head while the soldiers told me we had no permit to be in the area and that our ship would be impounded in case we were spies. I shook Naverdi and she heaved herself up on her elbows to argue, but one of them pointed a weapon at her and told her to get dressed. He said there was a military transport waiting for us. It would take us to the nearest refugee camp. He said we'd be safe there, as if we'd been in danger.

When Nav could stay on her feet, they marched us into a transport packed with sullen, silent people. We stumbled down the narrow aisle, me wide-eyed and mute with terror, Naverdi with blood all over her clothes, and found two cold metal seats in the back. The transport pulled away and I watched the storeship through the window until it disappeared between stars. I never found out what happened to the doctor and the red-haired woman. I didn't see them again.

Later, when the transport was quiet and most of the other passengers seemed to be sleeping, Nav nudged me. She was visibly larger, an early 'pregnancy' which might pass at a casual glance, but her largeness was lopsided, as though the grub wasn't sure how to orient itself.

"We have to talk about this *organism.*" She kept her voice steady with an effort, so low that I could hardly hear her. "You said it could manifest in Mesh."

I checked to see if anyone nearby had heard the word 'Mesh.' The couple in the row ahead of us lolled against each other, a blanket tucked across their knees. They didn't turn to stare. No one leaped up to point me out. Everything was still.

I leaned closer to Nav's ear. She smelled of sweat and sterilizers from the storeship, and underneath, of blood. "It wasn't just one organism," I whispered. "Well—it *was* just one, but it looked like thousands."

"You're not making sense," she said tightly. "How did it look, physically, when you landed?"

"Worms," I said. "Corey called them grubs. They were all over the place. They had a symbiotic relationship with a kind of moss. They fed off each other."

"And these grub things had the presence in Mesh?"

I nodded.

"How?"

"They—it—can assimilate foreign organisms," I said. "Propagats have an organic component and the grubs absorbed them, too. It might have had a kind of consciousness already, but when it tapped into the propagats, it became much more aware."

"And it had access to whatever information the old propagats could convey?"

"Right."

"But they didn't tell it about reproducing?"

"It didn't understand reproduction," I said. "It's probably immortal. It doesn't have to know how."

"What's it doing now?"

I thought she meant for me to drop into Mesh and find out. I could, I realized. Away from the nanovirals on her shuttle, I had access to the same waning population of ThreeSys 'gats as I'd had on the Medusa.

She saw what I was thinking. "That's not what I mean," she whispered. "I mean, do you *know* what it's doing?"

"It's analyzing your body's defenses," I said.

"Analyzing?" She held her hands taut, fingers spread, encompassing her belly. I was sure she was in pain. "It's *eating* me."

The last thing I wanted to say was yes, but I didn't want to lie. "The virtual part of it wants to learn how to reproduce," I said. "It won't . . . eat you until it figures out how that works."

She shivered. "How long?"

"Corey gave it a piece of fungus and that was gone in six hours."

She took a couple of short breaths like she was going to start crying.

"But you're way beyond that," I said quickly. *"Days* beyond that. And the doctor on the storeship said Staze'd slow it down."

"Staze?" she echoed.

"It's as addicted as you are."

She tried to make sense of that. "Because it's in my body? It sucked in a dose of Staze along with everything else?"

"Not just that," I said. "Before I left, Corey spilled a bag of Staze on Paradise. It went into the pools, all over the grubs and the moss."

She blinked, not comprehending.

"Every grub on the planet and every piece of moss was connected through the aquifer, and on a virtual level, like propagats. You could see that in Mesh. Corey spilled Red into one pond and it affected the entire planet." I made a hesitant gesture at her swollen abdomen. "That one, too."

"I can slow it down with Staze?" she whispered. "Did you bring any?"

I shook my head and watched her eyes travel over the rest

of the passengers, as though she could find kindred spirits just by looking.

I wanted to tell her—and at the same time I was too scared to bring it up—how the succubus might be wandering through the networks in Jack, using the storeship doctor as a vector, spreading like a contagious disease. On the other hand, the doctor'd acted like I was out of my mind when I started screaming about 'seeing it.' Maybe I was wrong. I rubbed my eyes and tried to think. Had Nav been Jacked in between Paradise and the storeship?

Of course she had.

She'd unplugged herself when I'd switched her monitors on the bridge, days ago.

The succubus had already released itself from Naverdi's physical limits. If it could contaminate the Medusa's onboard 'gats before the ship even touched down on Paradise, the Jacked networks were certainly infested by now.

"Eve?"

She'd been saying something. "What?"

"What did it look like in Mesh?"

You, I thought. "It looked a little like me," I lied. "I guess because it saw me first."

"Like parental imprinting." Nav showed her teeth in an unhappy grin. "What'd Annmarie say when she found out it looked like you?"

"She never saw it. Corey told it to stay away from her."

"Why?"

In my heart, I knew exactly why, and from a great distance, Corey's reasons made surprising sense. Annmarie would have found a way to torment the succubus, niggling away at its pitiful self-importance until the creature buckled under the force of her will. "She would have figured out how to control it," I said. "She would've found a way to make it depend on her."

"It's an alien," said Nav. "Why would it need her for anything?"

"It wanted to learn," I said. "She would've made it think she knew things no one else could teach it."

Nav rubbed her knees. "Did it have . . . I don't know . . . a presence? Could you feel it before you saw it?"

I touched the ham of my thumb. "I felt it all right. It bit me right here."

She frowned at my unmarked skin. "It attacked your avatar?"

I nodded. "It sampled the Mesh's defenses through me. It corrupted every system on the ship, including data partitions. By the time we got to the planet, we could walk through each other's environments."

"You could go into Annmarie's world and she could go into yours?"

I nodded. "And Corey's."

"And the manifestation was there, too?"

"Not at first. I could feel it, though."

"Like eyes in the sky?"

"What?" I said.

She ran her nails along the arm of the chair. "That's what's happening in my Staze place."

I smiled stupidly. "That can't be." I said. "Not in Staze. Just because the fish've changed color . . ."

"It isn't just the fish," she said. "Something's watching me. But I can't look up to see what it is. I can't move."

I felt the smile freeze on my face. "You're imagining things."

She let her hands drop over her belly and closed her eyes. "No," she said, and she sounded exhausted. "I'm not."

I woke up from a silent nightmare, sweating in the packed transport. I hadn't meant to fall asleep. The dank air, humid with body warmth, was still cold enough to make me stiff. I straightened up and swallowed against the change in cabin pressure. Outside, the blackness wasn't quite so black, and a soft crescent of atmosphere was just visible in the corner of the window. Around us, people spoke in low, nervous voices.

Nav was awake, staring at the next row of seats. Her eyes were bloodshot and I could see where she'd wiped the tears off her cheeks.

"Are you okay?" I said.

She shrugged.

"How long was I asleep?"

"Five or six hours."

I tried to estimate when she'd need her next dose and came up with another five or six hours. "Where do you think we are?"

"I don't know."

"How're you feeling?"

She leaned back in the seat. "I could puke up everything I've ever eaten."

I looked out the window again. By my feeble Meshless reckoning, we were three or four days from Paradise. I tried to make a map in my mind of where that would put us, but had no clear idea. The need to *know* washed over me and it was an effort to keep myself from testing whatever shreds of the Mesh might still be here.

The woman in the next row made a vague gesture out the window. "Bet they let us off down there," she said to the man who was with her.

"Bet they don't." He opened one of their suitcases and took out a bag of dried fruit. He stuck a wrinkled brownish piece into his mouth and jerked his thumb over his shoulder, pointing at us. "There's more coming. They'll let us out when they're damn good and ready."

Nav crossed her legs, uncrossed them, and kicked the man's seat as she shifted. The woman turned to us, chewing broadly. "You girls got any Red?"

Nav shook her head. All her desperation showed in the motion.

"We do," said the woman.

"Good for you," said Nav.

"We'll take money for it or trade," she said. "Doesn't matter which."

Nav stared past me, out the window.

"We don't have anything," I said. "Leave her alone."

"Everybody's got something." The woman chewed, studying me with sharp green eyes. "First time in the camps?"

I nodded.

"We've been to seven so far," she told me.

"Six," said the man beside her.

"Seven," she said to him. "You don't remember anything. First they evacuated us from the camp at Triez and put us on a transport to YonSou. I told you we should have left Triez two weeks earlier, because everyone knew the RMC was going to make a surprise attack on Moisa. Then the Moisans retaliated, but *we* were on the damn transport, and instead of YonSou we had to—"

"Shut up," he said.

She ignored him and turned to me. "We've been on this transport for two weeks. *We* should get housing priority at the next camp, because *we're* chronically displaced, but it never works that way." She shoved her Jackless wrist at me. "This is all they care about."

I nodded, afraid to say anything.

"It's always been that way," said the woman. "We killed off the Meshed because we thought things'd change. But they didn't. And unless someone stands up and *says* something, it'll always be that way." She got to her feet, ready to shout her politics across the crowded cabin, but her companion yanked her down into her seat.

"Shut *up,*" he said.

"I *won't* shut up!" she shouted at him. "I told you we should have left Triez. I *told* you!"

"Fuck!" he shouted back. "They wouldn't just let us *leave.*"

"*'Fuck!'*" she repeated, mocking him. "We *could* have run away."

He made a disgusted noise. They didn't say a word after that, just ate until the fruit was gone. Nav and I watched all of this, staring probably, but they didn't seem to care.

Outside, the crescent of atmosphere widened as the ship arced downward. White clouds rushed past the windows and below, I could see a river outlined in chalky shades. The floor shuddered and the pitch of the engines deepened. I hung onto the arms of the chair as the transport vibrated. Far away, the river widened to a sandy delta. A beach stretched into the distance. Buildings loomed dully in the haze. I saw an island, a boat. The transport seemed to pick up speed closer to the ground and the landscape rushed by, too fast to see.

Lights came on, throwing every exhausted face into jagged relief. The ship lurched, groaned, and slowed so abruptly that we had to grab the seatbacks in front of us to keep from being thrown into the next row. The couple ahead of us snatched up their luggage as the ship quivered and was still.

I peered out the window. Gray fog hid everything. All I could think of was the last place I'd landed.

"Here is the new world," I whispered to myself, because there was no one else to Say It, but Naverdi elbowed me in the ribs.

"There's going to be some kind of intake screening," she said and lowered her voice. "Don't tell them anything. We'll say we're sisters."

"Sisters?" I echoed. "What's your last name?"

She gave me a bleary, tired look as if I should have known. "It's Kadesha."

"What else are they going to ask?"

"Who your parents were. Where you were born. I've done this before. Just listen to what I say. And remember—" She touched my Jackless wrist.

The rest of the passengers jammed themselves noisily into the narrow spaces between the rows of seats. The couple in

front of us had already shoved their way into the aisle and
vanished in the crush. Babies squalled like they were being
tortured. Two teenage girls shoved into the open space at the
end of our row. One saw Nav's protruding belly and the nausea
in her face and moved to make room for us.

I helped Nav to her feet. She felt overbalanced and unsteady
and her palms were slick with sweat. She leaned against me as
we shuffled to the end of our seat row, concentrating on her
breathing, trying not to throw up.

"Why's everyone rushing?" I said to the girls. "For housing priority?"

"You have to get out quick as you can," said the taller of
the two, tow-headed and light-skinned. "Quick! If there isn't
room here, they'll send you on to the next camp."

"Where's that?" I said.

"Azier!" said other girl, and heads turned, nodding grimly.

"Azier?" I repeated.

Pressure seals hissed open somewhere toward the front of
the compartment and a hint of cooler air drifted in. The two
girls got a good grip on their luggage and the tall one lunged
over the backs of the seats in the next three rows. Her partner
gathered herself to follow.

"Azier is Olda's moon," she said to me. "It's hot as hell
and you have to buy oxygen from a syndicate. And you'll spend
months getting there." She leaped after her friend and disappeared in the boil of elbows, knees, and backpacks.

The rest of us shambled forward, one incremental step at
a time.

"Isn't this the camp with the swimming pool?" said someone not far ahead of me.

"You'll be washing in it," said someone else.

"Drinking out of it," said another voice.

"Pissing in it," said a fourth.

Armed guards in red berets herded us off the transport and
down a pink gravel service road. The road followed a high

meandering wall, covered with crumbling pink stucco. To the left, gray waves beat on a deserted strip of beach, and the cold sea wind smelled of rotting fish.

We passed a sign:

CAMP 3690

REFUGE FOR THE DISPLACED

Briny mist clung to my hair and seeped into my clothes. Nav and I were last in line and we followed the rest of the transport passengers as they straggled around a curve in the wall and out of sight. The line moved along, steady for a while and then stopped.

In the distance, the transport's antigravs whined and its bulky shape rose into the low-hanging fog, vanishing into dense haze. Half a dozen guards in riot gear marched up behind us in a tight little phalanx. They came to a halt, bristling with weapons, but they didn't even look at us, just stood there like statues.

I glanced around, but no one else seemed to care about the sudden appearance of heavily armed men. The people in front of us were eating greasy meat out of plastic bags. Others had stretched out on the ground to sleep.

"Do you think we're going to get shot?" I whispered to Nav.

"You don't get shot unless you try to leave." She sank down on the gravel. "Guess we're off the hook for Olda's damn moon."

I huddled next to her, awkward and close. The top of the wall was too high to climb, but still low enough for us to get a glimpse of the buildings inside. Old brick with red-tiled roofs. Ornate lintels over broken windows. I could see the edge of a balcony draped with laundry, and downspouts with animal faces peering out from under rain gutters. Dirty tattered streamers flew from a weathervane shaped like an outrageous bird. What

I could see of the place seemed weirdly festive and uncomfortably familiar.

I thought there should have been ancient elms and maples. Instead, I smelled wood smoke. There should have been a froth of roses in tended beds along the base of these walls. Instead, there were weeds and windblown garbage. I watched the sea and thought about how the sound of water had hushed my childhood nightmares.

It was a long time before I could admit to myself that I knew exactly where we were.

This planet was Mara-Isla.

And this place was the Sanctuary.

When evening fell, the guards herded us forward until we joined the rest of the transport refugees in a boxy courtyard. The courtyard was open to the sea and walled on three sides, with a gate in the center wall. Hot floodlights shone down from the ramparts and the warmth would have been a relief, but Nav held me back, and the two of us sat in the sandy gravel, as close to the seaward side as the guards would allow. The more-or-less orderly line along the road disintegrated into a nervous jostle of people with luggage, babies, even birdcages.

Evening settled into night. More lights came on and more guards appeared. The gate stayed shut, and despite what the angry woman on the transport said, no one—Jacked or not— seemed to have priority for anything. It was just as well, I thought. Someone would start asking personal questions the minute there was something to distribute, and I knew nothing about being Naverdi's sister. Even the name sounded wrong. Eve Kadesha. Raised by cousins in a refugee camp. I tried to remember which world she'd grown up on and realized how scared I was when I simply couldn't remember.

I held Nav's clammy hand in mine, our backs against the crumble of stucco. Down by the gate, hundreds of refugees surged like waves on a dark beach, desperate for food, I thought, or water. Or Staze.

"How many of them are addicts?" I said.

Nav shifted and groaned. "All of them are addicts, Eve. They're waiting for manna to fall from the goddamn sky." She let her breath out through her teeth. "You have to find me some."

I squeezed her cold fingers uselessly. In front of the gates, the mob was growing, louder and more frenzied, which said to me there was no Staze anywhere.

"*Find* some," said Nav and she pushed me away.

I got up and started for the thick heat of the lights, stopped, and turned to make sure I knew where she was.

Even at this short distance, the sight of her shocked me. Thin, sick-looking, sunken into herself except for her belly, which swelled up from her body like a tumor. I barely recognized her. Annmarie's words whispered in my mind, so clearly, she might have been standing right beside me.

You can do a lot better than that one.

I turned away and headed into the crowd. A gang of dirty-faced children eyed me as I shoved past. Farther ahead, two lanky women shared a box of dry pasta, nervously chewing the stiff ends of noodles. I passed a man with four perfectly matched white dogs on chain leashes. The dogs were terrified and cowered between his legs while he stood over them, explaining in great detail the reasons for their deportation. I made my way between piles of luggage and clumps of people too sick, or tired, or too long overdue for a dab under their tongues to join the agitated masses.

An extremely pale woman with short brown hair caught my eye and waved me over. She seemed to be watching a group of small children, and maybe she was selling Staze—not that I had anything to pay her with—or maybe, I thought uneasily, she was one of Annmarie's customers and had recognized me.

I picked my way toward her, nervous and feeling utterly exposed, but she gave me a friendly enough smile.

"Didn't I see you on the transport?" she said. "You and your friend were the last ones onboard."

I nodded. I found myself searching her wrists for a plug, or no plug, but her long sleeves were pulled down and I couldn't tell. I put my hands in my pockets, self-conscious, expecting her to examine me. Instead, she scooped up a little girl barely old enough to walk, swung the child onto her hip, and kissed her. The child had amber skin and a mop of black hair. I didn't think she was a blood relation, but she put her arms around the woman's neck and hid her face there, like this was her mother.

"I know your friend," the woman said. "I believe she's in the *supply* business."

Everyone here wanted the same thing. She had no idea who or what I was. I shrugged, but I felt hugely relieved. "She doesn't have any supplies."

The woman arched an eyebrow. "Better for both of you. This place has its own monopoly on *supplies* and they'll rob you if they think you're holding."

She seemed patently unafraid of the multitude, the guns, the lack of Red. I made a vague motion at the guards. "You mean they'll take everybody's 'supplies' and then make them pay for more?"

She laughed. "You don't need money. They'll start handing the stuff out when everyone's hurting enough. 'Confiscate and make them wait.' That's what they do in these places."

"The Staze is *free?*"

"Nothing's free." She hugged the little girl closer. "You have to listen to the damn speeches before they'll give you a single grain."

"Speeches?"

She nodded. "Some camps, they just want to go on and on about God—they pretend it's a moral payoff—we listen to the same old lecture about evil, slothful Red. Then they toss it out like holy water so we won't tear the walls down." She nodded at the pack of soldiers on the ramparts above the Sanctuary gates. "This one, though . . . she calls herself Queen Red, and she's got *philosophies.*"

"What kind of philosophies?"

"The end of violence. Paradise and evolution."

I gave her an amazed look. "What does she say about Paradise?"

She laughed again. "I don't pay attention. I just wait for it to be over."

Which was disappointing, but only a little. "So . . . Queen Red makes a speech, they give out Staze, and then they let us in?"

"That's right."

"Do you know if they have a doctor?"

She nodded. "They have everything. There's even a pool."

It was a relief to find someone who seemed to know what to expect. "How many times have you been here?"

She cocked her head, counting to herself. "I couldn't tell you. They keep moving us." She smiled. "You can stay with us if you'd like. Bring your friend over."

"Thanks," I said. "I will."

I headed for the seaward opening of the courtyard, feeling better, or at least better informed. I passed a flock of elderly women building a small fire. Nearby, two men played a game with pieces of gravel arranged between stick marks in the sand. I trudged along, thinking things might be looking up. I could pass for Jackless. In fact, it didn't even seem to be an issue. Getting into the Sanctuary didn't sound hard. I could find a doctor while Nav was Stazed, and a real doctor might have a real solution.

"Anything yawanna know!" Just ahead, a tall woman with wild yellow hair shouted into the crowd, interrupting my optimistic thoughts. There was a man with her and she held his arm straight up, like a fighter at the end of a match. He was unresisting, limp, and a chrome plug gleamed in his wrist. I tried to push past, but I was moving against the tide.

The blonde woman waved a Jackwire. "Anything yawanna know, anything, ask here! Ask here! Anything at all yawanna know."

People pressed around me, behind me, and in a minute I found myself practically at the man's shoulder in a ragged, gawking circle of refugees. He stood impassively, blue eyes focused into some long distance well beyond the Sanctuary walls. He was thin, with a roughed-over sort of physical elegance, hazy in the eyeballs, and I thought he might be blind. His skin seemed waxy, bloodless, like a corpse, I would have said, except I could see him breathing.

The blonde woman slid one end of her Jackwire into the man's wrist socket. "Well?" she said. "Any questions?"

Silence. Then someone spoke up.

"How do we know he's real?"

The woman made her mouth into a wide smile and pulled her jacket open. A dozen stamped silver medals hung from a single chain around her neck.

A dozen Annunciates.

Trophies.

I stared at the medals and I stared at the man standing in front of me.

"He's Meshed, all right," said the woman. "Plugged into the secrets of the universe, you bet." She gave him a big open-handed clap on the back. "Most of the Meshed may be gone, but their propagats are still here. We can't use them, but this guy can." She tapped her own wrist socket and grinned. "Think of him as the ultimate upgrade."

"Is he Stazed?" asked someone else.

The woman shook her head. "Waste of time and money." She pushed his thinning hair away to reveal the scars on his temples.

My knees felt weak enough to drop out from under me. I made myself not move, afraid to look for a route of escape. My own medal felt like it might burn its way through my shirt. I put my hand over it to make sure it was hidden and felt my heart pounding.

"How much you charge for answers?" asked someone else.

"Special situation," she said. "This time the first one's free."

An elderly frail-looking man pushed forward. "I'm trying to find my son," he said. "We were separated during the evacuation at YonSou. I thought they kept him at the camp there, but when I asked, they told me he was gone." He voice trembled and he held out his wrists, tight with sinew and Jackless. "I don't know where he is."

The woman smiled. "Give me your son's ID number."

He recited a long string of numbers and letters, inflected with dashes and parentheses. His tone was even, overly careful, and he wound his hands together as he spoke.

When he was done, the woman gave a brisk nod and closed the Jacked-Mesh man's eyes with her fingers. She pulled a datascape out of her pocket, plugged herself into one end, and connected the Jacked-Mesh man to the other, the same way the storeship doctor had plugged into Nav.

She shut her eyes and her mouth tightened in concentration. I could only imagine what kind of software she'd invented to make this connection work—if it did work. I watched the indifferent Jacked-Mesh man; waxy, stolid, nothing but a receiver, and wondered if there were enough 'gats left in the Sanctuary to lead me and Nav to a safer place.

The woman snapped her eyes open and pointed at the elderly questioner. "Your son is alive and well," she announced. "He's been transferred to Azier."

Scattered cheers behind me, but the old man's face fell. "He's on Olda's moon? But how can he survive there? He doesn't have the money for oxygen."

The woman made a soothing gesture. "Open an account on Azier and you can transfer funds for him."

"Funds?" said the old man. "I don't have *funds*. Look where I am! I'll be begging for Staze in an hour."

"It doesn't have to be your money." The woman patted the Jacked-Mesh man's arm. "Just like the old days. He can steal from anywhere."

The old man hesitated. "But what do *you* charge for that?"

She told him, and the rest of the crowd muttered at the amount. The old man turned and shuffled away without a backward glance. For the price, he probably could have bribed the Sanctuary guards, escaped, and bought a ticket to Azier himself.

The woman smiled, broad and false. "Next? Whaddaya wanna know?"

Around me, people pushed closer or backed off, discouraged or intrigued, or simply disbelieving. I crept past the Jacked-Mesh man, head down. I was afraid to touch him, afraid he would sense me in some remaining capacity, open his eyes, and cry out in recognition.

"What'd you find?" said Nav.

I'd been gone for less than an hour and I wasn't prepared for how much sicker and hollowed-out she was. "Nothing," I said.

"Nothing?"

"I found a woman who says she's a customer of yours. She invited us to stay with them."

She squinted into the floodlit dark. "Stay where? In their cozy little bungalow?"

"You shouldn't be sitting out here all by yourself."

She angled her head toward the line of guards in riot gear, between us and the rush of surf. "I'm not alone."

"You know what I mean."

Nav snorted. "She probably wants to go through my pockets."

I didn't say anything.

Behind us, the sound of waves on sand faded under a tone more intent and rhythmic, deep enough to feel in the roots of my teeth, echoing between the courtyard walls.

Nav pushed herself up, listening.

A signal, I thought. Finally the speeches would start, the Staze would appear and life could move on.

Nav scrambled to her feet with sudden, surprising energy
and pointed to the far corner of the courtyard, just to the left
of the Sanctuary gates. "It's coming from over there." She
steadied herself, swollen to a pear-shape around her middle.
"Let's go!"

"What is it?"

"It's the Staze-Fakers."

"The what?"

"I told you about them. They're religious nuts. They have
this ritual—they pretend to make Staze, but they have to hand
out some of the real stuff, or they'd get lynched." She leaned
on me, pulled on me. "If anyone's got Red, they do."

Over by the far wall, a hundred nervous, hungering addicts
watched three men in loose red pants dance to the booming
drumbeat, their faces set in a weirdly rigid ecstasy. Nav and I
shuffled forward between elbows and luggage and sweaty, unwashed bodies until we were close enough to see where the
drumming was coming from.

In front of the dancers, an old man with an iron-gray beard
to the middle of his chest drummed on a long black packing
case. The sound billowed upward, reverberating off the corner
walls. He pounded out a final-sounding roll and the dancers
came to a standstill. A few people applauded. The old man got
to his feet.

Nav leaned close to my ear. "Guess what that old Faker's
got in the case."

I couldn't even imagine. "What?"

"An industrial-grade hot unit. He's going to boil Kevake in
a pot, throw in some sand, pray over it, and call it a miracle."

"They have Kevake?"

"They have Staze," she said, like she could declare this and
it would be true. She cupped her hands around her mouth and
shouted through the cold, dense air. "Get on with it!"

The old Faker closed his eyes and began to sway. *"What is
the color of the dream we have?"*

"Red," echoed the people behind me.

The dancers began a soft, solemn clapping, marking the rhythm of his words.

"The dream in Red is the dream of peace."

"Dream of peace," his audience echoed.

"Red will make us all as one . . ."

"All as one . . ."

"Red is eternal life," intoned the man.

"Red is the end of death," replied the addicts.

I glanced around uneasily. These were Annmarie's words. Of the three standard harangues for addicts and potential addicts, this was the one she'd composed in the least amount of time. There had to be a holy mantra, she'd decided, for those who aspired to be disciples of the drug. I remembered her pacing up and down the Medusa's main corridor when I was fifteen or so, tapping out the rhythm of the words on the walls while I made suggestions.

The old Faker dabbed at his forehead and bent to open the packing case. Inside, sure enough, a large silver bowl sat on a hot unit, rippling with heat. The cloying stink of Kevake drifted with the salt breeze.

Beside me, an elderly woman watched at the steaming contraption as though she had seen this miracle performed before and could hold off her need until the act was over. Two emaciated teenage boys stood close together, eyes wide as saucers, one sucking his own fingers for stray grains of Red. I took Nav's arm, nervous. Even if the real thing was hidden somewhere in the trunk, there probably wasn't enough Red for everyone, and I could almost taste the impending riot.

"Let's get out of here," I said in her ear.

She leaned heavily on me. "Wait."

The old man reached into the case and moved the steaming silver bowl to a smooth place in the gravelly sand. He squatted beside it and pushed up his sleeves to the elbows, revealing Jackless wrists. *"My dream in Red is the dream of water,"* he chanted. *"I stand alone on the bridge and watch the fish and their glitter of scales."*

A few people nodded, sharing his vision, I thought, but beside me, Nav didn't budge. She might not even have been listening, focused on the appearance of Staze, not the trappings of ritual, or prophecy, or whatever this would turn out to be.

The old Faker scooped up a few fistfuls of sand and sprinkled them into the steaming Kevake. *"Behold the sanguine mix; the tears of virgins, blood of infants, the promise of water in a great desert. To this is added the very grist of man, dirt, sand, gravel and stones . . ."* His voice trailed off. He brushed his hands on his knees and ran one finger all the way around the edge of the steaming silver bowl, as if trying to remember what to say next.

"You want the miracle of Red," said the old Faker, "the way we all want it, the way we always will, as long as we live. Nothing changes for us. Not the need, not the vision. The illusions are always the same. Except now."

The dancers cast sideways glances at each other. Apparently this wasn't part of the script.

Beside me, Nav took a sharp breath. Pain. Impatience. Revelation. I couldn't tell.

"I have something more important to show you than a miracle." He scooped up more sand, mixing it into the Kevake, shoveling the red muck until it was as stiff as dough. He wadded the mud into a fat reddish egg shape, pressing and squeezing with awkward fingers and stood up, unsteady, holding the muddy form against his chest. "Something's changed in my Staze place," he blurted.

Around me, there was utter silence. I couldn't tell if it was belief or doubt, or stunned disappointment that Staze was no longer on the agenda.

"I'm not alone on my bridge anymore," he said. "There's another reflection in the water next to mine. It's a girl. She sings to me. It's the old Song. You know it. *'Raise up thine Unknown Child for all and shout . . .'"*

"Hail," cried someone in the crowd, spontaneous, like a reflex.

The old Faker held out his damp sculpture. It was a human shape, roughly formed with arms and legs splayed. With unmistakably trembling hands, he reached into a pocket and pulled out a tiny gleaming stone. Floodlights high on the walls touched it and it flashed, a profound and sanguine red as he pressed it into the mannikin's soft belly. "The Unknown Child," he said, as if he could hardly believe the words coming out of his mouth. "She told me that these are the last days of unhappiness and death." He held the muddy figurine up like an offering. "Here is the new world."

There was a silence. A long silence.

"I saw her, too," whispered someone, out of sight to my left.

"So did I," said someone else. "I thought I was dreaming."

Nav's grip on my arm went painfully tight. "Get me out of here." Her voice rose. "Get me out, get me *out*!"

The conversation, the whispered testimonials, stopped. People turned to stare.

The old Faker pushed toward us and opened his mouth to say something, but he never got the chance. From up on the walls, sirens started a low warble, wailing into the salty night. There was shouting, the heavy tramp of feet, and the crowd of rapt addicts split as soldiers and guards in red berets swarmed out of the Sanctuary gates.

I grabbed Naverdi as they cleared a path for themselves, knocking old people and screaming children out of the way. They pounded toward us, faces masked in shadow from the harsh overhead lights. I dragged Nav to the nearest part of the wall, shoving her down on the coarse gravel as people stampeded past us. I had a clear view as two of the soldiers kicked the old Faker's packing case to bits, glass and electronic shrapnel from the hot unit flying everywhere. Two more grabbed the old man and dragged him away, pounding him over the head with short clubs until they disappeared through the gates.

The dancers in the loose red pants were gone, scattered or captured.

I crouched over Nav, as close to the wall as I could get, deafened by the sirens and screaming. A long way off, guards dragged away the couple who'd tried to sell us Staze on the transport. The man was bleeding and unconscious. The woman was sobbing, her wrists in shackles.

Nav struggled out from under me, her hair puffed out in wild, chaotic twists, eyes wide, her face the color of ash.

"We can't stay here!" I shouted, but she pointed to the top of the wall, just over the gates.

From the Sanctuary ramparts, a heavyset woman in a gold-flecked scarlet uniform stood in the focus of a single spotlight. Below, the guards and soldiers began herding addicts toward that part of the wall, but most were already running that way. Women with children on their hips, old men with canes, people dropping luggage, all shoving through clumps of slower folk.

"Come on," said Nav. She heaved herself to her feet, grabbed me for support, and we lurched together across the courtyard to the edge of the accumulating mob.

The woman in the glittering jacket raised her arms for attention. The guard beside her hefted a big cardboard box onto the edge of the wall, reached into it, and held out his hand so everyone below could see what was inside.

They looked like tiny golden beads. At first, I wasn't sure what they were supposed to be. Then I realized they were gelatin capsules. At the base of the wall, people stirred and moaned. And then I understood this was a dosing method for Staze. One capsule, one addict. Any minute now, they would start tossing the stuff out by the fistful.

The woman in the red and gold uniform leaned over the ramparts, surveying the addicts as though she was judging livestock.

"I am Queen Red," she intoned, and the courtyard echoed with her voice. "I have what you need."

The entire crowd shoved forward. Naverdi wrenched herself

out of my arms, awkward and swollen, and bolted into the press. I lost her in the forest of outstretched arms and up-turned faces.

Queen Red pointed down at the addicts. "It's time you people started thinking about the consequences of your actions. Before I give you what you want, I demand that you *think*."

A man in front of me groaned.

"Now," said Queen Red. "We all know that Staze is sup-posed to be the end of violence. But the fact is—and I have come to this conclusion through a great deal of objective re-search—the nature of man *is* violent." She eyed the hungering addicts, put her arms behind her back, and paced a few steps. "In order to achieve real peace, we must remove something essential from ourselves. We must *compromise* our own nature."

Silence from the addicts.

She put her fists against the ramparts and nodded at the cardboard box. "You agree?"

"Yes, damn it," muttered someone beside me.

Queen Red straightened. "Staze is the end of conflict. Staze is Stasis. Staze is Paradise; endless days in a beautiful place. It sounds *good*, but this quest for perfect, peaceful, endless beauty has hamstrung our evolution from the beginning. What do we accomplish if we achieve the end of violence?" She smacked her palm on stone and the clap reverberated around the court-yard. "Nothing!"

Beside her, the guard with the cardboard box nodded with obvious awe. Below, hopeful faces shone in the floodlights.

Queen Red scrutinized them, flushed and judgmental, not happy with the response. "How many of you are addicts of drugs not yet synthesized?" she demanded. A few hands went up—appeasement, or weird honesty. "You're borrowed meat," she snapped. "You're rented flesh. You belong to the drug and nothing else. We, as a species, will never improve with people like you holding back the rest of us who are ready to fight our way forward at any cost. *I* aspire to *hellish* things. I *implement* the Algebra of Need on a daily basis, solving for unknown variables with an ocean of Red. But for *you,* the Algebra of Need is simply an analogous equation. For you, *Staze* equals *Staze* equals *Staze.*" She drew herself up. "*You* and your self-contained eco-system of Red hold back people like *me.* Your religions and sequels. Your metabolisms and beliefs—I spit on it all."

And she did, with precise drama.

Maybe I was the only one paying attention. I knew exactly what she could see from up there. I'd seen it myself every time Annmarie and I had wrapped ourselves up in red and black, dispensing Staze to the masses, making whatever promises they wanted to hear—peace, revenge, and justice—the things we wanted so badly for ourselves.

For the first time, I wondered if all of Annmarie's plots and plans and machinations to save the surviving Meshed hadn't made things worse for everyone. Staze was for the masses and would keep them sedate, but this Queen Red didn't fall into the category of *masses,* and neither did Annmarie.

Those not addicted would be the most focused, the most willing to fight at all costs for anything. Red. Not the end of violence, but a finessing of it. A sharper edge to the sword. A further defining of the lines between thinkers and doers. Fighters and addicts. Haves and have-nots.

I stared up at Queen Red, invisible to her in this sea of needful flesh, and wondered if I could make myself swallow one of those capsules.

Behind me, one person began to clap, hesitant, as though they weren't sure the speech was over. Someone else joined in and the rest of the crowd began to applaud. There were whistles and shouts and Queen Red smiled, arms wide, scanning her captive audience to make sure everyone had joined in. I beat my hands together, half-deafened by the noise, which was anything but congratulatory.

Queen Red made a magnanimous motion at the guards, and they raised the cardboard box off the ramparts. The shouts turned to cries of relief. Queen Red reached into the box, pulled out a handful of capsules, and threw them at us.

Hands shot up. A man in front of me leaped as high as he could, missed, and came down hard, his elbow in my chest. I staggered backward, stepping on other people's feet. Another handful rained down closer, and another, scattering in my hair, over my shoulders.

Hungry eyes turned toward me. I tried to shove myself out of the way and squirmed around to see an emaciated woman scrabbling for the capsules caught in the folds of my shirt. Sharp nails dug against my scalp and I heard myself scream. Someone kicked my knees out from under me and I fell between bare feet and sandals, bruised knees and torn pants. A far-off yell as more Staze pelted down. The mob jolted away, leaving me gasping, blood in my mouth, cuts on my face.

I sat up, looking for Naverdi, and couldn't find her. A lanky young woman dropped bonelessy into the dust between floodlights and milling addicts as the Staze took effect. An old man slumped next to a woman with a baby, already stretched out on the ground. Two boys leaned together, still and quiet in contrast to the distant shouts and surges as Staze showered down from above. I sat in the gravel, catching my breath, cataloging my hurts until there were more people lying down than standing. When I finally got up, I felt something small and soft roll under my palm. A Staze capsule. The gelatin surface was ingrained with dirty sand. I wiped it off as well as I could and stood.

The guards at the far end of the courtyard were gone. The only other person standing was the Jacked-Mesh man. I limped between Stazed sleepers, looking for Nav. When I found her, she was crying.

"I couldn't get one," she wept.

I held out the dirty capsule.

She stopped crying. She touched my cut lip, but it was only a distracted motion. She put the Staze in her mouth and closed her eyes. Her body sagged. Her knees splayed open, exposing her swollen abdomen. If I watched, I was certain I would be able to see the slow motion of the grub, growing.

I crouched in front of her, desperate to leave. If the Jacked-Mesh man could access the local 'gats without hordes of soldiers descending on him, maybe I could, too. I peered at him, standing like a concrete post. He had no will of his own, and in my gut, I knew spies and hunters could triangulate on nothing more substantial than my volition.

Floodlights dimmed above the Sanctuary gate. The ramparts were vacant, but now the gate was open. I expected soldiers to rush out and forcibly dose the few left standing, but the only motion was a man in a long dark coat.

He picked his way slowly through the Stazed sleepers, stopping to adjust an arm from an awkward angle, or to straighten a leg. He glanced at the Jacked-Mesh man but didn't stop. In a while, I realized he was working his way toward us.

I squatted down, terrified of dirty fingers cramming a capsule down my throat, and tried to get a grip on Nav. She was heavier than she should have been, a dead weight with the added density of the grub and its succubal intentions. I managed to lift her and tottered into deeper shadows, searching for someplace to hide outside the walls. In a minute, there was wet sand under my feet. Cold seawater rushed up to my knees. I waded deeper, to the left, and realized that the tide was high enough to cover the beach outside the courtyard.

Nav and the grub got heavier and heavier as the back and forth of the breakers chewed sand out from under my feet. I turned to see if we were being followed and saw the man in the long coat wading into the cold water, not rushing in the least.

He splashed out to me and smoothed Nav's hair out of her eyes. "Is she all right?"

I shook my head.

He took her out of my arms, as though she didn't weigh anything.

"Wait . . . !" I said.

"Come on. You must be frozen."

He turned toward the beach and I rushed after him.

I thought he would put her down in the sandy gravel, but he kept going. His long coat—except it wasn't a coat, but a kind of mannish dress, made of heavy material and tied at the waist—slapped his legs as he strode away. I staggered after him, squashing water out of my shoes. He got to the Sanctuary gates well before I did and I made myself run, clumsy and soaking, terrified I would be locked out of my memory of safe places, this time forever.

Instead, he waited. Between the tall gates, there was enough light for me to see his thin fringe of white hair and the pale gray color of his eyes.

He smiled at me. "Who are you?"

I hesitated, shivering. "I'm Eve."

"Hello, Eve," he said. "I'm Father Dunne."

As a child at the Sanctuary, I wasn't allowed beyond the gates, but I remembered watching the ocean through the bars, and now I tried to bring up a mental map of this part of the grounds. I thought Annmarie's lab and living quarters had been to the right, but the man, Father Dunne, was heading left, where my recollections were vague. I wasn't sure my memories would have done any good. What I remembered of the Sanctuary was old trees, rose hedges, and comfortable brick buildings. Now the trees had been replaced by thick stands of security floods and the hedges had become high wire fences. The old buildings had vanished, giving way to hideous prefabs and organized rows of blue tarp tents. The cobalt blueness of the tarps intensified under the harsh lights until the color saturated everything else, making the pink gravel path and the briny air glimmer in phantom shades of orange.

"Is that where we're going?" I said. "That . . . camp?"

He shook his head. "I have a small compound. You'll be safer there." He seemed to notice Naverdi's unlikely heaviness and shifted her weight with a grunt. "When is your friend due?"

"I don't know. Soon. I think."

We were closer to the tents and when I squinted, I could see bodies splayed on the ground. We passed the near side of a fenced compound where two women lay curled in the dirt and I felt my throat clench. But they were breathing easily, faces dreamy in the orangey blue night. It was Staze-time for everyone. The addicts here were under the kind of strict control Annmarie would have envied.

We made a sharp angle, away from the wire fences and blue tarps. Dunne stepped off the path and I followed, feeling packed dirt under my feet instead of gravel. The harsh lights faded and the salt air softened. I thought I could smell flowers.

Dunne slowed so I could walk beside him. "You're not an addict," he said.

I hesitated. "No."

"It's unusual these days," he said, "but there's no shame in addiction. Some people think Staze is the greatest blessing ever bestowed upon mankind. Others say it's punishment for the most profound of our sins."

I wondered if he was an addict himself. His title, *Father*, and his clothing made him a priest, I supposed. And *Dunne*. Like Father *Done* in The Landing Song? I was too tired to decide how to ask.

"What do you think?" he said.

"About what?"

"About Staze." He nodded. "Philosophically speaking."

He obviously had free run of the Sanctuary and Queen Red's blessing. "Peace is pointless," I said. "That's what I think."

He gave me a doubtful look.

The security floods faded to a gentler glow. Dunne stopped in front of a small light-colored stone building with a domed roof. It was surrounded by a high iron fence instead of wire. Inside the fence, roses bloomed profusely. Neither Annmarie nor Rose had ever brought me here. I would have remembered.

Dunne pushed the iron gate open with his foot and nodded

to me as I followed him in. "Shut it tight," he said. "Can you work the latch?"

I could. The metal latch fell into place with satisfying solidity.

"This is the chapel," said Dunne. "The whole place used to be a refuge for the Meshed before they were killed. This is the oldest structure on the campus. Quite historic, actually."

Instead of benches or pews, there was a scatter of sleeping mats. The building was circular, and the only sign that there had been an altar or some focus for worship was a chipped-out hole in the middle of the floor, as though something precious had been removed. The building seemed forlorn and stripped until I saw the dull gleam of gold leaf, hidden in the shadows of the domed ceiling. Paintings. Eyes and hands and faces.

Dunne laid Nav gently on one of the thin pallets and covered her with a blanket. "You won't be disturbed," he said to me. "You're welcome to stay as long as you like."

I sank to the floor beside Nav, exhausted. "Why us?" I whispered. "Why didn't you leave us out there?"

"A good deed is a good deed. There doesn't have to be a reason." He brushed off his knees and straightened. "Tomorrow I'll come back and tell you the story of the Annunciate."

NINE

Late morning light streamed in from three high windows in the chapel's dome, making the gold leaf on the ceiling shimmer. A man and a woman and a young girl draped in red stared down at me from their painted heights. A family portrait, I thought sleepily. So heavy, stern, and symbolic, they might break free of the dome and fall to pieces on the floor.

It was the painting of the girl that caught my attention as I lay on the thin pallet with my arms behind my head. The longer I looked, the more sure I was that the two sides of her face were different. One was tense with fear. The other serene, focused on something a long way from this circular room. It was almost a before-and-after view of her response to an unseen threat. Confusion and fright. Then calm understanding. Two reactions painted into a single face. Or one person existing in two simultaneous situations.

She was like me, I thought. Meshed, passing for Jackless. Or maybe she was like the Jacked-Mesh man, existing on two societal levels while not really existing at all. Or like the Staze-Fakers, faced with something new in their changeless places. Or maybe this was Naverdi, not pregnant but infested.

I rolled over and found Nav sitting beside me, fingers laced across her belly.

"I saw it," she said. "Like the Fakers. I saw it."

I struggled to sit up. "The succubus? In your Staze place?"

"Succubus. Is that what you call it?" She rubbed her eyes, but the motion had more to do with wiping away images still visible on the insides of her lids. "It . . . she . . . it kept asking questions."

"Questions?"

"It wanted to know how I decide what genes to pass on when I reproduce. How to convey nutrients through a uterine wall." She uncrossed her legs, crossed them the other way. "It sounds stupid when it talks. It says 'you-ter-in.' "

"Did you answer it?"

"How could I? I can't move." Her voice shook. "It's ruined everything. The trees are gone. The fish are getting caught in the net."

"What net?"

She held her hands out, miming a hand rail. "In Staze, I stand on the side of the bridge, watching the water. Now I can see a red string coming from under my feet. It drops into the river and gets tangled in a thousand other strings. I can't tell where they're coming from. I can't turn around."

If the succubus was testing its skill at virtual metaphor, a thousand red strings had to do with other addicts, and other sources of Staze. I tried to remember what the old Faker had said last night, but the most vivid thing in my mind was the muddy mannikin. The Unknown Child.

"Where was the succubus?"

"Right next to me. I could see its reflection in the river."

"Was it an adult?"

"It was a kid," she said. "About twelve or thirteen. It's covered with red dust and it isn't wearing anything." Nav dragged her nails across her shirt where the fabric stretched over her abdomen. "*How* could that old Faker see this thing?"

"I don't know," I said.

She studied the air, laden with dusty motes. "It broke down your data partitions in Mesh. What if it can do that with Staze?"

"Red can't work like Jack or Mesh," I said. "It's hallucinogenic. It can't convey information." Even as the words came out of my mouth, I knew I was wrong. Whatever the succubus had discovered about Nav physically, technically, it'd found something new in Staze as well.

Nav tried to get up but only managed to get her knees under her. "We're leaving, right now. I need a datascape. You can scramble the local defenses and I'll call in my ship."

I looked at her in surprise. "They'll find me if I Mesh."

"Not if you're fast enough," she said, but she sounded too scared to consider the consequences if I wasn't fast enough.

"Your ship could be weeks away," I said. "They were going to impound—"

"We'll find some *other* ship," she said. "We'll hijack something. You're Meshed, you can do whatever you want." She stopped herself. "Do you *want* to stay here?"

I shook my head.

"Then let's *go*." She shoved herself upright with a huge ungainly effort and headed for the door.

Maybe twenty paces beyond the chapel gates, we had to stop so Nav could catch her breath. We sat in the dust, in the warm sunlight, looking past the campus walls to the meander of blue-green mountains in the distance. Inside the walls, wire fences squared off endless blocks of blue-tarp tents. Cooking smells drifted in the morning breeze and we could see the addicts lining up for breakfast. It was too early for Staze. The next dose would be at nightfall.

I heard footsteps and turned to see Dunne laboring up the shallow hill with a metal tray stacked with covered dishes.

Nav caught my arm and struggled to her feet. "Who's that?"

"Father Dunne. He's the one who brought us here last night."

"He's a Meshie?"

"I don't know if he's Meshed," I said.

"He must be," said Nav. "Can't you people feel each other?"

"No."

"You must've given him some kind of hint. Why else would he help you?"

"He said he was doing a good deed."

Naverdi gave a cough of a laugh. I could feel her pulling herself together. By the time Dunne reached us, a smuggler's smile was plastered across her face.

She took in his cassock, his dusty feet. "Father Dunne, I presume?"

"At your service." He couldn't keep his eyes from darting to her belly. "I hope you both slept well?"

"Like babies." Her eyes were focused on his right wrist, where a Jack might have been, but the long sleeves of his robe covered anything that might place him in the social order. "We appreciate your help."

Dunne made a little mock-bow. "My pleasure."

"I hate to ask you for anything more," said Nav, "seeing as how you've obviously gone out of your way for us."

"No trouble." Dunne smiled. "What do you need?"

"A datascape," said Nav. "Nothing fancy. Just to borrow for a while."

"I could certainly dig one up for you." Dunne started for the chapel. The smell of hot food trailed behind him. I tagged along, my mouth watering. The last thing I remembered eating was the sweaty cheese on Nav's ship. "You'll have to be careful how you use it, though. It's safe enough to check records or references, but Those In Charge wouldn't be pleased with an unauthorized communication. For example, calling in a personal transport and attempting to leave the camp would have serious consequences."

"I wouldn't dream of doing that," said Nav.

"You can borrow mine, then. It's in the chapel."

So he was *Jacked*. I tried to catch Nav's eye, but she wouldn't look at me.

Dunne put the tray on the chapel floor, helped Nav sit, and uncovered the food with a flourish, as though the crumbling building was a private room in a fancy restaurant. There were fried breads and sweet chutneys, sliced vegetables, cottage cheese, and a pot of strong, fragrant tea. I tried not to cram everything into my mouth at once. Nav polished off three helpings, wiped up what was left on her plate, and licked her fingers.

When we were finished, Dunne pointed up at the ceiling. "Have you seen our mural?"

Now that the sun had reached a higher angle, the paintings hung over our heads in sharp detail: flatly drawn, heavy with gold leaf, caked with paint.

"A beautiful example of the artistry of its period," said Father Dunne. He seemed to have forgotten about Nav's request for a datascape and pointed to the stern-faced woman: *O' Mother,* I assumed. She held a rose in her right hand and reached for a glittering sunburst with her left. Stars gleamed above her, sharp and lush against a midnight background. At her feet, ebony stones were half-obscured by emerald vines, which formed the lower border of the mural.

"Of course, this is a highly stylized, mythic interpretation of the Landing." Dunne followed the vines from the woman's feet to where they tangled around the ankles of the man beside her. He held a bowl of seeds in one hand and scattered them with the other. A few seeds had been painted in between rocks and viney leaves. None of them had sprouted.

"Naturally," said Dunne, "the vines represent the Mesh, but it also refers to the sense of unity among the Generation Ship pioneers. Not many people know it, but all three social classes were equally represented on the Ship. The Jackless, Jacked, and Meshed, all focused on a future without hate or violence." He smiled at me. "Every image is representative of a deeper concept. It isn't important to comprehend every detail—the gist of it is enough for most people. But I've studied this particular work, so I know a thing or two about the intentions of the artist."

Nav didn't bother to pretend to be interested. She pushed one of the sleeping mats against the wall and sat against it, damp under her lower lip with sweat.

"The two adults represent the old ways," said Dunne. "They're parental, two-dimensional, without flexibility. You can see it in their faces and the way they hold themselves. No matter how well meaning, no matter how visionary, they're limited by their attitudes and prejudices."

He put his hand on my shoulder and I could feel the heat of his palm. This was like listening to a different version of Queen Red's speech. Applause was the price for Staze, or a datascape. I wondered if this would finally turn into a sermon about how I should submit to whatever Staze-gods he believed in, and dose myself at last.

Dunne nodded toward the third image; the girl, dark-skinned, hooded in red cloth, haloed in gold. Her right hand closed on the ornate bars of a gold leaf gate. Her pose was the same as the woman stamped into my mother's medal, except instead of facing the gate, her head was turned to make eye contact with the viewer.

"The daughter. The new generation. The Annunciate." Dunne led me across the ruined chapel until we were standing just below her. "What's most interesting about the image of the Annunciate is the variety of ways she's been interpreted." He turned to me. "What do you think? Is she closing the gate or opening it?"

"I have no idea," I said.

"Think about it," he said. "If she's closing the gate, what does it imply?"

"No contact with the outside?"

"Isolation," he said. "Exactly. Sometimes interpreted as the confining social separations between Mesh and Jack and so on. And if she's pushing it open?"

I shrugged. "Open-mindedness?"

"Good," he said. "But rejecting traditional prejudices is an old idea. I believe the Annunciate stands for uncharted change. She's a revolutionary on the brink of action, a virgin in the most archaic sense of the word; a woman of free will, unbeholden to anyone." He pointed to the girl, frozen at the moment of decision. "If she does nothing, the three of them are trapped together forever, in stasis, in the garden, where nothing ever happens. There's speculation that the Annunciate is a symbol for the moment of conception—of ideas, or children." He turned to Naverdi. "In fact, one of the interpretations for the walled garden is uterine."

Nav flinched at the word 'uterine.'

"From that point of view, the responsibility of the Annunciate is to give birth to a new world, clean of sin and violence," said Dunne, and his voice rose into song. *" 'Raise up thine Unknown Child for all, and shout . . .' "*

Nav held up her hands. "Please! Where's your goddamn datascape?"

Dunne stopped, deflated. He went over to the narrow entryway, and I thought he was going to walk out on us. Instead, he pulled a datascape out from under a dusty vase full of dusty flowers. He brought it over to Nav and gave it to her. The 'scape was filthy, with a circular clean spot where the vase had been sitting for who knew how long.

The Jackwire was sticky and stiff with age. Nav unwrapped it gingerly.

"You should take better care of this," she said. "When was the last time you used it?"

Dunne twitched up the long sleeve of his cassock so we could see the socket in his wrist. Unlike Nav's, the chrome had dulled. The opening of the Jack itself was filled in with dust and dirt, and instead of a healthy pucker of scar tissue, his skin seemed to be closing over the metal.

I saw Nav's eyes go wide.

"I haven't used the Jack since I joined the Order," said Dunne.

"What order?" I said.

"The Order of the Annunciate," he said. "We foresee a day when there are no social separations between the levels of technology. We take a vow of informational poverty to show our faith."

Nav opened her mouth in amazement. "You *volunteered* to be Jackless?"

He pulled down his sleeve. "Informational poverty or abstinence of necessity. My choice isn't much different than yours."

A chill went down my spine. Did he mean *me*? Did he know I was Meshed? How could he *know*? And if he did, why hadn't he turned me over to Queen Red, or the woman with the Jacked-Mesh man?

Dunne nodded at the 'scape. "Before you use that, you should be aware, things are different in Jack today than they were even a week ago."

"You're getting distortions," said Nav. "That's what happens when you let your plug fill up with gunk."

"That's not what I mean," said Dunne. "Our visions in Staze are spilling over into Jack. The gates are open. Everything's different."

Nav aimed the plug defiantly at her socket.

"Opening a gate can be the same as coming down from a bridge," said Dunne. "Was it different last night in the dream of fishes?"

Nav looked up at him, eyes flat.

"I've seen you there," he said. "We all have. We know what you're carrying. Your daughter has shown herself to us."

"My *what*?" said Nav.

"Who's *we*?" I demanded.

"The others in the dream of fishes," said Dunne. "The addicts. But my colleagues in Jack have seen her, too. If there were any of the Meshed left, she would have shown herself to them. She's everywhere." Dunne put his hands gently on Nav's shoulders. "You're carrying the Unknown Child. A being without aggression—a break from our genetic past. The gates between Jack and Mesh and Staze are open. The social and technical separations are disappearing because of her. You're the Annunciate, the vessel of Paradise itself."

"It's *not* a child." Nav grabbed him and shook him by the front of his cassock. "And I'm not a fucking *vessel* for anything!"

She didn't say another word until he left, and he took a long time to leave. There was more he wanted to tell us, and he probably thought we would run away if we could.

"He's out of his mind." Nav jabbed at her wrist with the datascape plug, missing half a dozen times. "He's nuts."

"He's seen the succubus," I said. "Like the Fakers."

"I don't give a damn what he's seen," said Nav. "As soon as I find a ship, we're getting the fuck out."

As if she could get away from the grub. "You can't land a ship inside the walls," I said.

"I'll set it down a couple of klicks from here. We'll need some kind of ground transport. Let me see what I can find, then you can hack their security. Just wait." She shut her eyes.

I waited.

Her body stayed tense, forehead furrowed, mouth pressed into a tight line. She grunted. Her fingers clenched. Once she said, *"Oh!"*

It would have been so simple for me to drop into Mesh and do what she was working so hard at. Her virtual audacity would probably attract Queen Red's attention faster than if I was the one smashing through security blocks. After all, I was extinct.

I glanced nervously at the chapel's closed door and then up at the Annunciate on the ceiling. No matter how Dunne praised the artistry, the painting was stiff and amateurish. Instead of hidden truths and layers of metaphor, what I saw was a young girl with a distorted face, staring off into nothingness.

Beside me, Naverdi jerked. I thought she'd unplugged herself, but the wire was still stuck in her wrist. Her eyes were wide. Her mouth stretched in a silent yell. Her body was stiff, braced against invisible things.

I shook her. "Nav?" Her pulse bobbed fast in her thin neck. "Nav!" I yanked out the Jackwire, expecting her to blink and sag and come into focus, but none of that happened. "Naverdi!"

It was the succubus doing this—dragging her even farther down so I would follow. The minute I touched the surface of the Sanctuary's virtual pool, I would be seen and that would be the end of me. Of both of us. Of all three of us.

I gripped Nav's damp, hot fingers, scared witless. I could feel her drowning.

I squeezed my eyes shut and fell in with her.

From the far side of Naverdi's temple, someone yelped in pain. I blundered through the metaphors of furniture and torchières, ducking under low crystal chandeliers, through long fringes of hangings. The Jack interface was more crowded than I remembered. Armchairs, ottomans, and oriental throw rugs everywhere. I passed two doorways, which I was positive were new, and finally found Nav and the succubus wrestling in the narrow space between the back of a couch and the temple's virtual wall.

Nav was on top, distinctly not-pregnant. She saw me and started yelling. *You said it looked like you!*

I opened my mouth to apologize or explain.

Nav slugged the succubus in the stomach. *How'd it get into Jack?* she shouted.

I'm in you. The succubus rolled its eyes and cackled. *I'm in Jack and Mesh and Staze. I'm* everywhere.

Nav pushed herself off the creature and crawled over the

sofa, past me. *I need a knife.* In a minute, I could hear her opening drawers and slamming cabinets.

The succubus got up, brushed itself off, climbed over the couch, and sat down. It was stark naked, still smeared in red powder. It'd finally mastered facial expressions, and now it seemed far too pleased with itself. It took an embroidered red cushion off the couch and began picking out the stuffing. In the dim light, I thought it looked bruised around the face.

You're hurt, I said hopefully.

I'm not hurt, it said. *This is a virtual environment.*

Nav was still searching noisily for a weapon. She could have just imagined one, then cut the succubus to pieces. It wouldn't have made any difference to the succubus. In the real world, nothing would change.

Why're you fighting with her? I said.

She started it, said the succubus.

You're killing her, I said.

Killing? It pulled out a handful of threads. *Mother Eve, you told me she was like food.*

Mother Eve? I nearly choked. *Like food. I didn't say she was food.*

What's the difference? said the succubus.

I didn't know how to argue that. *What're you going to do if she dies?* I wondered if it understood death yet and waited for it to react, but I might as well have been talking about the weather. *You'll be stuck inside a corpse,* I said. *Should I explain decomposition?*

The succubus dropped a hank of red thread on the floor and made an airy, dismissive wave. *Before that happens, I will be born.*

Nav kicked her way across the room, shoving aside furniture. *You can't be born!* She swung a kitchen cleaver back and forth. *I refuse to let you be born!*

The succubus eyed her impassively.

I'll be goddamned if I'm going to be eaten alive by a fucking alien parasite.

I'm not a parasite, said the succubus. *And if I'm eating you, it's because you refused to tell me how to transfer nutrients through the you-ter-in wall.*

Nav let out an inarticulate yell and charged with the cleaver, but the cleaver vanished as she flung herself forward. Nav stopped, backed away, bunched her fists, and started in again. This time her hands disappeared, cut off bloodlessly at the wrist. Then her arms, up to her elbows.

Nav froze, staring down at the missing parts of herself. *Stop it,* she whispered.

You stop it, said the succubus. Nav gave a quiver of a nod. Her arms and hands reappeared. She dropped into the nearest armchair, knees hugged against her chest.

I cleared my throat. *When will you be born?*

Very soon, said the succubus. *I am still forming myself according to your genetic codes.*

You are? I said uneasily. *What will you look like?*

Stuffing spilled out of the pillow, which was halfway unraveled. *The Unknown Child, of course,* said the succubus.

Nav snorted, but she didn't say anything.

What does the Unknown Child look like? I asked.

The succubus frowned, like it was a trick question. *My physical and virtual manifestations will be different. Which are you asking about?*

The one that's going to be born.

After enough gestation, it will look like a human baby.

So much for the vague hope that it might slide out the same way it'd slid in. *That's amazing,* I said.

No shit, said Nav.

I've learned a lot, said the succubus with outrageous modesty.

Nav clenched her fists.

So, I said, *I assume you've made plans for after your birth? Have you found someone to take care of you?*

What do you mean? said the succubus suspiciously.

Babies are helpless, I said. *They depend on a mother for protec-*

tion outside the womb. *If you gestate much longer, you'll kill your only parent. What're you going to do then?*

It hesitated. *Mother Eve.*

The idea gave me chills. I pointed to Nav. *The one who gives birth is the mother.*

It gave Nav a sideways glance.

Fuck you, whispered Nav.

The succubus fidgeted with the dismembered pillow, its feet tangled in scarlet thread. I wished hard for it to be disillusioned, depressed, and sad. I wished for it to want to go home.

Finally it looked up. I expected some defiant variation of *I know everything.* Instead, it said, *Mother Eve, you're an orphan.* It turned to Nav. *Your mother killed your sibling and abandoned you.*

Neither of us said anything.

I don't need a mother, it said. *I formed myself. I will birth myself. I will protect myself. I will grow up on my own. I will even give myself a name.*

Did it sound scared? The image of the succubus as an anxious, lonely little girl swam up in my mind so clearly, it might have been my own memory.

Listen, I started, but it shook its head.

I don't want to listen. You lie to me because you think I'm simple. You try to trick me, but you're the simple ones. I know how to extract Red from your bodies. I know how to make you peaceful, and I know how to make your bodies part of mine.

It tugged at the tangle of embroidery between the legs of Nav's armchair and Nav let out a yell as a strand looped her ankle. She leaped out of the chair and jumped up on the nearest table.

Kill it! she yelled at me. *Do it while I'm still Jacked in, Eve, just do it!*

You're not Jacked in, said the succubus.

What? shrieked Nav.

Your eyes were open, I said unwillingly. *Something was wrong. I unplugged you.*

How can I be here if I'm not Jacked in?

The succubus pulled apart the last strands of red silk. What was left of the pillow fell at its feet. Scarlet thread raveled under the furniture all over the room. *Because you're not in Jack anymore. And, Mother Eve, you're not in Mesh.*

If it hadn't been so frighteningly serious, I would have laughed. I opened my eyes to drop into the real world, intending to come right back, but nothing happened. I blinked and rubbed my eyes and pinched myself. The disorganized furniture and tacky chandeliers stayed as solid as ever. Nav watched, wide-eyed, as I didn't disappear from her interface. I held on to the wing of the sofa to keep from falling over.

Okay, I said, and felt my tongue stick to the roof of my mouth. *How're you doing that?*

It spread its hands to show a cat's cradle of red thread between its fingers. *My net lays over Jack. It lays over your Mesh. It is unity between the addicts. I am the dream in Red.* The succubus pointed languidly across the room. *Go outside,* it said. *See how things are different.*

There's no outside, said Nav. *I never put in an outside.* But she jumped off the table and bolted away.

I ran after her, between chairs, swag lamps, and knickknacks, afraid if I stayed with the succubus a minute longer, I'd make one more stupid assumption about its level of intelligence.

The twisting coil of red thread followed Nav's wake, clumping in a thick skein. It ran past a kitchen table where raw dough lay in wrinkled, comma-shaped lumps, slowly rising, as though the succubus was trying to form new grubs from salt and flour, yeast and water.

The thread made a sharp turn and disappeared under an enormous armoire. I found Nav on the other side, standing in a doorway I knew had never been part of her scenario.

Look at this, she whispered.

There were stairs. And at the bottom of the stairs, there

was sand to the horizon. Nothing broke the view except a few dead trees and a small pond reflecting the sapphire sky.

The place was so familiar and at the same time so foreign, all I could think of was the gauze of atmosphere between my world and Corey's after the data partitions on the Medusa had disintegrated. I swayed in the doorway, dazzled by the brightness and the fact that Nav could see it, too. I glanced down self-consciously to see if I'd become my usual naked, dusty avatar. To my surprise, I hadn't.

Nav kicked at the red yarn where it spilled over the threshold and down the stairs, twisting through the sand to disappear into the pond. *What* is *all this?*

The thread has to be a metaphor for Staze. The desert . . . I hesitated, embarrassed and feeling exposed. *It's my place in Mesh. The pool is my interface.*

Not possible, she said flatly. *You can't walk from one level of technology to another.*

Everything's different now. The succubus appeared in the doorway and pressed between us, down the stairs.

Nav and I followed it warily. I stopped at the bottom and turned around for a better view of the building that had never existed in my space before. It loomed over us, weathered boards nailed together and planted on thick wooden pilings. The roof was conical and there were vague carvings under the eaves. It had elements of both Annmarie's cottage in the woods and the ruined cathedral on Kigal, but it wasn't supposed to be either one.

What the hell is that? said Nav.

Your temple, I said.

My what?

All the mirrors and chandeliers and carpets, I said. *Isn't that what your Jack interface was supposed to be?*

She shook her head. *It was a sitting room.*

Another one of my offhand perceptions, solidified by the succubus's literal imagination. Add that to its versions of the apple, its weird concepts of pregnancy, parenting, and childhood. It was like a distorted reflection of my own distorted life.

A temple, said Nav. *Does that mean it wants to be a god, or a goddess, or something?*

Be quiet, I said. *You'll give it ideas.*

We started for the pool and Nav nudged me.

What if it never lets us leave? she whispered. *We'll lie in that chapel until we starve to death.*

I shook my head. *It wants to be born. It can't let you die.*

What about you?

It thinks I'm its mother. It thinks I'll take care of it.

That's not what it said.

No, I said, *but that's what it wants.*

How do you know?

I've been around it for a while, I said. *I just know.*

The succubus turned and beckoned from the edge of the pool. It crouched by the water, studying its own reflection, or things far below.

Nav squatted at the water's edge, keeping her distance from the red yarn. I hunched beside her and saw myself—a dark young woman with wild, twisting black hair, still not wary or wise enough. There was no sign of the dusty child.

The succubus touched the pond's surface. Reflections vanished and the water cleared to a crystalline depth. The view widened, expanding into the standard schematic of ThreeSys. Three suns and the usual colorful tangle of borders and battle zones.

Paradise showed, too, but differently this time. Not a dull chunk of rock. Not a phantom comet, or a wobble of gravitation. This time the planet was a ruby gleam between diamond stars, the way it appeared to the succubus.

The yarn twisted toward Paradise under the ersatz water. Its licorice smell rose up, sweet and pure. I reached over to touch the skein where it lay in the damp sand, coated with grit. Half-dissolved red crystals came away on my fingers. Nav looked at the yarn, the stain on my hand, with real despair.

That's Staze, she said. *From my body.*

Not just yours, said the succubus.

Dunne and the Fakers, too? she said. *All the addicts in the courtyard?*

The succubus nodded.

You'll suck us all dry, said Nav bitterly.

I stared at the yarn, suddenly understanding. The grubs on Paradise needed the real thing, not just the essence of Red. Not a simple metaphor, or the sensations that went along with the dose. What I could see, winding down the temple stairs, lying in the sand by the pool, was Staze. Actual Staze.

How're you doing this? I whispered. *How can you move a physical substance through the Mesh?*

You're not in the Mesh, it said. *Don't you remember how I moved you?*

I nodded. Nav eyed me.

Corey ditched me on Paradise, I said. *A hundred klicks from the Medusa.*

And?

I glanced uneasily at the succubus.

I saved you, it said. *You lied to me, but I saved you anyway, Mother Eve.*

Nav gave me a look of betrayed disbelief. *It saved you?*

I nodded slowly. Below, the rope of Staze wove through the ThreeSys schematic, thickening, winding in a net of scarlet filaments from other planets. Devi. YonSou. Azier. Anywhere there were addicts. Staze siphoned from a hundred thousand bodies, a million static dreams. A drift of red threads from all over ThreeSys, more dense than the ancient tangle of human borders.

Our view of Paradise was closer now, and the stringy connections between the grubs were visible. Red instead of black. The whole planet looked like it was wrapped in red cable, hawser-thick with the pleasures of Staze. I could see a gleam in a clearing between the strands, and I was sure it was the Medusa, but the ship was different. Not the bronze-colored bulk I was used to, but a circular wall of stone: a fortress in the wasteland. This was the way the succubus saw us, I realized, and as we swung around, I could see high golden gates, wide open, instead of the bay's airlock.

Inside, our point of view was from the ceiling of the drive bay, right over Corey's freckled bald spot.

There were other people in the bay and at first I thought with amazement that Annmarie and Corey had been rescued. But that was wrong.

Two women stretched out on the floor, gray-skinned and emaciated, not moving. There was another one lying in a long plastic tub filled with water and grubs. Only her head showed above the surface. Grubs lay all over her.

How did they get here? whispered Nav.

I lured them, said the succubus.

Why? I said.

I was hungry, said the succubus.

You're eating *those women?* said Nav.

I'm consuming them instead of you.

A fourth woman, separate from the rest, lay on a blanket, sleeping, or unconscious, her legs spread wide.

Annmarie knelt between the woman's thighs, probing at her privates.

They're trying to make another baby, I said in horrified amazement. *You'll have a—a sister.*

I won't let that happen, said the succubus. *I control my body, not them.*

Corey came over and crouched beside the unconscious woman. "How's it going?"

"You know how it's going." Annmarie wiped her hands and stood up. "The grubs can assimilate lower organisms, but humans are too complex. This one's being eaten from the inside out. They'll all be dead by morning."

"We need to keep trying," said Corey. "The possibilities . . ."

"Are pointless," said Annmarie. "Suppose one of your nasty little ideas works? A miracle happens and these women wake up tomorrow all bright and happy and genetically devoid of violent instincts. What do we do then? Send a grub to every Mesh-hating maniac in ThreeSys with a note that says, 'Shove this up your ass and find eternal peace'?" She pulled over a stool and sat. "If a slimy collection of cells can completely corrupt the Mesh, it's too dangerous to play with. We should be finding ways to get the ship off the ground so we can get back into the Staze business. I have customers waiting." She made a vague gesture at the dying women. "This is a waste of time."

"It isn't," said Corey. "This is the answer to every problem we've ever had. Staze has to be consumed. It has to be resupplied. If this thing knows how to use the Mesh, how much harder can it be to master Jack? It has to be trained, but if we do it right, it can be everywhere, in every informational system. We can control everything in virtual space."

Annmarie shrugged. "I'll grant that the grubs and moss have assimilated the organic aspects of the elder 'gats. I'll buy that they've developed a limited intelligence as a result—*very* limited—and that's the avatar you showed me in Mesh." She leaned forward on the stool. "But it's not any smarter than a virtual virus. It behaves like a predator, and it's certainly not going to change its biological priorities because you flirt with it."

From my ceiling viewpoint, I turned to the succubus. *She's seen you?* I whispered.

He lured me, said the succubus.

"It has intelligence." Corey tucked his fists against his hips. "And it's hungry. If we can't figure out how to control it, we may never get off the planet."

"You sound worried." Her voice took on a dangerous edge. "Eve told me you'd given it 'seeds.' "

"I'm sure Eve told you all sorts of things," said Corey.

Annmarie's mouth twitched up at one corner. I couldn't tell if she was laughing or agreeing. "You're right. We *do* have to figure out how to control it, and the first thing is to get it out of the Mesh." She crossed her arms. "I'll tell you how we're going to get off the planet."

"Purge the Medusa?" said Corey.

"Not a chance." Annmarie got off the stool and went to the other side of the bay, where the bioboxes were lined up against the wall. She reached into one with a pair of tongs, pulled out a grub, and dropped it on the floor. She pulled out another and another until there were six or seven grubs lying in puddles. "The grubs are like propagats," said Annmarie. "Right? They provide a physical foundation for a virtual world."

Corey gave an uncertain nod.

"We have to establish a few limits." Annmarie raised one foot and brought it down hard on the nearest grub. The thing burst like a plastic bag full of water. Pieces flew out with the force of impact and stuck to the walls, the bioboxes, Annmarie's pants. She brushed them away.

"Want to join me?" she said.

He took a step to one side. "I don't understand."

"Hunters have been exterminating propagats with nanovirals for years," she said with exaggerated patience. "Has that affected us?"

He blinked. "Of course."

"We run. We hide, but basically, we're at their mercy." Annmarie prodded the next grub with her toe. "I'm betting we can disable your naked little friend in Mesh the same way." She raised her foot.

"Exterminate its 'gats," he said softly.

"Not all of them," said Annmarie. "Just enough to scare it. I think it has the intelligence to be afraid. In fact, we can make it an experiment. How many grubs do we have to kill to get the Medusa back?" She slammed her foot down. The grub exploded in a gooey spurt. "Help me," she said to Corey. "We'll do it by fifties. Then we'll go into Mesh and see if anything's changed."

*   *   *

The view dimmed to grayish tones and the killing motions in the Medusa's bay became slow, watery. I got the impression that what we'd just seen had happened some time ago.

I glanced up to find the succubus watching me. In daylight, the bruises on its face showed as puffy places under dark coffee skin. It was hurt. Genuinely hurt.

Aren't you afraid? I said.

I'm not afraid, said the succubus with almost comical bravado.

You should be, said Nav. *Annmarie'd scare anybody.*

The succubus touched a tender place on its cheek. *There's one more thing I want you to see.* It sat up straight and pointed into the desert—or what had been desert.

Now, a hundred meters from the pond, sand blended into forest.

At first, I thought it was Annmarie's Mesh environment and I got to my feet, terrified that Annmarie had slaughtered enough grubs to coerce the succubus into bringing us to her. But the longer I gawked, the less familiar the woods were. Annmarie had never put in a stream, for one thing. This one gushed in rust-colored torrents from between the trees. Not rust. Ruddy. Red. The stream emptied into the pond, carrying a tangle of red strings that joined the ones coming from the temple, knotting into the cable far below.

Something caught my eye in the shadow of the trees. A fish with iridescent scales flashed over the surface of the stream. Another one leaped into clear view and Nav scrambled to her feet.

That's mine, she yelped. *My Staze place is here. It's fixed!* She bolted around the edge of the pond, running upstream, headed for the woods.

Wait, I yelled after her, but she didn't even break her stride. I turned to the succubus. *Mesh, Jack,* and *Staze? But . . . how can they all be together in one place?*

The succubus smiled and helped me to my feet. *The separations are gone, Mother Eve. I don't need them.*

It held my hand as we followed Nav to where she had stopped at the boundary between her woods and my desert. Her joyous abandon seemed to have evaporated.

This is backward. Nav pointed upstream where fish broke the surface in rainbow hues and the river cut straight as a highway between immense trees. *I swear the water used to go the other way.*

It did go the other way, said the succubus. *Staze dreams used to flow out of the pool. Everything's changed. Now the Staze flows into it.*

Like a pool of dreams? I said. *Where did you get that idea?*

I thought of it myself, said the succubus.

Nav gave me a doubtful look. *Rose,* she mouthed, and I nodded.

There was enough of a path for us to walk in single file along the riverbank. Nav went first, anxious, too fast, tripping over stones and roots. Every time a fish jumped, I heard her catch her breath. I let the succubus walk in front of me, not trusting it to bring up the rear. It trotted along barefoot, slim, smeared with dust, perfectly at home in this strange mishmash of virtual worlds.

What're you going to do if Annmarie kills all of your physical manifestations on Paradise? I asked.

I can make more, said the succubus. *I understand re-pro-duc-tion now.*

Well, you'd better start re-pro-du-cing pretty soon, I said. *Once Annmarie gets an idea like that, she doesn't waste time.* I waited for it to say something, but it just kept walking.

How are you going to reproduce? I said. *You don't have the anatomy for it, as far as we could tell.*

I could almost hear it thinking. *Seeds,* it said finally. *Maybe dough.*

It was so ignorant, so innocent in its own way, I couldn't help but feel sorry for it.

Do you even know where you come from? I said, but the succubus didn't answer.

The river cleared as it widened, and instead of murky water, I could see a dense ripple of scarlet reeds covering the bottom from bank to bank. Naverdi's fish darted through the stuff, gleaming silver, opal, steel-blue. One rolled to show gill, mouth, and eye above the water and I was surprised at its expression—a pure, contemplative solitude.

The wind gusted, bringing us the unmistakable licorice tang of Staze, and Nav let out a yell. Just ahead, a spidery bridge arched through the air above the river. Even from a distance, I could see hundreds of people standing on it, jammed together between the railings.

This isn't fucking possible! Nav stopped. *Anybody who takes Staze could be here.* Her eyes widened. *The addicted Jackless could be here.*

Keep going, said the succubus.

Nav started walking again, but reluctantly. The path narrowed between saplings and dense undergrowth. In a moment, she was lost in the thick vegetation, but I could hear her, snapping twigs as she pushed through green brush. She must have been visible from the bridge because heads began turning in her direction. Someone let out a surprised cry.

The succubus laughed.

What's so funny? I said.

You'll see, it said and trotted off, disappearing into the bushes.

I ran after it, trying to keep up, and lost sight of it. The path vanished altogether and I found myself fighting through weeds and shrubs and thorns. I kicked and tore my way through them and crawled out, dirty and scratched, into sunlight and green grass.

The bridge was just ahead, so packed, it would have been impossible to cross. The people—the addicts, deep in their Red dream of fishes—were elbow to elbow, pressed so tight against each other, I expected half of them to jump off into the river. Red threads hung from them, tangling under the arch of the bridge, draping in a net over the water, no doubt tangling with vegetation along the bottom.

I looked for Nav and saw her, not far from the near edge of the bridge.

Instead of her usual loose shirt and trousers, she was draped from head to foot in a piece of red fabric. She struggled with the cloth, which clung to her in graceful folds no matter how she pulled. It draped her hair, wound across her shoulder, and fell to her ankles. An accent of bright gold ran along the border and when she turned, a trick of the light made an arch like a nimbus, gleaming around her dark face. Cries of sheer joy erupted from the people on the bridge.

Harvest now thy fruitful womb . . .

A man in dark clothes pushed through the crowd and started toward her, arms thrown wide. He was like a cork pulled out of a bottle and the dense pack of bodies broke, streaming down to the riverbank, shouting and singing.

O' Daughter, one
night reveals all future days . . .

I sprinted across the grass, afraid they would mob her. The succubus was nowhere to be seen.

Nav! I was close enough to recognize half a dozen of the refugees from the Sanctuary's courtyard. The bearded Staze-Faker and the wild-haired blonde who owned the Jacked-Mesh man. I saw the pale woman with her amber-skinned little girl. In front of them all, Dunne belted out the lyrics to The Landing Song, jubilant. He dropped to his knees in front of Nav.

Raise up thine Unknown Child for
all, and shout, Hail!

No! I tried to yell. Raspy noises forced out of my mouth, but no sound.

Nav turned to me in desperation, still ripping at the unrippable cloth. Her eyes widened at something behind me and I spun around, ready to grab the succubus and bang it against a tree trunk until everything vanished, but the forest wasn't there.

Only the river remained, arrow-straight and filled with leaping fish. A stone's throw away, the wooden temple pierced the desert sky, reflecting in the surface of my former pool. The temple doors opened and the succubus stepped out.

It didn't look like Nav anymore, or an arcane combination of the two of us. It shone with prepubescent, girlish beauty and opened its arms in welcome, teeth gleaming as it smiled.

I stood as still as a block of stone, unable to budge as the crowd rushed toward her, carrying Nav along with them.

Only Dunne stopped. He touched my face. *Won't you come with us?*

I tried as hard as I could to tell him what the Unknown Child really was, where it came from, and what its plans were.

But the best I could do was sing.

Here is the new world.

TEN

I opened my eyes to the sound of someone hammering outside. The noise echoed under the chapel's dome and I had the impression it had been going on for quite a while. I pushed myself up from where I'd been lying on the crumbling concrete floor. Naverdi sprawled beside me, pillowed on a wadded sheet, half-covered with a dirty blanket. She was damp with fever and her skin was the color of wet cardboard. The datascape lay beside her, filthy and unplugged.

I shook her until she moaned. "Nav?"

She pushed me away.

More hammering. Not quite close enough to make me think someone was trying to break down the chapel door, but not that far away. I went over to the door and pulled it open, just wide enough to see out.

On the other side of the high iron gates, a crew of workers pounded together a wooden platform with walls on three sides, the open front facing the chapel. A handful of guards stood by in the golden light of late afternoon, but they weren't exactly guarding. One put down his weapon and helped move a dozen long boards into place while the rest peered at the chapel or checked the time. Even the guards were addicts, I thought, and recognized one or two of them from Nav's dream of fishes.

The workers conferred and banged with great intensity. They were building a stage, I decided. Circular, planted on timbers, with a vaguely conical roof.

Not much different than what the succubus had come up with.

I shut the door and went back to Nav.

She was awake. "What's going on?"

"They're building something."

"Who is?"

"The addicts."

She groaned. "They're actually doing it."

"What do you mean?"

"That succubus thing of yours. It told them to build its temple. It told them to bring everyone in the Sanctuary to see it being born." She pressed her hands over her face. "They were all yelling *Hail! Hail!*" She let her arms drop weakly to her sides. "Weren't you there? I *saw* you."

"It left me by the bridge. I saw them dragging you down the river. Dunne stopped and asked me what was wrong, but I couldn't talk."

"Then what happened?"

"That's all I remember," I said.

Footsteps crunched in gravel outside the chapel and the door swung open. Not crazed addicts come to take Nav away for birthing or tormenting, but Dunne.

I was just as scared of him, I realized.

He came over to kneel beside Nav. "How're you feeling?"

"I feel like shit," said Nav.

He pulled a small leather-bound breviary from his cassock and opened it. A plastic bag, dusted inside with Red, was tucked between the pages. Dunne pressed the breviary into Nav's hand. "Use it when you have the most need," he said.

Nav clutched the book and lay down on her hard bed, gray with exhaustion.

Dunne turned to me. "Come outside. I need to talk to you."

I glanced down at Nav, who closed her eyes. "Just for a minute," I said.

Around the far side of the chapel, the banging wasn't so loud. Fragrant untrimmed roses crowded along arches of thorny branches. Occasional bees blundered past, weighted down with pollen. The flowers, the high fence, even the sky were gilded with early evening light, but to me, it seemed like a virtual overlay that might peel away in strips at any minute.

Dunne brushed dead leaves off an ornate bench and motioned for me to sit. "You and Naverdi have been together for a long time."

He said it as though he'd sized us up as lifelong partners. Hardly, I thought. At this point, I wasn't at all sure what we were to each other. "It's been a while," I said.

He sat next to me and plucked a red blossom with white veins. "She's lucky to have you. It's encouraging to see two people so devoted to each other, especially since it's her hour of need, so to speak."

He patted my arm. It was a dry, chaste little pat, but it reminded me of Corey's transparent interest in my sex life. I felt my face getting hot. I put my hands in my lap where he couldn't reach them.

"How did you meet?" said Dunne.

"Staze," I mumbled.

He nodded. "I saw you come out of the forest last night in the dream of fishes. You told me you weren't an addict."

"I guess I lied."

"Why didn't you come with us to the temple?" he said. "It must have been as big a revelation for you as it was for the rest of us."

Because the succubus wanted me quiet. "I couldn't," I said, which was, at least, the truth.

"You should have come." Dunne's voice went soft and serious. He pressed his fingers over the middle of his chest. "The Unknown Child touched each of us."

The succubus might as well have sunk its teeth into him. I started to get up, but he pulled me back.

"I know you're worried about Naverdi," he said. "You have every right to be, but you have to understand. She isn't entirely yours anymore."

I knotted my fists together in my lap, wondering if this was a subtle invitation for me to leave. If I walked out of the Sanctuary—of my own free will or not—Dunne would probably take care of Nav if she survived giving birth, but she wasn't his main interest. She was mine. Somehow it'd turned out that I was the only one in a position to protect Nav from the people who wanted her so badly. She needed me. And when I thought about it, I wasn't sure that could ever change back to the way it'd been before.

"She needs a doctor," I said.

"When this is over, I'll make sure she sees one," said Dunne.

"But what if she dies?" I said. "Can't you see how sick she is?"

"If Queen Red found out about Naverdi and what we believe she's carrying, your friend would be killed," said Dunne.

"What exactly *do* you think she's carrying?" I said.

"The common vision," said Dunne. "I thought you understood that."

I shook my head.

"So far, the Unknown Child has only shown herself to those of us with the dream of fishes," said Dunne. "But if she manifests in all twelve visions supplied by Staze, and if every addict who sees her is freed from stasis, then the old world of technical segregation is gone. Forever."

"What do you mean?" I said uneasily.

"I mean," said Dunne, "that the virtual community which used to be reserved for the Meshed is now open to everyone who takes Staze—rich or poor, Jacked or Jackless." He leaned forward on the bench. "When I went up to the stairs to the temple in the desert, I could see into the room behind the Unknown Child. Would you like to know what I saw?"

I nodded, too dry in the mouth to say anything.

"I saw the rest of the universe," whispered Dunne. "Things beyond the boundaries of ThreeSys. Things outside the reach of Generation Ships. She showed me the end of our containment. And she showed me Paradise."

From the front of the chapel, the pounding intensified.

"Paradise?" I echoed.

"The outflung star," said Dunne. "It's come back to ThreeSys and that's where we're going next."

I had a startlingly clear vision of a hundred thousand addicts on a pilgrimage to a wrecked planet, marching headlong into the succubal maw. Addicts plunging into pools full of hungry grubs for a self-sacrificial dip.

"You can't," I said.

Dunne raised an eyebrow and I wondered what kind of lies I was going to have to come up with in order to tell the truth. He'd given me and Nav shelter. He deserved a warning.

"It's not a child," I said. "I *know* it's not a child. That's what it looks like, but that's not what it is."

He studied me, uncertain of my position as Naverdi's personal acolyte. "Perhaps you're our first heretic, Eve."

"I've seen it before," I said.

"We all have," said Dunne. "Looking down from the bridge. We could see its reflection before we could move."

"I saw it even before that."

"In the dream of fishes?"

I shook my head. "The dream I usually have is a desert."

He almost smiled. "How can you have two dreams?"

"It isn't common," I said, "but it happens."

He nodded at the rose between his fingers. "Go on."

"The thing you're calling the Unknown Child came to me the same way it came to you in the dream of fishes." I was trying to be careful, but I barely needed to lie. "It showed me its . . . different aspects. It's not human. It's not even close to being human."

Dunne plucked at the flower. Petals fell around his feet. "Are you saying this 'thing' is an alien of some kind?"

"Isn't that just as likely as a miracle?"

He eyed me and I thought he might be taking me seriously for the first time. "Why does it have all the trappings of the Annunciate?"

"You already know it's gotten into the Jacked networks," I said. "It has access to all the information there. It's found a good story to hide in. It's found addicts who want to believe in it, but it's a predator. It's opportunistic, and it's *not* the Unknown Child."

Dunne cleared his throat. "So, it's going to eat the addicts?"

I felt myself flush.

"And are you really telling me that Naverdi's pregnant with an alien being?"

"What do *you* think she's pregnant with?"

Dunne pulled off the rest of the petals and the rose drooped between his fingers, pared down to its knotted core. "I'll tell you what I think, Eve. I've been taking Staze since I joined the Order, and in the Order, we talk about a community of addicts. But up until now, what I've seen in my dream of Red isn't community. It's a cycle of dosage and isolation." He touched the overhang of blossoms. "The drug isn't salvation. It's a method of control, and it's no accident that Staze appeared as the majority of the Meshed were killed or imprisoned. I'm certain we could trace its production to some tiny group of survivors if we tried." He looked up at me. "What's happening in Staze is a miracle in the truest sense. For me to see every addict in the dream of fishes, talking, singing, able to touch each other *while Stazed,* after so many years of being alone . . ." He toed the heap of torn petals. "When the Child put her hand over my heart, everything changed. The old world disappeared. The sedation Staze gives me was gone. I felt a real, honest peace."

"Losing your will to fight isn't *peace*," I said. "Once that's gone, we're *food*."

He shook his head. "I saw the truth when she touched me. Whatever she is, she'll be the foundation of the greatest peace the human race has ever known."

"You're wrong," I whispered.

"And you're afraid, Eve. You're like Queen Red. What the Unknown Child offers is the end of violence and you're afraid of that."

I couldn't think of anything else I could possibly say and he seemed to take my silence as assent. We sat together in the sweet evening perfume of the roses for another long minute and then I got up to go inside.

He followed me to the front of the chapel, where the workers had been joined by a growing crowd of addicts. A few of them squatted on the ground outside the gates, watching as Dunne opened the door for me.

"We'll start the birthing ceremony after dose time," said Dunne. "It won't be long."

Dose time was after sunset and the sun was sinking fast.

I pointed at the stage with its conical roof. "What're you going to make her do?" I demanded. "Have a baby in front of everyone?"

"You take care of your friend," he said. "We'll take care of the Child."

He shut the door behind me.

Nav lay on the floor, awake, knees splayed, breathing hard. Sweat filmed her face and neck. "Where did you go?"

I crouched next to her. "I tried to talk some sense into him."

"I'm in fucking labor," she panted. "Isn't there a fucking doctor?"

"Yeah," I said. "Dunne says there's a doctor."

"He's a lying son of a bitch," said Nav. "This is just a circus for him."

I pulled her close so her head was cradled in my arms. Her pulse pounded in her throat. She was sweaty and hot and cold, all at the same time. She shivered and I pulled the blanket up around her chin.

"Whatever comes out," she whispered, "you have to kill it, Eve. It isn't human. It's not murder."

"I know," I said.

She stared up at the figures painted on the ceiling and squeezed her eyes shut. Tears trickled down her cheeks. "I'm sick of looking at them," she whispered. "They're so goddamn judgmental."

The evening deepened and the light from the chapel windows crept across the image of the Annunciate, turning her robes to scarlet. Outside, the hammering finally stopped as the evening's ration of Staze was dropped off, no doubt by complicitly addicted guards. I expected things to quiet down as soon as the addicts dosed themselves, but after a while, the hammering started again, this time with such speed and intensity, it sounded more like tenor drums.

The chapel door swung open, and a boy no older than five stepped into the room holding a bowl of white cereal mush. Behind him, a cluster of skinny old women pushed each other for a glimpse of the Annunciate.

The gates were open. Dunne had let in the addicts. The faithful, whatever he wanted to call them. They reminded me of the painting in the Sanctuary's virtual gallery, where monsters galloped toward the garden.

The little boy came across the crumbling floor, knelt beside Naverdi, and dipped a spoon into the food.

"Let us feed the Unknown Child," he said to me. The audience, his cherubic face, and the fact that he'd so clearly been coached on what to say made my shoulders ache.

"It isn't the Unknown Child," I said hopelessly.

He gazed at me with an expression I'd seen in addicts far older.

"Please," he said.

The last thing I wanted was a rush of old women cramming mush down Nav's throat in hopes of atonement.

"Not them," I said. "Just you."

Nav let out a moan, but when the spoon touched her lips, she opened her mouth and swallowed it down.

In the doorway, the grannies and nannies muttered their approval.

The little boy put the bowl down, reached into his pocket for a gelatin capsule of Staze, and offered it to her. Nav eyed it dully.

"Isn't that your dose?" I said.

He nodded. "Tonight we're supposed to wait."

"Wait for what?"

"For the testa . . . testam . . . " He squinted, trying to think of the word. "Some people are going to talk," he said finally.

"Testimonials?" I said. "About the . . . the Unknown Child?"

He nodded gravely, gripping the capsule in his fist, as though it took all his will to keep it out of his mouth.

"You saw it—her—in the dream of fishes?" I said.

The boy nodded. "She said I would never have to fight or die—ever—in my whole life. She said she's the end of violence."

He might have been quoting Annmarie. Or Rose.

He got to his feet and picked up the bowl. He touched Nav's hair shyly and walked out of the chapel into the excited cluck and mutter of the women at the door.

As soon as he was gone, a group of younger women pushed through the elderly gaggle. They were as lean and as ravenous as the succubus, and they arranged themselves around me, visibly stressed from the lack of drugs. One pushed lank blonde hair behind her ears, over and over. Another kept her arms stiff, fists clenched. A third had chewed her lips until they bled.

They wanted their Annunciate and I was an obstacle.

"She's very sick," I said, knowing they didn't care. "She's dying."

"We need her," said the one with bloody lips.

The stiff-armed one grabbed me. I yelled and she almost let go. The blonde and the woman with the bitten lips didn't waste time. They scooped Nav up and rushed her out the door, where the grannies and nannies made way for them and then closed ranks against me.

They grabbed me with withered bony hands, holding me, shrieking in hoarse old-woman voices until a huge man with a torn shirt appeared. He clapped a big sweaty palm over my mouth, pinned my arms, and pushed me outside.

Between the chapel's gates and the temple, there were a thousand people. Jammed together, shouting and crying, desperate for Red. The last rays of sunset were just fading and the faces of the needful swarm glowed in shades of dull maroon from distant security floods.

The man pushed me forward until we both had a view of the wooden stage. Whatever the addicts thought they were copying from their vivid new world, the three-sided stage with its conical roof looked like a ramshackle collection of precariously balanced boards. Dead center on the stage was a battered chair with the seat cut out. As I watched, the little boy who'd brought the bowl of mush appeared and knelt to place a pillow directly underneath. A birthing chair. With a cushion for the Unknown Child to drop onto.

On one side of the stage, the crowd began shouting and waving as Nav was dragged through her admirers. I kicked the man who was holding me as hard as I possibly could. He grunted, but his shins were like concrete.

Naverdi's three abductresses clambered up onto the unfinished boards, half-carrying Nav between them. They were at least gentle and eased her into the birthing chair, where everyone could get a good view. They'd taken her clothes and dressed her in a long red gown, which they arranged with great care. Nav struggled to pull herself up straight. She was withered like an old, old woman, well beyond her fertile years but somehow surreally huge with child. What would they do when her part of this event was over? Send her to a hospital with 'the baby' at her breast? Let her crawl away under her own remaining steam? Sing praises over her—*O' Mother, none*—while she hemorrhaged to death?

I squirmed, but the hand over my mouth crept up to block enough of my nose so I could hardly breathe.

Half a dozen men trooped up behind Nav, each with a dirty white plastic bucket. They knelt in an uneven row and turned the buckets upside down. For a second, I had a horrifying vision of the succubus birthing itself, emerging not as the child it wanted to be, but as an unholy combination of grub and baby. These men, I thought wildly, were prepared for that and would whisk the mutant away in a bucket and replace it with something more wholesome before anyone had a good look.

The men with the buckets tapped the bottoms tentatively and a baritone drumming sound echoed between the temple and the chapel, but the abducting midwives waved them into silence. A few of the addicts in front of me peered nervously over their shoulders. It was easy to imagine what would happen if Queen Red noticed that the addicts in this part of the Sanctuary had decided to hold a religious ceremony instead of dosing themselves.

Onstage, a young man, shaved to his scalp, moved into the light. The crowd became absolutely silent.

He cleared his throat. "I've always been an angry person. I've hurt some folks. I even killed one."

Nods all around me. My captor grunted in agreement. His grip felt less focused. If I waited and was still, I could get away.

"I've never been religious, but I've seen her. *Her.*" The young man took a step closer to the edge of the stage, hands pressed over his heart. "I feel different. I can't explain it. She

told me I'd have peace from now on in my life and I *feel* it."
He spread his arms and the chrome plug in his wrist glinted.
"I'll say that to anyone. I'll be a messenger. I'll show them
how to find her."

By throwing a couple of kilos of Staze into a reservoir, I
suspected, if he could get his hands on that much. I had a
sudden dizzying vision of Annmarie and Corey producing Staze
as fast as they could, supplying a demand they couldn't fathom.
Addicts would bring Kevake by the ton to Paradise. Annmarie
and Corey would spew Staze into the equation of need. The
succubus would feed on the slough of addicts and the addicts
would absorb its distorted mythologies until ThreeSys was a
perpetual and circular ecology, just like Paradise.

The crowd cheered. The hand came off my mouth and my
keeper shouted, *"Yeah!"*

His grip on my elbows was sweaty and loose. I slammed
my foot on top of his. He jerked in surprise and I tore away.
He grabbed at my shirt, but I ducked, flinging myself into
the surge of addicts, who paid no attention to the big man
yelling.

I squirmed and shoved between elbows, breathing sweat
and dust and briny air. I plunged through testimonial eddies
as people practiced to each other in shy, confessional tones, or
loud, like gossip. *"I saw HER too, and what SHE told ME
was . . ."*

On the stage, the little boy who'd brought Nav a bowl of
mush stepped forward and said very clearly, "I would die for
the Unknown Child."

Behind him, the men with the buckets started a rumble of
palms on plastic. Dozens of people shoved onto the stage,
jumping and dancing to the half-coherent beat. I struggled
through the dense pack of bodies as the noise echoed between
the chapel and the ramshackle temple.

My clearest plan was no plan at all. I would grab Naverdi
and carry her away. I didn't know where. I didn't even think

I could get her onto her feet, but there was nothing else I could do, except slink off, and I couldn't do that.

I elbowed my way to the right side of the stage and clambered up over rough studs and broken boards with the rest of the addicts, half of them chewing their own fingers with Red need. A haggard old woman pulled me up onto the platform, where the addicts pounded in time with the drums and the rickety wooden floor shook. She yelled something, but I couldn't hear a thing she said. She made motions toward the birthing chair, mouthing instructions, *"Go on! Go on!"*

In the middle of everything, Nav squirmed in agony, pale beyond ash. Offerings of Staze capsules by the dozen littered the wooden boards at her feet. The drummers sweated over their plastic buckets, hands moving faster than I could see. The stage thundered under the dancers, loose construction adding baritone to plastic percussion. The noise was deafening. I stood still, dry in the mouth, jaws clenched hard enough to hurt. I could have shouted out my entire life's story. No one would've heard.

Somebody touched my arm. I turned to see Dunne sweating in his cassock.

"I couldn't hear what you were saying," he shouted in my ear.

"I haven't said anything yet," I shouted back.

"Take your time," he said. "When you're finished, we'll pray."

"Pray for what?" I yelled.

"For the name of the Child." He pointed and I turned to see Nav, hands wire-tight on the arms of the chair, gasping with effort and pain. Her grim, needful team of midwives surrounded her and there was already a bloody puddle on the pillow.

"It's started!" shouted Dunne. "I don't want to rush you, but we're running out of time." He gave me an encouraging smile. "Say what you need to say."

Over the noise, over everything, the night air vibrated with a chorus of voices, rich and translucent, a dense tonality inside my chest, resonant with salt and body heat.

Ma-ka-LI-ma
ka-LI-ma-ka
LI-ma-ka-LI
ma-ka-LI-ma

The name they wanted was hidden in the song, broken into parts, dispersed and disguised, like grubs and moss and yellow fungus. Like me, Annmarie, and Corey. I stood there, wanting to scream out everything I knew about the beginnings and ends of things. The Jackless, Jacked, and Meshed—all of ThreeSys— on the verge of being distilled by the succubus to our basic elements. In the deafening roar of voices, I could have told them what they really needed to know about balanced ecologies and the mathematical codependence of predator and prey.

Ma-ka-LI-ma
ka-LI-ma-ka
LI-ma-ka-LI
ma-ka-LI-ma

I turned to the seething audience of addicts, their bodies a rhythm of motion, more articulate than I could ever hope to be. At the foot of the stage, mothers shouted *MA-ka-li-MA* and shoved their wailing children up on the splintered boards so they would be witnesses to the new world the second it dropped out of Nav's body. A man with scars all over his face masturbated into the crowd. A woman tore at her clothes, shrieking in a wordless frenzy. I stood on the trembling planks, too frightened to watch anymore. There was nothing I could say to make any of this change. Let the succubus birth itself. Let these people have it.

I closed my eyes.

And found myself in Mesh.

The addicts swayed in front of me, infested head to foot with Sanctuary 'gats long forgotten or ignored by Queen Red and her cronies.

I expected the vision to hollow into the succubus's imitation, but it *was* the Mesh. The Sanctuary's tactical schematics laced the air. Addicts shimmered, gleaming scarlet in their need. The sky opened to me, revealing orbital paths of ships and shuttles.

I was everywhere. In everything. And now I could hear the way the Name really sounded.

Kali-ma
Kali-ma
Kali-ma

I turned, expecting to see the Mesh version of the succubus attempting to birth itself. Instead, I saw Nav laid out in schema. Nav turning blue from lack of air as she tried to exhale the thing from her body. Nav with her arms flung out, fists clenched, legs kicking, crowned with light. Nav thrashing so hard that her limbs blurred to a half-dozen afterimages.

Not Nav.

The succubus.

She spun in front of me, lushly female, blue as sky, a hundred arms spread in a nimbus around her numberless heads, a hundred legs poised to dance. A necklace of tiny human skulls swung against her blue breasts. A skirt of human arms rippled along her thighs. She was immense and delicate, disorienting and huge—thousands of her, overlapping into infinity, like an open book of mirrors.

She turned her beautiful, terrifying eyes on me.

I've named myself, she said.

Kali-ma, I echoed.

It's a good choice, said the succubus, as though she wanted my approval. *I found its definition in your Mesh. Shall I explain it to you?*

She was teeth and tongue. Inescapably huge. She smelled of scorched dirt.

I am Kali, the Beautiful One. Kali, the Destroyer. I am Kali-ma, the Dark Mother, older than the Annunciate, more ancient and powerful than the first woman.

A threat. Or admiration. I couldn't tell from the endless reflections of her faces.

I am the physical, the spiritual and the virtual, said the succubus, but I could have sworn she was quoting from somewhere. *The beginning and the end of the world.*

In real time, under the shouting addicts, I could hear an ominous, keening wail, which sounded like Queen Red's sirens. Nav writhed in childbirth while the addicts surged at her feet. The minute the grub-baby dropped, they would abandon her, and the succubus could not have cared less.

I am birth, life, and death, said the succubus, oblivious to everything.

You don't know about any of those things, I whispered.

She stared at me with her hundreds of eyes and despite the necklace of heads and the skirt of arms, her vulnerabilities were painfully obvious. She was naïve enough to trust me. *Mother Eve . . .*

I'm not your mother, I said. *How could I be? You're an alien. You've had an accidental encounter with an invasive technology and an addictive drug. That doesn't make me your mother and it certainly doesn't make you a goddess.*

Her long red tongue darted out in a nervous motion.

You're a genetic anomaly. A parentless organism. I pointed at the addicts. *It won't take long for them to figure out you're not the Unknown Child.*

I will be born, declared the succubus.

Go ahead, I said. *We'll preserve you and study you. We'll keep you in a . . . a . . .* Jar, I wanted to say. A green glass jar, like the one in Annmarie's kitchen. The one filled with wormwood.

I will grow up on my own, whispered the succubus.

You don't know how, I said, more afraid of the words coming out of my mouth than I was of her. *I'm going to show everyone what you are.*

They know what I am.

You told them a story they want to believe, I said. *That's nothing.*

Her faces twitched like I'd slapped her. A hundred tears seeped out from the corners of her beautiful eyes. A hundred blue hands came up to brush the tears away.

I turned to the addicts. In real time, seconds had passed. Dunne still hovered somewhere to the left, waiting for me to speak up, ready to lead his masses in prayer as soon as the succubus clawed free of Naverdi's womb. I wouldn't have to speak. I only had to think. The propagats would do the rest.

I focused on the 'gats and felt them lean into my intentions.

The addicts felt it, too. Their wild, slow motion dance came to an uneven halt. The singing died away. Behind me, the drummers crouched over their plastic buckets.

In Mesh, I made the silence visible—a darkness like cupped hands, covering the stage, the chapel, and everyone in between.

From inside the succubus's vast interface, I showed them the beginning of things: the shape and form and hidden sense of Paradise. Indigo sky, ebony cairns, the ruins of ancient cities and blackwater pools. I laid in the slimy fringes of moss and the behemoth rising of the first grub in the shadow of the Medusa, showed them my *piscae,* turned to gray rags and the grubs floating with them. I showed them everything.

Staze caking in cold water.

The succubus, and how it'd manifested in Mesh.

Naverdi, and what was in her belly.

The insatiable hungers of the Unknown Child.

I showed them the *Kali* she'd named herself after; the Name pared down to its definition in Mesh, blue-faced and ravenous, sensual and soft, an ancient goddess with her arms stretched across the sky, Kali-ma, descending as a hawk among pigeons.

Hail! I said inside the mind of every Staze-hungry addict. *Here is the new world.*

I opened my eyes. I could hear Nav gulping and panting in labor. In the distance, a siren warbled over a low rumble, which I thought was the sea. No one was moving in the audience, and the silence between me and the chapel was thick as paste.

Father Dunne rubbed his eyes and came to me across the creaking stage. He reached over to touch me, then changed his mind. "That was you?" he said. "But that was Mesh."

It didn't matter that he knew. Now everyone knew. It only mattered that I'd planted a doubt.

Wind ruffled his thin white hair. He frowned past me at Naverdi. "She said she was the end of violence."

"She's not," I whispered. "She's the end of everything."

Over by the chapel, the rumbling was closer, deeper. Someone let out a surprised yell. Dunne and I turned in the direction of the sound in time to see two immense troop vehicles grinding over the chapel's iron fences, burying the roses. One had a cannon turret and as it swung toward the stage, it crushed the chapel's dome like the top of an egg.

Someone screamed and the silent wake of Mesh dissolved.

Soldiers piled out of the carrier and rushed into the crowd. One figure in a glittering uniform—unmistakably Queen Red—climbed to the top of the vehicle and stood there making wide rallying gestures.

Addicts rushed past the stage, away from the chapel, down the hill toward the wire fences and blue tarp tents. Dunne leaped forward, waving his arms for attention. I grabbed Nav and tried to get her onto her feet. She was heavy as a stone, too weak to lift herself. I tried to position myself under her arms, but I was hurting her and she started to cry.

Dunne shouted for the addicts to come to him, bellowed at the soldiers to *stop*. I turned in time to see him leap off the stage, cassock flying. The last I saw of him was his outspread arms and balding head as he fought his way toward blue flashes of gunfire.

"I can't move." Nav grabbed my hands and held on. "You have to go."

Bitter smoke drifted across the stage. More horrified shrieks and the smell of burned skin. Dozens of addicts lay dead on the ground. The rest were fighting, or trying to. There were more blue flashes, which left glaring afterimages inside my eyelids and, when those cleared, more bodies.

"Run," said Nav. "I can't. You have to *go*."

Her grip was just as tight as ever. She didn't mean what she was saying. It occurred to me that she'd never meant anything she'd ever said to me.

Soldiers came toward the stage, hunkered over their guns. They stepped on the bodies like they were part of the landscape. Not a woman's arm, but a dead branch. Not a little boy, just a soft place in the ground. There was a second when I thought they might not have seen us. Then one of them pointed at us and raised his weapon. I had time to believe that this man would never shoot if he knew anything about the Mesh.

Naverdi let go of my hand. I heard her yell out in fear.

I closed my eyes.

Propagats everywhere. In the dirt, bright with detail, swarming through the carrier vehicle where Queen Red shaded her eyes against the floodlights.

'Gats in the volatile mechanisms of their guns.

I didn't have to study how it should happen. Just willed it, and in Mesh, electronic safeguards failed on every weapon in the compound.

The soldier who had us in his sights gave an agonized cry as his weapon erupted into his face. I threw myself across Nav as flaming bits of gun landed all around us.

Soldiers ran screaming, falling over the bodies of the addicts, their clothes and hair burning. Gritty smoke blew across the stage, stinking of plastic and flesh and wood. I slapped away sparks from the wooden birthing chair and Nav's clothes. Small but respectable fires caught here and there on the stage's wooden planks and licked up from the plastic bucket drums.

Naverdi braced herself and together we managed to heave her to the edge of the seat. Another heave and she was on her knees on the rough splintery stage. She crouched there, stark and bloated, quaking as a languid tongue of fire rose to ignite the stage's wooden roof. I wondered if the succubus had any conception of fleeing for its life.

Nav yanked on my sleeve. "*Do* it!"

"What?" I caught her arms, thinking I could twist underneath and carry her, but she yelled again.

"Tell it to come out *now*. I can't move! Tell it how it's going to *die*."

I took a breath of smoke and plunged into Mesh. The succubus was waiting, spread like a fan. Around us, the fire and mayhem slowed to the pace of a painted landscape, framed with streamers of smoke, rippling with heat I couldn't feel in Mesh.

You want to be born? I shrieked. *Get out of her now! You understand?*

The succubus shook her heads. *You'll leave me.*

Behind it, a torpid ball of fire bloomed upward and the stage's conical roof spiraled gently with flame. Nav crouched in terror at my feet. Smoke rose from her smoldering hair. The last thing I was going to see would be her face stretched in agony, gasping, blistering as her clothes caught fire. The last thing I was going to feel was my own panic.

I grabbed the succubus by its nearest arm. *You're going to die if you don't do something!*

Mother Eve, said the succubus, as if I was the one who didn't understand. *I'll be alive long after you're gone.*

Hot white fire rushed up between us. I yelled and let go and opened my eyes in a veil of black smoke. I flailed for Naverdi, expecting the heat to scorch my lungs, but the smoke was vaguely moist, and cooler. Not like fire. I'd passed out, I thought, without saying goodbye to Naverdi, without a chance to apologize for whatever part I'd had in killing us both.

I groped in the dark, expecting burning, splintered boards, but what I found instead was a half-frozen thickness. The hot white flame widened, cool and enveloping, until it phosphorized into a blinding distance. I felt the stage give way to nothingness, felt myself falling. The brightness opened into stomach-wrenching emptiness, like a tear in an airtight container. Sickening and familiar.

Like being yanked across Paradise.

I wanted to yell with relief. The succubus had plucked us from the fire. It was going to *save* us, after everything I'd said, and all of Naverdi's threats. I twisted, trying to find Nav, but there was no direction and I might as well have been staring at the insides of my own eyelids. It *would* save her, I told myself, at least long enough to drop out of her body. I tried to imagine it emerging as a normal human child, but the only image I could come up with was an ugly grayish infant with a maggoty face and tail. It seemed funny in spite of everything and I heard myself giggle hysterically as I fell at breakneck speed toward the jagged stones of Paradise.

ELEVEN

"Eve!"

I opened my eyes in a panic, staring up at the night sky.

There was no fire.

Nav shrieked again. I sat up and found her writhing on her back, speckled with ash, fingers clenched deep in warm sand, the red dress bunched up at her waist. Watery blood smeared her thighs.

"Eve!" she screamed with more strength than I thought she had. "Mesh with it!" She surged up on her elbows, sweaty and furious. "Make it *leave!*"

I crouched beside her with no idea what I was supposed to do. Of course the succubus had brought us "home" to Paradise. We were in the middle of a bright oasis of sand; an island in the freezing dark. A glassine shimmer separated us from the ancient ruins, but except for that, we might have been in the middle of my Mesh environment.

Her face pinched up in desperate agony and she rolled back and forth in the sand, pounding her own abdomen with both fists.

I couldn't watch that. I shut my eyes.

Waited for the vast weightless entry to the greater Mesh.
Waited.

Took a breath and made myself concentrate as Nav let out
another bellow, but there was nothing. No Mesh. Not even
the succubal 'net.' It felt like a door had been nailed shut.

"*Help* me!" she yelled. "You're not *helping*!"

I crawled between her legs and grabbed her knees. She
grunted and more reddish fluid surged out of her vagina. I
edged backward to see if anything else was visible. She felt it
when I moved and wrapped her bare legs around my waist.

"You're not leaving!" she shrieked. "Don't even think it!"

"Damn it," I yelled back. "If I was going to leave, don't
you think I would have left already?"

"You *couldn't*. I wouldn't *let* you. Your *sheltered* little
life . . ." She gasped for air. "And that's what you've had, you
know. Annmarie made sure you never learned *anything*. . . ."
She arched her back and wailed. More blood, and this time
something more solid.

"Push!" I yelped. "I can see it!"

She was sobbing now, fingers daggered into the sand, feet
splayed out. I knelt between her legs, practically wringing my
hands, not knowing what was right or wrong or dangerous.

"Push!" I shouted.

She shoved and howled and the top of a bloody little head
crowned out of her body. A forehead. Squinched-shut little
eyes. I wanted to reach in and grab it and pull, but I was scared
to death to touch it.

"Push!" I screamed instead.

The wrinkled rest of its face came out, stippled in blood,
half-veiled in mucus. Tiny lips. A chin.

Nav heaved up in agony and the motion was enough to
force out the rest. The grub child slid into my hands, hot and
wet and slick, so thin that every rib stood out. It—she—the
grubby baby—was unmistakably female, squirming at the end
of a scarlet umbilical. I wiped away the mucous, coaxed her

mouth open, and she let out a sticky cry. Nav dropped back onto the sand, gasping.

I couldn't stop staring. She was so small. Barely twice the size of the grub it had been to begin with. She wriggled and breathed, and I could feel the live pulses of her body.

"It looks human," I said. "It's a girl."

I thought Nav wanted to see. I raised it up so she could get a clear view. She stared, dry lips opening and closing. Sand stuck to the tears and trails of sweat on her face.

"Eve," she whispered, and I could hear her tongue sticking to the roof of her mouth. "You have to kill it."

"Oh," I said. "No. It saved us from the fire."

"It's a monster," she hissed. "It only wanted to save itself." Her head lolled to one side and her eyes closed. I leaned over her, the grubby, bloody baby in the crook of my arm, and grabbed her wrist, afraid she was dying. Instead of a pulse, all I could feel was the warm metal of the Jack, planted between tendons. I put my hand on her chest and found her heartbeat, fast and hard, like a runner at the end of a long, exhausting race. I kept my hand there, awkwardly crouched, with the grub child cradled in my other arm. I was afraid to move, thinking if I did, they would both die.

But they didn't. The baby felt warm and Nav's heart beat steadily. Her belly sagged, still bloated, but not painfully distended. If not for the blood, she might have been asleep on a beach somewhere. If not for me, kneeling between her knees with a weakly squirming infant. Finally I took my hand away and sat cross-legged on the ground.

The tiny convincing creature wriggled against me. I could feel it concentrating on the flow of air and blood and lymph, the electricity between nerves. Its umbilical, red as Staze, looped stiffly from between Nav's legs. Afterbirth, I thought. Placenta. There was more I should do, but I didn't know what, and it seemed wrong to wake Nav just to make her more uncomfortable.

I wondered how long we were supposed to stay here. The

grubby, bloody baby was making silent *wah-wah-wah* motions with its mouth. It was hungry, but unless Annmarie and Corey had been sowing Paradise with Red, once the umbilical was cut, its only physical conduit for Staze would be gone. Could it really stay connected to every addict in ThreeSys through its own virtual spaces and thrive on a diet of second-hand Staze? Or would it have to find a different way to feed?

What if it couldn't?

Was it my job to lay it against Naverdi's breast to nurse?

As if she would have let it touch her.

I stared out into the dawnish twilight of Paradise, at the glint of distant pools, and wondered if I should just put the grub child into the nearest murky pond and let it find a new symbiosis with its old body.

Something moved outside our desert bubble. A darting motion across the indigo sky.

Not birdlike. More confined. Fishlike.

It cut under a swath of purple cloud and landed on the stones just outside our fishbowl bubble. It wasn't wearing a helmet, just goggles.

Corey. He unbound himself, kicked off his fins, and trotted over to the edge of our bubble. He tested the airy membrane with a finger. It went through without an effort or a tear.

"God *damn*," he said. "Look what it learned to do."

He came inside, careful not to kick sand. He peered at what I was holding and then at Naverdi.

"God *damn*," he said again. He unzipped his suit and pulled out a sterile glove, a couple of torn towels, and a plastic bag of what seemed to be milk.

"How did you know we were here?" I said.

"Same way I knew you were at the Sanctuary," he said and spared a glance at Nav. "Fatherly intuition." He held out a clean strip of towel and tried to take the grub child, but I edged away from him. He tried not to act disappointed. "You made good time from Isla without a ship," he said. "How'd you manage that?"

I ignored him.

"It'll tell me, you know." He nodded at the grub child.

"Then maybe you should ask her," I said.

He straightened, theatrically affronted. "I'm here to save your neck, Eve. There's no need to be hostile."

"I'm not being hostile," I said. "Where's Annmarie? Did she fall for that trick with the tea again?"

He gave me his most serious, most wronged look and changed the subject. "The Mesh isn't working."

"I noticed."

"Do you know why?"

"No," I said. "And I don't think you do, either."

"That's what's doing it." He pointed to the baby. "It's hiding."

"From what?"

He raised an eyebrow. "From Annmarie."

"Oh, yeah?" I said, but I hardly needed an explanation. Corey was hiding from Annmarie. So was I.

He bent to examine the drying umbilical. "This has to be cut." He took a sterile-sleeved knife out of his pocket.

"She'll die if you cut it," I said, but he shook his head.

"This thing is so *connected*. It's everywhere. The grubs and moss are one manifestation. This *baby* is another. It has a presence in spaces we can't even describe. It's more than an alien. It's like a *god*. It doesn't need her." He meant Nav. He made a quick, nervous motion with the blade. The umbilical dropped between Nav's thighs like a dead snake.

Corey knotted what was left clumsily against the grubby belly and shook out the towel. "Give it to me."

"No," I said.

He made an impatient noise in his throat and coughed to hide the sound. He put the towel down and poured the milk into the sterile glove. He pricked the thumb so that the milk beaded out and offered it to me. "Don't hold it like that. It's not a serving dish. You have to . . ." He made cradling motions.

I adjusted my grip and he nodded. He gave me one of the towels and I wrapped her in it. He gave me the glove and I dribbled milk across the grub child's lips. She stared out of dark filmy eyes, not sucking or swallowing. The milk ran down her neck and into the towel.

"No mammalian instincts whatsoever," mused Corey. "Or maybe it doesn't need to eat?"

"She," I said. "It's a girl. And it isn't a mammal. She just looks like one."

He grinned. "Have you thought of a name?" It was the same tone he'd used to needle me about my nameless *piscae*.

I wondered if he knew anything about the addicts and their holy applications of Staze. "Kali-ma," I said. "Someone suggested Kali-ma."

"Kalima," he said and chucked her under her tiny chin. "Pretty name! Pretty girl!"

I half-expected her to rear up and bite him.

He lowered his voice as though we could confide in each other. "I might as well tell you. Annmarie found out about your friend's 'pregnancy.' She tried to duplicate it."

What we'd seen from the ceiling of the drive bay through the succubus's vision. "I'll bet anything it didn't work," I said, already knowing I was right.

"She tried all sort of things. Insertions, injections, immersions." He touched the baby's forehead, still making sure she was real. "There should have been another 'merging.' Our results were just . . ."

"Your results were food," I said.

He nodded and glanced at Nav, wasted in her face and arms, consumed from the inside out. I could see him trying to decide how much I knew, and how much I might be guessing.

"It doesn't want to merge with us," I said. "It wants to eat us. Like the yellow fungus. Like my fish. It's a predator and it's adapting to a new kind of prey. I'm holding its eyes and ears. Maybe even its mouth."

That made him think. He'd been edging closer, bit by bit.

Now he gave himself more distance. I tried to come up with
something that would scare him enough to run away and leave
us alone.

"There was one thing we didn't try with our, ah, subjects,"
he said. "We were so focused on finding a workable genetic
mix, we forgot how the virtual aspect of the grubs and moss
introduced itself to you."

The succubus, he meant. "It *bit* me."

He nodded. "What do you think would have happened if
you'd bitten it back?"

I frowned at the grub child.

" 'Man bites dog,' " he said and gave me a strange smile.
"Or maybe 'woman bites dog' is more accurate. The dog's so
shocked, it runs for its life."

"I should've attacked the succubus?"

"If you had, Paradise would be our place right now, and
that"—he raised an eyebrow at the baby—"would still be an
anomaly in Mesh." He rubbed his knees. "*That* is a *lot* bigger
than we are, Eve. Annmarie says it's at the top of the entire
cosmic food chain. She's going to change that."

"How?"

"Think about it," said Corey. "How does Annmarie handle
anything bigger and more powerful than she is?"

I had an astonishingly clear vision of Annmarie and the
succubus, face-to-face in the ruins of Paradise. No matter how
big the succubus was, or how old or confident, Annmarie could
find a way to make it feel insignificant and useless.

"Annmarie's taking steps to stay in charge," said Corey.
"You know how she is."

"Taking steps?"

"Biting back." He made a squeamish motion with his
mouth.

"Biting *what* back?"

"She's showing your succubus who's boss," he said. His
voice actually shook.

"What's she *doing*?"

"Annmarie's on the Medusa, eating grubs," said Corey.

"*Eating* them?"

He nodded. He'd been a rotten actor for as long as I'd known him. An accomplished liar, yes, but this was well beyond his normal machinations. He looked genuinely scared to me.

He started to get up. "We can get away. There's another ship. It's just a Jackless transport, but it has a nanoviral program."

Annmarie would kill him if she found him escaping alone. He needed hostages: human, alien, or a combination of both. He reached for me to help me to my feet. I pushed his hands away.

"I'm not leaving without Nav."

He eyed her. She groaned, awake enough to understand what was going on.

"She won't last," said Corey.

He would have left her to rot. I wanted to kick him. "Then I'm staying here."

He hesitated. "You can stay. She can stay. But the baby's coming with me."

"Like hell," I said.

He squatted next to Nav and put the scalpel blade of the sterile knife against her throat.

I stared at him, open-mouthed, not sure if I would scream or throw up if I tried to tell him how disgusting he was.

"It's your call, Eve," he said. "Come along if you want. We might even need each other one of these days, but I don't have time to argue."

"Get *away* from her!"

He held out his free hand. I clung to the grubby, bloody baby. If I refused to leave, he'd work up the nerve to cut Nav's throat and then attack me with his little knife. He'd take what he wanted and Nav would die anyway.

I gave him the grub child. He lurched to his feet, backing away with her through the glassine separation between us and the rest of Paradise. He couldn't fly and hold the baby, but he could run. He took two long strides away from the little bubble of air and light, ready to run for his life.

"Corey!" I yelled after him. "If I tell that thing to tear your fucking heart out, it will!"

He didn't say a word, but he did stop.

I helped Nav sit up. She slumped forward and the motion of her body forced out the afterbirth. It lay between her legs, gray and paper-thin, as though the grub had shed an entire version of itself to take on human form. I managed to sling her across my shoulders and staggered across the warm blood-speckled sand, draped in her dead weight.

Outside the bubble, the air was thin, but not so insubstantial that I thought I'd suffocate. It was cold, though, and the sweat under my arms felt like trickles of ice. Nav's ribs grated across my spine, hot ridges compared to the rest of her cooling bones. Her uneven breathing went *huh-huh-huh* as I slogged between piles of debris and blackwater pools. Grubbish bodies broke the surface, taking note, I was sure, of our speed and direction.

Corey rushed ahead, clinking through shale and gravel. I couldn't see him half the time, but at least I could hear him. I knew more or less where we were; climbing the planet's central rill toward the ruins of a city. The broken skyline was the same one we could see from the Medusa, but now Corey and I were coming from the opposite side. As I labored up through loose stones, I caught a glimpse of basalt plains stretching to the horizon, punctuated by an island of light. That was the Medusa and the lights were Corey's halogen forest.

He waited at the top of the rill in the shadow of one skewed wall.

"Where's the other ship?" I panted.

"Over there." He pointed, but I couldn't see anything except black stone and craters. It occurred to me that he was lying about the ship. But then he would have been lying about everything, from Annmarie eating grubs—which I had no problem believing—to his own plans for escape. The only thing he needed to do was to get rid of me and Nav. As I swayed under her weight at the top of the rill, I knew he would take us down the narrowest, most dangerous path he could find. I would fall and he would flee to the Jackless ship with Kalima, the only piece of Paradise Annmarie couldn't put into her mouth.

"Wait," I said as he started to move off. "I can't breathe."

He shuffled nervously. "We can't stop. She's looking for us."

For you, I thought. If Annmarie knew Nav and I were here, she would've put off her dinner plans. Instantaneous interplanetary travel was far more appetizing than grub, no matter who was boss.

Nav moaned as I shifted under her weight. Her hands clenched feebly at the air. She needed her dose. Nothing else would bring her back from the dead.

"Is there Staze on the ship?"

"Of course there's Staze." Corey stopped fidgeting and frowned at the baby in his arms. "It's an addict, too."

"Obviously," I said. "She's been feeding off Nav and—" *And every other addict in ThreeSys.* I stopped before I could say it. "Did you tell Annmarie about the Staze you spilled?"

He blinked with glib innocence. "What? Of *course* I did."

But he hadn't.

And then I understood why he hadn't left already.

If Annmarie was eating grubs, she was dosing herself with Staze.

It might not be a big dose, or a pure one. She was swallowing what was left after the grubs had absorbed their portion, which put Annmarie *way* down on the Staze chain, but Corey obviously thought it was enough to keep her stone-still until he—and we—were gone.

I bowed over the sharp stones. Annmarie, Stazed. I tried to picture it. How much *happier* she would've been in a beautiful place. How much happier *I* would have been if she'd spent half her time there.

But Staze wasn't the trap Corey thought it was—not anymore. Would Annmarie have the dream of fishes and follow the addicts to Kalima's temple? How long would it take for her to realize that Staze—*her* weapon, *her* tool—had been appropriated by the succubus? And how would she feel, standing in my desert, surrounded by addicts from every rung of the social ladder, when she figured out that the upshot of addiction was a virtual common ground between Jack and Jackless and Mesh?

The grub child let out a muffled squall. I looked around for Corey and didn't see him. I stumbled in the direction of the noise, still carrying Nav, and dropped to my knees at the crumbling edge of the rill. The baby howled again, a thinner, more distant sound.

Below, Corey scrambled through runnels of loose gravel. There was no way I could follow him with Nav, and no way I was going to leave her. I knelt there, heart pounding so hard I was afraid I would start bawling out of sheer panic.

Nav stirred across my shoulders. I slid her onto the ground, trying to be gentle, and let her slump against a cold boulder.

"What's happening . . . ?" She huddled into herself. "What're we doing up here?"

"Corey took the baby." I could still see him, loping between boulders, heading away from the lights of the Medusa at an oblique angle. "And Annmarie ate . . . Annmarie took Staze." I wanted to tell her everything. I wanted her to shout at me, *'Go after him! What're you waiting for?'*

Instead, she rubbed her eyes like she was dreaming. "So much for her."

"She'll find out what's going on in Staze," I said.

Nav let out a hoarse laugh. "She'll beat the crap out of your succubus."

She was right. I could picture it. In Staze-Jack-Mesh, she'd throw Kalima down the temple stairs. She'd kick and bite until the succubus gave in to whatever she wanted.

Nav touched the sticky smears of blood on her legs as though she'd forgotten what had happened. "Corey took that—*thing*. Didn't he?"

I nodded.

"Let him have it." She sounded relieved.

I slumped on the stones, huddled between her and the wind. "He'll use her to control Annmarie," I whispered. "He'll make her work for him and she'll learn from that. She's like a weapon, or a tool."

"He'll kill it," she said. "Or Annmarie will. They'll all kill each other, Eve, and then we can get on with our lives." The solution seemed to satisfy her. She leaned against me and her breathing became calm and slow against my neck. "All we have to do is wait."

I held on to her, trying to keep her warm but feeling her body lag as the cold crept in. Corey and the grub child vanished in the distance and I watched them go, knowing that if I hauled Nav onto my back again, she would die in jolting agonies long before I reached the plains.

Maybe Nav was right. In the long run, what difference did it make who controlled a bunch of useless addicts? Annmarie? Corey? Or a seductive alien who saw ThreeSys as an endless meal? Nav wouldn't survive to suffer the consequences and I could leave the costs and benefits of Staze behind forever.

I put my cheek against her scorched hair, stroking the brittle dreads. She seemed weightless, almost insubstantial. I touched her face. She quivered, as if something in a dream had surprised her. And then she was gone.

Really gone.

No warning sound. No disturbance in the cold night. Just not there anymore, like a light turned off.

Nothing left but the burnt scent of her hair.

I shoved myself to my feet, alone in the ruins at the top of the rill.

"Naverdi!" My voice echoed between the sharp naked rocks and the ruins of ancient buildings, screechy and amazed. I ran back and forth, as if she could've crawled away. I scrambled to the top of the highest, most unsteady pile of rubble I could find and hopped around like a crazy woman, screaming her name.

"Nav!"

Nav!

The echo was thin and mocking. I made myself stop, tricked or blindly stupid. The succubus had done this. It'd been listening every time Nav had said, "Kill it." In a final act of self-preservation, it'd thrown her into a pool full of hungry grubs.

I squeezed my eyes shut in utter desperation, but there was nothing.

I slid down the heap of rubble, found the trail Corey'd followed down to the plain, and plunged after him through loose shale, cutting my hands, bruising my knees. I came to the bottom, panting, and fled after Corey at a dead run, the glimmer of light from the Medusa just visible to my left.

Annmarie eating grubs. I pounded along, trying to imagine that. Was she sitting in the crew room with a fork and knife, transfixed by Staze, or was the drug so diluted in the contaminated grubs, all she would feel was a tingle of calculated pleasures? I couldn't decide if I was outraged that Corey'd let her poison herself with such offhand ease, or angry that I hadn't thought of dosing her myself.

The ground flattened, less rocky, with fewer pools for me to trip into. I kept looking for Naverdi as I ran, certain she was drowning, or freezing where the succubus had left her. But maybe that was wrong, giving the succubus credit for understanding revenge. Nav might be safe, dropped onto the Jackless shuttle, well ahead of Corey, well ahead of me. Maybe this was a roundabout alien way of asking for company. Or family. Two mommies and a dad. The only arrangement which might be more dysfunctional would be a Medusa family reunion. If a family was what the succubus wanted, I told myself, it would have sucked me away with Nav.

The ground smoothed under my feet. Rubble heaps scattered into gravel. I slowed down, sweating in the icy air, abruptly aware that I had no idea where Corey might have gone. The glow of the Medusa's lights were a long way behind me. I was on part of the basalt plain I didn't remember seeing before, and the ground was smooth to the point of being almost featureless, like a slab of black ice. There wasn't a grub-filled pool in sight. The only thing I could see was one round little rock. I trotted over to it, thinking Corey might have dropped something. As soon as I saw what it was, I let out a yell.

An apple. It lay on the ground, red as a beacon, perfect and shiny and bizarre.

The same piece of fruit from the first time I'd come through Rose's virtual gates?

At least this time I knew what the message was.

I turned and looked behind me. In the distance, the crumbling ruins of human habitation stretched to the horizon. The Paradise of our perceptions. In the opposite direction, beyond the border marked by the apple, was the succubus's weird blending of realities. Here, featureless and smooth. Farther ahead . . . it was difficult to say. I was certain the separation wasn't visible from orbit. But it was here. And I could go on, or turn back.

I skirted the apple and started walking.

The landscape got flatter and flatter. Even the curve of the horizon went flat and when I looked over my shoulder, the ruins were out of sight. I kept going. There was no way to judge distance or direction, and after a while, I felt no bigger than an insect on a sheet of paper. I slogged along, expecting to see Corey. If the succubus had any sense of strategy, it'd have him running in circles until I found him.

Or maybe I was the one walking in circles. I stopped in the smooth blankness.

"Show me where you are," I said to the empty air and waited.

Nothing happened, as far as I could tell. I turned, feeling stupid, and under that, hopelessly lost, and then I saw a gleam in the distance. I started toward it.

The gleam solidified into a stretch of white walls. Closer, I could see a familiar archway draped with blossoms. Closer still, the scent of flowers crystallized in the chill air.

I stopped and squinted at the all-too-solid illusion, close enough to hear the music of the fiesta.

The only reason I was here was because the succubus needed help. Mother Eve to the rescue. But if the succubus could break the barriers between virtual and real, and mix up Jack and Mesh and Staze into one coherent vision, how much help did it need? So what if Annmarie killed every grub on Paradise? Wasn't the succubus's "greater aspect" great enough to survive that? So what if it lost its capacity to manifest in everybody else's vision—was that such a loss? The temptation to let it fend for itself washed over me, and I would have run in the other direction, except for the blinding image in my mind of Annmarie, bloated on a diet of grubs and moss, emerging from the temple in Staze to declare herself Goddess of Everything.

I ducked under the heavy swag of flowers and went into the plaza.

At first, I thought nothing had changed. The fountain sparkled and splashed. The two vendor women chopped vegetables, wrapped them in dough, and tossed them in hot grease, but this time the drunken dancers swayed to a drumbeat which sounded like plastic buckets, and underneath, familiar lyrics.

Tether now the outflung star . . .

Some of the faces were familiar, but they weren't the people I expected. When the woman in stiletto heels turned, she looked like Doctor Rose. The children trailing colored streamers . . . didn't I know them from the orphans' dorm?

I stepped into the courtyard. Beyond the plaza, a curtain billowed from an open window over a balcony. A girlish cry of pain drifted with the scent of flowers. I hurried across the cobblestones and went up the winding staircase where the succubus had taken me the first time.

Eve, said Annmarie from where she was sitting on the bed. *I knew you'd come.*

She was unfocused and out of proportion, as though she hadn't quite mastered the details of appearance in this new environment. Her head and hair and mouth were bigger than they should have been.

The succubus sat beside her. This time it wasn't spread out in multiple images. Its grisly necklace and skirt were gone, and it was crying, naked, and bleeding from its left hand where the thumb and forefinger were missing. It looked scared and incomplete. Most obviously missing was its outrageous self-confidence.

Annmarie patted the mattress where she wanted me to sit. *I was just having a little heart-to-heart with your friend.*

I moved closer but didn't sit. I knew what she was doing. Back on the Medusa, she was gnawing grubs; a physical assault on the succubus. Here, in the arcane combination of Staze and Mesh, she would browbeat it into submission. A two-pronged assault.

The succubus held out its bleeding hand so I could see and burst into fresh tears. *She bit me.*

It serves you right, said Annmarie. *Eve should've bitten you.* She stroked the succubus's hair, but eyed me. *If she'd told me the truth about you in the beginning I would have bitten you. We could have avoided a great deal of trouble.*

The succubus just whimpered.

What if it bites you back? I said.

Annmarie shook her head. *It doesn't understand how to turn and attack. Its instinctive paradigm is 'eat or assimilate' not 'fight or flight.' It's not very smart, but it seems to be learning. I don't think I'll have to hurt it much more.*

The succubus gave me a look of confused misery. *What is 'fight'?*

See? said Annmarie. *It's not capable of the concept. It's never had enemies. It can't learn to fight any more than humans can learn to assimilate other organisms through selective digestion— to eat without eating. We don't even have words for it.*

I felt sick to my stomach. Annmarie raised an eyebrow at me, wolfishly frightening in her present distortion.

It's not very articulate, she said. *When I ask questions, it always says the same thing. Watch.* She took the succubus's bleeding hand. *You brought Eve and Naverdi here without a ship. How did you manage that?*

I'm everywhere, said the succubus, as if that was enough of an explanation, then moaned as its middle and ring fingers vanished.

Well? Annmarie said to me. *Can you explain how you got here?*

I shook my head and fought the urge to check my own fingers.

Annmarie squeezed the succubus's hand until the creature groaned. *Speculate for me, Eve.*

I think it's like a giant collection of propagats, I said. *Different parts of it exist in different spaces and I guess it can move physical objects like the 'gats move information.*

Annmarie pushed a lock of hair behind the succubus's delicate ear. *You're not limited to four dimensions, are you? You're very, very big, I think. Maybe you really are everywhere.*

The succubus tried to pull its wounded hand away, but Annmarie wouldn't let go.

You keep telling me how you know everything, said Annmarie. *Now that you're an addict, can you tell me where Staze comes from?*

The succubus chewed its lips. *Corey.*

Annmarie laughed. *Oh no. It comes from me. When you want more, you have to come to me.*

The succubus looked up at me in despair. *Mother Eve . . .*

It calls you 'Mother'? Annmarie let out a bark of a laugh.

Nav doesn't want it, I said. *I was there when it was born. Why shouldn't it think I'm its mother?*

You're not even responsible for yourself. Annmarie clapped her palm across the creature's bloody knuckles. *You'll stay with me. I'll teach you everything you need to know.*

The succubus tried to smile, but it hadn't mastered bravery and began crying again.

Stop that, said Annmarie. *Pull yourself together and show me where Corey is.*

The succubus sniffed. Outside, I heard the baby squeal like it was being stuck with pins. I glanced out the balcony window, hoping to see Corey in the plaza. Instead, the fiesta downstairs had vanished and turned to a telescopic view of the flat feature-less world beyond the walls. A long way off, Corey plodded toward the Jackless shuttle. The front of his environment suit bulged out where he'd tucked the grub child against his chest. The shuttle's airlock was wide open and someone lay sprawled on the floor inside. Naverdi. When Corey found the ship, he'd shove her out. He didn't need her.

Hide the shuttle, said Annmarie. *Hurry. I won't let him leave.*

The ship disappeared. Corey stopped dead in his tracks. He ran a few steps and spun around, right, left. No ship. His bel-low of frustration drifted in through the window and the plaza reappeared as the vision faded.

Annmarie patted the succubus's head. *There's a good girl.*

The succubus gazed at her, just as doomed as the luckless yellow fungus. If it tried to resist, Annmarie would slaughter grubs until Paradise was barren and the succubus was a writhing stump of its former self—still alive and usefully addicted—but not in any shape to argue. When Corey finally realized he couldn't escape, he would bring the grub child to Annmarie as a peace offering, and its capture would be complete.

Annmarie would give it my cabin on the Medusa. It would have my place at the table in the crew room. It would spend the rest of its life hiding in a hand-me-down desert, surrounded by worshipping addicts until Annmarie decided there was nothing left to learn from it, and then she would find a way for it to die.

I could see those terrors in its childish face.

Come with me, I said to it, as though we were the only ones in the room.

Annmarie snorted. The pinkie disappeared from the succubus's remaining hand and it yelped in pain. *Get out, Eve,* said Annmarie. *Find that shuttle and get the hell out. I won't stop you.*

I turned and went down the stairs, out of sight. Their eyes stayed on me as I wove through the crowded plaza and I tried not to think, because I could feel Annmarie probing for my intentions. I ducked under the white archway and the flowers faded. I was back in the ethereal flatland. Annmarie's scratching curiosity vanished, but I could still feel the succubus. Her fear was a taste under my tongue. There was only one thing left for me to do.

Show me the Medusa, I whispered.

The pearl-colored landscape gave way to the Paradise I was used to: cold stones and ruins. Not far ahead, the Medusa gleamed bronze under the halogens. It was the real ship, not a metaphor in the succubal net, and it wasn't any more than a fifteen-minute walk.

I heard something move to my right, and turned to see Corey, arms crossed under the bulge where the grub child was tucked into his suit. His mouth opened in dismay when he saw me.

"What're you doing here?"

I pointed to the Medusa.

He angled his thumb over his shoulder. He was tired and

cold enough for his thwarted plans to show on his face. "The shuttle's back there. Naverdi's in it."

"I know." I made a motion toward the Medusa. "After you."

"Oh, no," he said. "We can walk together."

I started toward the ship and he fell in step beside me, just out of reach, expecting me to jump him and wrestle for the grub child.

"You've decided to make up with Annmarie?" he said.

"Have you?" I said.

"I can't," said Corey. "She doesn't trust me anymore."

I wondered if he had plans to kill her.

Ahead, the Medusa loomed under the lights. We were close enough to see steam rising from the halogens, drifting in plumes over the barren stones.

Corey braced his hands underneath the bulge in his suit. The weight of the grub child drooped lower, it seemed to me, down to his stomach until his belt was holding it up. He moved like it was heavier.

"She's growing," I said.

"She's not," he said. "She's sleeping."

"She's starving," I said. "What're you going to do when she figures out you're edible?"

He tugged at his belt. He still had the strength of will to make the motions pensive, thoughtful, but I could see him calculating how fast he could strip off the suit.

We came over a low heap of shale, passed a dozen empty pools, and picked our way between the stalky poles of the halogen forest.

Ahead, the bodies of Annmarie's four victims lay in a neat row on the ground. Inside, the bay was scrubbed down and the lab tables had been stored away. There was no sign of grubs or moss.

"Where is she?" I said.

"In the crew room," said Corey.

I followed him down the hallway, past his room and mine. The crew room door was open.

Annmarie sat at the table, facing us. A grub lay in pieces on the plate, leaking thin, reddish liquid. There were more in the casserole to her right. Bioboxes filled with grubs surrounded her on the floor. To her left was a tall plastic container we normally used for garbage. The smell of vomit rose out of it.

Annmarie gave me a bleary, nauseous glare. "You shouldn't be here. I told you to find that shuttle and get out." She saw Corey behind me. "Son of a bitch," she said.

Her dose of Staze, metabolized through the grubs, was too dilute to incapacitate her—I wasn't even sure if she was officially addicted—but it'd definitely slowed her down.

I stood in the draft from the corridor, choking on the smell of half-digested grubs. Corey pushed past me, digging in his pocket.

"I can defend myself," she said to him in a hoarse voice. "I could kill you both if I wanted to."

Corey didn't say anything, just pulled a rolled-up plastic bag out of his pocket. It didn't have much Staze in it. Just enough to form a streak of red powder. He hitched up his sagging suit and opened the bag.

"Get away," said Annmarie.

He ignored her and coughed against the stink. The bulge in his suit, the grub child, hours past its dose, squirmed.

"Eve," said Annmarie. She groped at the tabletop, knocking the fork and knife to the floor, but she couldn't get up.

I didn't move. I could see everything with utter clarity, events unrolling in front of my eyes in slow motion. Corey fumbling with the bag, trying to get a dab of Red on his finger. The infant, Kalima, on the verge of starvation, close enough to smell her own elixir. The way the bag dangled over the seam in his suit. The distance between Corey's smudged hands and Annmarie's lips. It might as well have been light years.

Corey yelped in surprise as a dark arm shoved out of his suit, grabbed the bag, and snatched it inside. He stood there, frozen between tearing the suit off his body or reaching inside to grab away the Staze. He waited a second too long.

We all heard the plastic rip, and then the low, rumbling sigh from his belly.

The air in the crew room went cold. The smell of vomit vanished and the real Medusa gave way to the succubus's version. The rectangular room turned round. Colorless walls shifted to a vision of stone and mortar. The ceiling telescoped upward and I could see stars high above. When I looked down, I was standing knee-deep in flowers.

Annmarie, wolfishly distorted, leaped to her feet, released like any other addict in this new mix of realities. I took a step backward and felt the metal gates. To my left, Corey squirmed in a thorny bed of roses, tearing at the straps and buckles of his suit as the succubus's head emerged, smeared with red powder.

She clambered free of him, pared to a naked essence, black as charcoal, tall as a tree. She arched her body and shook out the coiling snakes of her hair. She smiled at me, but her teeth were like knives.

She swung around to where Corey was still goggling from the roses.

You don't want me, he shouted. *I'm your father.*

'O' Father,' whispered the succubus, *'done are thy tasks.'* It took a step toward him.

Corey let out a scream like his hair was on fire. He shoved me out of his way and hurled himself against the gilded gates. The metal seemed to bend. The gate creaked and abruptly, he was on the other side, where blank landscape had replaced the rest of the Medusa.

He stared at me from outside the garden, at Annmarie and the looming succubus. And then he seemed to understand that there was no way he could ever come back. He turned and raced away into the unchanging distance. I saw him stop long enough to strap himself into his antigrav unit, but he'd forgotten his fins and as he flew off, his body spiraled uncontrollably into the featureless sky.

Annmarie eyed the succubus critically, its teeth and new talents. *Why did you let him go?*

I can find him anywhere, said the succubus, fluid as a serpent.

Annmarie laughed with her exaggerated mouth. She was taller than she'd been seconds ago, swaying and unwieldy, like a four-legged creature trying to balance on its hind legs for the first time. Her nails curved into claws and she arched her fingers. *I thought you were hungry.*

I am, said the succubus, *but you are the aggressive one, and I will eat you first—without selective digestion.*

Annmarie leered into the succubus's face.

You'll have to fight if you want to eat me, she said. *Do you understand that?*

Fight, repeated the succubus, but it glanced down at me for help.

I hesitated and threw a weak punch at the air. Annmarie watched with complete contempt. I tried another one. The succubus made a few swings and Annmarie laughed at us both.

You can't teach what you can't do, little Eve, she said, and she threw herself at the succubus.

It yelled in pain as Annmarie sank her claws into its belly, ripping upward to its ribs. She bit deep into the succubus's neck, and the succubus flailed and squealed.

I pressed myself against the imaginary gate as their feet trampled roses and lilies, grinding flowers into the dirt. If Annmarie was unfamiliar with this virtual environment, the succubus was utterly at sea with the basics of combat, and I could already see it losing. It stared skyward, mouth wide open, eyes bulging, gasping as Annmarie hung on to its throat.

Even for me, the air seemed too thick to breathe—but dense enough to focus everything with the precision of a lens. When this was over, Corey would show up on his hands and knees, and while I watched, he and Annmarie would slice the infant Kalima open to scrutinize her inner workings. They could always make another, and if Naverdi was still alive, she'd be drafted to carry the replacement.

If she wasn't, it would be my turn.

The succubus fell to its skinny knees, croaking in fear, Annmarie's wolfish avatar still clamped to its throat.

I took a step forward and made myself bigger.

Annmarie's eyes flickered toward me, squinting through folds of flesh with a combination of fury and real dread. I crouched beside the succubus and pulled its hands away from Annmarie's bristling forearms. I guided its fingers to the delicate ridges of windpipe beneath Annmarie's animal jaws and helped it wrap its fingers tight.

Annmarie slashed at me. Her claws raked the side of my face with incredible scathing heat. I yelled and jerked away. She'd *never* hit me, but now, in the fiery depth of the wound I could feel how much she'd *wanted* to. And when I saw the red smears on my hand, I felt every shred of my own mercy—seven years of timid endurance and false forgiveness—evaporate.

I reached past the aching places in the succubus's chest and closed its fists around Annmarie's neck until its fingers wound into her skin.

Here, I said, this *is how you fight.*

Annmarie dug in deeper with teeth and claws and will. The succubus hung on, and they held each other in a murderous balance until the succubus gasped and finally let go.

It let go. Its fingers fluttered over Annmarie's twisting hair. It ran its hands down the length of her spine to caress her buttocks and thighs. It wrapped her in its arms. Intimate. Gentle.

Annmarie's eyes closed, not in deadly concentration or fear but in relief. Her jaws came loose from its throat and she laid her face against its neck as the succubus stroked her. It pressed Annmarie's long, distorted body close to its gangly torso and in a minute, there was less of Annmarie; a layer of her presence diminished. Her arms wrapped loosely around the succubus's back, thinning with each breath, peaceful and serene. Without effort or struggle. The succubus held her until Annmarie was barely a shadow. A flicker at the corner of someone's eye. A last whiff of perfume.

The succubus opened its arms and Annmarie was gone.

It got to its feet, solid and unscathed, and turned to me.

Is she dead? I whispered.

She is in me, said the succubus.

I don't understand, I said.

It came closer and put its narrow black hand on my chest. *She is in me.* It looked at me with the same eyes I'd seen in my portrait in the Sanctuary gallery and put its arms around my neck. I stood stiffly against the gilded bars, waiting for the sensations of being absorbed, eaten, or assimilated because there was no way the gates were going to spring open for me.

I waited. The succubus's warm cheek rested against mine. I could feel the dusty dryness of its skin, the strong, girlish warmth of its body. I wrapped my fingers into the bars of the gate, wanting to hang on to the illusion of something solid before I dissolved.

Its breath brushed my ear. Its heart pounded hard where our bodies touched.

You don't want me, either, it whispered.

What?

You said Naverdi didn't want me.

I gripped the bars, afraid to say anything.

It hugged me more tightly and I squeezed my eyes shut for any distracting thought, but what I saw inside my own lids was my mother. Not the blood loss and stolen jewelry I remembered from inside the Mesh, but the way she'd really looked as I'd stared down in uncomprehending terror from my father's arms. Everything I'd felt as he carried me across the room trying to cover my eyes, the pure unfiltered agony of a frightened little girl, alone in the world for the first time.

The succubus pressed her face against my neck, damp and hot.

I let go of the gate and put my arms around her.

I'll never leave you, I said.

EPILOGUE

I never did find Annmarie's body, but I did find Naverdi, wandering along the basalt rill, wrapped in a red blanket. She was haggard, in need of drugs, and in a terrible mood but otherwise in remarkably good shape, considering.

"Where's Corey?" I said.

"No fucking idea," she said. "He gave me a blanket and kicked me off the shuttle." She huddled deeper in the scarlet folds. "Is there any Red?"

There was plenty on the Medusa, and enough Kevake to make half a ton of the stuff. When we got to the ship, I sat Nav down in one of the control room's soft chairs and trickled a pinch into her palm.

Nav's eyes flickered from the red crystals to the baby. Kalima, no bigger than a large doll, lay swaddled in a cut-up sweater, half asleep in what had been Annmarie's chair. Nav wouldn't come within an arm's length of her. Would barely look at her.

"All I ever wanted out of Staze was a little peace and quiet." She shook her head slowly, like she was in pain. "I guess that's gone."

I nodded.

"You know," said Nav, "even though you showed all of Dunne's addicts what that *thing* really is, they still have to take their dose and that *thing* still has to eat. In a couple of weeks, it'll be in every single Staze vision. Anyone who takes Red's going to see . . . it."

"I know."

She eyed the baby. "You could save us all, Eve."

"I won't turn into your mother for you," I said, because I'd anticipated this conversation and found I knew exactly what to say to make her shut up. "You'll have to do that yourself."

Nav grunted and her face twitched. It was a low, effective blow.

"Killing her wouldn't help anyway," I said. "What's going on in Staze isn't going to change unless she learns that human beings aren't food."

"*It's* an alien," said Nav. "It's hungry. You can't teach it to go against its nature."

I pointed to the plastic glove full of powdered milk which was warming in a bowl of hot water. "It—*she* can eat other things."

"Sure," said Nav, "but it has a taste for *us.*"

I picked up the baby and sat down with her in my lap. She was heavy for her tiny size, and warm. Her hair was as soft as fine velvet. Her skin smelled ever so slightly of fruit. When I held her, I could feel my heart expand inside my chest. Protective. An emptiness finally filled with something constructive.

"Take your dose," I said to Nav.

Nav let out a bark of a laugh. "It's got you, too, Eve. Analyzed your defenses. Sucked you in. You're the next course on the buffet table." She leaned over and lapped up every last grain in her palm. "We're all fucking doomed." Her eyes closed and she slumped into the cushions.

I reached for the plastic glove and gave Kalima the thumb-end. Once she'd figured out how to swallow, powdered milk seemed to satisfy her. Solid food would be a different story. I didn't want to think about how she might respond to meat.

In the other chair, Naverdi snored. The baby suckled noisily, and I tucked her little body against my chest while I stared out the window. The barren ruins of Paradise stretched into night shadows, not a shade lighter than when we'd first arrived. One languid comet marked the indigo sky, which made me think of Corey spiraling away in his finless environment suit. If I ever saw him again, I would loose Kalima's hungry avatar on him.

He'd escaped by accident, I told myself for the hundredth time. He was alive because Kalima'd been distracted by Annmarie. Not because she had any feelings toward him. Not because she believed he was her father.

I took a deep breath and tried to relax. The smells of the ship, the sounds of its subtle mechanisms, the insulated feel of it were all the same, homey and familiar. What was different was me. The next decision was mine. We could stay on Paradise forever, swathed in the corrupted safety of the elder 'gats, or I could purge the ship and leave.

We could follow Annmarie's supply routes. Her old customers would remember me, but beyond that, they would recognize the Unknown Child. The next time I stood in front of a crowd of potential addicts with a bag of Staze, my reception would be vastly different.

Kalima was finished with the glove. I wiped her tiny mouth and reached into my pocket for the bag of Staze. Her dark eyes watched me, no longer filmy and vague but attentive. I kept wondering if she'd ever smile and couldn't quite imagine that. It was even harder to picture her growing up as a normal little girl. She stuck out her tongue and I gave her two grains.

Kalima sighed and closed her eyes, entering the new world where her mother and her acolytes waited at the temple door. I kissed her on the forehead and held her close. Between us, my medallion was a warmth against my chest, like a comforting touch from someone long gone. Outside the comet dropped slowly behind the horizon and I was left with my own reflection and Kalima's in the curve of the control room window—a foreign image of us both as *mother* and *child*.

Beyond that, the stony garden gleamed under Mara's distant light.

Secret and eternal.

The old world and the new.